RACING HEARTS

BENNETT BOYS RANCH

LAUREN LANDISH

Edited by
VALORIE CLIFTON
Edited by
STACI ETHERIDGE

CHAPTER 1

SHAYANNE

"You ready for this, Shayannie?" my dad asks. In his middle age, Paul Tannen, with his big personality and bigger belly paunch, is not a man I can lie to. In this case, I don't need to.

I'm ready, though I wish he hadn't used that nickname. I've hated it ever since I was about eight years old.

After all, is it still a nickname if it's actually longer than your given name? I'm not sure on the rules of that, but it's what he's called me since I went through a curly hair phase as a kid, even though my light brown hair has zero red and my tanned skin has no freckles, unlike the famous orphan.

"Yes, sir. I've got this," I call back confidently.

Today is a big day. I'm finalizing a deal to stock my goat milk soap line in the gift shop at the mountain resort in town. This country girl is going big time! Well, as big as I can right now, since my business is a one-woman operation run out of a farmhouse and I plan to keep it that way.

It's my baby, and no one else's.

Daddy eyes me critically, his judgment heavy. "Maybe I should come with you? Help smooth it over." He pulls his hat off, running a handkerchief over his greying but still full head of hair before putting his hat back in place.

I'm rough around the edges, but I don't need his cowboy slick style mucking up the business meeting that I set up. I know refusing is bad manners and will likely set off a domino effect I don't want to deal with, but I'm adept in my own way, and I know my dad's weak spot.

He doesn't feel comfortable around 'city' types. He thinks it puts him at a disadvantage, and Daddy never likes being at a disadvantage . . . ever.

"Daddy, this is a done deal. I'm just going in to answer questions they might have so they can represent the brand appropriately. Do you know about goat milk benefits for skin care? What scents I create? Can you tell the cute story about the logo I drew by hand?"

I eye him back just as harshly, having learned at his knee and knowing he can't answer any of those questions.

"Okay, Shayanne. I'm trusting you with this. We need this to go well."

The words hit like stones, weighing me down because if anyone knows how much the family needs me to succeed with this venture, it's me. I'm the one who does the books for the family farm, sees every penny going in and out, and has to pinch those pennies till they scream to feed my dad, three hard-working brothers, and myself.

We've had years where it was lean and times when it was easier, and after my mom passed seven years ago and I took over her household duties, I've successfully financially guided us through them all.

There was a point where Daddy's personal issues meant we really were tight, but Daddy, bless his heart, is doing okay with the love of his family. And while things aren't tight now, a little more income is always a welcome padding to the bottom line.

"I know, Daddy. I've got this." I inject hard assurance into the words, making them a vow I can't, and won't, go back on.

He dips his chin once, giving a stamp of approval that I don't need, and then spins on his booted heel to walk out the front door toward his truck.

I don't know where he's off to today, which is worrying because I almost always know exactly where he is and what he's doing. Even when he's gambling.

Yeah, that's his demon. Cat's out of the bag. No Schrodinger's cat question of 'is he or isn't he,' this one. Dad's alive and therefore betting, for sure. He keeps it separate from our household budget, maybe because he's responsible, or maybe because he doesn't want me to see how much he's winning and losing, but most likely, it's a mix of both.

I watch him leave, mentally checking the family calendar, and decide he's probably going to lunch with the boys in town since he didn't ask for anything to eat.

From behind me, I hear heavy bootsteps. "He's right, you know. But I trust you," my oldest brother, Brody, says softly in his deep timbre.

"I know, Brody," I tell him for the millionth time since I first got serious about this idea. "I've got this under control, just like I always do."

He nods, then studiously ignores the fact that he's repeating back to me damn-near verbatim what I've told him my plan for the day is. But I recognize that it's more for him than for me. He's excited, understandably so, and I am too.

"So, take the batch of soaps into the resort, double-check the order and set them up, and make sure to touch base with the manager and give them the purchase order so we get paid. If you run into any problems, call me."

As he talks, he makes a thick sandwich with the supplies from the fridge and sits down at the kitchen table, mouth already full and sandwich already half gone. Brody has always eaten fast and hard, never sitting down for too long unless I put my foot down about it.

I take two steps in his direction, closing the gap between us physically even as I know the other gap between us will likely never be bridged. We're on the same team, a part of the same family, but we both know the roles we play. And they're nowhere near equal. Placing my hand on his shoulder, I growl out, "I can handle this."

I squeeze the thick muscle a little harder than I should, but it seems to drive home my point.

Brody has the graciousness to look the slightest bit sheepish. "I know, Shayanne. This is just a big deal, and I don't want anything to mess it up. Especially Dad."

This is my goat's milk soap business.

My baby, that I started from the ground up with the help of Google, a lot of trial and error, and a small but growing herd of goats. Those first batches were barely good enough to wash our hands with before dinner, and I'd felt bad about wasting my precious goats' milk that way, but I'd learned. And for almost a year now, I've been selling soap like hotcakes at the farmer's market.

Well, Brody has been because I don't usually go into town for that since he's already there, selling our family farm's produce. To his credit, Brody could answer every single one of those questions I put to Daddy without issue because he memorized all the answers I gave him and was the one listening to me ramble as I worked my way deeper into this hobby-slash-business. And now, Brody sells my soaps almost as fast as I can make them, which is why I'm expanding.

I like to picture my pretty soaps going from my little slice of dirt to the resort, to the world. Not for some global takeover, because I don't have dreams of being a big dog in the specialty soap marketplace, but even if I'm stuck here, some little piece of me can go . . . somewhere, anywhere, everywhere.

"Brody Tannen, are you suggesting that I will mess this up? Let's review. Who's more likely to appropriately handle a bit of public handshaking and salesmanship? I'll give you a hint. It sure as rain ain't you unless grunts and dirt are the angle you think we should go for?" I challenge him. "Further, who has handled every one of our contracts and financial affairs since the day she turned thirteen? Unless you or Daddy suddenly dropped your balls in favor of ovaries, it's been me."

Brody winces at my crass language, but he knows I'm right. I might be trapped in this house, on this farm, looking after my daddy and three brothers, but I'm an important part in this machine we call a family. Even if they sometimes forget it and I have to get a little loud with my reminders.

Well, either that or I slip the tiniest sliver of Ex-Lax in their chocolate chip cookies. Not enough to keep them in bed the next day, but just enough to keep them regular, you know? A girl's gotta do what a girl's gotta do to keep her menfolk in line.

We country women have had our ways going way, way back. And Brody, once again, gives me my respect.

"Fine, I'll leave you to it, then. But, for real, call me if you need anything, Shay." His voice is softer, kinder this time. And there it is, the gooey heart center of my rough-and-tumble, more likely to fight than talk, eldest brother. I'm closer to him than I am to either of my other brothers, mostly because while I run the house, Brody is in charge of running the thousand acres we own.

He mostly cares for the critters, as he likes to call them. The herd of cows, the barn full of horses, my goats, a flock of chickens, a few herding dogs and mouser cats, and a partridge in a pear tree. Okay, not that last one, but I tried one Christmas when I was little. Mom had said no, and I'd pouted a good fit, but I'd gotten over it when I'd gotten a kitten instead. 'A working animal', my daddy had called it, but Brody and I had turned it into a lap-sitting pet with milk and catnip. Meow-ser never caught a single mouse in his too-short life.

That's Brody, though, all venomous spikes outside and honey-flavored caramel inside. Not that he'd let anyone but me see that.

"I will, Brody. I promise. And remember, I'm hanging with Sophie tonight. Dinner's already in the crock pot, so you boys will just have to spoon the stew into bowls when you're ready."

"And dessert?" he asks, his sweet tooth known far and wide. Too bad we're on bad relations with the neighbors. Mama Louise's desserts would be a perfect match for him.

"Cobbler in the fridge, ice cream in the freezer," I say, mentally making sure that I've done my list of chores before I head out.

Bills are paid, bank statements checked, floors cleaned, bathrooms scrubbed—no small feat with four men—and dinner cooked. Check, check, and checkity-check-check. Shayanne out, finally!

"Okay, be good, girl. Or don't get caught being bad." He grins wolfishly, likely thinking there's no way I'd get myself into any trouble. I'm a good girl, except for my mouth. But that's mostly the boys' fault, anyway. They've all had their hand in showing me how to curse creatively.

That's me in a nutshell, anyway. Though I might be female, my tight circle of family is all male and has left me decided-ly . . . not feminine? Like a tomboy who didn't know how to indulge in her girly side beyond her soap operas.

Thank God for Sophie, my best friend and the girliest girl I know. Not to say that she doesn't get down and dirty with the best of us, especially when her vet job requires it, but she's got a fancy-schmancy spa-loving side to her, too, and I've been converted to the joys of foot soaks and face masks.

"As long as Daddy don't catch me, I'll be just fine," I volley back, though it's the God's honest truth.

"Shayanne," Brody warns.

"What? Not like I'm gonna climb on the tables at Hank's and start shaking my moneymaker. And even if I did, whatcha gonna do about it?" I grin big and wide, hands on my hips as I give a little shimmy shake, daring him to say that he'd tattle on me because we both know he won't.

Once upon a time, he would've been running to Daddy faster than a kerosene fire lighting up. Back when we'd all thought Daddy was a good man, an honorable one whom we could look up to with pride and respect.

But that changed a while back. It's not so much the Tannens against the world, but us 'kids' against Daddy *and* the world. At this point, Brody and I mostly work together to make sure our father isn't getting us into any financial trouble with his gambling and big mouth.

I get the irony of my saying he has a big mouth when I'm sassy as fuck, but my mouthiness is cute and crazy. Daddy's is dangerous and daringly dumb, especially if he's had a few beers in him.

"Maybe I need to come with you," Brody hedges. But he's already rising from the kitchen table, moving to put his lunch plate in the dishwasher because I trained my big brother right. Thankfully, he means to dinner, not the business meeting, since we've apparently moved on from that part of my plans for today.

"You ain't coming and you dang well know I ain't dancing on tables. So do your job and let me do mine. And we'll both blow off some steam so we can do it all again tomorrow." He narrows his eyes, swallowing like he's tasting the air to see if I'm lying to him. I shove at his wide shoulders, shaking my head. "Now, get. I'll be late. Don't wait up."

He grunts, which sounds like an agreement, but he'll wait up anyway. He's protective in a sweet and smothering way. But he goes outside, grabbing his old, oil-stained Rangers hat on the way and smashing it down on his head. I wait one beat, then two, waiting for his constant humming to start, and then I'm hustling my fine ass upstairs to get ready.

A quick brush through my hair and then I pull it into a ponytail at the nape of my neck. Looking in the mirror, I pull it tight, making it as perky as possible. Sophie calls my tone 'bronde', not quite blonde, not quite brown, but somewhere in between. I call it blah, but what I lack in pretty color is made up for with thick waves that, even corralled in a band, wind down my back to below my bra strap.

Some mascara that Sophie showed me how to use and some tinted lip balm, and I'm ready, or as ready as I'm going to be. I've got my nicest jeans on, my freshest boots, and a button-up shirt tucked in behind my braided leather belt. In short, I look like a country girl, which is exactly what I am.

I toss a pair of denim shorts into my bag for my night at Hank's with Sophie, and I'm out like trout. I clomp down the stairs like a herd of cattle and let the screen door slam behind me. A quick peek in the passenger seat tells me that one of the boys helpfully loaded up my boxes of soap, and I'm ready.

A cloud of dust stirs up behind me as I pull out of the grass and onto the dirt driveway to the front gate. I hold my breath, not even realizing I'm doing it until I hit asphalt and it whooshes out like freedom.

I press the gas pedal to the floor like there are demons chasing me, but it's not Satan's goons out. It's responsibilities and expectations, this role I play in my family. One I'm proud to have, but one that keeps me chained to a plot of land I could ride in a day. One that doesn't have the whimsy and unexpect- edness of 'out there'.

"Whooooo!" A hoot of exuberant joy escapes my mouth, but really, it's from my soul as the wind rushes in through the open windows, tearing wisps of hair from my ponytail to whip them around. Each lash is a welcome reminder that I'm floating on the wind, buoyed by the sunshine, free to chase forever with home in my rearview mirror. If only for today.

———

"OH, MY GOD, TELL ME ALL ABOUT IT," SOPHIE SQUEALS from across the table, clapping her hands, and from beneath the table, I hear her heeled booties stomping.

I grin, excited to have something different to share today than my usual farm life update. Not that Sophie's ever minded my chatter about goats since she's an animal lover herself.

I squirm in my seat, the vinyl making an awkward peeling sound against the bare flesh of my thighs. After my meeting at the resort, I'd changed at Sophie's and she'd helped me add a bit of flirtiness to my barely-there makeup. I feel a bit like a rhinestone cowgirl now, but knowing that I could out ride, out rope, and out shoot most of the guys in this room helps me relax into the sexier-than-I'm-used-to getup.

"Brianna and Gavin were so nice and even excited to carry my soaps. Bri read each and every label, set them up in a prime location right inside the door, and let me leave a bowl of sample slivers in the lobby restrooms with a sign that read, *Tannen Goat Soap is for sale in the gift shop.* And I saw your sis-in-law, Katelyn. They're putting mini soap bars in the honeymoon suites!" I freeze, the full weight of the awesomeness hitting me at once. My jaw drops open and my hands lift to cover it as my eyebrows shoot high.

"Oh, my Chee-sus and crackers, Soph! I'm doing it!"

She grins, truly happy for me. She should be, especially since this whole thing was her idea. When we met, I was just excited to have another girl to talk to and had hoped for a friend for the summer while she was here. But she fell in love with a local boy and stayed.

Okay, not quite just a local boy, but one of the neighbors,

the youngest of the Bennett brothers. So that made it a lot easier to get together with Sophie on the regular. She was the one who suggested I sell my soaps other places besides the market, and here I am . . . actually doing it!

"I'm not only a domestic goddess of the farm species. I'm an entrepreneur!" I proclaim, proud of both titles.

"You sure are!" She does a happy dance in her seat that I copy until a deep chuckle comes from beside the table.

"I take it this means the meeting went well?"

I look up to see James Bennett, Sophie's husband, standing beside the table. He's a tall drink of water, a little thicker than he used to be, but still, all muscle these days since he's not keeping lean for the rodeo, and he's hopelessly smitten with Sophie. Which is only fair because that girl is ass over teakettle for James too. They'd be sickening if they weren't so adorable.

I don't answer James in words, just a squeal and a nod.

He smiles back, turning over his shoulder to call out to Hank. "Round of 'special' strawberry margaritas for the girls and a draft for me, please." Hank nods but points a gnarled old finger at me, so I know I'll be getting that 'special' version too. One sans alcohol.

It makes sense for Sophie since she's five months pregnant, but for me too?

Come on, twenty-first birthday! It's literally weeks away, and at home, I have beer and wine coolers when I want, and the good lord and Sheriff Downs know I've had more than my fair share at pasture parties. All of which Hank damn well knows. But neither he, nor I, will risk his liquor license and the only honkytonk in town for me to get a little José Cuervo in my margarita.

Seconds later, the waitress drops off our celebratory drinks, ours with paper umbrellas and James's in a frosty mug. We raise our glasses, toasting my victory.

"To the goats," I say, my cheeks flushing with joy.

"To dreams coming true," Sophie says, always one for pretty words.

"To the goat soap girl," James answers, laughing like he said something hilarious as he winks at me.

"Not the worst thing I've been called," I singsong back as we clink glasses and take sips of our respective drinks. "Besides, we know what you did with the goats during your younger days."

Even James has to laugh at that one. It's not really a dirty joke. He used to practice riding on the backs of the goats and fell off more than a few times. Seeing him on his ass was good fun for the younger me, before everything between our families went so wrong.

"Did you order yet?" James asks Sophie as we set our drinks down. At her nod, he guesses correctly. "Special of the day?"

"Ham steak, potato salad, green beans, and a roll," I say, a worry trying to worm its way into my head about the guys back home feeding themselves tonight. It's not that they can't or don't do it when they need to, but it's part of my daily checklist, and even though I know they're fine and full of beef stew, I love them and worry whether they'll get enough after a long day of work.

Because make no mistake, I might work hard keeping the house running, but they work just as hard, sometimes even harder, keeping the farm and ranch running. It takes us all together.

But I fight the urge to text our group chat to make sure they ate. They're grown men. They don't need me checking up on them. Besides, it's a chance for me to lead by example. If I leave them alone, maybe they'll occasionally leave me alone too. Let me have a bit of wild child freedom tonight.

In my hometown . . . in a bar where the bartender remembers me in diapers . . . in a room full of people I've known my whole life. Sitting at a table with my literal next-door neighbor and his wife.

Some *rebel* I am.

But I only let a single bite of bitterness chase the margarita down, determined to celebrate tonight. After all, I'm here because I'm making my mark now.

And I do . . . chowing down on delicious food I didn't make and burning it off by dancing with every cowboy who'll spin me around the floor. There's quite a few, and while one of them looked like he might be wanting to push a few boundaries, one glance from James has every man in here on their best behavior.

Nobody wants to piss off both the Tannens *and* the Bennetts.

I might not be the rebel they write books about, but I'm a good country girl, and besides, no one sits out when the jukebox plays *Cotton-Eyed Joe*.

I let the music take me away, kicking my worries to the curb, two-stepping away from the chains of rules I'm expected to follow and celebrating that today, I took a chance and it paid off big-time. James might've thought he was being funny, but I'm damn sure glad to wear that crown today.

"Goat Soap Girl," I whisper to myself, almost needing to pinch my arm at the dream come true.

CHAPTER 2

LUKE

A huge sigh works its way free when I see the lights of Great Falls. Just beyond that crest, way on the outskirts of the city in the surrounding rural area, is my destination.

Home. Finally. After weeks away, I've missed this growing little mountain burg.

But with as late as it is, I need to eat dinner before crashing into bed. It's not like anyone's expecting me at home, anyway. I come and go as I please, my brothers and me and an occasional seasonal ranch hand working the family ranch.

As long as I'm there for chores bright and early in the morning, no one gives a shit what time I roll into town tonight.

So I pull into the parking lot at Hank's, ready for a bite to eat, a cold beer, and a minute to relax. But damn, the lot's full. And as I go inside, the loud music and chatter of the crowd greet me. So much for relaxing. What day is it, anyway?

I glance up at the specials board to see that it's Friday. Huh. I would've guessed Wednesday at most, but the days on the road are long, and when I'm away from home, I usually work the entire week. So it's no surprise I lost track.

I sit down at the bar, and Hank, the owner, saunters over. If you didn't know better, you'd think his hip-swinging gait was from years of horseback riding, but I know his secret that his ambling walk is from a bum hip that acts up sometimes, product of his time in the Marines and a river called the Hue. But he doesn't tell that story to many folks, so I don't share it either.

"Usual?" he asks, his hands drying a freshly-washed glass with a white towel.

At my nod, he leans in, lowering his voice. "Your brother's over there. Not sure if that makes you wanna go over or leave, but there ya go."

My lips twitch, appreciating the warning, but I've got no bad blood with my brothers. We get along well, aside from the usual Alpha-male shit from our teens. It was well established then, and continues to be the case now, that my older brother, Mark, is the boss of us all. Now that he's the stand-in for Pops too, he's even more the leader of the Bennett family. The only one with a hope and a prayer of making Mark do something he doesn't want to is Mama. Or maybe his girl, Katelyn?

Yeah, Kate's got Mark wrapped around her pretty little finger.

But it's not Mark I see when I glance over my shoulder. It's my younger brother, James, and his new wife, Sophie. She's feeding him bits of her roll and he's sucking at her fingers like it's damn near foreplay in the middle of Hank's.

Never one to miss out on giving James shit, I lift my glass toward James's table to let Hank know I'm moving over. He smirks knowingly, trusting that we Bennett boys won't get too far gone. We're a little crazy, my youngest brother most of all, but we're not troublemakers.

I slide into the round booth, sneaking up to lean in close to Sophie's other side. "Now what's a nice lady like you doing with a degenerate like this?"

James sputters for a half-beat, bowing up instantly before seeing that it's me and settling. Slightly. "Fucker, can't you see you're interrupting here?" he growls, but Sophie's already got a hand on his arm, encouraging him to stand down with a sweet smile.

I chuckle, cocking an eyebrow paired with a grin. "And that's the point. You think Mama's gonna be happy to hear about you and Soph mauling each other in the middle of Hank's?"

He bites his lip, looking at Sophie like she's a steak and he's a starving man. "I ain't mauling her . . . yet. Just politely nibbling as she shares her dinner with me." He's got sex dripping from every rumbled word, and I don't need to hear that shit from my brother. Hell, I hear enough when they visit the pond out on the ranch. Sophie ain't . . . quiet.

So I poke and tease, the way brothers do. "Oh, just sharing dinner, you say? Then you won't mind if she shares a bit of her biscuit with me too?"

Sophie is on to our brotherly games by now and holds out a bite for me, barely restraining her laughter. I chomp it from her hand, making sure to not get too personal and touch her with my teeth or lips, but it still devils the shit out of my brother, who's watching with fire in his eyes though we all know I'm just joking around.

"You leave her biscuit to me, Luke."

I laugh, chewing open-mouthed just to drive home the point that I already got a bite of her biscuit, even if it's not the one he's mouthing about.

I sit back up straight, no longer invading Sophie's space but still preening at getting one over on James. I can't help it. He's too easy, and Sophie's so easygoing. It's why their playfulness works, I guess, not that I'd know anything about what a relationship takes since my grand total of serious relationships is zero.

Casual? Okay. Short-term? Sure thing. No strings? I'm your man. Because I'm gone next week, anyway.

Not that I'm leaving a trail of women everywhere I go.

No, most trips I take, it's me and a couple of old guys watching and praying our work takes and another generation of racehorses is born. For a guy who spends the bulk of his time on procreation, I do very little of it myself.

"You just getting into town?" James asks, pulling Sophie's legs over his under the table. She leans back and relaxes, letting her stomach pooch out a bit.

Even in the two weeks I've been gone, I can tell her baby bump has grown beneath her shirt. Give her a month, and she won't be able to sit in a booth here but will have to use a chair.

Speaking of the next generation, she's got a Bennett growing in her belly. Never would've thought it'd be the youngest Bennett to hit that milestone first, but James has never done anything in small measures. It's in for an ounce, in for a kilometric fuckton with that guy since he was a kid.

Hell, Mark's probably not far behind. I get the feeling he'd have his new wife, Katelyn, knocked up twenty-four seven if he could. Their relationship was a bit of shock to everyone since Mark had all but declared himself a perpetual bachelor in the town square, but Katelyn hadn't taken no for an answer. And now, they're living their happily ever after, to everyone's surprise.

I can't help but think that if even grumpy, grunting Mark can find someone, surely, I can too.

But not many women want a man who's here and gone all the time. I've got roots, and they run deep, but I've got dreams that take me far and wide too. And that's a lot to ask of a woman.

But I'm here now.

"Yeah, drove back from Tennessee," I answer, knowing he

probably didn't keep up with where I disappeared to this time. "But things went well."

"You get that filly knocked up?" Sophie asks, knowing she sounds more frat bro than nice girl. I think that's one of the reasons James likes her. She can keep up with our brother-hood of boy shit, though we might've corrupted her a little bit. "She's young, right? Three?"

And that's one of the reasons I like Sophie. Other than she keeps my brother on his toes while somehow loving him, she can talk horses with me, cows with Mark, and bulls with James. She can carry on a conversation about ranch maxi-mization, check your pigs' health, and get dirty in the mud without a second thought before getting gussied up in heels and a dress. James is a lucky man. We're a lucky family to have her as a sister.

"Almost four," I correct her. "So if it takes, she'll be just shy of five for delivery. Should be good."

The waitress sets my plate down, and I basically hoover it into my mouth. I've got manners, and even use them occasion-ally, but right now, I just need food in my belly. Lunch was a few hundred miles and an Interstate rest stop ago.

I tell Sophie and James about the ranch I visited, their horse stock, and how we'd decided on a particular stud for their filly, hopefully soon-to-be mare. They return the favor, telling me about what I've missed at home on our ranch.

"What brought you two lovebirds out tonight? Planning on some dancing?" I ask as we wrap up our ranch business update.

Sophie grins, shaking her head. "Shayanne got the soap deal at the resort. She put everything out today, so we're cele-brating."

I nod, pushing my empty plate forward a few inches. "Good for her," I say.

I know Shayanne more in name than in person these days. When we were kids, she was the annoying squirt who followed us boys around, demanding that we include her in our roughhousing play.

Later, the families drifted apart, even though we're technically neighbors. But lots of acres and well-tended fences mean that neighborly distance is pretty far, and the Hatfield-McCoy vibe our families maintain has kept us even further apart.

I hadn't seen Shayanne for years until she was a bridesmaid at Sophie's wedding this past summer. My impression then had been that she'd grown into a stunning firecracker of a woman. In her bridesmaid dress, she was all curls and curves and bright eyes that dared a cowboy to fall under her sway.

But she's young and a Tannen, so I mostly just hear about her from Sophie since they're best friends. We've struck somewhat of a tenuous truce with them, mostly because of Soph, but that doesn't mean I want to poke that particular bear.

Until . . . speak of the devil and she will appear.

Shayanne herself plops down beside me, her tanned and toned bare thigh pressing up against mine as she leans in, breathlessly proclaiming, "Whew, that last one near did me in. I need a water, stat, before round two starts."

I can see a thin bead of sweat running from her collarbone down to her cleavage, and thankfully, her attention is on Sophie as I watch its winding trail. My mouth waters to chase it, track it like a hunter, and lick it up as I devour her lush tits.

I inhale sharply. *Where did that come from?*

But I can smell her. A sweet combination of sweat and sunshine, dirt and perfume. Nothing fancy, not this girl . . . just honest.

Honestly sexy.

I want to breathe her in, explore her every nook and cranny to see where her uniquely personal perfume originates.

I clear my throat. Fuck, this trip must've hit me harder than I thought. I need to get laid. And not by the Tannen woman sitting next to me.

Her cheeks are pink with exertion, her smile wide and dazzling. She looks pleased with herself, though I'm not sure if that's from her achievement today with the soap or her spins on the floor. Maybe both.

"Here, you can have my water," I tell her, pushing the glass I haven't touched her way. I purposefully pick up my beer and take a good pull on it so I don't watch her throat work the cool liquid down. Instead, I scan the area behind her, wondering who she was dancing with.

I see a guy in a dusty, curled ballcap eyeing our table like he's trying to figure out the relations between us all. With Shayanne sitting by my side, I'm sure he's hoping we're kin so he's not cockblocked for the night. I give him a glare over my beer bottle, and he spins in place, walking away.

That's right, buddy. Hands off the girl.

Wait . . . what? Why?

I'm not sure why I care. She's certainly entitled to dance with anyone she damn well pleases, but I feel a bit protective of her for some reason. Not that she needs any sheltering. Everyone knows her daddy and brothers keep her on a short leash. Hell, she rarely even comes into town unless it's to hang out with Sophie, and that's usually for girls' night in.

But something about her makes me want to throw my arm over her shoulders, pull her to my side, and keep her safe. In realizing that she's all grown up, I see that other guys are checking her out and it doesn't seem right. She's not innocent, but maybe unjaded? I don't want anyone taking advantage.

Except for me, maybe, I think selfishly.

I don't know what it is tonight, but something about Shayanne, the girl I've known distantly for years, seems different, and that's a problem. A growing one in my jeans, which are getting uncomfortable as fuck.

She swallows greedily, gulping before sighing in satisfaction. "Thanks."

"No problem," I say, hoping speaking the words will make them true. Because I'm not looking to get in a fight tonight over her honor, especially considering that for all I know, she's hoping Ballcap Boy is on his way over for round two on the floor. "I hear congrats are in order? Happy for you, Shay."

The nickname falls off my tongue unbidden. I don't know this girl well enough to run around shortening her name, but I did it anyway.

She doesn't seem to mind, or even notice, too excited to tell me about her soaps being in the resort gift shop. And though Sophie basically just told me the same thing, I listen to the story again, happy to hear her share her excitement and wanting to hear it from her lips.

She seems to catch her breath because I can feel her booted foot tapping beneath the table, and when the next song starts, her eyes dart to the floor.

"All right, I'm up again. Love this song!"

Like a flash, I can read the future for just a split second and know I'm fucked as fucked can be. She's going to eyeball me for a dance, and I'm going to do it. Mama raised a gentleman, and if a lady asks you to dance, you'd best get off your hiney and cut a rug.

But this is a bad idea. A *really* bad idea.

For one, Ballcap Boy is still stalking around on the other side of the room last I checked, which was just a second ago. And two, her last name is Tannen and my last name is Bennett, and everyone knows that's like playing with dynamite and fire and hoping shit doesn't blow up. Only Sophie exists in the gray area.

Hell, half the folks in here have probably already texted her brothers that we're sitting together, even with James and Sophie on the other side of the table.

But most importantly, and most dangerously, I'm finding that I quite like the idea of pulling her curvy body against mine and sharing space for a little longer.

Before I can make an excuse to get the hell outta dodge, she turns those eyes on me. They're hazel, not quite blue or green or brown but some amalgamation of them all, and I'm struck with an urge to map each fleck of color.

"Come on, Luke. Scoot me around the floor," she orders. And though she's asking me, it feels casual, like if I say no, she'll just hop over to the next cowboy. Like nothing ever gets her down. Like she's not remotely affected by me the way I am by her.

And for just a minute, I want to hold her sunshine in my arms and let it chase through me, lift me up with her exuberance. And test my limits, and maybe hers too.

"All right, Shay," I say, knowing it's simultaneously the politest and stupidest thing I can do. For me, for her, and for our families.

I can already imagine the 'conversation' I might have with her brothers about this.

She has a sort of pass to be friends with Sophie, and by extension, James, but even then, they keep the family business chatter non-existent to respect the tension between our families. Tension they planted, watered, and helped foster.

I damn sure shouldn't be here publicly thumbing my nose at the whole thing by dancing with Paul Tannen's youngest and only daughter.

Yet, here I am with her in my arms as a slow country waltz plays. Luke Combs's *Beautiful Crazy* plays from the jukebox, and while some couples are getting mighty cozy, I hold

Shayanne a mostly respectable distance away. Not quite the hard-armed frame Mama taught us, not quite the bumping uglies grinding some other folks are doing to the sweet song, but somewhere in between.

You can see daylight between us if you look, but there isn't much.

I can read that she's about to say something, and right now, we're not fighting like our families tend to do, so I spin her, doing a complicated switching of hands that has her grinning in surprise. Then I dip her, sweeping both of her feet off the ground for a moment.

To her credit, she's a great follower and goes right along as I lead her like we've been dancing together forever.

When I set her back right, whatever she was going to say is wiped from her mind, and she's laughing and breathing hard.

"That was awesome. Luke Bennett, you can dance!" Her declaration is one of pure delight. "Where'd you learn that one move?"

"Denver," I say with a shrug, though I know I'm on the other side of the bell curve as far as dance partners go. I've spent more than my fair share of nights alone in country towns, and bar dancing is one way to make friends. I might've even taken a bar-session class or two after a beer, not that I'd admit to that.

The song ends and the next one starts, a fast one, thank fuck. After a quick eyebrow lift to ask if she's still in, we dance several more rounds, working around the floor as I show her off. She's not my girl, but she is the prettiest girl in the bar, and I'm the lucky guy dancing with her right now.

But her hand in mine feels nice, the curve of her lower back as I lead her is completely proper but feels naughty, and the heat from her skin singes me to the core.

From the table, I see James lift his hand, and I pause. "Looks like James is flagging me. You want a break?"

She pauses, her bottom lip disappearing behind her teeth, but she's smiling like the world is her oyster. "Nah, I've got a couple more in these boots. But will you order me another water?"

I nod, stuck somewhere between disappointed and relieved, and then spin her loose.

Finally free of whatever spell she was weaving, I run my fingers through my hair. *What the hell was that?*

I've never looked at Shayanne like that, never wanted her that way, but tonight, all I can think about is her curvy body sinking onto my cock as she rides me like a cowgirl. I don't know what changed, but I need to stay far away from her and her witchy magic that makes me think with my dick and not my head. Because she is danger with a capital 'chop off your D'. Her dad and brothers would happily feed my cock to their goats and leave me ball-less for daring to even fantasize about their baby girl.

But damn, their baby girl grew up. She grew up good.

Before I've taken two steps away, Ballcap Boy is catching her hand, and she flows into dancing with him like it was choreographed that way, like something out of a movie.

Oddly, I feel torn. Part of me feels like I'm leaving her to the wolves, but it's only a dance and I have no right to tell that guy to step off. He just rubs me the wrong way, a bit too predatory for a sweet girl like Shayanne.

I'm still watching over my shoulder as I sit down with James and Sophie. "You didn't have to sit out for us. I was just giving you a five-minute warning that we're almost out. That's what the parenting books say you're supposed to do so the kid doesn't throw a tantrum."

If glares were daggers, he'd be bleeding out right here at Hank's. "You calling me a kid? And trying to use your kid tricks on me? Shithead."

There's a beat of tension before we both laugh. "You really reading parenting books?"

James nods, and I'm honestly not surprised. He's full throttle—with Sophie, with their wedding, and he'll be the same with their baby. I give that kid two years before he or she will be on a horse.

"Yeah, I figure I had pretty good examples with Pops and Mama, but now that it's my turn, that's a lot of pressure to live up to. I mean, how am I gonna compete with Pops, you know? Especially with this new generation of kids?"

He's right. Our father was the best . . . rancher, husband, dad. He was the best man I've ever known, and we all miss him dearly. Hard to believe it's been almost a year and a half since he died under the tree in the front yard, right where he proposed to Mama so many years ago.

I tell him earnestly, "You do what you can, and when you fuck up, Mama and Sophie will tell you. Just listen to them, say 'yes, ma'am', and get your shit straight."

He knocks my knee under the table, and I grin, knowing that I'm right. But more importantly, he knows I'm right too.

Shayanne reappears at the table, grabbing her fresh water and chugging it like it's a beer guzzling contest before wiping her mouth with the back of her hand. Damn, if I could be a glass of water right now . . .

"James and Sophie are out for the evening," I say instead, forcing myself to stay polite. "I probably should head home too. I've been on the road all day."

Shayanne smiles. "Oh, me too, then. This was fun. Thanks!"

We get up, and the girls hug and make promises to talk tomorrow. James gives me a handshake, handing out advice like he's the boss of me. My little brother . . . the boss.

Like hell.

"Head on home now, Luke. Drive safe."

I flip him off, and he grins like he never had a doubt in my ability to make appropriate decisions. Like he's such a responsible adult now that he's married with a baby on the way.

Sophie hugs me too, and I swear her eyes are ticking from me to Shayanne with hope. I can almost see the heart emojis jumping out like in a cartoon.

"Best you toss those thoughts out the way you should've tossed my brother before he put a baby in you," I warn her with a deep growl just between us. "Tannen. Bennett."

The two words, just our names, are a reminder to us both, one I definitely need. They're also enough to dampen Sophie's scheming. "Yeah, yeah," she whispers, but maybe not as resigned as I'd hoped. "*Never the 'twain shall meet.* Still, can't blame a girl for hoping for her best friend and her brother. But yeah, I kinda like you, so probably not a good idea to get yourself killed by dipping the wick so close to home."

Sophie. The girl who can be as prissy as a princess one minute and as crass as a ranch-raised cowboy the next.

In the parking lot outside, I sidle up next to Shayanne. "Hey, I'm not a creeper following you, but we're going the same way, so I'll be on your ass the whole way home, you know?"

She laughs like that half-assed joke was actually funny, playfully slapping my chest. I imagine for one second that she's feeling my muscles because she actually wants to touch me, not because she's clowning around.

"I know, neighbor."

The whole way home, I follow those red, glowing taillights, knowing they should be telling me *stop, stop, stop*, but when I reach our ranch gate, it takes all I have to turn in and not see her the rest of the way home.

I might be crude, a dirtier cowboy than most, but I'm still a gentleman with manners.

Sometimes.

I just want to make sure she gets there safe and sound. That's all, I tell myself. But even I can't believe my own lie.

I see her tap her brake lights twice, a good night salute, and then she's gone, red orbs getting further away from me.

Probably for the best . . . but I don't like 'for the best'.

CHAPTER 3

SHAYANNE

*O*ur kitchen can get hot as balls. And this is one of those times. I'd love to get out of here for a little bit, cool down, and cool off.

My lips screw up as I look around and then check the clock, wondering if I have time for a short break. It's not like farm life is a clock in, clock out, scheduled break type of job, but it's important to get everything done in a timely manner. Our lives and livelihood depend on it.

Today is canning day. Well, it's canning prep day, which is more than half the battle. If today's prep goes right, then the actual canning can be fun . . . ish. If not, it's the third circle of Hell.

I've got dozens of jars boiled and ready for me to start the real work tomorrow, along with lids, seals . . . the whole works. I glance down at the list of recipes I'm planning, some tried and true, some new for this year. I might not have gone to a fancy culinary institute, but any country woman worth her salt has a repertoire that'll please the hungry masses.

And this month's farmer's market sales will be instrumental

in getting us through the lean months of winter. Farming is feast or famine, and when times are good, you'd best put some away for a rainy day.

Well, except that we like rain because then the fields green right up and the cows get nice and fat, but the metaphor still works.

"Fuck it. I'm out for a bit," I tell the empty room.

I tend to have a foul mouth at times too. Three brothers and all.

And yeah, I talk to myself.

I talk to everything—people, animals, and inanimate objects. Daddy finally had to ban me from the living room during football season because I kept yelling at the TV too much.

Mom used to say it's because I have so many words in my head, a constant cacophony of chatter that needs an outlet.

In hindsight, I think she was just happy for me to share the wealth with any and everything around me so that she didn't have to listen to me wax poetic about every thought that ran through my mind. But she never made me feel like I was annoying her in any way. She happily listened to me. She was a good mother, and I miss her.

I look over to where our only inside dog is lying on a braided rug by the front door, watching for Bruce to come home. Murphy might be a family pet in theory, but we all know his heart belongs to my brother.

For a guy nicknamed Brutal, and rarely called by his given name of Bruce by anyone outside of family, he's a pushover for that pooch. Only that dog, though, as anyone who's tried to get one over on him has learned.

I drop my voice to my adopted dog-ish gravelly sound. "You sure that's a good idea, Miss Shayanne?" Murphy is old-school, calls me Miss like I'm a proper lady. He's the only one that does that. I laugh at my own weirdness.

"Yes, Murph. I'm sure, and don't you go telling on me neither, or there will be exactly zero pumpkin puree in your dog food this week, and we both know how much you like a little fall flavor. You're almost a basic Starbucks girl, fangirling for her Pumpkin Spice Latte."

Okay, that's pushing it, and he lifts his head at the insult, huffing before his chin returns to his paws. I take that as a sign of his agreeable silence.

I grab my notebook, part diary, part recipe book, part scrapbook, and my near-constant companion. I scratch Murphy's head as one last bribe and hit the barn to saddle up.

My favorite horse is a chestnut mare named Embers for her brownish-red tinted coat that's capped with a black mane and tail. She whinnies as I come closer, as ready for a ride as I am.

"Hey there, girl. You wanna get outta here?"

She has a voice too, but considering my imaginary conversation with Murphy, I hold back from speaking for Embers too. I lay a blanket on her back, saddle her up, and climb aboard.

The afternoon sun beats down on me, but the fall wind blows through my hair and over my face, refreshing and cool. The land stretches out before me, nearly flat with a few gentle rolling hills, and wide to the horizon in the distance. It's beautiful, it's home, but at the same time, it's a cage.

A pretty one, of course, with family and friends. But sometimes, I think it would've been nice to be one of those city kids with a mom and dad who told them they could be anything they wanted. Sure, there would've probably been a lot of extra baggage . . . Girl Scouts, piano lessons, primping, and SATs. But I could be anything, an astronaut or a firefighter, a ballerina or a businesswoman.

Well, I am that last one now, a businesswoman in my own right. If I wasn't sitting astride Ember, I'd do a happy dance at that thought, but I restrain myself, just barely, so I don't fall off the horse like a newb.

But I've also never been off this plot of land, not for long, anyway. I've never considered that I'd be anything other than exactly what I am.

The stand-in for Mom, a replacement after she died.

The glue that holds the Tannens together.

The last bastion of civility to keep my brothers from going feral.

I hope I've done her proud, taking care of the family the way she would've been happy to do. I'm happy to do it too, truth be told. I do something meaningful here. It just would've been nice to get to choose it myself, which seems like a small but important distinction.

Ahead, I see my destination. Far away from the house, over a hill and to the slight valley below, sits a big shade tree. It's my refuge, my hideout where none of the boys ever look, mostly because it's right on the line of our property and the Bennett ranch next door.

I can already feel the long day of work drifting off my shoulders, my load lightening, and with a little encouragement from my heels, Ember stops beneath the canopy of leaves. They're still mostly green, but the edges are turning a yellowy color that'll darken to orange before they fall to the ground, leaving my sanctuary bare for the winter season.

I let Ember roam freely, trusting that she won't go too far and will answer my whistle when I'm ready to leave. I approach the tree like an old friend, placing a palm to the rough bark of the trunk.

"Hey, there. I've missed you," I tell the tree. "Mind throwing me a little shade?" I grin at the silly joke, but the tree doesn't so much as sway. I'm weird but not crazy, and I know the tree won't talk back. Not in words, at least.

I slip my boots off, reach up, and grab a branch, hoisting

myself into the canopy to find my favorite spot. It's like the tree grew a chair just for me, a spot to lean back against the trunk, but with a wide enough limb that I can sit comfortably. And hidden by the leaves. I can't see out or be seen.

I pull out my notebook, flipping through the pages of my own penmanship as I dream of far-away places, of new scent combinations of soap, of Daddy getting his shit straight and being a stand-up guy.

You know, the basics.

Time passes slowly here in the cocoon of my tree until I hear hoofbeats coming. Then time somehow both stretches and speeds up at the same time as excuses and justifications begin running through my mind. Depending on which brother, or God forbid, my dad, has found me, I'll have to adjust on the fly.

I slowly move a leafy branch, peeking out, but I can't see anyone. I can hear a horse snorting, though.

And then a deep voice rumbles, "What the fuck?"

That's not one of the Tannen boys, not one of my brothers and not my father. Which means only one thing. A Bennett.

The voice pitches softer, higher. "Come here, girl. What are you doing out here?"

Shit. He sees Ember, fully saddled, so it's obvious there's someone out here. I debate keeping quiet, but when I hear him cooing worriedly, asking the horse where her rider is, my conscience takes over.

"She's fine. I'm here," I say from the treetop.

I can't see him, but I can hear his boots scuff quickly on the grass. "Fuck!" I get the impression that I just scared the shit out of him and made him jump, which makes me giggle.

I wonder which Bennett it is? Surly, grumpy Mark? Funny, love-smitten James? Or . . .

I hop down from my hidey-hole to the soft grass and turn around.

"Luke?" I say, not surprised to see him since I'm right up by his property line, but also somehow shocked too. I haven't seen him much besides the few minutes here and there in the crowd of people at Sophie's wedding, so running into him twice in one week seems weird.

"Shayanne? You almost gave me a heart attack." He holds his chest dramatically, which draws my attention to the broad width there.

I'd noticed it when we danced too, how he'd dwarfed me but held me softly, like a gentle giant. And when I'd been kidding and slapped his pec right over his heart, it'd been like touching a brick wall. I'd had to hold myself back from asking if that was real and patting him again just to double-check for myself.

"Sorry, just hanging out. I'm canning tomorrow, so I had to escape the hot kitchen for a bit."

"To our property?" he asks, his eyes narrowed, but he seems more curious than angry.

Usually, folks are pretty kind out here in the country. Welcoming and hospitable even. But not so with the Tannens and Bennetts.

A while back, Mr. Bennett passed and Daddy tried to buy their land. It was in poor taste, and he was a bit heavy-handed with Mrs. Bennett and the boys, thinking he could take advantage in their time of need. Not that things between the families were good before that. It just reignited tensions a bit.

We hadn't known about Daddy's tactics at first, had only heard him ranting and raving about 'those snot-nosed Bennett boys that think they're better'n everyone else.'

There'd been hard words and a tense moment where my brothers and the Bennetts nearly came to a full-on brawl. In the long run, though, Mark Bennett had been the better man, and after accidentally stirring up some trouble with his questions around town, he'd filled us in about Daddy's secret gambling habit.

It'd been a turning point for our family. The time 'before' and the time 'after', when our image of our father had been not just tarnished but shattered.

I'd always been a bit of a Daddy's girl, but now, I can see that he's slick and opportunistic. Within twenty-four hours of that newsflash, Brody had taken over the family reins with me at his side. Daddy is a part of this family, of course, but business-wise, it's mostly in name only, though his word still carries some sway. Too many years of listening to him makes it hard to completely dismiss him. Especially when he gets loud.

And so the cold war continues. I think mostly because no one wants to rock the boat. Or piss off Daddy, since he's moved on to threatening to kick Brody out in some 'who's the boss' battle. *As if this place could run without Brody*, I often think with an internal eye roll.

But years of being the youngest and being the only girl mean I can't help but argue and stand my ground, literally. "I'm not on your land. This tree is Tannen property." I pat the trunk like an old friend.

Luke's eyes darken, but I can see a smile hinting at the corners of his full lips. I think he likes this verbal sparring. "The trunk, maybe, but that branch you were lollygagging in is definitely over the property line."

He might be right. Hell, the whole tree might be on Bennett property. I never really thought about it, and there hasn't been a fence in this area to delineate the property line in decades because it's not a pasture that's used for the cattle. It's just open space, sort of a buffer zone between our land and theirs.

So I hedge my bets because Mama didn't raise no fool and my daddy's a gambler. "Well, unless you're here to tear it down, I don't reckon it matters one bit. So, are ya?"

"Here to tear it down?" Luke asks, his blue eyes swirling with confusion like he's not following my train of thought. I'm not surprised. Most folks don't. "Of course not. I like this tree."

I nod once. "Glad we got that settled. Second matter—you never saw me here. I've been in the kitchen all day. You got that?" I point a blunt-nailed finger his way. "Capiche?" I sound like a Hollywood version of a mobster, but with a twang instead of an Italian accent.

But he gets me instantly this time. "Never saw you. Understood, loud and clear, ma'am." He stands straight, clicks his boots together once, and throws a half-assed salute my way. A shitty impersonation of a soldier, but then he relaxes back into his usual cowboy stance. He's laid-back and mellow, but he has little biting surprises, like vanilla ice cream with pop rocks in it. It's a thing. I had it once on the Fourth of July.

He scratches at the sexy scruff of blond along his jaw, his brows pulled together over eyes the color of cloudless summer skies. "So, why are you hiding out here? Everything okay?"

He sounds like he cares. I remember how kind he just was with Ember, who can be skittish around new people. But she walked right up when he called her and is currently nibbling at his heels, hoping for scratches behind her ears.

Horses are a good barometer of a person. If they like you, you're probably all right. If they don't, chances are, you're a bad egg. It's not a perfect test, but I trust Ember's instincts.

"All good in the hood," I say for some reason. I think I heard it on a television show once or twice. I try to play it off, laughing at myself before Luke laughs at me. "I mean, just been a busy morning getting ready for canning tomorrow, and the kitchen was so hot, I had to escape for a little. The next few days are going to be doozies with Triple-P on the agenda. Even with the radio going, it's gonna be five kinds of ugh."

My words are rushed, each one falling on the one before it

like it's a train coming in to the station too fast. Surprisingly, Luke follows until the end.

"Triple-P?" he asks, his teeth flashing white. But he seems interested, not like he's laughing at me, which is a good thing because I'm thinking I like that smile. Like he's trying to figure me out, but I'm the simplest of simple. What you see is what you get with me.

"Pears, peaches, and pumpkins. Bobby and Bruce are doing all the harvesting. I've got all the recipes ready, and the jars are cooling on the counter, ready to be filled. Today's my last day of freedom before I get chained to the stove for the rest of the week, at least. And that's just round one. Ding." I make a sound like the boxing match can start, tapping an invisible bell with my fingers.

I'm joking, of course, but Luke looks a little horrified as he looks down at my bare feet, or maybe it's my ankle he's checking out?

Either way, I clarify. "Not literally, like ball and chain" —I drag my pink-tipped toes through the grass like I'm lame— "but because of the cans. I've seen your mom's jellies. You know what I'm talking about."

Recognition dawns on his face. "Yeah, but she usually just does a batch or two at a time. Maybe fifty jars a year. How many you doing?"

I know he doesn't give one single shit about my canning plans, but what else am I gonna talk about? Goat soap? The way he looks at me with those blue eyes that make me want to melt into the grass? Or how it felt when he'd catch me solidly against his muscled chest after a spin that reset my world's axis?

No, definitely not that last one, and I'd best stick to the safe topic at hand and not ruffle any feathers. Especially mine, which are itching to do a bit of a sway his way.

"I've got two different pear recipes, cinnamon spicy for

cobbler and a sweet jelly. Peaches? Three, I think, including a new bourbon one I'm excited to play with. And more pumpkin recipes than humanly possible, but since it's a once a year thing, I do it up big."

I flip through my notebook, showing him the recipes, but I flash them too fast to reveal my secret ingredients. "My favorite is this smashed pumpkin, though. I've got almost a hundred orders for the special pie filling I make and twenty more Thanksgiving orders already. Lots to do, lots to do . . ."

My voice trails off awkwardly, heat running up my cheeks as I for some reason feel like I'm babbling. But Luke is steady as can be, just watching me ramble and taking me in like I'm a show he wants to watch on repeat.

He even seems impressed, whistling softly. "Damn, you are busy. All that and soaps too?"

I shrug, toeing a rock in the grass. "Well, Brody wouldn't dream of letting me near his animals, and Daddy won't let a girl help with the harvest." I drop my voice low, mimicking my dad's. "Get in the house, young lady. Let those boys take care of the fields."

My eyes roll unbidden, and Luke laughs, a deep chuckle that vibrates in my belly too. "Yup . . . Sophie had to kick a little butt to earn her respect from James back when they first met. Some people . . ."

"So up to my eyeballs in pumpkin pie it is." I hold my hand flat, just below my eyes to highlight my point.

"I get it. I'm playing catch-up too. Mark and James play favorites and only ride their horses most of the time, so while I'm gone, the rest of my babies get a little too lazy. Fed, brushed, and pampered too much . . . but they need the exercise. I'm letting Duster stretch his legs a bit." He looks at the horse fondly. "But I didn't think my ride was gonna lead to me catching a trespasser in our tree. Even if she's a cute one."

Oh, we're not back to this, are we? Wait, did he just say

I'm cute? Is he teasing about the tree or about my being cute? I'm not sure.

Both of us busy as beavers building a dam before winter but neither of us making a move from beneath the shade of *my* tree.

Interesting. Exciting.

Those are the words that keep running around in my head when I think of Luke, and I really do wonder what he thinks of me. I know I'm not the usual type of girl that guys go for. I'm a little too rough, a little too odd. But I'm looking at Luke like I'm sure women all over the continental US have, like I could eat him up with a spoon for supper.

I take a moment to really feast my eyes on him, from his mop of overgrown blond hair that's starting to have the barest hint of curl, to his blue eyes squinting against the sun, to his full lips and chiseled jaw. Broad shoulders, as we established at Hank's, taper to a slim waist where his T-shirt is tucked in behind his belt, and his long, thick legs are encased in work-worn denim.

Yep, a girl could definitely work with that, I think. *He's all honest to goodness, authentic man.*

Thankfully, the thought manages to stay in my head and not pass my lips, but judging by the amused smirk on Luke's face, he's reading my mind loud and clear. The air between us crackles with new, electric tension, our eyes meeting and all humor falling away as it registers that we're both thinking the same thing.

Well, I'm thinking Luke Bennett is a genuine horse riding, cowboy hat wearing, someone call Bonnie Tyler because I've done found a hero that I wanna ride all night long hunk. Hopefully, he's thinking some sexier, sweeter version of that, because in my mind, he's smoother than I am.

But suddenly, his look darkens like he just remembered

something, and when his eyes drift off to the distance, toward our homestead, I know what it is . . . my last name.

"Shay," he says, his voice soft and quiet, but it might as well be a siren, warning me off.

My gut drops, a sour feeling taking over. "Yeah, you're right. I'd better get back to the house before anyone misses me. Uh, I'll see ya around."

I toss him a careless wave, grabbing my boots but not bothering to put them on as I whistle for Ember.

She scurries over to me, thankfully sensing my need to get out of here. I climb up, and though I want to slouch in defeat, my training kicks in and my spine straightens.

Out of the fiery kitchen and into the fire itself. Because I think Luke could burn me to ashes, with no poetic phoenix rising in rebirth. I'd be just plain toast in his wake. And while he'd be a hell of a way to go, based on his obvious rebuff in the silent but heated moment, I don't think he's interested in the girl next door.

"Hey, Shayanne!" he calls out, and for a heartbeat, I consider pretending not to hear him, imagining that it was just the wind or my own wishful thinking. But I know it was his voice.

I glance back, jaw hard. "Yeah?"

He smiles, sweet and sexy and stirring my guts into mashed potatoes all in a single look. "Think you could save a jar of smashed pumpkin for me?"

An olive branch.

Daring. Stupid. Sweet. All thoughts that rush through my mind, but in the end, I smile and give in because a little bit of something good is better than none of it. And Luke is good, even if he's not good for me.

"Of course. But I don't do delivery service." That's a lie. I deliver stuff all over town with the boys' help. But I can't exactly roll up to the Bennett house in my truck because I'd get busted for sure.

Luke tilts his head toward the tree. "Meet you here?" He still looks uncertain, like even though I agreed, he thinks I'm going to bolt like a jumpy foal. Or maybe like he's questioning himself on whether asking for some pie filling was a smart move or the dumbest thing he could've done.

I blink, telling my heart to slow the hell down because it's beating in my chest like the hooves of a thundering herd of cattle. *Not a date, not a date,* I keep telling myself, trying to get the thuds to match my mental pace.

"Okay, gimme three days to get the first batches done, so . . . Thursday? Around three?"

I choose the day and time knowing my brothers' and Daddy's schedule. They might think they're the boss, but I'm the one who keeps the whole train chugging with everything running smoothly. And by Thursday afternoon, Daddy'll be gone for his weekend of gambling up north and my brothers will be busy with chores of their own. I should be able to sneak away without a problem and get back before dinner. Easy peasy, lemon squeezy.

He nods, giving me a full smile like he's happy I agreed. "See you then," he says, confirming our little peace treaty.

The trip back to the house is faster than I want it to be, my mind ping-ponging and replaying the expressions that chased across Luke's face.

He could've just let me go after he caught me blatantly giving him the once-over. It would've hurt, but it'd be like ripping a Band-Aid off.

But he'd called me back, made plans to see me again. I can't decide if he's just trying to pull the sticky bandage off slowly so it doesn't take skin with it or if he's actually interested.

In my pumpkin pie filling? In me? While that moment had

felt like something, his wanting the pie filling is more likely, rich and thick, creamy and delicious, while I'm just . . . me.

Shayanne Tannen, the odd-duck, fast-talking tomboy.

I know folks in town think I'm some sheltered little girl, but I'm not. I'm a woman with a backbone of steel, big dreams, and a dirty mind. If only they knew.

"Hell, if only Luke knew," I tell Ember. She whinnies in response like my good girl.

CHAPTER 4

LUKE

*B*y lunchtime on Thursday, I'm damn near chomping at the bit for the sun to get to chasing its way through the sky toward mid-afternoon.

I don't know what it is, but my mind has returned to Shayanne about a couple of hundred times over the last few days. Our conversation had been like a roller coaster, ups and downs and twists and turns as the words rushed out of her pretty mouth like she couldn't wait to have someone to listen to everything she had to say. I was glad for it. I hadn't wanted her to control it but had rather been interested in what was running around in her head. Even about canning, for fuck's sake.

Everything had been comfortable and casual, and when I'd seen her eyes tracing over my body, I wanted to puff up like a damn stallion. Whatever protective urges I'd been having at Hank's had caught fire in an instant when she licked her lips like I was an ice cream cone she was ready to suck down. I'd been on the verge of making a move, had felt the desire running hot through us both in the small space between us.

And then reality hit me. Hard.

41

That girl doesn't need my protection, and she sure as hell doesn't need my attention. She's got three brothers who are big, bigger, and biggest. And none of them exactly like me.

So it's not good for either of us. But she'd looked so dejected, and I couldn't hurt her, so I'd done the stupid—or maybe brilliant—thing and asked for pumpkin pie. No euphemism intended, mostly. I just really hoped, deep down, that I could see her smile again.

And she did. It'd been beautiful, and my heart thumped proudly that I'd done that for her.

Me. Luke Bennett.

And now I keep torturing myself in my few idle moments with memories of her cute little bare feet digging into the green grass, her wavy hair blowing in the breeze, and wondering if her skin would taste like sunshine.

More than once, I've nearly been caught daydreaming by James or Mark, and I know my luck can't hold out forever. They won't know why, but they aren't as stupid as they look.

Fuck. What the hell is wrong with me?

I shove away from my desk, which is basically just a table in the back stall of the barn with a fan to supplement the air conditioner. I stalk over to the nearest stall and offer up an oat cookie to Mama's favorite mare, Briarbelle.

"You up for a ride today, girl? We'll get going here *soon*." She snorts like she can hear the lie in my voice as much as I can, because three o'clock can't come fast enough, but she takes the cookie delicately before chomping down. I give her few scratches and brush along her flanks, more for something to do to kill time than because she needs it.

My phone rings in my pocket, and I have a momentary surge of hope that it's Shayanne calling me, which is ridiculous. *She doesn't have my number*, I think.

I glare at the phone like it's responsible for the offense until I see who's calling. Talk about an important call. My heart leaps into my throat as I push the *Talk* button, my mouth suddenly dry.

"Hello?"

"Luke, it's Russell Quinlan." The voice sounds like exactly what Rusty is, a pack-a-day, sixty-year-old cowboy who could chew nails and hit a bullseye when he spits out the crumbs.

"Rusty, how's it going?" I say, my breath making my lungs tight.

"Not good, unfortunately, Luke. Sad to say, it didn't take and my Apie ain't got a foal in her."

Rusty's Appaloosa horse is a stunner, sure to create a genetic line of superior horses. But not this time, it seems.

I research the matches I make to an obsessive degree, checking pedigrees and genetic lines. The work I do is important, to breed for desired traits but also to do it safely and ensure the resulting animals are healthy, strong stock.

"I'm so sorry to hear that. She's a good one, though. We'll try again when she's ready." It's true, but it's a pitiful promise when we're talking the thousands of dollars my clients invest in this process. There's great joy when it succeeds, but when it fails, it feels like a personal failure. Like I let my client and the horse down.

"We will," Rusty vows. "Probably won't get a chance for another try this year, but add us to your rotation for spring and we'll cross our fingers."

"Will do," I say, making a mental note to do just that.

I like Rusty. He's authentic, a straight shooter, but not one for small talk, so once the business conversation is done, he says his goodbye and we hang up.

Well, shit. I thought that was going to be a good match. I recently used the same stallion for another mare in Colorado, so I really hope this was just a one-off.

I glance back to the phone, realizing that Rusty's call was just the distraction I needed and that I can head out to the tree to meet Shayanne without being too early or looking eager. Nothing worse than showing up looking like it's the first time I've ever talked to a girl before.

I saddle up Briarbelle and take her out, letting her go in a casual loping ramble across the fields. I make it a point to whistle before I come over the ridge by the spring-fed pond, just in case. Sophie should be at work, so it's likely clear, but since she and James have claimed the spot as their own, we're always better safe than sorry.

Mark and Katelyn have the courtesy of doing it at his house, at least. Most of the time.

But the pond is empty save for some ducks that should be flying south any day now. I encourage Briarbelle to pick up the pace to run her a little bit, stretch her underused legs out, and to get to the tree faster. The anticipation is killing me.

But when the tree comes into sight, Shayanne's not there. She might be hiding up in the canopy again, but I don't see her horse either, and my gut drops as disappointment winds through my veins.

I ride on over to the tree, though, hoping she'll somehow magically appear. I wouldn't put it past her to have some sort of parlor trick the way she surprised me the other day, her disembodied voice scaring the bejesus out of me.

I hop down and look up into the leaves, and a white piece of paper catches my eye. It's sitting on a branch, a rock holding it down.

I can't remember the last time someone wrote me an actual letter or even a scribbled note, but she did.

Alone, with no one to tattle on me but Briarbelle, I let my smile loose as I grab for the paper.

Running late but got a good reason. See you at four. I'll bring dinner. – S

Her handwriting is round and bubbly, cursive but bits of print mixed in so it's unique, like her. There's a smiley face and a messy heart by her initial, and I try not to read too much into them. Maybe she signs everything that way, for all I know?

Dinner, though? We definitely hadn't planned on that, but now that she's suggested it, I'm excited to share a meal with her.

I send Mama a quick text that I won't be at her dinner table tonight, and thankfully, she doesn't ask questions.

But she does send an emoji back, a silly looking face with one big eye, one little eye, and its tongue sticking out of a smile. What the hell does that mean? She rarely texts us anyway, usually preferring to call us on the carpet in person, so maybe she just picked the first one that appealed to her?

But I don't question her choice of emoji lest she question my evening plans. Give me a choice between angering God or Mama . . . well, the Almighty had better get ready.

I climb back in the saddle and ride Briarbelle around the pasture for a bit, working with her on responses to the reins and then getting down to walk her, judging her ability to be gently led.

One part of my specialty is breeding premium horses, but the other just as important part is training them. Briarbelle is still pretty young. Her first foal, Polka Dottie, is barely a year-ling. But she's doing well and will likely be able to take a rider among the cattle soon, which is a big step for a horse and makes me feel a bit like a proud father.

But even as I work with her, I don't lose sight of the tree or my watch. At 3:57, I hear hoofbeats running hard right before I see Shayanne come over the ridge.

Shayanne is in her element as she directs her horse my way. She's a natural, clearly as easy in the saddle as any of my brothers. I can see the flush in her cheeks, her hair flying behind her like a banner, and her eyes lit up like diamonds. Unfortunately, that look also has me thinking of other things she can ride . . . but I stay under control for now.

"Hey, Luke! Guess what? The boys took advantage of Daddy being gone and went into town too. Dinner's on me!"

Her voice carries across the air between us, but it hits more than just my ears. Between the image of her riding and her innocent words, my jeans get just a little tight, my mind conjuring images of eating her for dinner, tasting the sweetness of her lips, nibbling the candy peaks of her breasts, drinking her like a fine wine.

Fuck. No. Down, boy.

I remind myself again of her last name, and when that doesn't seem like such an important hurdle, just how young she is does the trick.

She's twenty, I remember Sophie saying, and I'm twenty-eight. Not much, by adult standards. It's not like back in the day when I was in high school and she was still running around in her My Little Pony T-shirts. But the difference comes in the type of lives we've led and the experiences we've had, and I'd do well to remember that when I'm imagining rolling around in the grass with her.

I swallow that image down and force my mouth to stretch into a smile I know doesn't reach my eyes.

Most folks would let it pass, polite manners requiring you to not call people on their shit when they're putting up a nice front. Shayanne must not follow the rules of civilized society because she hops down from Ember and struts right over to me, poking at the corner of my lip with a finger and a wrinkled nose.

"What's wrong?"

I chuckle, gently pushing her finger away. "Nothing. I'm happy to see you. Dinner sounds great. What'd you bring?" I hope the redirection will stick.

"Sandwiches. What's wrong?" she repeats.

No luck, apparently. I can't tell her what really got me spun as she came up. That's a dangerous no-man's land of territory I'm not willing to traverse, but I can give her something else.

"Got some bad news this afternoon. One of my breedings was unsuccessful. Good Appaloosa, quality stud . . . it should've taken."

She looks at me, her eyes narrowed like she's looking into my mind. Lord help her if she sees some of the thoughts I've just had in there. A good girl like her would run screaming for her daddy and there'd be a shotgun in my immediate future for thinking such impure thoughts.

"Ain't your fault, but you take it personal, don'tcha?"

Perceptive thing, that one. "Well, yeah. It's my job, and my clients pay me a helluva lotta money to do it well. So when it doesn't work, I need to figure out why and do better."

"You do all you can, but you're not God, Luke. You can do all the studying, time everything just right, but at some point, nature takes over and it's out of your hands. I mean, it does come down to two horses making babies. Doesn't always happen."

A bark of laughter bursts free from inside me and Shay jumps in surprise. "Believe it or not, you're not the first person to tell me that. Mark has accused me more than once of having a god complex when it comes to my horses. He likens what I do to a mad scientist mixed with a proud father, with a little bit of art and a dash of science thrown in for good measure."

I rub my thumb and fingers together like I'm sprinkling salt, no, fairy dust or something magical like that, because that's what I sometimes feel like.

I shrug, tucking my hands into my pockets. "He's not wrong. Actually, that's pretty accurate."

Her lips purse prettily, and she looks at me with full respect while at the same time, she's amused. "And nowhere in that description does it say Luke Bennett, Horse God. So quit thinking you're the shit and admit that sometimes, you can't pull a miracle out of your ass on command."

Why did I think this girl needed my protection again? She's an absolute ball buster, in more ways than one. But damn if that doesn't make her sexier and more exciting.

Giving up, I hold my hands wide, dipping down in a semi-approximation of a bow. "When the lady's right, she's right."

She preens at my lighthearted praise, regal except for the button nose she thrusts up in the air haughtily. Her voice is full of fancy English-sounding tones as she reminds me, "And don't you forget it." The persona drops away and the real Shayanne returns. "Now sit your ass down and let's eat."

Roller coaster, party of one.

I look down at our booted feet, the long line of her denim-covered legs leading me to the green grass, and I need to get the upper hand back, not that I ever had it to begin with.

"You planned dinner but didn't bring a blanket?" I tease, clicking my tongue in a *tsk-tsk* sound. "How . . . gauche."

She huffs a growl of frustration, but I can hear the humor in her voice. "No, I didn't bring a blanket. Didn't take you for a pansy who couldn't sit his ass in the grass. But by all means, if you're worried about a little dirt on your Wranglers, feel free to stand."

She says it sweet as pie with a saccharin smile and then promptly plops down in the grass beneath the tree, zero fucks given to grace. Her legs crisscrossed in front of her, she starts digging in the bag I hadn't even noticed she was holding.

I can't help but grin as I lower down to the grass next to her, measuring the distance between our hips carefully to find the proper Goldilocks distance. Not too much, not too little, but just right.

Still . . . was it just sass, or did she really notice that I'm a Wranglers man? And if so, how closely was she checking out my backside?

"Whatcha got in that bag of tricks?" I lean forward, trying to get a finger in the corner of the bag like I'm going to peek, but she swats me away, laughing.

"Fancy French dip sandwiches."

I lift one brow, slightly worried. French dips? That takes prep, and if that's the case, I could be in trouble. "What makes them *fancy*?"

Admittedly, it's not a word I'm used to hearing or saying in this side of my world. Sure, with some of the horse breeders, the jodhpur wearing crowd who don't consider their riding gear complete without a frock coat, they talk 'fancy,' although they rarely use the word. And their food is most certainly fancy, considering they wrap a perfectly good piece of beef in biscuit dough, calling it a 'beef Wellington' that can't hold a candle to Mama's roast and biscuits. But here at home in the country? That's more of an insult than a descriptor we'd use on purpose.

So for Shayanne to use the word to describe her food makes me a little nervous.

It's just not a word that fits Shayanne in any way. But I think I like that about her, like she doesn't give a rat's ass about what a lady *should* do or what people will think of her. She's just herself, and everyone else can take it or leave it.

Take it. Take it double, if I can.

Shit. To distract myself, I look at the sandwich she's handed me, examining it with squinted eyes like it holds the meaning of life.

"Horseradish," she says with a big grin. "Get it? Because you like horses? I thought it was kinda funny."

But she blushes slightly, her chin dropping, and I can see that she's schooling herself on making the silly joke.

"I do like horses, but I've never had horseradish on a sandwich. What am I getting myself into here?" I mean that in more ways than just about this sandwich, which honestly smells delicious.

"Just roast beef on crusty bread. Usually, you dip it in the au jus, but that's too messy for a picnic, so I drizzled it on the bread to make it to-go. But the horseradish is the secret ingredient. It's kinda . . . twangy. You'll see." She looks at me encouragingly.

"I think you mean *tangy*," I correct and then take a big bite of sandwich. Spicy, bright, sour . . . she's done something to sass up this horseradish, maybe pickled it with some vinegar or something? "Mmm, okay, maybe twangy is right," I say as I press my tongue to the roof of my mouth to get the too-big but tasty bite down.

I think for a moment, deciding whether I like it or not. Kind of like a sour candy, it's a love-hate thing. So I go in for another chomp. "Really good, Shay. This meat is awesome, fall apart tender. Needs lettuce, I think. Like the crunch and coolness would balance it out."

Listen to me, sounding like a damn chef or something. *Hey, Gordon Ramsay, let me tell you what's up.*

I pull a slice of the roast beef from between the bread, tilting my head back to get it down in one gulp. If she ain't about manners, then I'm not going to worry about them either. As long as Mama doesn't see.

She tilts her head, looking at own sandwich like she's imagining that. "Never heard of putting lettuce on a dip, but I don't see why you couldn't. Then it'd be extra-fancy."

"Just like us," I reply, smiling with a mouth full of food. She returns the smile, but it's a small one because she's got a bite hidden behind her teeth too. "Fancy as dirty Wranglers sitting in the grass, at least."

She laughs, thankfully having just swallowed so she doesn't choke. But I force my bite down, swallowing hard before laughing too.

We sit, talking and laughing about everything and nothing, watching the sun sink lower into the sky. I don't want to go home, don't want *her* to go home. I don't want this meal to end.

It feels like we've fallen into this perfect pocket of time and space where she can be her, I can be me, and nothing else matters.

In here, the world doesn't exist beyond the green around us.

In here, our names are just Luke and Shayanne, no surnames to complicate things.

In here, how many years we've been on this Earth, swinging around the sun that's turning to orange fire before our very eyes, doesn't mean a damn thing.

Honestly, the more Shayanne talks, the older she sounds. She's not worldly, but that doesn't mean she's immature. I've met plenty of 'worldly' people in my travels who seem to think their bank accounts matter more than their maturity. Hell, I'd venture to say that she's more responsible than I am, given how many balls she's juggling at any given moment.

Regardless, I want to let my fingers trace up the legs she's stretched out beside me, trace every inch of her skin, tease higher until we get to a place where even the cool moon that's rising over the horizon can't put out the flames that would spark between us. I want to swallow her unfiltered words, hear her gasp and taste my name on her breath.

Inwardly, I feel my guts twist.

I am so fucked. Majorly. Royally. Epically.

Knowing I'm reaching my limit, I push up from the ground, letting myself indulge in the gift of grabbing her hand to pull her up too. It feels small in mine, but she's no dainty lady. Shayanne's hand is strong, a working hand. I bet this girl can give as good as she can take.

I inhale sharply, not letting that idea blossom.

"Better get home before your brothers," I warn, though I'm

LAUREN LANDISH

feeling reckless and careless. Right now, I think I'd take one of Brutal's hard right fists to the gut in exchange for Shayanne's soft kiss.

She bites her lip like she's trying to test out the possibilities of what might happen here. Or maybe I'm reading into an innocent gesture because my mind's in the gutter.

"Luke," she says huskily. And my name on her lips, especially in that sexy tone, hits me low and hard. She . . . she wants me, too. I know it as sure as I know the sun's gonna rise up in the morning.

I can't let her say whatever's about to come out of that mouth, but this time, instead of spinning her on the dance floor to disorient her, I pull her in for a hug that'll have to be enough for us both.

Her head hits my chest, her arms instinctively going around my waist and her mouth clacking shut, thankfully. The length of her presses against me in the barest hint of what I want.

I pat her back instead of skimming along her skin like I'd like to, trying to give the impression of a neighborly goodbye when I feel anything but neighborly to the spitfire in my arms.

"Shay, we can't. You know that as well as I do." I'm trying to be kind. I'm trying my damnedest to do the right thing as I say the words softly over her head because I can't look her in the eye as I speak them.

"Luke," she whispers again, and it nearly breaks my heart. It's just my name, but I can hear all the other meanings behind it.

"This was . . . uh, thanks for dinner. Leave me a note or text me if you want." It's ridiculously weak for what I'd like to say, but my brain is fogged over, swimming in her aura. Still, I know I sound like an awkward kid with no game on his first date.

I want to make plans to see her again, but that's only

52

playing with fire, so I let her go. I stare at her ass as she climbs aboard Embers, noticing that just like I'm a Wranglers man, she's a Wranglers girl, but lift my eyes just in time for her to turn around.

Her hazel eyes catch my blues, and she gives me that heart-stopping smile again. "Thanks for the dinner date."

The word *date* hangs heavy between us, and I can feel that she's pushing at me to see what I'll say, what I'll do if she throws out some obvious signals.

"I appreciate the smashed pumpkin, too." I hold up the jar of orange-brown puree she brought with her. "I think I'll have it for dessert tonight."

She nods, soft and sweet, but there's a hint of sadness in her eyes that I hate. I especially hate knowing that I put it there. But really, it's not my fault and not hers, either. But I don't want to make problems for her, and seeing her again will undoubtedly do that.

"Let me know what you think," she says, her gaze drifting to the jar, but it feels like she's asking for more insight into my mind. And she might be feeling a little something in the air between us tonight, but I'd bet she'd be shocked by the filthy thoughts I'm wishing I could give in to.

CHAPTER 5

SHAYANNE

This is, by far, the stupidest thing I've ever done in my life. Bold, brash, brave, and as stupid as a cow looking up into the rain and drowning. But I've committed to doing it anyway, even if only to myself.

With Daddy gone gambling and the boys all out in the far fields for the day, I'd thought about going to my tree. But I knew that wasn't where I really wanted to go, and after a good pep talk, I decided to follow my gut.

I look left and then right, though if anyone were nearby, I would've already seen them and they would've already caught me. But there's nothing for acres besides green grass and dots of cattle to my left and the old country road to my right. I bend down, carefully pulling the two lengths of barbed wire apart so I can sneak between them without getting caught by a sharp barb.

Booted feet firmly on the other side, I breathe a sigh of relief, knowing there's no turning back now. I'm in 'enemy territory'. But in for an ounce, in for a pound, and I'm going whole hog.

I cross the acres, though they seem like miles, until I see

the dull shine of a metal barn against the horizon. I pass it slightly then loop back toward it, keeping my eyes open to make sure no one is around, but the coast looks clear.

I skip the sliding door, assuming it'll be loud on its track, and choose the regular door off to the side. Luckily, it's unlocked and opens easily, without a sound. Whoever does the maintenance here knows their business.

Inside, the lights are on, but compared to the bright sunlight, it's dim and my eyes take a moment to adjust.

"Hello?" I call out.

I'm greeted with only silence and defeat seems suddenly imminent.

I'm such a dork. I'd considered getting caught, I'd considered getting turned down, and of course, I'd thought about what success might look like. But this, a total strikeout, with me standing in the middle of an empty barn, wasn't on my possibility list.

But just before I leave, I hear a faint tapping and hope breaks free from its restraints in my chest again. I follow the sound deeper into the barn, carefully peeking around the corner and into the stalls as I pass by.

I find success in the back corner. Luke is in some sort of makeshift office, a stall dominated by a desk and computer. He's working on something, his eyes focused on the glowing screen and his hand tapping out a rhythm on the desk to the music playing through his earbuds.

Jackpot! I'm the youngest sibling of three brothers. I know how to play this game. I slowly and methodically move closer, easing my way toward him without catching his attention like a bobcat until . . .

Boom!

I hop up on the desk right beside him, my denim-covered ass sitting down on his paperwork and a big smile on my face.

He jumps a foot into the air, yelling, "What the fuck?"

His eyes meet mine, and I grin as I see the anger of the jump scare melt away to surprised recognition, then delight, then confusion. He pulls the earbuds from his ears. "Shayanne?"

I wiggle my fingers at him in a silly little wave. "Hi! Whatcha listening to?"

"Uh, hi. What are you doing here?" he asks, but his mouth is already breaking into a smile. He's happy to see me, even if he is confused about why I'm here. "And I don't even know, just an old country tune."

"Well, I wanted to see what you thought of my pumpkin puree," I say, using the excuse I'd preplanned for this ambush. "You ate it, right? For dessert?"

"Pumpkin puree?" he repeats. "I did. It was delicious," he says automatically, all polite like his mama taught him, but it also seems truthful.

"I know. My smashed pumpkin is the best there is. I'm not bragging. It's just true," I say, shrugging like perfecting that recipe didn't take two seasons and about ten different variations.

He leans back in his chair, hands linked over his belly as he laughs. "Humble much?" He looks long and lean, knees and elbows spread wide like he's taking up as much space as possible, like he wants me to see him in all his cowboy glory.

He's got a pair of jeans so worn there's a peekaboo tear high up on his leg, but his pocket sadly covers any bit of skin I might've gotten to see, and a white T-shirt with a logo so faded I can't even read it anymore, but it fits him like a second skin. But most importantly, he's wearing that smile that's some mix of cocky and sweet that does it for me. He's comfortable, confident in a way I may never be.

He looks around the office, like he just remembered where we are again. "Seriously, though, what are you doing here? Trying to get me killed by one of your brothers?"

He doesn't sound scared in the least, but I shake my head anyway. "No, I was thinking about you and wanted to see you again."

There's a lot tied up in those simple words, a question and a promise. At the tree last time, his name was a promise, a plea, and I could hear the hesitation in his voice when he pushed me away.

So I haven't been able to accept that. Now, I'm being as blatant as I can be. I'm already going further than I ever have before with putting myself out there, and this limb is getting mighty skinny. Luke's warned me off before, but I'm not easily led astray, not by him or by anyone. And I've never been accused of being subtle or scared.

"You were thinking of me?" he parrots back like he's still processing that idea and deciding on whether it's a good thing or a bad thing. He swallows like he's trying to keep words in, but they come out anyway. "What were you thinking?"

His voice drops a bit when he asks me that, deeper and rougher, and I imagine it's his bedroom voice.

I squirm a bit, crinkling the papers I'm sitting on but needing to squeeze my thighs together for some relief at the ache that's already building from being this close to him. Luke's eyes follow the movement, and the pull between us snaps back into place, filling the air with crackles like a summer sky primed for lightning.

This is it. The moment I've dreamed of since I was a little girl. He's going to push me back on his desk and take me like in one of my soap operas. I can feel it in my bones that every-thing's about to change. For me, for him, for us. If only he'll let it be.

I'm not stupid or naïve. I knew that he wanted me under the tree. His jeans certainly didn't hide that at times. And he all but acknowledged the buzz in the air, but it was with a refusal to do anything about it. For some reason, my heart doesn't care that he's not brave enough to battle our names. It's beating so hard there's a roar in my ears.

"Luke," I say again, and even over the roar, I know my voice is too soft and breathy, the desire woven in the single syllable.

He pushes back from the desk, scooting his chair a little to the side, and suddenly, I find myself caged in by him. His hands are on the desk, his arms on either side of my legs and his knees framing my feet where they dangle. He looks up at me, his eyes diamond hard and his jaw working, making a bump appear and disappear beneath the scruff.

Shit just got real, dangerously so.

"What were you thinking, Shayanne?"

It's an order, but a pleading one, to put us out of our misery and either move this chemical reaction forward or to stop it before it combusts. I choose both, to move us leaps and bounds forward with fiery flames lighting the way. I put my hands on his shoulders, feeling the tight muscles there as I bravely tell him everything.

"I was thinking about your dancing me around the floor at Hank's and how it made my whole world spin. How *you* made me spin. The whole drive home, I wished our last names were different so we could just be two people who met at a bar and got along. I was thinking about you at the tree, looking like you'd been working hard, and how sexy that was." He groans quietly at my confession, but I don't stop.

Whole hog, I remind myself, though I'm scared I'm making a fool of myself. The little girl he'll never see as anything more than an annoyance with a family full of assholes.

"I was thinking how much I wanted you to kiss me, not hug me like you couldn't feel this thing between us." I lick my lips, wanting his kiss now too. "I want you to stop being a gentleman and give me more than a nod and a tip of your hat."

He can't deny that he feels this, right? There's no way this is my imagination, not with the way his jagged breath is heating the space between us.

A dirty thought wanders through my mind, wondering if he can smell my arousal, because sure as he's damn close to me, my panties are wet with want for him.

I take a steadying breath, noting the way his eyes track the rise and fall of my breasts in my long-sleeved T-shirt. If I were a different kind of girl, I probably would've dressed better for a mission like this, but jeans and T-shirts are who I am, and I want him to accept that. No, I want him to *want* that.

Me. Plain old Shayanne Tannen. Nothing fancy, all real.

I can feel him battling himself, both wanting and not wanting me, his body and his brain at odds. Such a gentleman, but I want him wild for me, as wild as I feel right now, on the edge of something amazing.

He moves a hand to my knee, both of us watching his thumb rubbing at the soft denim, and even the slight contact feels delicious, filling me with fresh desire. More importantly, it feels big, like it's his silent confession that he wants me too and I've never been wanted before. The breath I was holding, awaiting his decision, releases in a sigh.

"Shay? Are you sure?" he says, tension winding through his shoulders as he gives me an out that I don't want. "There's no going back from this. You know that, right?"

I tilt his chin up, forcing his eyes to mine. My voice is steady, though my stomach is full of butterflies bouncing off the walls. "Kiss me."

Whatever control he was holding onto evaporates into the warm air at my request, and we ignite in fiery passion. He surges up from the chair, standing in front of me. He grabs at my hips, scooting me to the edge of the desk, and my thighs naturally go astride his. His hands delve into my hair, and before I can even think to be nervous, his lips are on mine.

With that first touch, I feel just how much restraint he's been using to hold himself back from me.

His kiss is devouring, a melding of our breaths as his tongue tangles with mine, invading my mouth to explore and claim territory. I kiss him back, wanting to taste him too, explore his soft lips, and sear his mouth with my own.

"Fuck, Shay." His moan is slightly more recognizable than my own mutterings, but it feels like we're both jumping into the wilderness of possibilities together.

He lays kisses along my jaw and down my neck as he guides my head to give him room. It feels like dancing with him, like I somehow instinctively know what he wants me to do, though I've never done this dance before.

His hands cup my breasts, his thumb rubbing over my taut right nipple twice before he's grabbing at the hem to whip the T-shirt over my head.

I gasp as the breeze from the fan licks at my bare skin, goosebumps popping up along my flesh. Luke's rough fingertip brands me as he traces them, his eyes burning with intensity. "I want to taste each and every one of them."

He bends down, fulfilling his promise and kissing my right wrist where I know he can feel my heart racing. He moves up, pressing his lips along my inner arms, which doesn't sound sexy, but when Luke does it, it becomes the most amazing erogenous zone, an anticipation of where he's going and what he's going to do.

When he gets to my shoulder, he begins the trek down my chest to the full lushness of my breast. He's thorough, taking his time and appreciating every square inch of my skin but doing so with searing heat that brands me with every press of his lips and lick of his tongue.

He teases at my nipple through the simple cotton fabric of my bra with his nose, nibbling at the nub while his hands slip behind my back to unhook it. The fabric drops away and I'm bared to him.

"Fucking gorgeous," he whispers reverently before licking a loop around my nipple, tasting my skin. I grasp at the soft curls at the nape of his neck, holding him to me as I arch into his mouth.

I grab at his shirt, wanting it off, needing to be skin on skin with him. He reaches behind his neck to grab it, pulling it over his head and dropping it to the floor. He's stunning. The strong chest I felt beneath my cheek as we hugged is topped with flat brown nipples, and the ridges of his abs are divided by a dusting of a blond happy trail that I want to follow to the promised land.

"See something you like?" he asks cockily, teasing me as he runs a rough hand over his chest. I'm jealous he's getting a feel and I'm not, so I grab him by his belt, pulling him back close to me, and then wipe that smirk right off his face when I run my hands over his skin.

"Yes. I like." I let the blunt edge of my nails scrape along his skin, and he shudders, making me feel powerful.

He kisses me again, our hands exploring, mapping, and burning trails along our skin. He nips at my lip, then soothes it with gentle sucking that I want him to repeat all over my body.

He presses in closer, his hand trapped between us where he's teasing at my breast. I feel his cock pressing against my belly. He's hard, long, and thick, and I moan in delight at the obvious proof of how much he wants me.

It's too high to be where I need him, but my hips buck anyway, wanting and needing. I can't stop the whine for more that comes from my throat.

Luke pulls back, looking between us at my rolling hips. "Jesus . . ."

He picks me up like I'm light as a feather, sitting back

down into his chair and planting me on top of him. "Do that again. Roll your hips on me."

I nod, moving my heated core against the ridge of his cock. Even through the two layers of denim, it's so good. He guides my hips, pulling me up and down as we both pant. But it's not enough. "More," I demand, unbuttoning my own jeans. "Now."

I don't know where this wanton woman is coming from. Maybe Luke is drawing her out of me, but I'm on board with the plan for more. I'd hoped for maybe a flirty conversation today, to tempt him into seeing me again. I didn't dream this was going to happen, but I'm so glad it is.

Luke follows my lead, undoing his belt and then his jeans, but then he sits forward and helps me stand. "Take them off. Leave your panties on."

I kick off my boots and drop my jeans to the floor. Standing before him, mostly nude, I'm struck with a bout of nerves and pull my hair over my shoulder to hide a bit. I fidget with it nervously, already knowing I won't stop. I want this, want him.

While I undressed, Luke stayed in the chair but has shoved his jeans down his hips, his cock still covered in cotton boxer briefs. He palms himself through the cotton, like a magician about to do his big reveal, prolonging the moment before the oohs and ahhs.

I watch, mesmerized and wanting to see him, feel him, taste him.

"Shay," he says, soft and low, commanding my attention. Though my eyes don't want to, they flick up to meet his. "Have you ever?" He lifts his chin, gesturing toward his cock.

I bite my lip and consider lying but answer truthfully. "No, but I want to." An embarrassing thought runs through my head, and I know I'm blushing to the roots of my hair. "Oh, God, did I do something wrong? How did you know that?"

I cover my face with my hands, feeling the heat for an entirely different reason. But before I can back out, Luke reaches up, forcing my hands down. "You didn't do anything wrong. There's nothing to apologize for. But you deserve better than this for your first time, Shay."

His voice is steady, sure, not laughing at me in the least, which helps dissolve some of the mortification.

"Better than you?" I query, guessing at his meaning.

He smiles and his left shoulder goes up the slightest fraction of an inch. "Probably, but certainly better than a quick fuck in a dirty barn."

My jaw drops, but not in shock. In want.

A quick fuck in a dirty barn . . . those filthy words are like hot drops of arousal to my brain, and he can see it written plain as day all over my face. His hand drops back down to his cock, the slow strokes up and down hypnotizing me.

"I'm not going to fuck you, Shayanne. Not like this. But do you trust me?"

I have virtually zero reason to do so. He's a Bennett. I'm a Tannen. By our very nature, we're adversarial for some reason beyond me. I barely know him, having only spent one long evening watching the sun set over his hard features as we talked about our lives. But then my memories remind me of the kind smiles he'd give me when I was an annoying kid, the way he'd been a perfect gentleman at Sophie's wedding, the gentle but firm way he guided me at Hank's, and the way he looked at me under the tree. My gut tells me everything I need to know about Luke Bennett.

I do trust him. And I want him for whatever he has in mind, though I'm disappointed I'm not getting fucked right here and now by him.

"Yes," I tell him, looking directly into his eyes, daring him to betray that trust while demanding that he earn it.

"Sit on the desk."

I have a moment of hesitation. *Am I really doing this?* But then I look in his eyes, so dark with lust, and I can feel the needy pulse in my center.

Be brave, Shayanne.

I hop back up, but this time, he opens my legs wide, placing one of my bare feet on each of his spread knees. It's a weird kind of diamond shape, keeping us apart but also somehow connecting us in a deeper way.

I feel vulnerable and exposed, even though my most private of parts is still covered by a slip of cotton. I'm trying to relax, but the nerves and need are all spiraling in my belly and I want him to do something, anything.

I want the rushed urgency, the devouring feel of his lips on my skin, the barely bridled passion rushing through us that obliterates my every thought.

But Luke is power personified. I know from the explosion in his kiss earlier that he's working hard to restrain himself, that he is sitting in that chair through sheer force of will, not because he's not as desperate as I am.

"I'm not going to fuck you, Shayanne. But if you'll trust me, I want to do something else," he says.

My mind runs away from me with wishes and dreams as fantasies and ideas from every dirty book and sexy movie I've ever seen whip through like flashcards of excitement. "Anything," I vow, meaning it because at this point, I'm game for anything that will ease this ache in my core.

"Touch yourself for me," he says, shocking me.

Okay, thought we were heading toward some oral action, maybe some finger play, but not myself. I blush because though I've obviously done that a lot, and I've even got a little toy hidden in my dresser, I've never had an audience.

Before I can argue, he leans back in the chair, his hand running down his chest like I did earlier, and he slips a thumb beneath the waistband of his underwear. And I realize that it's not only me who'll be touching myself.

This idea just got a whole lot better.

"Show me," I demand, not because I need some tit-for-tat arrangement but because now that he's planted the idea of watching him jack off, I desperately want to see it.

I want to learn how he touches his cock, how he teases and draws out the pleasure for himself so I can do it to him too. And I realize that's how he feels about watching me. We're exploring, learning each other, just differently from what I expected.

He slides his hand under the cotton, cupping himself, and I groan, hungry to see. He lifts his hips again, using his other hand to slip the fabric under his butt until he's bare-assed on his office chair. He's still covering himself, but his hand moves to stroke his length and several inches peek out the top. I have zero experience to compare to, but I think that means Luke Bennett is hung like a horse.

He pumps his hand up and down, revealing more of himself. He's thick and hard, and there's a vein that runs along the underside. Obscenely, I wonder what that vein would feel like as he thrusts into me.

He groans, and my eyes jump to his, but his are focused on my core poised inches away from his cock. I curl my hips up, and his lips part, a jagged breath escaping unconsciously as he murmurs what he'd like to do.

Unbidden, my hands slide up my thighs from my knees to the crease where my center begins. Hesitantly, I rub through my panties, feeling the wet heat through the fabric.

"You feel that? You're soaked through," Luke growls, like it's a personal achievement on his part. Hell, it is, because every bit of this desire is for him.

I slip my fingers beneath the cotton, testing and teasing myself. Am I really going to do this? It seems crazy as fuck, but I am. I'm too far gone, too needy for him. I buck into my own touch, wishing it were his.

"Tell me how you feel."

My words falter, and I try to think of a sexy way to say this, but my brain is only thinking *yes, yes, yes* and nothing comes to mind. "Hot, slick, so wet," I say.

It must be right because he squeezes at the base of his cock, shivering as he fights back his orgasm. And suddenly, I don't feel shy and uncertain. I feel powerful and desirable.

And I want to show him too. I want him to come looking at my pussy. I want him to be the first man to see me there and watch me come apart.

I pull my panties to the side, pausing while he looks at me. "Goddamn, Shayanne. Your pussy's so pink and pretty. Look at how wet you are."

I think any other time, that would embarrass me, but he says it hungrily as his tongue slips out to wet his lips. I run my finger through my folds, gathering my juices, and then hold my finger out. "Want a taste?"

He dives at my hand, that primal urge testing his restraint as he sucks and licks at my finger to get every drop. His hand jerks faster up and down his cock in powerful strokes as I watch, memorizing every movement.

Pulling my finger out of his mouth, he actually *groans*, like I'm taking something from him that he wants as madly as I want him. He sounds like he needs me with a deep hunger that can only be satisfied in just one way.

I drop my finger back to my pussy, running circles around my clit and then occasionally tapping at the hard button. My hips jump every time I do, getting closer and closer to coming.

My breath is ragged, eyes locked on him stroking himself in front of me as I slide a finger inside myself, feeling the warm, silken tightness of my inner walls.

"Wanna know what I thought at Hank's?" Luke asks through gritted teeth, his hand never stopping.

"Uh-huh," I cry, unsuccessfully trying to make my brain

concentrate on words, but they float away like feathers in the wind.

"I thought you were the sexiest thing I've ever seen and wondered how I missed your turning into such a stunner. I held your hips so I wouldn't grind against you like an asshole, and when you drove away, I wished the night hadn't ended so soon. I jacked off that night, just like this, the smell of your sunshine and shampoo on my shirt."

"Luke," I whisper, on the edge. "Please . . ." I don't know what I'm begging him for. I'm the one touching myself, feeling each pulse of my pussy as I get closer, but I need something from him. I just don't know what it is.

"And then the sun set over our tree as I watched it turn your hair to red and blonde highlights, fiery like you are. And I wanted to fuck you right there in the soft grass while you cried out my name. The one that matters, my first name, just how you said it against my chest. Because I don't want our last names to matter. I left because I couldn't take it anymore, was on the verge of losing it, but I teased us both with that hug, knowing it was all we should do. But here you are, riding your fingers like a goddamn cowgirl, about to come all over my desk, and all I can think is that I want *everything*."

I buck hard, a shiver racking through my body, and I force my eyes to focus. "Are you going to come?"

His teeth gnash, his face contorted in pleasure. "I'm doing everything I can to wait for you, Shay. Make that pussy come for me, and I'm gonna fucking come like a damn freight train. Come, Shayanne. Please." His voice is strangled, like he's gripping the edge with all his might, but his words send me flying.

"*Yes*, Luke," I cry out, my pussy quivering beneath my blurring fingers as I come apart. I'm riding a fierce wave, lost in a star-spotted dark abyss of pleasure, but I force my eyes open, wanting to see him come too.

The muscles in his neck stand out in strain as his jaw

clenches hard. His brow furrows deeply, but he keeps his eyes on my core. "Fuck, Shay," he rumbles, like the words are forcing their way free as his cock jerks in his hand. White cum jets from the crown, covering his hand, and he spreads it along his shaft, working himself for more.

It's glorious to see him this way, vulnerable and lost to the pleasure we wrought together. I only wish we'd done this sooner, like on the way home from Hank's, or hell, in the parking lot. Fuck, I just came and I'm already wanting more.

Luke reaches for my hand with his left, pulling my honeyed fingers to his mouth and licking at them as he moans in delight. After a second's hesitation, I do the same to his right hand, pulling it to my mouth.

"You don't have to," he reassures me, but I want to know what he tastes like too.

I lap at the creamy fluid, that's a mix of salty and sweet, and smile. I suck one finger into my mouth to clean it, and Luke pulls it back and grabs his dropped T-shirt.

As he wipes his hand, he grins. "Woman, if you keep that up, we'll be going for round two . . . and I'm thinking we might need to slow our roll until your mind catches up with our bodies."

Still sweet and thinking of me, not wanting to push me too far, too fast. But for such a gentleman, Luke has a filthy mouth that promises more, and I love it.

He wipes my hand too, and I press the cleaned fingers to his chest. "That was . . . wow." Words to adequately explain the bubbles in my body escape me, but I try again. "Wonderful," I say seriously because it feels like he's looking at me uncertainly, but the high I'm riding right now makes me feel ten feet tall and bulletproof. "Everything I could want and more. And yes, I want more."

He nods. "I know, but I don't want to pressure you. Shit's gonna hit the fan. You know that as well as I do."

LAUREN LANDISH

He's talking about more than what we just did. He's talking about who we are, where we live, and our family histories.

His words hit me hard, piercing my armor of happiness as doubts painfully rip their way through my heart and responsibilities slam back onto my shoulders. He's the enemy, but he doesn't feel like it. Not at all.

CHAPTER 6

LUKE

*C*oming all over my own hand while Shayanne rubbed her sweet, gleaming pussy in front of me is damn near the best orgasm I've ever had, and that's dangerous. I don't care about getting myself jammed up. I can handle her brothers and dad and whatever hassle they throw my way.

But I don't want to get her in trouble, and I really do want her to think about what the hell we're doing because now that I've had a taste of her, I'm not letting her go.

That I can't wait to have another taste of Shayanne is a sentiment I'm not all too familiar with. I'm usually more of the 'love-'em-and-leave-'em' type, but with one glance, one taste, one earth-shattering moment, Shay's got me tied down tight.

It's left me feeling like tying her to my side and daring her family to try and take her away from me is a damn fine game plan. I know, it sounds pretty damn caveman-ish, maybe even more Mark's style than mine, but I'm feeling a good Neanderthal grunt coming on.

Still, I'm trying to be gentlemanly, even though what I really want is to flip her over my desk and fuck the shit out of her, then hold her in my arms and learn every single thought that's ever run through her pretty head. Okay, I could prob-ably flip-flop the order of those.

Maybe. If I have a cold shower first.

I tuck myself back in and pull my jeans up, zipping them but leaving them unbuttoned. I grab my T-shirt to wipe the last traces of evidence of our activities from my chest and then swipe along her pussy, knowing this will be my new favorite shirt even after it's been through the laundry. A reminder of the first time we gave in and admitted to what's happening between us.

She pulls her T-shirt over her head. I help her get her panties situated right, inhaling her sexy arousal, and my mouth waters for another taste, but I force myself back.

"Fuck, you smell good, Shay. I want to eat you up," I tell her, eyes on the way her panties dip down in a V right above her mound.

She wiggles a bit, but when I look up, instead of hunger, her hazel eyes are wide with . . . something not-good that I can't decipher. Shock? Fear?

"Shayanne?" I say quietly, like I'm talking to a wild animal because that's what she looks like right now. Hair a mess from my fingers, shirt on but hanging haphazardly, mouth dropped open, showing me her little white teeth. Teeth that only moments ago were biting her lip in pleasure.

"I have to go," she says, pushing at me. I can read her face loud and clear now. It's panic, pure and potent.

I move, letting her hop down from my desk, but I reach for her hand. "Hey, talk to me. What's wrong?"

She shakes her head, silently reaching for her jeans and pulling her hand from mine to yank them on. She puts her boots on just as fast. Faster than I can find words to make her stay, to make her explain what just happened.

We were fine—hell, way the fuck better than fine—then

bam . . . like someone flipped a switch, she's pulling away from me.

Fuck.

Our families. That's what I said that spooked her. Well, her family.

Because I suspect I could waltz Shayanne right up to Mama's dinner table tonight and she'd be greeted with open arms and a double helping of peach cobbler. Some questions, for sure, but open arms.

I'm sure that's not the case if I were to show up at her house, though. If I didn't walk in with my friends Smith and Wesson, I'd be walking into a bloodbath. Mine.

She's walking away, already at the barn's back door as I run after her. "Shayanne, I don't care about our last names. I care about you. What we just did . . . that was something. You felt that too."

I don't have fancy words and sweet poetry. I can't strum a guitar, and when I sing, it's off-key and only the horses and cows hear me. I'm just a plain old cowboy, but what I want right now is to have all those words, all those skills. I pull at my hair, willing the words to pour out, but my mouth just opens and closes like a fish.

She turns back, and I see the tears shining in her eyes. Those glimmering diamonds tear my guts out. She presses a kiss to my cheek, catching the corner of my mouth, and I turn to kiss her back, but she's gone.

She's literally running across the field, knees high and elbows pumping, jumping over the big trough hose to get away from me. The sight leaves ice in my heart and pain in my soul.

I almost call out, scream her name, but the sound would carry and alert everyone in a several-acre radius. That would definitely lead to questions. Questions she doesn't want, apparently.

"Shayanne," I say quietly, though to my heart, it sounds like a booming drum.

What the fuck?

I'M A GROUCH ALL AFTERNOON, TORN BETWEEN STOMPING my way over to Shayanne's house and demanding an explanation or leaving her alone, since that seems to be what she wants. One minute, I'm reaching for my hat and heading for the door, and the next I'm slumping behind my desk, trying to work and getting nothing done.

I'm man enough to admit that trespassing onto her family property to see her is a scary proposition, knowing what I do about her brothers and their 'hit first, ask questions never' style. But right now, I'm so twitchy with all this pent-up frustration coursing through my veins, I feel like I could put my fist right through the big maple outside the barn.

Luckily, there's no one in the barn but me and the horses, and I'd never hurt them. My brothers are out on the acreage somewhere, leaving me to do my own thing, same as always, not knowing that today, it's probably saving them from a therapeutic knuckle buster.

I use the unrest to fuel me, punishing myself with manual labor. I muck the stalls, one by one, until they're as clean and cozy as a stall can be. I brush each and every horse, talking to them as I carefully care for them until their coats gleam like they're ready for a show.

"What the hell happened, Briarbelle?"

But the horse doesn't answer, the universe doesn't answer, and I still don't know any more than I did when Shay high-stepped it out of here.

I lead Briarbelle outside, letting her run freely in the front pasture I've claimed for my training. I watch her mane bouncing and streaming behind her, wild as the wind she creates as she runs. It makes me want to run too, not away this time, but just as freely as Briarbelle is. She's got no worries, no concerns, just the feeling of her hooves on the grass and the wind in her eyes.

But I'm not free, and neither is Shayanne. We both have restraints holding us back, keeping us in place, no matter how much we might want to fight them.

I skip dinner at Mama's, well aware that I'm not fit for company since I couldn't make polite conversation right now if I tried, not wanting the interrogation about my piss-poor mood I know would be coming. Instead, I hide away to lick my wounds and heat up some chicken and mashed potatoes in the ranch hand house, my makeshift home.

The night is long and empty as I toss and turn in bed. I'm used to sleeping alone, always do, and I've never felt lonely in my sheets. But tonight, instead of spreading out like I usually do, I want to curl up with Shayanne in my arms.

But she's not here. And next door has never seemed so far away.

With a grunt of frustration, I throw the blanket off and stalk to the kitchen. I grab a beer from the fridge and pop it open, guzzling half of it in one go as I stare out the window over the sink.

"Fuck this," I tell the night. The moon's clear and bright in the sky right now, a yellow harvest moon that casts a faint light over the fields outside. If I were younger, and if it were a few weeks later, I'd call it a Halloween moon.

If I can't sleep, I'm going to do something productive, something to distract myself. I pull on my boots by the back door, letting my plaid flannel pajama pants puddle at the top and not caring in the least to right them. A flick of the switch on my flashlight lights my way to the barn, which I stalk to with fast strides.

I use the side door so I don't wake the horses, leaving them in relative quiet darkness, but in my office, I turn on the over-heads so I can see. Out of habit, I sit down in my chair, but then I'm stuck, not knowing what to do.

I slide my fingers through my hair, staring at the mess of papers on my desk. Right on top are the ones crinkled from Shayanne's ass perching on them as she teased her pussy for me and watched me jack off. My hand gently splays on the papers, a connection to her I need. "Fuck. Fuck. Fuck."

I'm so damn sorry, but I don't know what for, exactly. The scene from today replays in my mind like a movie—perfect, frame by frame, until the end, where everything went so very wrong.

"You forget to order the hay and decide to do it in the middle of the night before anyone realized what a fuckup you are?" a familiar gruff voice asks from the doorway. He's amused, although you'd have to have known him your entire life to recognize it.

I lift my eyes from my desk, telling the interloper, "For a big fucker, you're damn quiet, you know that?"

Mark grunts, his lips pursing, which is basically a full-wattage smile for him. My big brother has always been the most serious and staid of the three of us, and somewhere around his early twenties, he took a serious run at the Asshole of the Decade award. Then Katelyn, his new bride, got ahold of him and quite literally forced him to speak in complete sentences, which he does more often than not these days.

It's a good change, usually. And one that'll come in handy when he and Katelyn get around to having their first baby. Honestly, when the time is right, he'll be one hell of a father. So I support him as best I can.

Until he shows up in my doorway when I want to be left alone to wallow. Ignoring my huff of displeasure, he drops into the chair on the other side of my desk and puts his feet up like he owns the place.

"So, did you?" he asks from behind closed eyes as he tilts his head back and crosses his arms over his broad chest. He looks mighty comfortable in my office, especially considering he's got on shorts, a T-shirt, and his dirtiest boots. Which, again, are *on* my desk like he's got zero manners. Or more likely, like he's trying to irritate me and doing a fine job of it.

"Did I what?" I volley, a tiny piece of me afraid that he knows what I did on this very desk today. Nerves make me shuffle the papers, stacking them neatly, and I'm struck with a bout of disappointment that I can't see the evidence of Shay's ass on my desk anymore.

Mark pops open one eye, suspiciously glaring at me since he has no real clue why the hell I'd be out here unless I've fucked up.

To be clear, I pull my weight around here. I just tend to take care of things without a lot of fanfare. Mark might have learned how to run this ranch at Pops's side, but I was only a half-step behind him. I never wanted to step into Pops's shoes, but I could if I needed to. I know how to run everything on this land damn near as well as Mark does.

But my dreams lay elsewhere, and what I bring to the table with horse breeding and training is so far outside of what our family ranch usually does that Mark doesn't always get it. He doesn't understand that putting the stallion and the mare in the stall is just the last step of a very complicated process.

No one in the family really gets it, though Pops supported my dreams and thought I could do damn near anything I set my mind to. Although Sophie sort of understands since she works with Doc. So that's progress too.

I've had a way with horses since I was a boy, able to get even the wildest big animal to calm. From there, it'd been a logical step to begin training them, and I'd done so with our cattle wrangling horses since I was a young teen. In high school, I even helped the other local ranchers with their horses and word had spread. At eighteen, I started traveling and training far and wide, usually for ranches but eventually for racing.

That's when the bug really bit me hard. Race horses are a different thing altogether, requiring finesse and study to achieve the best results. And that's all before training begins.

It's amazing to see a horse go from no more than an idea to a rose-wreathed winner. I've been able to work with everything from quarter horses to harness racers. Even the big Clydesdales.

"Order the hay. What the fuck else are we talking about?"

See, complete sentences. It's progress.

"Of course I ordered the hay. It'll be here in a couple of weeks, just like it's supposed to be. You think I'm some sort of newb?"

He lifts one shoulder, not commenting either way, but the lift of his brow gives his opinion quite clearly.

"I ordered the hay, mucked the stalls, checked the lists of cattle available for the fall sale, reorganized my trip since that filly didn't take, and sorted the vaccines for the herd. Anything else you need?" I know my tone is a little aggressive , but c'mon, I do this shit all the time and don't need anyone checking up on me.

He opens both eyes now, looking at me reproachfully. "What crawled up your ass?"

"Nothing," I bite out, sounding like I meant to say *everything*.

I can't meet his gaze anymore and spin in my chair, opening the top drawer of the filing cabinet to lay the stack of papers inside. They're not sorted, so I'll have to refile them later, but it's a good break from Mark's X-ray eyes.

"Man, you sound grumpy as hell, and coming from me,

that's saying something. What's got you working late if not the hay?" He sounds genuinely curious now, not like he's giving me shit.

Oddly, I prefer the other way, because with him being nice, it's harder to tell him to fuck off. It feels like he's prodding at a wound that hasn't even had a chance to scab over yet, and I'm not sure how deep it goes.

"Just couldn't sleep, so I thought I'd do some work." It's the truth, but not the whole truth. That's only for me and Shayanne. A secret for us.

Mark grunts, not believing me for a second. "You getting itchy?"

I have no idea what he's talking about, but my hand naturally moves to scratch at my bare chest and his eyes light up like it's some big tell.

"That's what Katelyn calls it when she wants to smack someone, 'itchy palms'. You look like you got itchy feet, like you're ready to hit the road again. Where're you going next and when are you leaving?"

He's astute, though I'm gone for jobs sometimes more than I'm here, so his guess is a safe bet.

But I'm not ready to run, or at least not to hit the road like I usually do. All I'm thinking is that I could run next door in a heartbeat. But the fact that I don't want to go anywhere that'd add more distance between me and Shayanne seems more telling than anything else.

I get up, coming around to the other side of the desk to shove Mark's feet off with a glare. I sit where his boots just were, staking my territory. He's got his own damn office. "No, I don't have itchy feet, and that's a weird saying."

He shrugs, no skin in the game about whether it's odd or not. And a thought occurs to me.

"What're you doing up in the middle of the night to even

come over and give me a hard time? You got something itching you too?"

He does smile at that, rubbing his hands together like they're tickling him something fierce. It takes me a second to get his joke because his sense of humor is damn near non-existent. He's saying his hands itch. Katelyn says that's what happens when you want to smack someone . . . ergo, Mark wants to smack someone.

If that were it, I'd be scared my big brother was ready to roughhouse like we used to when we were kids. Or hell, like we did last week before Mama stopped us with a threat of no dessert.

But that's not it. Mark and Katelyn are, to put it lightly, kinky as fuck. I truly never needed to know that about my brother, but I learned the hard way, hearing and seeing shit I'll never forget. Still, they both seem inordinately happy together so I'm not judging.

"Then go home, asshole," I tell him, kicking at the chair and hoping he'll be the one who leaves this time.

He answers my previous question about why he came over, moving on from the delicate conversation about him and his bride. "I was awake, out on the porch, and saw the light pop on. Thought I'd check on you is all."

"I'm fine. Just couldn't sleep. Everything's all good." It's as much of a promise as I can give to alleviate any concerns he might have.

He dips his chin, and I can tell that though he doesn't believe me, he's respecting my need to keep quiet. For now.

He gets up but pauses in the doorway to look back over his shoulder.

"Luke, if there's something going on, something that'll take you away from us for longer than usual . . ." He pauses dramatically, saying more with the intensity in his blue eyes than his mouth. "Just let me know. I want you here, by my side and James's side. That's all I've ever wanted, us working together to carry on Pops's legacy, and it's finally happening. But only if it's what you want too. When push comes to shove, if this isn't it for you, we'd understand. But we're always here for you. This is your home, no matter where you go or how long you're gone."

Having said his piece, and more words than he usually spouts off in a week, he finishes with a grunt and walks out, leaving me feeling like shit.

He thinks I'm having some existential crisis about being here on the ranch. The reality is, I love this ranch and this family. I want to see both grow. I want to become Uncle Luke in a few months. And while my work may take me all across the country, the Bennett Ranch is home.

No . . . what I'm obsessing about in actuality is the off-limits girl next door and how to get her to come back. And if I can't do that, I'm wondering how I can sneak onto her property without getting shot in the ass by her family.

CHAPTER 7

SHAYANNE

"*B*obby, watch the bows as you're packing those!" I holler, responding to his dark glare by sticking my tongue out at him. If my hands were empty, I'd stick my thumbs in my ears and wave my fingers at him like a moose too. Yeah, I'm twenty, but sometimes, these guys make me feel half that old.

"Why the hell did you put ribbons on the jars this year, anyway?" he grumbles.

I'd give him a smart-mouthed reply, but he's a little bit right. Usually, the jars pack into the boxes cleanly, but I'd thought an extra touch would look good.

Selling the canned goods from the farm has always just been something I did, but this year, it'd seemed more like a 'business' and I'd wanted to treat it as such. Hence, the cute little stickers I printed out and stuck to every lid and the ribbons I'd tied on every single jar of smashed pumpkin puree.

But Bobby doesn't care about any of that, so I just tell him the one fact that'll have him running for the hills. "Because I thought it was pretty," I say in full falsetto, batting my lashes.

Nothing scares my brothers more than a reminder that I'm

a woman and that as such, I sometimes like feminine things. Most of the time, I think they just pigeonhole me into some classification chart as an asexual lump. Admittedly, I do the same to them. 'Brothers' and 'sex' are two words that do not belong in the same sentence. A full-body shiver of disgust runs through me.

From the hallway, Brody appears, tall and dark-haired like all my brothers are and Daddy used to be before his hair turned into a distinguished salt-and-pepper blend. The Tannen boys are the hallmark tall, dark, and handsome in a gruff, barrel-chested, country boy sort of way. No six-pack abs in this house. I feed them too well and they work too hard to be that sort of lean. But I'd put my brothers up against any trio in the world when it comes to chucking hay bales.

"She put the damn bows on them because they cost twenty-five cents each, but she raised her prices two dollars a jar. Now shut your pie hole and get to packing."

Brody is certainly all charm. Hashtag sarcasm.

But he's right, quoting off the figures we discussed like he came up with them himself. In a way, I guess he gave his blessing, but it was the two of us who made the call to amp things up and treat this as an actual business, not just a hobby to pad the bottom line. My soap success is carrying over into other areas of our business.

Go, Shayanne! I cheer myself mentally, but outwardly, I realize I'm doing a happy dance when Bobby looks at me like I sprouted a second head.

He sets his box down on the stack by the door and ruffles my hair. I scoot away, trying to get out of reach, but he grabs at me, locking me in his arms and tickling the stuffing out of me as I scream and laugh. "Bobby! Stop it or I'm gonna pee on you!"

I'm not, really, but he stops near-instantly. Well, until he reaches out from a safe distance to muss up my hair one more time, grinning like a loon. He's my closest in age brother, so we fight more than I do with the other two boys.

"Load 'em up, boys!" I singsong. "We've got at least fifteen deliveries each today."

They grumble, but we get it done, half going into Brody's truck and half going into Bruce's so we can divide and conquer. They think I don't notice that they've given me and Brody all the old folks who want to chatter the day away, but I don't mind.

We roll out, and the automatic gate closes behind us with a push of a button. It's one of Daddy's additions to the farm that I was thankful for when he installed it, but now that I know it came from his gambling wins, it seems expensive and excessive. There's nothing wrong with hopping out to swing a fence closed.

"What's your bottom line so far this year?" Brody asks once we change from dirt to asphalt, all business as his eyes never leave the road.

"Better than last year, for sure," I reply as I set my little notebook with my notes for the farmer's market aside. "Orders are up, and profits are up too. All the orders from today are prepaid except for the big one for the elementary school PTA. They'll give me a check and we can deposit it in the bank before leaving town. We need to transfer money out of the main account too."

He nods, neither of us mentioning why we keep the farm's primary account balance as close to zero as we can. Daddy has a separate account for his gambling, but he plays big, win or lose, and the last thing we can afford is for him to lose the farm. Literally or figuratively.

So we transfer as much as we can to our personal accounts. Makes hell on me sometimes when I have to figure things for tax purposes, but better safe than sorry.

"How're you doing, Brody?" I ask him quietly.

His fingers tighten on the steering wheel and his jaw goes hard. He's always been a good brother, but I see the wear and tear on him. He's been disappearing into town more frequently, and I don't know what he's been up to, which makes me nervous. I'd thought maybe he finally had a girl, but Bruce said he didn't think so, and he'd know better than I would. Again, we don't talk relationships and sex. We stick with the farm and family.

"He's a piece of work, you know?" It's obvious that he's talking about Daddy, so I nod in agreement. "Did you know he asked to borrow a hundred bucks Thursday before he left?"

My jaw drops in shock, and I turn to look him in the face. "He did not."

Brody laughs but it's mirthless. "Sure as shit did. He had some story about not having time to make it into town before the bank closed, but I'm guessing he's just low on funds. I don't know what's worse, that he asked or that I gave it to him."

"Oh, how the mighty have fallen," I intone.

Once upon a time, I'd quoted Daddy so often that Sophie had threatened to smack me if I said the words 'Daddy says' one more time. She'd even made good on the threat while I worked that bad habit out of my vocabulary.

But honestly, back then, he'd been larger than life, and his word was like the gospel. I mean, he's my daddy.

Now, though, I can see behind the curtain, and I've all but given up on his ever being that force in our family again. But Brody is stepping up, in more ways than one. "Brody, don't let him get to you. You're doing so much, and we need you, but don't take on so much that you crack under the pressure. We're a family, a team, and we've got your back the way you've got ours."

He reaches a hand over, patting mine where it rests on the console between us. "I know, baby girl. Don't worry. I'm fine. And as long you keep the finances in ship shape, the farm's fine. Tannens never give in. We're like roaches. Too tough to die."

My nose wrinkles up at the metaphor. "That's disgusting, Brod. How about we *not* talk about bugs, 'kay?"

He inches his hand up from mine, tapping fingers that make goosebumps pop out along my flesh as he threatens, "They're gonna getcha!"

He laughs, and the smile stays on his face, but his shoulders are still an inch or two too close to his ears like he's working hard to carry the weight of the world.

Our first five or six deliveries go off without a hitch, people oohing and ahhing in excitement for their special treat. I get a few compliments on the updated packaging, which makes me feel like the hassle of packing up the jars was worthwhile.

"Where to next?" Brody says, climbing behind the wheel as I hop in the passenger side.

I look at my notebook, following down my bulleted list. "Doc Jones's clinic."

"Ah," Brody says with a smirk. "Guess I'll get time to talk over the entire football season with Doc then . . . or just grab some lunch with him while you girl gab with Sophie."

I roll my eyes, smirking. "Just drive, Brody."

Once there, I grab jars out of the emptying boxes. "Doc ordered two for now and a pie later, and I told Sophie I'd bring her a jar too."

Brody takes two jars and I grab the last one, heading inside.

But as I walk in the door, I stop stock-still. I would've expected to see James here, visiting Sophie. But that's not the Bennett brother standing before me.

As if fate is conspiring against me, or maybe it's *with* me, Luke is standing at the counter, chatting with Doc. "And then I said—"

Luke sort of drifts off mid-sentence, his full lips parted

slightly like he's lost the words he was saying when he sees me and our eyes lock. Everyone else in the room disappears, and it's only me and him again, a string pulled taut between us.

I haven't slept well in days, thinking about him and what we did, wishing things could be different. I've even stayed away from the tree, knowing that if I went there, I'd spend the next two hours perched up in the branch, wishing the whole time that he'd come up the rise like something out of a movie. I told myself that if I stayed away, I wouldn't know if he was looking for me, or worse, has just written me off as a silly girl who literally ran like a bat outta hell at the worst possible moment.

Well, maybe not *the worst*. During would've been worse, but immediately following having his fingers in my mouth is a pretty close runner-up for the crown of Awful Moments in Shayanne Tannen's Life.

"Luke," I say, my voice obviously belying our more-than-acquaintances situation, at least to my ears. Everyone in the surrounding county must know, or at least everyone in Doc Jones's office. And Brody's right here.

Shit.

Sophie comes to my rescue, overacting and squealing in a high pitch that makes me wince. She's got a good squeal. I've even heard it from the tree, although I don't let her know that. "Shayanne, so good to see you, honey!"

She gathers me a hug, basically shaking me to bring me to my senses.

But it's enough to break the staredown I'm giving Luke, trying to decipher what he's thinking. His face is blank, and I can't decide if it's in shock or because he doesn't care about seeing me. Of course, right now, I can barely focus my eyes on anything because my head's being whipped around so hard.

"You too, Sophie," I reply, but it's nowhere near as

exuberant as I usually am and is in stark contrast to her excitement, even if it's forced.

Doc bangs his fist on the countertop, a thick piece of oak that rattles loudly enough to draw everyone's attention. "All right, you young'uns, gimme my pumpkin pie before I kick the bucket."

It breaks the tension further, and Brody steps forward to hand over his two jars to Doc. "Here you go, Doc."

But as he steps back, Brody is eyeballing Luke, well aware of the reaction we had at seeing each other. So much for secrets. Brody's disapproval is coming in . . . what's the opposite of loud and clear? Silent and deadly? It's not a fart, but Brody sure looks like he smelled something rank.

"Bennett," he manages.

Luke nods, and his voice is slightly warmer, at least. "Tannen."

Both are speaking through clenched teeth, but that's as much of a greeting as they're likely to give each other, and honestly, it's friendlier than usual. Hell, not too long ago, Brody punched James in the jaw at the Fourth of July festival. It'd been a drunken misunderstanding courtesy of Dad's shit, but still, it's not exactly roses and rainbows with my brothers and any of the Bennett boys.

But there's no need for all these dramatics, so I jump in the middle of them, lilting my voice like a coffee-fueled kindergarten teacher. "That's right, boys and girls. Tannen," I say, pointing to Brody's chest. "Bennett." I point to Luke's, pointedly ignoring Brody's growl at the contact. "Tannen." I touch my own chest. "Bennett." I wrap my arm around Sophie. "Cute little Bennett," I continue, rubbing Sophie's stomach. "And Jones," I finish, smacking the palm Doc holds up for a high-five.

Thanks, Doc. You read my mind beautifully.

He's a slick one, sly and spry despite his age, and he's

watching the showdown like he wishes he could have some popcorn, but I'm guessing his dentures don't allow for that anymore. Sophie would eat some, though, because she's standing next to Doc with the same ticking eyes. Luke. Me. Brody. Luke. Me. Brody.

I decide to try and push things along peacefully, even if that means making a fool of myself. I keep the too-high-pitched teacher voice. "Now that introductions have been handled, let's move on to small talk, shall we? Remember, that's where we talk about mundane things and *do not* shed blood."

I look back and forth between my brother and Luke, daring either of them to disagree with me and praying neither of them throws the first punch.

But they stay silent, eyes locked and jaws hard, and I can see Brody fisting and unfisting his right hand. So much for killing them with kindness. I smack him on the chest with the back of my hand. "Manners, asshole."

Yeah, I get the irony of me calling someone else on their manners with language that would sound right coming out of a Marine's mouth, but I do what I can to keep my family semi-civilized.

It's a work in progress, me included.

Brody cuts his eyes to me, fiery smoke rising in their black depths like he can't believe I just did that in front of a Bennett. Chastising a grown man while he's mid-dick measuring before a fight is in poor form and I know it. But I glare right back. I might be almost a foot shorter than he is, but you don't fuck with the person who cooks your food. Ever.

And I'm no shrinking violet little lady, which he's damn well aware of.

"Play nice," I try again, a bit more syrup in the words. "First of all, we're in Doc's place. Second, Sophie's baby don't need that stress."

My excuses get through to him. Brody might be a hothead

sometimes, but he's not completely without manners. Brody takes a deep breath, and I can see him fortifying himself because to a guy like him, saying the first kind word is an admission of forfeit. But he'll do it for me. "How're your horses, Bennett?"

He spits the name like it's the filthiest kind of curse, but the question is nice enough. It's a baby step, but one in the right direction.

Luke nods, his voice sounding a little more relaxed too. "Doing okay. I was just here to talk to Doc about a stud. How're your animals doing?"

"Great. Thinking about getting a few more goats so we can keep up with Shayanne's soap production."

It's stilted, but damned if it's not the politest words they've spoken to each other in years, which is major progress. And just as importantly, that's news to me.

"Really?" I ask Brody, my eyes wide with hope. "I didn't know that. Are you sure?"

He nods, eyes still on Luke. "Figured we could use some of the pumpkin money since you did so well."

"That's because it's delicious!" Sophie pipes up, and I realize that instead of popcorn, she's opened her jar of puree and is digging in. I didn't even see her get a spoon, but she must've pulled it from somewhere. Probably a pregnancy thing. See-food diet and all. Or maybe she's having those pregnancy urges, in which case I'll have to bring her a half dozen jars just because.

And like a train wreck I can see coming but am powerless to stop, both guys nod their heads at the same time, agreeing with Sophie. It takes zero-point-two seconds for the meaning to dawn on Brody.

"You've had Shayanne's smashed pumpkin?" It's an accusation. He might as well be asking Luke if he fucked me. Bam, and Brody's on his guard again.

I butt right into that bomb about to explode, stepping between them to explain. "Mama Louise bought some last year." It's not a lie, but it sure ain't the whole truth either.

Luke smiles, cocky arrogance on full display like he's baiting Brody. "Yeah, Mama must've given me some before . . . or something."

"Not helping," I tell Luke, but I can't help but think I'd sure like a repeat of that 'something'. Even if I did hightail it out of the barn. Ugh. My brain and my body really need to get on the same side of this thing if I have any chance at not going mad.

But any chance at 'something' happening again is only possible if I can get everyone out of here alive. It's time to go.

"Okay, well, we've got another delivery and a stop by the bank before it closes, so we'd best be going. Thanks again for the orders, Doc." I'm basically shoving at Brody's chest, not that I could move him if he didn't want to let me, but he takes a few solid steps toward the door. Enough for me to relax my guard ever so slightly.

And just like the punk he is, Brody takes advantage of my laxness and turns back to Luke. "Rule stands, Bennett."

The left corner of Luke's full lips quirks. "Yep, rule stands, Tannen."

The 'rule' being that they stay on their land and we stay on ours. Grunt, grunt, rawr, rawr, and to hell with what *I* want.

But when Brody bursts through the door, pushing it a little too forcefully, Luke's eyes meet mine, already dismissing my brother's bad attitude. He looks hurt, or maybe pained at seeing me, and the questions are mentally telegraphing from him to me.

Why? What the hell? Wanna do that again?

Okay, that last one's probably my thought, not his. But it stands either way.

Seeing the curious looks from Sophie and Doc, Luke shuts

his mouth. His jaw clenches, that little bump appearing and disappearing once again. He really shouldn't grind his teeth so much. He'll end up making them into nubs if he keeps at it.

Or maybe he only does that around me? Maybe I'm the only one who drives him that crazy?

I can't decide whether I like that idea or not.

CHAPTER 8

LUKE

*M*y phone buzzes on the coffee table and I ignore it. I don't want to talk to anyone. I want to dissect what the hell happened and figure out why Shayanne went from seductress to scaredy cat in the crack of a whip.

Seeing her today at Doc Jones's clinic was the most painful salve I could imagine, too. At least I know she's okay. That's what I told myself after she waltzed out the door after her brother. But if she's okay and I'm definitely not, what does that say about me?

Nothing good, that's for sure.

Maybe Mark's right and I should get out of here for a bit. I don't have any jobs pulling me away, but that doesn't mean I can't grab my go-bag and take a vacation for a few days.

The beach, maybe? It's been a long time since I've been anywhere near an ocean, not since a breeding trip down in the Tampa Bay area, and I was too busy to worry about the beach then.

I picture me with cutoff jeans and boots, laid back in a lounge chair by the ocean with my hat pulled down low over my eyes. I could even try one of those fruity girly drinks with an umbrella in it. Hank always says they're tasty, but no cowboy worth his truck would order a piña colada at a country bar. He'd be laughed out of the place before one rum-flavored drop hit his tongue. But maybe a little sunshine and a beach are what I need.

I grab my phone to look up possible travel deals when it buzzes again.

Holy fuck, it's her.

I had your number from the wedding. Hope this is okay.

Of course, I text back, my thumbs actually shaking for some reason. *Are you okay?*

Those three dots have never seemed so ominous before, and I hold my breath until her reply pops up. They seem to roll on forever, one, two, three, one, two, three, one, two, three . . .

Tree in thirty?

She didn't answer the question, I notice. But even if she's fine, I'm going to go meet her and I know it. There's no question that I want to see her again. To apologize, to make her see reason, to talk to her, to fuck her, maybe to do all of that and more.

Yeah. See ya in a few.

I don't bother saddling up a horse since I already bedded them all down for the night, comfy and quiet in their stalls. But I do grab a blanket, thinking it'll be handy for us to sit on or to wrap around Shay's shoulders if she gets cold.

The walk's not far, and I use the cool night air to clear my head before I get there.

Don't be an asshole, man. She's inexperienced. Maybe she just got nervous after the fact. Be gentle with her.

Surprisingly, it's the last thought that does it. There's nothing about Shayanne that says she needs soft and easy. She's as tough as they come. But, in a way, she's like one of the horses I train, or maybe I'm just such a horse guy that everyone reminds me of one of my equine friends. But the truth is, even though they're big animals that could stomp you if they wanted, at the same time, they're incredibly fragile.

It's up to you to treat them right. If you do a good enough job, they'll come right to you and that connection can develop.

That's what I need to do with Shay. Be patient, give her what she needs to feel comfortable, and let her come to me. But damned if that doesn't sound like Mission Impossible when I just want to gather her in my arms and promise her the moon or whatever else it is she wants as reassurance.

The tree is a dark spot in the night, and underneath the branches is total darkness, but I can sense that she's already here.

"Shayanne?"

She hops down from the low branch and wordlessly steps into the night. Her sweatpants are pulled up to her knees, leaving a gap of curvy calf above her boots. She's got a flannel shirt over a tank top, and her hair is piled on top of her head in a messy knot. She's gorgeous, natural, and effortless, and I've never seen a woman so stunning by moonlight.

"Luke? I'm so sorry," she finally says, and I can hear her voice shaking.

"It's okay. Come here," I soothe her, pulling her to me in a hug. I still don't know what's going through her head, but I hate that she's upset. Especially if it's something I did.

She curls into me, her soft curves molding to the hard lines of my body, and I run my fingers over her neck, teasing at a tendril of hair that's escaped. "Shay, talk to me. Just talk to me. Help me to understand."

She steps back, putting an inch of space between us so I can see her nod. I take that as a sign that she's willing to talk, so I spread the blanket out, guiding her to sit down next to me. There are only inches between our hips, but where before it felt like I could feel her energy buzzing around her body, now it feels like the valley outside of town. It's a ravine that has to be traversed carefully, step by slow step, or you'll tumble down, banging your head on the rocks the whole way.

She takes a big breath, and I'm ready to hear her say something heavy and profound about how she got nervous because it was her first time or about how our families would never allow us to be together.

Instead, she laughs, but it's high-pitched and vaguely hysterical. "I freaked the fuck out."

She shakes her head and tries again. This time, her voice is quiet, tinged with sadness and worry. "I know this is gonna be hard, and people, A-K-A our families, are definitely going to have some things to say. I was all rally cries and ready for war with Mama Louise and Mark, but then you said shit was gonna hit the fan, and I realized this wasn't just about me. I didn't want anything to happen to *you*, so I bolted. I think I thought it'd keep you safe or be easier or something."

Her chin drops, her hair a curtain around her face, so I tilt her face up so I can see her in the moonlight. "You think you can take on Mama, who's literally the scariest person I know, but I can't take on your family? What kind of pipsqueak do you take me for?"

Her smile is weak but growing as I spread my shoulders wide and flex my biceps like I could fight the world for her.

Her giggle is lighter, brighter. "You think Mama Louise is scary?"

I look around, lowering my voice to a stage whisper. "Don't say her name again or she'll appear like Beetlejuice just to get us in trouble."

From behind her hands, she whispers. "Mama Louise!" She looks around the moonlit pasture, squinting to see toward our house. "Guess she's not as scary as you think."

But I can feel her unease at the true thread running beneath our silly joke. "Seriously, I know it can get ugly. Based on how Brody looked at me today, the odds are that shit's going to fly, and it won't be pretty. But I can take it if you can."

"I spent this entire time thinking about you and hating that I hurt you," she confesses, and then she apologizes. "I'm sorry, Luke."

I let out a sigh of relief, my chest loosening though I didn't even realize it was tight. "I'm sorry too, Shay. I thought I'd hurt you or pressured you — "

She interrupts, her hand on my thigh between us as she shakes her head. "No, not at all. It was everything I ever dreamed of. Well, not everything, but you know what I mean."

"Okay, so we're good?" I ask, needing to be sure because it feels like we just went through the wringer but came out the other side pressed a bit closer.

Her lips twist into an ironic grin as she says sarcastically, "Well, except that you're a Bennett and I'm a Tannen. Oh, and a 'fraidy cat, yeah."

"Girl, you're gonna be the death of me, aren't ya?" I tease, tucking another loose strand of hair behind her ear.

She flinches, and I'm not sure why until she says, "Don't call me girl, okay? Not to be weird, considering we've been damn near naked and all, but that's what my daddy calls me to put me in my place. I hate it."

Her voice trails off like this was more revealing than everything else we've done. For her, it just might be.

I've never been a fan of her father, and the way he tried to strong-arm our family into selling to him put the nail in his coffin as far as I'm concerned. But all those ugly feelings for him are nothing compared to the way Shayanne sounds small when she tells me about him putting her 'in her place'. As far as I'm concerned, her place is anywhere she damn well wants it to be, and I'd fight her whole damn family to make sure that's the case, if that's what it took.

I pull her around to straddle me, her legs wrapping behind

me as I cup her face. "Shayanne, I'm not trying to put you anywhere you don't want to be. And I don't think you're some silly little girl. We wouldn't be where we are right now if I did. When I look at you, I see a woman, strong and responsible, with a daring side a mile wide, who knocked me on my ass when I just opened my eyes and saw you again."

She rolls her eyes. "Yeah, I'm such a daredevil." She dismisses the idea completely as she throws her arms over my shoulders and fidgets with the curls at the nape of my neck. I've been meaning to get a haircut, but now I'm thinking I'll leave it because she seems to like it. And I like her hands gripping my hair too.

"Uhm, who exactly stomped her way onto private property, committed a little light breaking and entering into my barn, and then threw herself at me? That'd be you, Miss Shayanne Tannen, Daredevil." I boop her on the nose as I say her full name intentionally.

She blushes, although I can feel the heat more than see it in the moonlight, but she argues back, taking me on that roller coaster only she can get me to ride. "The door was unlocked, so that's only entering, not breaking. And you kissed me first."

I crowd in close to her, whispering hotly in her ear. "This started long before I kissed you, honey. And we both know it. It started the second you sat down beside me at Hank's, looking sexy and bright as the sun." That was the moment my brain short-circuited, and it had nothing to do with the trip away from home or the long drive alone.

Nope, it was all Shayanne, the girl who became a woman, who's become my obsession.

She rubs her cheek along mine, my scruff making a scratching sound against her soft skin that makes me think of doing it to her bare thighs as I sip at her.

"Honey?" she questions the endearment. "Is that what I am?"

"Because your skin is honey gold, your hair flashes amber in the sun, and you taste so fucking sweet," I explain, punctuating the words with a soft kiss.

"It'll do," she groans into my lips, accepting the name.

It feels like I just got the wildest mustang to take the slightest pressure of a halter, the first start of gentling her to not just want me but to truly trust me.

I reward us both with another kiss, harder and hotter this time, and the passion ignites instantly as she pulls me toward her, but I'm already in her orbit. I may have led her around the dance floor, but she's leading me around by other things that have nothing to do with music.

Our tongues fight for dominance, battling for breath as our teeth clack together. But neither of us cares, just wanting more of this. Suffocation finally wins over desire, and I press my forehead to hers, panting breathlessly. "Fuck, Shay."

I can see her smile up close, her cheeks lifting and her eyes flashing like fireworks. She looks like the cat that got the cream, but I'm feeling like I'm the lucky one here.

"Let's go for a walk," I tell her, pulling away before she can stop me. She makes a whimpering sound of argument, but I press a finger to her mouth. "If we stay here, I'm not going to be able to hold myself back from you, and I'm not fucking you for the first time in a dirty barn *or* on the hard ground. Not until there's no doubt in your mind, and not without a date first. So let's go, Shayanne."

It's heavy-handed, and for a second, I wonder if she'll recoil from me again. It wouldn't surprise me after what she's said about how her dad treats her, but I would never treat Shayanne like that. This isn't me trying to keep her down. It's me trying to respect her and treat her the way she deserves when I'm at the end of my rope.

"Well, all right then. Though I'm thinking a dirty, hard fucking sounds just fine too." She hops off my lap and bends down to grab the blanket, shooing me off it as her words freeze me where I sit.

Her round ass is in the air in front of me, and I can't help but remember that I'm the only man who's seen her naked, looked at her pretty pussy, and tasted her sweet honey. The only one who'll be fucking her in a dirty barn, too, but not yet. So I fight the urge to pull her back down to the blanket and stand up, getting out of her way.

She lays the folded blanket over the lowest branch of the tree, asking if we can leave it there. I agree, mostly because it's a sign that she plans on coming back here with me. Besides, it sort of marks the tree as ours, and I like that.

We walk in the night air, holding hands and whispering to each other even though no one is around to hear. But disturbing the sounds of the night feels intrusive, like this is a time and place we shouldn't be, but I'd go anywhere, anytime with this woman.

"How you doing now?" I ask, wanting to make sure she's solid now.

"Still in shock a little, I think," she answers, and because I can't see her face fully in the moonlight, I'm not sure how to take that.

"Good shock, like 'oh, my God, Luke is the best', or bad shock, like 'what the fuck have I done?'" I say lightly, though I'm holding my breath to hear her answer.

She laughs, and I feel the vibration against my side as she cuddles up next to me and I lay my arm over her shoulders. "Maybe a bit of both?" she says. "Luke, you're a lot of man to take in, and that's a good thing. Still, I think about how you and Brody looked at each other, and all I can think of is 9-1-1. That's not so good. But maybe I'm in shock because I think I can live with that."

I can't help but smile, thinking she's right. I'm a bit in shock too, I guess.

Just a few days ago, I was just working in the barn, researching horses and their success rates and admonishing myself to not think about Shayanne after our unexpected dinner. It hadn't been going all that well, my mind returning to her again and again. But I'd been holding strong.

Until she walked in, all long legs and wavy hair, damn near daring me to take her the way I wanted to even if she had no fucking idea what she was asking for. And then she ran, but now she's back.

As far as roller coaster loop-de-loops go, she is already my favorite unexpected twist.

"Me too," I tell her softly as I run my hand up and down her arm, letting her know that I'm leaning more toward the good kind of shock. "I think your strutting into the barn was the best surprise I've gotten in longer than I can remember. And I don't spook easily, at least not usually. Sorta helps with the horses, you know?"

Shayanne laughs quietly. "You surprised me too. I didn't know when I came over that it was going to be like this. I would've worn cuter lingerie or something." She laughs nervously, but I think she's talking about more than just what we did that let me see her panties and bra.

I stop her, turning to meet Shayanne's eyes. "I like you as you. Plain jeans, regular old panties, whatever. You never need to dress up for me. I don't need all that muss and fuss unless you do. I just wanted you . . . *want* you," I correct myself. "You might've come over to ask me about pumpkin puree, but I think we both know we wanted more. At Hank's, at the tree, at our dinner date, and right now."

It's the God's honest truth. I can virtually see the sparkles of desire dancing between us, but it's not just physical. Or at least, not only physical. There's something special about her, and I want to know everything about her.

I lean down, searching for her lips, and she lifts to her toes to meet me halfway. It's sweet and too short when she pulls back with a smile.

"Why did you stop it every time? I feel like I'm seducing you into something you're not sure you want." She drops her voice into a sultry tone, but it's cartoonish and playful. I can sense the real question underneath, though.

I tilt her chin up, bringing her eyes to mine. "I didn't see you before, literally and figuratively. Not even at Sophie's wedding, really. Not till Hank's, and then it hit me hard, Shay. But I know who your family is and who my family is. I didn't want to cause you problems. I still don't want to cause you trouble. And you're young, Shay."

I run my thumb along her cheekbone, tracing the smooth, tanned skin and wishing it was bright enough for me to see her clearly so I could analyze every bit of her expression. "I didn't want to take advantage of you, so I held back. Not because I don't want you but because I do. And you made it damn hard, literally, to walk away from you."

"I didn't see you either, but I do now, Luke Bennett. I might be young, but I know a good one when I see him, and you're one of the best. There's no way my daddy and brothers are gonna believe that." She sighs, resigned as she drops her head. "I'm gonna have to fight them, unless . . ."

"Shayanne Tannen, are you asking me to be your dirty little secret?" I tease.

I hadn't thought of it until just now, but truthfully, it'd solve most of the problems she's worried about and keep my nose straight and pretty instead of broken from one of the Tannen boys' fists.

Not that they'd get the drop on me. I haven't only spent my time in bars learning to two-step. There've been a couple of brawls in there too. Nothing serious, but I've been the new guy in town a few too many times. Some guys feel the need to piss on their territory just because you dared to cross the county line.

She grins, the moonlight glinting off her white smile. "What? No!" she says, laughing as she pushes at my chest. "You think I'm really worried about handling my brothers?"

I lift my eyebrows at her, amused at her little phrase at the end, probably one she picked up from Sophie, most likely. "It's fine, Shay. We don't have to solve all the world's issues tonight. We can start with just us. Do you want to see me again?"

Her nod is fast and furious, her hair actually whipping into my face she's so adamant. "Do you want to see me again?" she asks, repeating my words.

"Fuck yes, woman," I say, picking her up and spinning her around. "Every night, if I can."

She hollers, and I set her back down, covering the sound with a kiss, capturing her bubbly giggles. "You have to be quiet, honey, or we're gonna get caught."

I hear the tiniest moan in her throat and chase it, pressing my lips to the long column of her neck. "Ooh, I think you like that naughty idea, don'tcha?"

With a breathy purr, she says, "Yes."

And that tells me more than I ever thought I'd know about Shayanne Tannen. She's a daredevil, but with a soft heart of gold for her family. She's a good girl with a dirty side. Most importantly, she likes me, even though she shouldn't.

We kiss for several minutes, the moon the only witness to our shamelessly wanton need, and I memorize every sound she makes, learning what she likes and what drives her wild.

Realizing it's getting late, I reluctantly ask, "Want me to take you home? Or at least to the property line?"

It's a test and I damn well know it, but I offer it anyway.

She nods, confident and certain. "To the fence line."

It feels like a step in the right direction, but truthfully, it's a huge leap.

Today has been a fork in the road for us both, and I'm just glad we're taking the rest of the trip together, even if there are some serious potholes in our future.

"Come on. I'll walk you home," I say with a satisfied smile, leading her across the fields with her hand tucked into mine.

CHAPTER 9

LUKE

*T*he kitchen table is full, like it always is at its best. Full of food, full of family, and full of love, if you look close enough.

Sure, next to me, Mark's got Katelyn at his right, though only because Mama said she couldn't sit in his lap at the dinner table. They're still so possessive of each other. Well, more than that, but no one's mentioning that with Mama around, especially not at her dinner table. You'd be cut off from dessert for a month, maybe longer.

Across from me sit Sophie and James, who still look so wrapped up in each other that I'm surprised they're not tied at the hip and singing love songs to each other. At the foot of the table is Mama's place, across from Pops's seat until Mark had begrudgingly taken it when we'd needed the space.

But even with all the coupledom going on, you don't have to scratch too far under the surface to see the love between us boys. We pick and argue and needle like the devil himself, but that's just the brotherly way, or at least it is for us. But behind every veiled insult is deep love, acceptance, and belonging.

Even so, I always sort of disappear into the middle. And it's not because I've got some middle-child syndrome. Mark's this looming, gruff presence that everyone's always been aware of, even when he was a kid. And James is the wild child rebel who keeps everyone on their toes because you never know what he's going to do next.

And me? I'm not loud nor quiet, not impulsive nor cautious, and not bold nor timid. Just somewhere in the middle of it all. Call me Switzerland, neutral and forgettable.

It's never been something I've particularly thought about until tonight when Sophie is looking at me through narrowed eyes like she can see into my soul and I feel uncomfortably put on the spot in a major way.

"So, are we going to talk about the clinic, Luke?" she says, and though it's her usual voice, it seems to echo around the table as every eye turns to me. I swear I even hear silverware scrape across a plate.

That's probably Mark, if I had to guess, because he asks the follow-up. "What happened at the clinic?"

If I could shoot daggers with my eyes, I'd be launching automatic knife warfare Sophie's way right now. "Nothing happened. Just talked to Doc about a stud he wanted to see if I was interested in." I'm praying she's receiving my 'abort mission' message, but Mama scents blood.

"Aaaand . . . ?" Mama prompts. She has no idea what Sophie's talking about, but she'll excise the truth like a scalpel-wielding surgeon. The CIA should hire Mama for interrogations, she's that good.

"That's it. Doc has a friend with a retired racehorse. We talked about his potential." I look to Mama, making sure to meet her eyes fully so I don't seem like I'm hiding anything. "In my professional opinion, he won't be a frequent request because his results were spotty at best and he's on the shorter side of average. Maybe he'll be appealing to average riders or the endurance racers, though."

I shrug like that's all there was to the conversation and I have no idea what Sophie is hinting at. But Mama must hear something in my voice because I can see the crow's feet at the edges of her eyes deepen, and I know I'm in for it.

If you saw Mama walking around town, you might not think much of her. She's on the petite side, blonde hair that's starting to show a distinguished gray, bright blue eyes . . . all pretty packaging that houses the kindest disposition you've ever met. I've heard her described as a 'sweetheart' more times than I can count, and that's true. She's got a heart full of love and will share it with the world like rain falling on the earth.

Unless she's responsible for making sure you don't turn into an absolute hooligan. Us boys have never once been fooled by Mama's sweetness. We've always known it comes with a framework of steel. Her smiles might look like sugar wouldn't melt in her mouth, but I've seen her smile nice-as-can-be with her mouth while her eyes promised punishment my little hiney didn't ever want to know. She's a good woman, a tough mother, and unfortunately, she knows all of my games.

Mama looks into my soul with her lie-detector eyes, and I call on the experience dodging her during my misspent teen years and look right back unflinchingly. After a long stretch of three heartbeats, her brow lifts a half-inch. I win . . . for now.

"Mmm-hmm." She doesn't believe me in the least. There's going to be a round two. Mama's just letting me skate while James and Mark are around.

Sophie, though, is like a dog with a bone, going after me even harder than Mama and blowing the situation up even before I can dig my spoon into the mashed potatoes. "And then you nearly came to blows with Brody Tannen." She mimics boxing, her little fists punching at the air as she bobs and weaves her head left and right. "Bam, bam, pew-pew-pew," she says, adding sound effects to her mimed fight.

James leans forward, eager as a kid in a candy store. "Did

you hit him? Tell me you hit him and busted his nose." He turns to Sophie next to him, matching her air punches as they smile playfully. They're quite the pair, a perfect match.

"James," Mark admonishes him, simple but effective. And though James and Sophie stop their antics, their smiles only grow wider. Especially when Mark turns his attention to me, his voice not changing at all in tone. "Luke."

How he manages to only say our names but communicate so much is a testament to his position as the strong leader of our family, Mama aside. And though I still remember the days when we would goof around as kids, those days are few and far between now. In their place, Mark rocks his grumpy asshole vibe that's been softened slightly by Katelyn, who's currently placing her hand over his on their shared corner of the table.

"Mark," I continue his rollcall of names. He grunts once, a warning to get on with it. "Fine," I huff, leaning back and abandoning my mashed potatoes, knowing I won't get back to them until they're cold and the gravy's gloopy, dammit. "While I was at Doc's, Brody and Shayanne came in to make a delivery. He was an ass, as always, but we exchanged pleasantries and everything was fine. No one got in a fight," I finish, giving as few details as possible.

I also definitely leave out any details about Shayanne's late-night text and our rendezvous at the tree.

See, I'm good at being a dirty little secret, I think smugly. *These lips are sealed!*

I lift a brow at Sophie for starting this whole mess with her big mouth, and she grins back, not chagrined at all by my attempts to make the interaction sound minor but rather pleased with herself.

But then Mama jumps back into the fray. "Luke Bennett, first of all, language. And you be nice to the Tannen kids. They haven't had it easy, which all of you very well know, so don't go causing any problems when they've already got enough on their plates."

My throat closes, full of the arguments I want to throw out there, blaming Brody. But Mark and James catch my eye.

Mama doesn't know the full extent of the 'discussions' we had with the Tannens when Paul tried to buy our ranch after Pops died. But it was tense and ultimately led to the current bad blood between the families. Not that Mama would care in the least. She's a lover of all people, one of the good ones who will take care of you, whether you want her to or not. And she's likely already forgiven Paul for any 'misunderstandings' about his offers.

But I follow Mark's silent edict and swallow the biting words, instead offering Mama a dutiful, "Yes, ma'am."

We finish dinner, delicious pork chops with applesauce, mashed potatoes, and green beans, but I don't think I taste a single bite of it after that firing squad moment with me as the prisoner strung up before my family.

The ladies mostly carry the rest of the conversation, between Katelyn sharing stories about her latest bridezilla up at the resort where she's an event planner and Sophie talking about a llama farm she's going to visit with Doc. But Mark, James, and I have an entirely different conversation going, all through silent communication with eyes, eyebrows, and tensed lips.

I do my best to ignore them, feigning the utmost interest in whether Katelyn's bride chooses ivory or cream.

After a slice of pumpkin Bundt cake that only reminds me of Shayanne's smashed pumpkin puree, I excuse myself, thanking Mama for another tasty dinner. I'm basically making a run for it, not ready for the reckoning to come yet.

But before I can get out the door, my brothers are filling the frame and then some. They've let me keep my silence in

Mama's presence, being polite and familial, but that's over now.

"Okay, now tell the rest of that story," Mark growls.

I sigh, going to the kitchen to grab a beer, and Mama gives me a small smile. She knows what's up and that Mark and James are about to do some of her dirty work. Heading into the living room, I toss one to James and one to Mark, both of them catching them with ease and popping the tabs. We each sit down on worn leather, them on the couch and me in a chair. Dimly in the background, I can hear Mama gather up Sophie and Katelyn to start clearing the table, giving us a little privacy. Probably so Mama can get Sophie's side of the story before she talks to me.

I sigh and give in to the inevitable even as I still decide how I want to frame this. After all, they know I had words with Brody, but that's not unexpected if a Tannen and Bennett meet these days. Even down at the rancher's supply, things can be tense.

But they don't know that it has a single thing to do with Shayanne, and I don't want to spin that tale yet. Or maybe ever, depending on what she wants me to do.

"I was at Doc's, like I said. Brody and Shayanne came in. He was eyeballing me from the get-go, and Shayanne stepped in to referee. She forced some small talk, which was awkward as fuck since she was being playful and cute about it, and then they left to make another delivery. That's it."

I take a drink, not missing the glance my brothers give one another. I don't like being the center of their attention, the recipient of their judgement.

Shit. I said she was 'playful and cute.' For fuck's sake, don't let them catch that.

James breaks the stalemate. "I hate that fucker." He shakes his head and then takes a deep pull on his beer. "You should've punched him."

He raises his beer high, his other arm following so that it looks like he's celebrating his favorite team's winning touchdown.

"Hell, no," I reply, giving him a harsh look. "Not with your wife and baby there in that tiny ass reception room. I am not risking my future niece or nephew just because Brody Tannen's an asshole."

James looked abashed, then nods. "You're right . . . thanks. Still, Brody deserves a good smash in the teeth. Hell, we should do that next time we see them. Plain ol' three on three."

"And then we'd all end up in the clinker down at Sheriff Downs's office," I predict. "I'm sure Mama could afford bail for one of us." I point to my chest, making sure they know I'd be the saved one.

Mark chuckles, sipping his beer. He's got half a beer in him already, so he's a little looser-lipped than normal. "Hell, we all know that Mama would bail her baby boy James out before she'd bail you or my ugly ass. At least I've got Katelyn. You, Luke? Well . . . don't drop the soap."

James puffs up, knowing it's true, but hopefully, none of us is actually going to put that to the test anytime soon. "What can I say? She loves me," he says with a shit-eating grin. But then his smile dims, and he looks a little worried. "Hey, did Brody's hard-on for you have anything to do with your dancing with Shayanne at Hank's the other day? If folks were telling tales, that'd rile him up before he even laid eyes on you."

Technically, the answer to his question is no. It didn't have anything to do with anyone telling him about our dancing.

My guess is Brody could tell there were some sparks pinging between Shay and me, and her stepping in between us probably didn't assuage those concerns. But I'm not sharing that, and I'm crossing my fingers and toes that Sophie doesn't get too starry-eyed sharing that version of events either. "Nah, he didn't say anything about Hank's. Just a one-off, ran into each other unexpectedly, and you know how he is."

I shrug, trusting that my brothers will think the best of me and the worst of Brody Tannen, which they do.

Mark slaps his knee with his free hand, standing and suddenly resolute. In his boss man voice, he growls, "You two, stay away from anyone with a last name of Tannen. Got it?"

He points to me and then to James, but James is never done. "Well hell, Mark, I was planning on heading over there uninvited for dinner tomorrow night. That should be fine, right?"

Sarcasm coats every word and Mark rumbles deep in his chest.

Ever the peacemaker, or at least the one who pushes things past the line so that it's two on one, I add, "Oh, you're going for dinner? I was thinking of breakfast. I'm sure they'll welcome me with open arms."

Mark looks to the ceiling, or maybe he's seeing beyond to heaven, looking for some divine intervention. "See what I put up with? This is why I'm an asshole, because everyone else is a bigger asshole."

James and I look at each other, united in our teasing. "You are definitely the biggest asshole of them all," we say simultaneously, spreading our arms wide and then laughing.

Mark moves toward the door, shaking his head. "I ain't got time for your shit. Katelyn's probably ready to head home and is waiting on me."

There's a joke in there too, something about her waiting on her knees, but even as frat boy immature as we can be, that's a joke I'd never make. Especially not about my brother's sweet wife.

But when Mark throws up a middle finger as he struts out the door, I do call out, "Fuck you too!"

But it's with a smile. And a prayer that Mama ain't listening too closely.

James gets up too, pointedly putting his empty can on the coffee table like the heathen I know he's not. "Me too. Sophie and I need to drive into town. See ya tomorrow."

A few minutes later, I hear James's truck start up and rumble down the drive toward the gate. He'll lock it behind him, so we're secure for the night.

Mark and Katelyn in their little house. Mama in the main house. And me in the ranch house. But for some reason, I feel more alone than ever.

I finish my near-warm beer, realizing that if my family gave me shit for the little scene at Doc's, it's likely that Shayanne's did the same to her. Especially Brody, since he saw the whole thing firsthand. But she didn't say anything about that when we met last night.

It makes me uncomfortable that she might've had to sit through a dinner while they volleyed questions at her about my knowing anything about her smashed pumpkin puree or how our eyes locked when she'd walked in.

I stare at my phone sitting on the coffee table, inches away from James's empty can, wondering if I should do what I'm considering. Mark explicitly ordered me not to, but I also already know I'm going to do it anyway.

I pick up the phone, scrolling through my messages to find hers and type a new one.

Got a full interrogation at dinner tonight about Doc's.

A few seconds later, my phone buzzes in my hand.

Eek! Sorry. You okay?

I'm fine. You've got nothing to be sorry for. Brody say anything?

Tree at midnight?

Definitely.

CHAPTER 10

SHAYANNE

I wait for the house to be quiet, knowing that my up-at-sunrise brothers will be asleep long before midnight. Once the only thing I hear is the sound of the night outside, I slip out the back door, closing the door silently. I forego riding Ember, who's likely asleep too, in favor of walking, also in the interest of quiet.

The walk to the tree is quiet and peaceful as the bright moon lights my way and I know the path like the back of my hand. The tree stands tall in front of me, a beacon of peace, usually, but tonight, it seems like it's more. A promise of excitement, maybe? A hope for something new?

It seems insane that for being the quintessential boy next door, Luke definitely feels new and exciting. Since we've rediscovered each other, he's different in a way that doesn't make sense for a guy I've known my whole life.

And it's not the taboo of his being off-limits or the way we came together like fireworks. It's how his smile lights up his face, the kindness in his heart, and the surprise of the way he spun me around the dance floor but kept me secure in his strong arms.

It's the way he's respected me, taking it slow even though we both could be swept away in this tidal wave of desire that's smashing through us. The way he wants my first time to be something special.

It might be dumb, or at the least ill-advised, but I've got a full-blown, life-sized, hotter-than-three-PM in August crush on that man. The man who drove me to do the craziest thing I've ever done in the dusty quiet of his barn, the man who cared enough to check on me after my brother's spectacle, the man who should be here any minute.

And what's even crazier is that he has a crush on me too. Little old Shayanne Tannen. Who'd have thunk it?

I grab the blanket from the branch where we left it, thanking the tree for keeping it safe and then smiling as I realize that it smells like Luke. Hay, sunshine, animal, and cologne, and even though he's not here yet, it makes me feel surrounded by him. I lay it out beneath the tree, sitting down to wait while wishing upon the stars. Yeah, they're romantic girly wishes, but for Luke, I feel okay being romantic and girly. Or at least my version of it.

I watch the night, seemingly still and quiet but alive with lightning bugs and the occasional moos of cattle. The moon rises, tracing a shining path across the star-studded inky sky. I smile and wait until I hear the sound of grass moving and denim on denim as bootsteps draw near.

My heart jolts, for one second thinking I've been caught, and I realize I have been. Caught in Luke's eyes as he gets close enough that I can see him in the dark. He's wearing dark jeans and a black T-shirt, a black ballcap pulled down low.

"You trying to scare me, coming up like a country cat burglar?" I tease, laughing softly as the squirt of fear turns to molten desire at seeing him. He looks dark and dangerous, not because of the clothes, but the hard set of his jaw and wide berth of his shoulders.

"Just thought I'd dress for discretion, seeing as I'm your dirty little secret." He says it with heated promise and a cocky smirk that tilts up only one side of his mouth, knowing it'll make me squirm in a good way.

Ooh, he's playing dirty. Two can play that game.

"Well, come sit down then, Secret." I throw the blanket open and smile innocently when he hisses.

"What the fuck are you wearing, Shay?" he bites out like I've somehow wronged him with my chosen apparel.

Of course, I'll admit the tank top skims my curves nicely, holding the girls up so I can go braless, which is obvious by the diamond points of my nipples in the cool air, and I intentionally rolled the waistband of my flannel pajamas down a little bit, leaving a strip of my belly bare.

"Pajamas. It's part of my whole cover story, you see. If I were to get caught sneaking out or sneaking back in, I can say I was getting a drink of water and heard something outside." I gesture along my body Vanna White-style as I throw him a dazzling movie star smile. "Perfect cover story."

He mumbles under his breath as he takes his boots off, but it's quiet enough that I hear anyway. "Barely covering a damn thing."

He sits down and leans back against the tree, throwing out his right arm for me to snuggle up next to him. I lay my head on his chest, pressing my front to his side and throwing my leg over his. It feels natural, like we've done this a million times before. Or maybe like we'll do it a million times again. I hope it's that one.

He pulls at the blanket, covering us both and turning us into a Luke-Shayanne burrito, warm against the slightest chill in the air.

"Did you bring a jacket, at least?" he asks. "Or are you gonna freeze your tits off on the way home?" He growls that part like he doesn't like that idea at all.

I look up at the tree where my flannel shirt is hanging, and he follows my gaze. "You know, you could help me stay warm instead."

He chuckles and pulls me to him, his voice low and intense in my ear. "So, you knew exactly what you were going to do to me, didn't you, honey?"

His fingers are skimming along the stretch of skin between my pants and shirt, almost ticklishly light, but it's the casual way he calls me 'honey' again that makes bubbles rise like champagne in my belly.

"Who was I to know you had a thing for flannel PJs and tank tops?" I say coquettishly, thinking I'm getting good at this flirting thing. Thank God for books and movies or I'd be awkward as hell.

"Never did until about two minutes ago," he whispers against my hair before pressing a kiss there. "Or maybe it's just you."

It's quiet for a moment, and I don't know what he's thinking, but I'm thinking how much I like this. It's still head rattling how I could go from barely speaking to Luke Bennett one day to feeling like I'm missing a limb when he's not next to me. I've heard of insta-love and insta-lust, but always dismissed them as fairy tales.

But this is insta-something, and shockingly, it feels deeply real. From the moment he took my hand on the floor at Hank's to right now, he's suddenly my first thought when I wake up, my last thought when I go to sleep, and damn near every thought in between.

His quiet words break my reverie. "Sophie threw me under the bus tonight, making it sound like Brody and I were this close to blows." He holds his finger and thumb an inch apart. "And then Mark declared Tannens off limits."

He snuggles me in closer, pressing his cheek to my head, and I can feel the 'fuck off' message he's sending to his brother.

"You're a bad boy, not minding your brother like that," I tell him as I draw shapes on his chest with my fingertip.

"Guess that makes you bad too," he says gruffly, and I can feel his heartbeat thumping. I like that he didn't call me a 'bad girl'. It shows that he's listening to me, respecting me. Another sign that he's a good man, regardless of what my daddy says about the Bennett boys.

"What about your brothers? Did they say anything about the scene at Doc's?" he pushes, and I can feel the protectiveness blooming in him. It feels different from what my daddy and brothers do, though. Luke doesn't want to smother me. He wants me to feel safe to blossom.

"Brody was making all sorts of noise about your trying to look tough in front of him, but I reminded him how nice you both were with your small talk. I even ventured that maybe Daddy was wrong about your family, seeing as he's been wrong before."

I swallow thickly, years of hero worship of the man who raised me hard to let go of, but I can see the truth now. The pedestal I had him on started crumbling a while back, and now there's only rubble left surrounding him. "I only said that because he was gone. Figured it was a way to get my brothers to see reason, or at least the beginnings of it. Because I truly believe that Daddy was wrong. I started seeing that with the way James is with Sophie."

Luke squeezes my hip, his voice soft in my ear, contemplative. "I don't know what all your dad has said about us, but we're definitely not perfect. I suspect no family is. But all of this started long before any of us had anything to do with it, which means it's our right to either continue it or stop it."

I pick up, meeting his eyes. "I want to stop it, but I don't know how. Do you know what started everything? I mean, I know bits and pieces, but I feel like everything I've been told has been filtered through Daddy's lens, and I don't trust that anymore."

It's a painful confession, but it's the truth. I don't trust Daddy, having seen firsthand how willing he was to put us all on the line.

Luke gathers me back to him, taking a deep breath like he's about to tell me a bedtime story, but I sense this one won't be a fun adventure. Instead, I think the pedestal rubble beneath my father is about to be reduced to dust.

"I don't know a lot about when we were kids, but I think there was a little bit of tension. Nothing big, though, just between your dad and my pops. Mama says that everything was fine until a while after your mom died. She said Paul loved your mom, and he took her passing hard, especially since he had a lot on his shoulders then with the farm and you four kids. Mama was helping when she could, being neighborly and bringing over casseroles and school supplies. At some point, Pops felt like Paul was . . ." he pauses like he's not sure he should say whatever he needs to.

"It's fine, tell me. I want to know the truth." I do, but I strengthen my armor in preparation.

Luke sighs and continues. "Pops felt like Paul was getting sweet on Mama. He was probably just lonely, and she was around and helping, filling the role that your mom had. It's only natural, I guess. But Pops put a stop to that real quick. It was hard for Mama to back away from you kids. I know she liked all four of you, but she had to because of your dad." He squeezes me, and it feels like an apology, though he has nothing to be sorry for. The guys were just teenagers then, lost in the world our parents created for us.

"Then after Pops died, Paul showed up and tried to buy the ranch from us." I feel his flinch beneath my cheek as he swallows. "I think he made some moves on Mama then, but she's never said whether he was pushy about it."

"He . . . that's low," I admit.

"But she said she's only loved one man in her life and that she will always love only Pops. When that didn't work, he came after us boys. We shut him down fast and hard. That's when everything really went to shit and your brothers got involved."

He scratches at his scruff with his open palm, and I wait because I sense that he's trying to make sense of something. "Sophie told us all a business saying . . . 'he offered, we refused, no harm, no foul,' and as far as we're concerned, that would've been the end of it. But then things went really south with your brothers, and it got very . . . on edge. I guess I got it. Your dad's . . . issues are a point of pride. But I guess we've been hoping that things would thaw faster than they have. Just never got why."

He shrugs at the end of his story like he doesn't get it, and that's because he's never heard Daddy's version.

"Because that's a very different picture than we've been painted," I say, trying to make the puzzle pieces fit together between what Luke just said and what I've been told.

"After Mom died, it was hard. I remember Mama Louise coming over, being nice to us and taking care of us. She taught me how to cook a few more things, though I already knew a lot from helping Mom. She would hug on the boys even though they fought against it because I think she knew they needed that love. She even hugged Daddy a few times, though now that I think about it, he might've hugged her."

I close my eyes, trying to remember, but the details are lost to time.

"When Mama Louise stopped coming over, Daddy said it was because John only wanted her taking care of her kids, not us. We felt abandoned all over again, but we got over it, and I was old enough, so I started taking care of us. There I was, barely a teenager, packing lunches in the morning before school while the boys did their chores, and then I did laundry and made dinner while I finished my homework. I think the boys did their homework in the barn because I never saw them crack a book. They were always working, right by Daddy's side."

The memories come rushing back in waves . . . me with my nose in a book while simultaneously stirring something on the stove, the boys coming in hot and sweaty but with smiles as they roughhoused with each other, dinners around the table where Daddy would tell us that we'd survived another day. It felt like an accomplishment at the time, the Tannens against the world, and we'd win, a single day at a time. We missed Mom, but it felt like times were as good as they could be, like we were a team, a family.

"Then, soon after your father died, Daddy started talking about expanding. Brody and I were worried because we didn't see how that was possible. We've never had the manpower to run our farm and your ranch, and we didn't have the money to buy you out, but Daddy was so excited and kept talking about how our hard work was paying off, and it was infectious. I mean, on the surface, things were looking great. Daddy had that brand-new truck of his, and we figured he had a plan. Then he came home cussing a blue streak about you boys. That was probably the day you told him no, and this dream he wanted was crashing and burning right before his very eyes. He went mean, spewing ugly things about your whole family, and we just sort of nodded and went along with it. I mean, things were already at just that sort of icy polite stage between the families. What else were we gonna do?"

Guilt assaults me, that I should've seen, should've done something to stop Daddy's tirades, but at that time, he'd still been everything to us.

"Then Mark came over and told us about the gambling. We were shocked and Daddy was ashamed. But he didn't retreat quietly. No, he yelled and bitched for days after that. But the damage was done." I swipe at my eyes, remembering how my world had changed in an instant, everything I knew being shown not as a lie, exactly, but as a front.

"Brody and I really took over then. I did a deep dive through all the finances, and oh, my God, did I have some realizations then. That truck . . . he told us it was paid in full. It wasn't. And that was just the beginning of it. Brody forced Daddy to have some hard conversations, even threatening to go and take us all with him, leaving Daddy high and dry with a farm he can't work alone. Finally, Daddy basically just said 'fuck it' and he left us instead. He still lives in the main house with me and the boys, but he barely helps around the farm and he's gone almost every weekend to go gambling. He doesn't hide it now, even borrowed a hundred bucks from Brody. But we manage. Brody had a come to Jesus talk with him and put him on an allowance while I have all the passwords on the accounts. Bobby and Bruce take good care of the growing, Brody keeps the animals, and I run the house."

I let go of a breath I didn't know I was holding, a pain I didn't realize was still wound up around my heart releasing with the rush of words.

Scenes flash through my mind like photographs . . . of Mom and Daddy, of happy Christmases around the tree in the living room. And later, of the boys, gangly and grumpy through their teen years, and now the awkwardness we all feel around the dining table when Daddy sits down at the head like he's still in control of the ranch and himself.

When he's gone, it's fine, and we laugh and joke. We still sound like a family. But when he's there, the tension ties us all in knots.

"Do you know how amazing you are?" Luke's question is quiet, more breath than sound, and I can hear the effect my story has had on him.

I snuggle into his side, wanting to hide from the compliment, not sure I deserve it. "I just did what I had to do, what Mom would've done."

"Shay, you were just a kid. Literally. We all work our family land, it's what we do out here, but you stepped up in a way most kids don't or couldn't. I couldn't have pulled off what you did. Your mom would be so proud of you."

His certainty as he says words I didn't even know I needed to hear brings hot tears to my eyes. I know he can feel them dropping onto his shirt, making the cotton beneath my cheek damp and warm at the same time.

He runs a soft hand over my hair, stroking my locks soothingly. "I'm sorry if I overstepped. Losing a parent is a touchy subject. I know that. I try to live up to Pops's example every day, the same way you do your mom's, and it's hard. But you're doing a damn fine job, Shayanne."

I sniffle, trying not to get snot on his shirt even though whatever romantic, sneaky vibe we had going at first is long gone with our heavy stories. He reaches in his back pocket, pulling out a bandana and offering it to me.

"Are you seriously this prepared?" I ask, a smile cracking through the tears.

"Well, it's usually my sweat rag, but it's clean. I promise."

I use a corner to dab my eyes and then another corner to wipe at my nose.

"Every time I'm in her kitchen, I feel her. Like she's right there, hugging me," I admit. "I remember being so little, banging on her mixing bowls with wooden spoons like I was trying out for a drummer job, and then later, her first lessons, where she taught me to knead bread and make a salad. By the time I was in middle school, she'd sometimes sit at the table while I tried out recipes, and we'd talk about school, boys, and whatever random things ran through my mind. But that's what I remember of Mom. That probably sounds stupid. Sorry."

He follows my conversational jump back to talking about our parents like it was smooth.

I can feel him shake his head. "That's not stupid at all. Hell, I know James talks to Pops at the pond, which is kinda weird now that I think about it, considering he and Sophie also have a sweet spot for that particular place."

I giggle through the tears, his levity helping dry them up.

"Mark will go out front and 'check the tree' when he needs to think on something, and I'm pretty sure he's channeling Pops there. And me? I ride Duster, Pops's horse. He spent hours on the back of that horse, working this land. And every time I sit on Pops's saddle on Duster's back, he's right there with me. So no, feeling close to your mom when you're in her kitchen doesn't seem stupid at all."

I slip an arm beneath his back so I can squeeze him tight. "Thank you."

"For what? Telling you the truth? That loss is hard, and whatever you've got to do to get through it is okay? Because your family has done what you needed to, except for your dad. Can I still hate him and like you?" He looks down at me with a furrowed brow, comical confusion in his eyes.

I smile, not taking the bait. "No, for making me feel like there's something honorable in taking care of my family and making a home for them. I know you travel and see so much, and there are people who do amazing things. A lot of times, I wish I could be one of them."

"What do you mean?"

"It just seems so . . . I don't know," I admit. "Like there's a buffet of options that I wish I could pick from and live a life I chose." I spread my one arm, the one that's not hugged against Luke right now, wide, indicating all the choices I would have.

I look out to the night sky, not seeing stars but seeing endless possibilities before sighing.

"But in my heart, way down deep, as much as I hate that

I've never been anywhere, never done anything significant, I know I wouldn't leave my family. They need me and I need them. I like taking care of them. I never had any other choice, but I've made the best out of the life I have, and I'm proud of it. Of being a Tannen."

He sits up, and I move with him, sitting cross-legged between his bent knees. He cups my face, not letting me shy away from the weight in his stare.

"Shayanne Tannen, you can be or do anything you want, right here or anywhere. And your dad or your brothers or anyone else shouldn't even try to stop you. If you're happy here, taking care of your family, making soap and pumpkin puree, that's exactly what you should do. There's no shame in that. Be damn proud of what you do. Be the best damn goat soap maker in all the country if you want. I know you can do it. I believe in you."

No one has ever said that, not even me when I talk to myself, which seems sad and ridiculous when Luke makes it seem so obvious.

"Hell, my mama is the most badass woman I know — don't tell her I called her that, though, because she'll get onto me about cussing — but do you know what her resume has on it?" he asks pointedly.

I shake my head, though I think I know where he's going with this.

"Waitress. Wife. Mother. Rancher. In chronological order, though I suspect if we were going on priorities, it'd be wife, mother, rancher, and she'd conveniently forget the waitressing job she had when she was a teenager. Well, except that's how she met Pops, so maybe she'd keep it on the list." He pauses like he's considering what his mother would do, and I laugh.

He shakes his head, focusing again. "But nowhere on that list or in her life has Mama thought she was less than. She's strong, happy, stubborn as a mule, and smart as a whip. She had to be to keep us three boys and my Pops on the straight and narrow, and she has put her little size-seven boot in all our asses at one point or another. I suspect you're a lot like her, and just so you know, comparing you to my mama is the biggest compliment I can give. Don't tell her I said that, either."

He pins me with his eyes, making the direction an order of utmost importance.

I can feel my heart filling with light. I've looked up to my mom for so long, her pedestal still firmly in place as I tried with all my might to live up to her. And Mama Louise was a substitute in a lot of ways for that short time after Mom died. To hear that I'm in their company is powerful.

"What about you? Are you following in your dad's footsteps?" I ask, feeling like Pops Bennett would be so proud of Luke. I may not have been around Luke much, but his name's becoming famous in that sort of quiet way that people get when they're known in a relatively small circle that doesn't get a lot of press. He's the best around for breeding and training, making a name for himself with racing horses.

But Luke shakes his head. "Nah, that's Mark. He's Pops's shadow, version two-dot-oh. But Pops always encouraged us to do what we felt called to do. Hell, he damn near had to hold Mama back when James went off to join the rodeo at eighteen."

He pitches his voice high in a piss-poor imitation of Mama Louise. "My bayyy-beeee!" We both laugh at the exaggeration. In his regular baritone, Luke says, "Pops liked horses well enough, but I've always sort of had an affinity for them. So he used to take me with him when he'd visit folks so I could meet their horses, and he took me to the rodeo and races some. I remember the first time he got us into the barn to see the horses up close before a race. I thought they were like movie stars, and I'm not talking about the jockeys." He laughs at the memory, and I can see a teenaged Luke star-struck by a horse, so I giggle too.

"Biggest show of support he ever did was help me get Demon and Cobie, my thoroughbreds. I had enough to buy one, but their owner wanted to keep them together. They've always been stall-mates, and though they're not genetically related, they're as close as brothers. Pops paid the other half." I can hear the sentimentality he has for the memory, the horses, and how much it meant to him that his dad believed in him that way.

"Sounds like you have a lot to live up to, too. I'm sure Pops was proud of you," I say gently, and he nods.

Tonight has been nothing like what I thought it would be. I think I'd expected the passion from before to reignite and something physical to happen. Hell, I was hoping it would, fantasizing about us naked in the moonlight, wrapped up in the blanket and in each other.

Instead, we've shared things that make tonight seem even more intimate. We've shared our stories and our hearts, not just our bodies.

It's even better.

CHAPTER 11

LUKE

*W*e meet the next night, and the one after that too. It becomes routine for us both—dinner at our respective homes, where no one is the wiser, and then late-night meetups at the tree by cover of moonlight. I even head out there a couple of times mid-day to leave her slighty sweet, but kinda dirty notes under that rock on the lowest branch, hoping she'll find them before I get there.

Mostly, I work through the daylight hours, impatiently marking hours and getting stuff done simply to kill time until I can sneak off and see Shayanne. I want to hear about her day and share mine with her, hold her in my arms and taste her full lips. In a way, we started backward, our chemistry exploding quickly, but now it's burning low and slow, though the deli-cious torture of not taking her is damn near killing me.

I feel like a teenager again, driven to the brink of madness with wanting her so badly that the necessary daily jacking off does nothing but remind me that my hand isn't hers. Each release into the old hay behind the barn is a reminder that I'm not buried inside Shayanne and that I'm going crazy with anticipation.

But I wait. For her, for us, not willing to push too fast, do anything too soon. I want us to build this foundation, steady and strong, because an earthquake is coming, a big one, and there's nothing we can do to stop it.

"Hey," a voice says from the doorway, and I startle, not expecting anyone to be in the barn with me.

I look up, and it's like a birthday and Christmas gift all in one. Shayanne is standing there in the doorway in the middle of the day, like I conjured her up with a wish.

"Hey," I answer with a smile, scooping her into my arms and taking her mouth with a searing kiss. I press her against the doorframe, bending over her to cage her in before giving in and just picking her up.

My hands cup her firm ass as her legs go around my waist, and I shift, pressing her back to the wall to hold her steady. I'm starving for her, licking and nibbling down the line of her neck as she throws her head back to give me better access. "Fuck, I missed you," I murmur against her skin, the vibrations of my voice blending with the purr in her throat. I pull back to really look at her in the hazy brightness of the barn, her hair wild, her eyes dancing, and her cheeks flushed with excitement. "You are so damn beautiful."

"Missed. You. Too." Her hands are scraping circles on my back, her arms resting over my shoulders as she holds on to me for dear life.

"Gonna get caught sneaking over here in broad daylight, honey," I scold her. I don't really care, but the threat of the danger is deliciously hot. "But fuck, am I glad to see you."

Her body writhes against mine where I have her pinned between me and the wall. I grip her hips, guiding her thrusts and rubbing our centers together, hitting her clit through her jeans. My voice is gravelly, already lost to need. "Is this what you came over for? Need me to get your pretty pussy off?"

Her eyes darken and her full bottom lip puffs up around

her teeth where she bites at it. Shayanne doesn't have the words, not yet, but she likes it when I talk dirty to her, voicing her needs and wants. "Luke . . ."

My name is a plea, one I'm more than happy to fulfill.

I let her slide down my body until her feet hit the concrete floor, but I keep her pressed against the wall with a kiss as I drop my hand to her jeans. I flick the button open quickly but slowly and torturously slide the zipper down, tooth by tooth, enjoying the way she bucks against me, wanting me to get the show on the road.

I slide my hand inside her jeans, dipping inside her panties too, and follow the soft skin of her belly down to her core. She whimpers as I bump along her clit and feel the moisture already gathered there. "Fuck, honey. All this for me?"

Shay shudders, finding her voice. "I was thinking about you, about what we did last night under the tree, and I wanted . . ." She pauses, her cheeks pinking, but it's not in embarrassment. It's in heated memory of twelve hours ago when she came on my fingers. That she'd let me touch her was so meaningful, and now we both can't hold back. She meets my eyes boldly, demanding. "I want it again. More."

I growl at her admission, the honesty in her confession the sexiest thing I've ever heard. "Anytime, Shayanne. Any. Fucking. Time."

Her jeans restrict me a bit, but I manage to slip my fingers through her lips, teasing at her entrance. My thumb dances over her clit as I slowly press my finger inside her. "You're so tight, honey. We're gonna have to work you up to take me because I don't know if I'll be able to be gentle. I want you so fucking much."

Her hands fist my shirt at my shoulders, and then her hands open, fingers splayed wide. "Tell me," she whispers, her head thrashing and her eyes closed.

She's gorgeous, lost in pleasure and ordering me to give her more. I do as she needs, finding a rhythm as I fuck her with my finger, adding a second to stretch her and groaning at the way she spasms around me.

"Ride my hand, Shay. Ride it like you're going to ride my cock. I'm gonna fill you up, fuck you deep and hard until you shatter on me, your tight little pussy squeezing and milking my cock, so hungry for my cum. Take my fingers. Get ready for me, honey, because this pussy is going to be mine."

Her hands move, one to hold my forearm, her blunt nails digging into the skin to keep me there as if I have any intention of leaving her on the edge. The other moves to my head, gripping my hair as she kisses me like she wants to taste the promise I'm giving her.

I feel her whole body tighten, tense with possibilities, and for a long second, I don't so much as breathe, not wanting to miss the moment she falls apart for me. She shudders and then whispers my name. I hold her up as her legs give way, still teasing her clit and shoving my fingers into her to wring as much pleasure as I can out of her.

I wait until she comes back to her senses, letting her pretty hazel eyes focus so she can see me slip my fingers out of her and directly into my mouth. "Next time, I want to lick you off, Shay. Think you're ready for that?"

Her eyes track my mouth, watching the words form and my fingers disappear as I savor her sweetness. "I'm ready for something else too," she says. "I've been ready. I just didn't want to rush us." Her eyes betray the white lie. She's been trying to move us along faster than I have, greedy and needy and so damn gorgeous in her desire for more that it's taken all of my control to go slow.

I feel her hand palming me through my jeans, and I can't help but groan, on the edge of painfully rock hard for her. She squeezes lightly, teasing me and making me groan with need.

"Shayanne," I rasp, though I don't know if I'm trying to tell her yes or no. Fuck, I want her hands on me, want anything she wants to give me. Her smiles, her stories, her body, her mind, her future. I want it all. I just can't resist, and she's everything I've ever thought possible.

She unbuttons my jeans, pushing at them to get them over my hips. I help her, pushing them down my thighs and then doing the same with my boxer briefs. I've never been shy about being naked, and Shayanne's already seen me, but this is a big step for her, and I need to control myself.

I slide my hand up and down my rock-hard shaft, giving her permission. "You can touch me if you want, or I can do it if you're not ready." It's not a challenge, just an option, but she doesn't take it.

"I want to touch you, want to do to you what you do to me." Her palms are soft as they rub along my thighs, inching closer to where I need her. And then she wraps one hand around me and I instinctively thrust into her fist.

"Fuck, Shay. I've dreamed of you touching me," I growl, already on the edge from getting her off.

"What have you dreamed about?" she asks, her hand stroking along my length.

"Just this," I hiss, my eyes trying to slip shut, but I want to watch her. "Your hands on me, doing whatever you want."

She leans forward, nibbling at my neck and whispering, "I want to do what you see in your dreams, so tell me, Luke. Hard or soft, slow or fast? How do you want me jack you off?"

I grunt, not able to hold back when she says things like that. My teeth are gritted, and I can't keep my eyes open anymore at the onslaught of pleasure. "Hard, fast . . . I fucking need you, Shay."

Her little hand moves faster, my precum easing her way as she spreads it along my shaft with her tight fist. "Come for me, Luke. Come all over my hand."

She's getting damn good at the dirty talk, or maybe I'm

easy? I don't know, but she's doing things to me I've never felt before. I swear she's got my dick attached to my damn soul because my entire being is straining toward her, wanting her touch, her attention, her everything.

I manage to turn the slightest bit at the last second so I don't come on her belly and ruin her T-shirt. Instead, the cum pulses from my crown, covering her hand and shooting into the hay on the stall floor. My voice is strangled in my throat, but I cry out her name as I release, the orgasm hard and draining after days of need.

"Goddamn," I pant, blinking as I regain the ability to see again. "Holy shit, Shay. That was . . ." I shake my head, not finding the word I need when my brain is still on autopilot, barely maintaining life supporting systems. And right now, speech ain't one of them.

I look down at her, still pressed against the wall, her dirty hand held in the air and a victorious grin on her face. "Good. You'd better say that was good, Luke Bennett, or we're gonna have words. Keep in mind, that was my first time, so I'll get better."

I laugh, but she can see the heat in my eyes as I lean forward and kiss her softly. "Great, Shayanne? That was *fucking amazing.*"

She goes to do a fist pump, or at least I think that's what she's going to do, but then her face spreads into a grin. "Uhm, can I like wash my hand, or is that considered rude? I think I need a little bit of help with what's expected here. They don't talk about this part in my romance books, and it's definitely a fade-to-black moment on soap operas."

She's so fucking adorable, and weird, and adorable.

I plant a kiss to her nose. "There's a sink in the main aisle. Let me toss some fresh hay in here so there's no mess if one of the animals comes into this stall. I'll muck it out later. 'Kay?"

She nods and ducks beneath my arm, heading in search of the sink.

A quick dispatch of hay later, I follow her, only to hear her talking.

"Ho-lee shit! Did you hear that? He said I was, and I quote, 'fucking amazing'. You heard that too, but you won't tell, right?"

A deep voice that sounds vaguely like Shayanne says, "No, ma'am. I won't tell."

I'm confused for a second about who she's talking to, then I come around the corner to find her cozied up to Demon. Demon . . . who earned his name the hard way.

"Uhm, Shayanne. Back away slowly."

She looks my way, rubs her nose along Demon's in an Eskimo kiss, and then steps back. Demon lets his dissatisfaction be known with a snort.

"What's wrong? Why're you looking all freaked out?"

Now that she's a safe distance from the big, black beast of a stallion, I ask my first question, ignoring hers. "Were you talking to the horse? Or more to the point, were you talking *for* Demon?"

She drops her chin, but not before I see the flush overtake her cheeks. She talks into her hands, where she's brought them up over her face. "Yes, I do that sometimes. Talk to animals, trees, basically anything around me. And I have them talk back, but I'm not crazy."

I laugh, pushing her hands away from her face and lifting her chin so she's forced to look me in the eye. "You're adorable and weird," I tell her, repeating my earlier thoughts. "I love it."

Her eyes open wide. "Really? You don't think I'm crazy?"

My lips quirk, and I tilt my head back and forth like I'm considering. I pause long enough that she shoves at my chest. "Asshole. So I talk to myself. We all have quirks." She shrugs, no longer embarrassed but proud and confident in her weirdness. "I'm sure you have your own oddities too, like having to spin around three times before you lie down at night like a dog."

She says it with such certainty that I decide to do that if I ever get her in my bedroom at night, just to prove that I'm weird too. The thought of her in my room is a powerful one, but I let that go for now, sticking with the teasing. "Maybe, but I'm not telling."

"So if not because I talk to myself, why were you looking freaked out?" she asks, returning to her questions.

"Because Demon's not exactly the friendly and welcoming sort. In the field, he's fine, even did a photo shoot for one of Katelyn's brides, but when he's in his stall, he's earned his name as a bit of an asshole. But you're apparently a damn horse whisperer, getting him to let you love on him in two seconds when it took me damn near a week before I could touch him. He's picky about his people."

She looks over her shoulder at the big horse who's nuzzling her like a gentle birthday party pony when I know he's anything but. Shayanne steps closer, offering her hand to Demon again. He sniffs, and then, slow as molasses, she lifts her hand up and scratches at his cheek. "Who's a big, mean horse?" she coos as she cuddles him, and damned if that grumpy horse doesn't whinny back at her in answer. "Yes, you are, you big baby."

I come closer, petting along his flank. "Damn persnickety monster, but I'm glad you like her too," I tell the horse, knowing Shayanne is listening. "She's beautiful, isn't she?"

She pitches her voice low, pretending she's Demon. "I like her better than you."

My jaw drops in feigned shock, and I try not to laugh. "Rude! Who feeds you and gives you treats?"

Shayanne turns, sticking her butt out at me, and I can see she's got an oat cookie in each back pocket. Ahh . . . smart woman. "Is that how you got him to warm to you so quickly?" I accuse.

She gives Demon another rub, dropping her voice to a conspiratorial whisper. "We'll never tell, will we, boy?"

I feel on the outside of their quick friendship, but I like that she's an animal type. She gets it and likes them the way I do, too, which is something you can't explain to someone who's not a horse person. "Can we ride him?"

"Yeah, let me grab his gear." I get his saddle from the tack room and get Demon ready before climbing up. I settle in and make sure he's in the mood for a ride today.

For most of my horses, I'm the Alpha of the hierarchy and there's no debate. Demon is a different creature, and instead of dominance, we have more of an accord to help each other out.

But like me, he's totally enamored with Shayanne and is in a fine mood today, so I move my foot out of the stirrup and offer Shayanne a helping hand. She climbs up and settles behind me. The saddle is a tight fit for two, pressing her core up against my ass, her thighs aligned with mine, and her soft tits to my back. As her arms wrap around my waist, I rub at her hand. "Hang on, honey."

I lead us out of the barn, looking around to check for Mark or James. It's not that I care if they see us, but I want to respect Shayanne's wishes to keep quiet for now. Though her being here in the middle of the day, doing what we just did, is dangerous if that's what she wants. This powder keg is getting closer and closer to igniting, and I'm afraid she'll be the one to pay the price when it blows.

I don't see anyone around, but I head away from the barn, away from the Bennett homestead, and even farther away from the Tannen house. Instead, I head for the part of our ranch I call The Drop, a shallow valley that stretches out for miles, even beyond our holdings.

It's quiet for a bit, just Demon's breath and the clopping of his hooves along the grassy ground, but it's a comfortable silence. Just the two of us atop Demon, and it feels like we're alone in the world. Safe, together.

"I didn't get a chance to ask with you all bossy and demanding orgasms, but how'd you sneak away today?" I goad her.

She smacks my back, playfully fired up. "Luke Bennett, you did not just call me bossy."

I look over my shoulder at her. "Pretty sure I did, but I didn't say I was complaining." I give her a wink and a little smirk, which settles her indignant ire.

"A bit of a risk, to be honest. The guys all went out to our furthest pasture to check on the herd. Daddy's even helping, but they'll be gone until dinner." She looks up at the sun, judging where it is in the sky, and I do the same.

"Not much longer then, huh?"

"No, I threw a roast in the crock pot so dinner would cook while I was gone and the house would smell so good when they got home that they'd be distracted and not ask too many questions about my day." She taps the side of her head, snorting. "Not my first rodeo."

"Well, let's take advantage while we can," I tell her, wishing she didn't have to go home so soon but thankful for the unexpected visit today. "Hang on."

She tightens her hands around my waist once again, and after I make sure she's secure, I give Demon permission to let loose. He's a thunderer, known for his speed over uneven turf, and we're flying through the air atop him in the blink of an eye. Freedom blows through our bones, the wind chasing away any worries, and with Shayanne pressed to my back, all feels right in the world.

After a good mile, I turn him back at a trot and bring him home, far too soon, unfortunately. Giving him a rubdown, a cooling drink, and another oat cookie, we put Demon in his stall. Shayanne gives him scratches at his ears, and he flicks them in response, nuzzling her shoulder again.

"You've definitely made a friend."

"More than one, hopefully," she says, her brow lifting as she looks at me.

I crowd in, moving her away from Demon and to the gate to the empty stall next to Demon's. Pressed against her, I nuzzle her neck the way Demon was, but my intentions are decidedly less friendly. My voice is gravelly against her. "I'm not your friend, Shayanne. I want to be much, much more than your friend."

"Good," she says breathlessly. "I don't have a lot of friends, but I don't want you for one either."

Usually, a Tannen saying that to a Bennett would be cruel-spirited, but I know exactly what she means.

CHAPTER 12

SHAYANNE

I virtually skip home on a cloud of Luke's making. Our ride with Demon, our tryst in the barn, the words we shared . . . I'm in a heaven that lasts right up until I burst through the back door into the kitchen and see Daddy and Bruce sitting at the table.

I am so busted.

"Hey, Shayannie, where've you been?" Daddy asks, nose buried in his phone. He doesn't sound the least bit suspicious, but Bruce is looking at me with narrowed eyes.

"Just out to check on the goats since Brody's in the fields today." The lie falls off my tongue readily, though I hadn't planned it. Daddy hums like he's agreeing with me, but I don't think he even heard me. Bruce did, though, his head tilting, and then his eyes tick out the window toward the barn before returning to me.

He doesn't believe me. I can read it on his face. But I'm responsible and good, and I don't think any of them would ever suspect I'd snuck off to the Bennett ranch. Bruce likely thinks I was fucking off, but he wouldn't think I'd go against a family edict.

I just hope he continues to think that way.

Wanting to redirect their attention, I ask, "What are you doing back so quickly? Thought you had a long work day ahead."

Daddy looks up then, but it's to Bruce with a bit of a sneer. "I sat down for a quick break, and these young'uns thought I was done for. Damn near forced me to come in and said they could handle it themselves, so I'm gonna let them. If that's what they want to do, have at it."

He waves his hand dismissively, and it pains my heart. Not that he came in or that he might be tired out. It's the tone of his voice, an *Oh, I can't win the game, so it must suck* sort of thing.

Bruce, though, is not so forgiving. "You didn't sit down for a break. You almost passed out, Dad. You were sweating bullets like it's the Fourth of July in September."

I gasp, rushing over and pressing the back of my hand to Daddy's forehead. He's warm but not hot, and his color looks fine. "Are you okay?" I ask. "Should we call the doctor?"

He shoves my hand away, sighing heavily. "I'm fine."

Even so, I grab a rag and wet it under the sink. I wring it out and then whirl it around a little to get it to cool, just like Mom used to do when we were little. I place it around Daddy's neck, and he pats my hand like I'm the one who needs comforting.

I sit at the table, eyeing him and looking for any sign that he's lying, but he really does look okay. I look to Bruce for more information, but instead of analyzing Daddy, Bruce's eyeing me up and down. I glare back and hope he'll focus on the problem at hand.

After all, our father, despite his issues, nearly dropped in the field. Whether it was heat exhaustion or that he's gone a little soft from not working, I don't really care. Both are more important than where the hell I've been.

But Daddy's finally got his attention pulled from whatever

he's doing on his phone, and now he's staring at me too. "Did you say you were checking on the goats? I thought Brody did that this morning."

Shit. I knew that was too easy.

"He did, but they're my babies so I like to check on them too. Troll is my favorite, with his little horns and scruff." I wiggle fingers on my head, miming horns and then beneath my chin for the beard. "I just wanted to give him some extra scratches."

That sounds reasonable but also silly enough that Daddy won't question it too much.

Which he doesn't, but he does start up a lecture. "Shayannie, you have chores to get done and can't be lollygagging around, petting the animals."

He looks around the kitchen, and I wonder what he sees. Does he remember Mom cooking here? Does he see how I follow her recipes and scrub her counters and floors until they gleam? Does he think I'm doing a good job?

I don't know why I care what he thinks, other than he's my dad. I've fed this family, mended work shirts, patched up minor and not so minor wounds, and more. I think I'm predestined to want to please him and make him proud, even when he doesn't make me proud very often anymore.

He finishes his visual perusal and meets my eyes again. His voice is harsh, getting louder with every word. Once upon a time, I would've flinched, but now the effect of his hollering is like pebbles in a pond, a blip and ripples but no kerplunk of impact. "You made us lunches and then put a roast in the crockpot," he says as he points to the appliance like it's personally offended him. "Which I damn well know means you've had the whole day free. Even petting the goats doesn't take all day. So what have you been doing?"

The accusation is heavy. He doesn't know where I've been, but he knows I haven't been doing what I'm supposed to, and he expects me to pull my weight. I do, I know I do. Between the budgeting and bills, cooking and cleaning, and keeping track of my brothers and dad, I've got a full-time-plus job. I might not be doing the heavy lifting with the farm and animals like the boys do, but I make it so that they can do that and trust that literally everything else is taken care of.

We balance each other. The only one not pulling his weight is Daddy.

And that pisses me off. It has for a long time.

How dare he sit there and lecture me about doing my share when the one day in months that he's supposed to help the boys, he . . . what? He has some sort of spell and cuts out early? I may have taken today, and all right, a few nights out too, to hang out with Luke, but those are the exception, not the rule. I'm the literal opposite of what he does for the family.

"I went for a walk. Is that what you want to hear?" I spit out, palms slapping the table as I push to stand up. It's the truth, or at least as much as I'm willing to give him because I don't want to start World War III between my family and Luke's.

I go over to the crockpot, yanking an oven mitt on and pulling the lid off to check the roast. The hot steam blasts me in the face as I lift the lid, but I'm even hotter inside. I'm molten with fury that he dares to call me out.

He stands up too, but he keeps one hand planted on the table as he truly yells at me now. "No, of course that's not what I want to hear. I want to hear that you're handling things here at the house like you're supposed to." He slams his palm on the table, emphasizing his point. "What the hell's gotten into you, girl?"

He shakes his head like I'm the hysterical one, overreacting to nothing and flitting about like a teenaged girl, not a strong woman who runs this damn farm. Okay, I run it with my brothers, but it's been a long time since Daddy's run a thing besides a poker table.

My teeth grit, and in a display of pure will, I keep my eyes on the roast. "I am taking care of literally everything, Daddy. Dinner will be ready in an hour."

I slam the lid back onto the crock pot and instantly feel guilty for the abuse of the appliance when it's done nothing but what I ask of it.

Daddy huffs, though, still looking surly. "I think I'll eat out tonight."

He turns, walking through the living room and grabbing his truck keys from the bowl by the front door. Bruce whistles once, and Murphy hops up from the rug, getting out of Daddy's way a second before he would've stepped on the dog's tail.

The screen door shuts with a slam of finality.

"Well, that went well," Bruce says with sarcasm dripping from every word.

I turn to glare at him, but he's looking at me carefully. "You know what you're doing, Shayanne? You ready for the shit storm you're stirring up?"

I roll my eyes. "I just went for a walk. It's not a big deal."

Drop it. Leave it. Please.

His chuckle is rough, like he hasn't done it in way too long, which is probably true since the barest laugh brings a tear to his eye that he swipes with a thick finger. I put my hands on my hips, cocking my head to the side. "Why are you laughing? That was some bad shit with Daddy."

His laughter stops abruptly, and he leans forward, putting his elbows on the table and rubbing at his jaw. His scruff is getting long, more beard than shadow these days. He looks at me like he's seeing into my soul.

Bruce has always been the most misunderstood of my brothers. He got the nickname 'Brutal' playing football in high school after sending three guys to the hospital with knock-out tackles in one game. The last one led to the winning field goal, and he got dubbed with the moniker that makes him sound like a monster.

Part of it, I think, is that he's quiet and reserved. He doesn't say much, and when he does, it frustrates him that people assume he's some sort of Neanderthal because of his hulking frame. The truth is, he's probably the most sensitive of any of our family. He's a watcher, and he sees people, sometimes even when they don't want him to, and I forgot that.

"Sit down, Shayanne," he says, kicking the chair next to him out with his booted foot.

I drop into the chair, petulant. "What?"

He's quiet for a moment, waiting expectantly, but I don't know what for. And then he reaches into his back pocket and pulls out my little notebook, setting it on the table between us with a thick finger holding it in place.

My heart flutters in my chest as I realize what this means. He read it. I can see it in his eyes. He read my notebook, the one full of recipes but also of my thoughts. It's enough of a diary that Bruce knows about Luke.

"Bruce," I say, hoping against hope that I'm wrong.

He smirks, but it doesn't reach his eyes. "I thought you were being weird when Brody was bitching about Luke after the clinic run-in. Now I know why."

Well, there goes any dream I had that maybe Bruce just found my notebook and put it aside for safekeeping.

Shit on a shingle.

"Please." The word is snatched from my throat, pained because I don't know what he's going to do with this information. We've all been pretty brainwashed about the Bennetts by Daddy, and finding out I'm sneaking around with one of them isn't likely to paint Luke in a flattering light either.

He picks up the notebook, which looks comically tiny in his

big hands, flipping through the dog-eared pages. It's a violation of my privacy, even as close as we all are, but I don't dare call him on it. What good would it do now, anyway, when he's read it already?

"What are you going to do?" I ask, my voice shaking with equal parts fear and fury.

Not liking something he reads, his nose wrinkles and his lip curls beneath his dark moustache, and then he tosses the book to me like it's a hissing snake. I catch it easily from years of experience playing touch football in the yard as kids.

He leans back in his chair and sighs heavily. "Do you like him? Not the sappy, girly shit in that book, but for real."

I fight the urge to argue that the stuff I wrote isn't sappy. It's not like I'm writing out wedding fantasy scenes and dreamy sexy times like my favorite soap operas. It's my thoughts and feelings, hopes and wishes. I refuse to be embarrassed about them. My cheeks heat just the same, not getting the memo from my brain.

"I do," I say simply, though the fact that my words sound like vows doesn't escape either of our attention.

"And he likes you?" Bruce says. It's a good thing he doesn't make that sound impossible, like I'm some second-rate tomboy choice that no man would want, because if he had been that rude, I would've given him the rough end of the roast tonight.

"He does." I'm keeping with my stellar way with words.

Bruce closes his eyes, pinching his nose between his thumb and finger. "He treat you right?" he asks, but then he opens his eyes and points at me. "Do not say a single thing about sex. I mean, does he . . . is he . . . I don't know, nice and shit?"

The smile breaks across my face and I can't stop it. I bite my lip, not wanting to say things I shouldn't, especially to my brother because of our standing agreement that talking about sex is gross when it comes to family. But my wide eyes and nod seem to be answer enough.

Bruce crosses his arms over his thick chest, glaring at me as he thinks. The minute stretches to two, my fate in his hands. Finally, he shrugs as his head tilts to the side. "Okay, then. You do you, baby girl. But if you need me to, I'll beat the shit out of him for any reason. Good or bad, you just say the word. I've got your back."

I'm so gobsmacked, my jaw drops. It's too easy, too good to be true. My eyes narrow, and I lean in closer to him. "What's the catch?"

He smiles, and this time, his eyes sparkle. "Shayannie, the heart wants what the heart wants."

"That's a load of manure and you know it. Why are you being so nice to me, Bruce? I mean, you're always nice, but this is . . ." My voice trails off, and then I confess. "I figured if any of you found out, I'd be buried six feet under."

Bruce's eyes darken, and he nods. "If Dad finds out, you will be. Make no mistake there. He'll kill you and Luke too. But I never had the issues with the Bennetts that Dad and Brody did. I only threw punches because it was my brother. You'll have to fight that battle when, and if, the time comes. But you won't have to fight it today with me."

My eyes burn, pinpricks of hot tears that I blink back. "Thanks, Bruce."

He reaches for my hand, rubbing it roughly. "Don't mention it. Literally. Do not mention it. To anyone."

I smile, though it's watery, and he ruffles my hair like he did when we were kids.

"I see what you do here, baby girl. You're not invisible, not to me. You work damn hard and give this family your all, so if you have a chance to take a little piece of happiness for yourself, I'm not going to stand in your way. Just be smart, and be safe."

His words are sweet, but there's a sad undercurrent to them. All of my brothers are alone, I'm alone, and Daddy's alone. Together, but family is different from a partner. With Luke, I feel like I'm on the trembling edge of a completeness I've never felt before, and it's an amazing feeling.

It makes me wonder if Bruce missed a chance at taking a bit of happiness for himself.

Reaching over, I take a risk. "I will be. Smart. Safe. Got it. You too, you know? She's out there, the woman for you."

We're breaking all kinds of unspoken rules today, I guess, because Bruce just shakes his head. "She is, but she's not mine and never will be."

I'm shocked to my core. I was talking in generalized terms, but apparently, there's a 'she' I never knew about. "Brutal?" I'm not sure if I'm using his nickname or commenting on his sad statement.

He ignores my question, and I wonder. "The third step from the top squeaks when you leave at night, so skip it. And you're less likely to be spotted if you go left out the back door, around the house, and in front of the barn before you head toward the Bennett ranch. When you turn right out the back of the house, Dad's window looks out to the yard and there's a greater chance he'll see you. He's a heavy sleeper, but you never know."

I let the slip of truth about his girl go, focusing on his tips and advice. "Sounds like you've done this before?"

He winks, relaxing a little. "A time or two. Always got past Dad and never woke you or Brody up." He's bragging, proud at getting one over on us.

"What about Bobby? He sleep through your hell raising too?" I tease.

Bruce laughs, shrugging. "Hell, half the time, he was coming with me, and even when he stayed back, he knew when I was gone. He was my cover story and I was his."

I pout, crossing my arms over my chest. "I suddenly feel very left out of this brotherhood. You've got alliances and I'm just out here with my ass in the wind, hoping I don't get caught the one time I do something I'm not supposed to. And I got busted anyway!"

He gets up from the table but stops behind my chair. "First off, when we were pulling this shit off, you were too young to be doing any of it. As for now, I'll be your alliance in this if you need me to be. I'll even cover for you, if that's what it takes. Just be happy, baby girl. You deserve that."

And with that, he's gone. The screen door slams behind him, and the kitchen suddenly feels very hot, stifling with its quietness and what could've been.

I thought any of my brothers finding out about me and Luke would be catastrophic, only bested in awfulness by Daddy discovering the truth. Bruce seemed to take it in stride, though, giving me hope that Bobby, and maybe even Brody, would be just as unconcerned.

A girl can dream, I guess.

CHAPTER 13

LUKE

"So Brutal knows and doesn't care?" I ask, incredulous after Shayanne tells me the story about getting caught in the kitchen after our day ride.

Both her shoulders lift to her ears and she makes an unconcerned face. "Apparently, he's a lover of love. Who knew?"

She says the words airily, one hand moving through the air like she's an orchestra conductor, but they hit something in me.

Love. It's the most dangerous four-letter word I know. It feels too soon for something that heavy, but I know in the spectrum between 'yeah, she's a friend' and 'ring the wedding bells,' I'm a lot further along that arc than the 'like' she told her brother.

But we don't have to figure it out tonight. Not when the full moon is over us, round and white and bright, the crickets are chirping a song that the cows' moos occasionally join in with, and I've got my woman wrapped in a blanket beside me at our tree, our spot. It feels right, like meeting her here each night is *us*.

"Mmm, I like this," I whisper, pressing a kiss to her forehead. "This is the best part of my day, finally getting to see you, hold you, touch you."

She snuggles into me, sighing happily. "Me too. I'm going to hate it when you're gone."

It's the first time we've talked about the fact that I travel. A lot.

I've had this conversation with other women before, and it never goes well. Though usually, it's the whole package deal — I live in the sticks, far from the closest city, I travel on a near-monthly basis, sometimes for days, sometimes for weeks, and I'm shit at calling and texting. All of which add up to a 'See you when you get back, maybe?' level of relationship with every woman I've dated. A casualness that's always worked, for them and for me.

But I hate the idea of leaving Shayanne here when I go. "I wish I could throw you in my truck and take you with me. You'd love it."

It's not a bad idea, I think as I imagine showing her the world, introducing her to my friends across the US as my woman, and spending every night with her in my arms and on my cock. Sounds pretty fucking sweet. Business and pleasure, a perfect combination.

"I would, but I've got to stay here and help out at home. I can't just up and leave the way you can." There's no accusation in the words. They're just the truth of the way our lives are set up and the different ways our families need us.

Shayanne has to be there for her brothers and dad, day in and day out, to take care of them and run the house. Mark needs me to keep bringing in the money that my horse programs provide. I'm more valuable away than at home.

And I know it's a shitty thing to do to a woman. Especially to abandon a woman like Shayanne, whose entire being is caught up in caring for others and making a homestead. I'm going to be on the road too often for it to be anything but a hard cycle.

She's roots, and I'm wings, which sounds sweet and poetic. But I can feel that in the long run, we might pull at each other until it hurts, her roots ripping from the ground, leaving crumbles of dirt in her wake, or my wings clipped painfully, leaving me flightless.

It's not right. It's not fair. But it is what it is.

"Tell me about it," she says, her lips pressed to my chest for a sweet kiss. I'm thankful as fuck that I unbuttoned my shirt when I got here, wanting her on my skin, because now, she's tracing her fingertips through the dusting of hair along my pecs, and every scratch of her nails makes goosebumps threaten to pop up with how good it feels. "Tell me about where you're going or your favorite place to go. Tell me about what's beyond Great Falls."

I swallow, thinking about everywhere I've gone and all that I've seen. What would she want to hear about? What would take her away on an adventure, if only in her mind for this moment?

"There was this one time I went to the Grand Canyon . . ." I reply, telling her about watching the sunset dip into the red rocks and how wowed I was by nature's majesty and how it contrasted with the ranch I was working with in Arizona that was staffed by the rowdiest old cowboys I'd ever met. "They had me mouth open to the sky in the rain, promising it was some good luck charm. And I didn't want to be rude, you know, so I did it." I chuckle at the silly memory. "Felt like I'd been really accepted by their little group, warm fuzzies and all, right up until they all busted up laughing. I was a good sport about it, though. Sometimes, hazing the new guy is the norm. In making fun of me, they were bringing me into their fold."

She laughs too, tinkles of glee in the cool night air. "More," she whispers, doing a wiggly dance against me like she's happy. "Best horse you've ever worked with?"

"An Arabian from the Middle East, flown into the US for a showcase and breeding with another Arabian. Lord, she was gorgeous, fifteen hands tall, bright white with black skin underneath, but her coat was so lush, she damn near shone in the sun. Her tail was so high-set it reminded me of a cheerleader's ponytail, and she had the temperament too, always bouncing around and ready for action. Smart as a whip, too," I finish, remembering Badra, the sweet girl.

"Did it work?" Shayanne asks. "She have a foal?"

I nod, pleased with the question. "She did. Went home and delivered the next spring. Her colt's looking good, too, and will likely be a good racer."

The questions go on and on, each of them so innocent but eager. Furthest away from home? Longest time away from the ranch? Best meal on the road? Prettiest ranch? Where I'd go if I could go anywhere?

I answer them, each and every one without hesitation, giving her bits of myself with every detail. More importantly, I'm giving her pieces of the world she's never known beyond her television or maybe a schoolbook. It makes me want to package up the entire globe with a big bow and give it to her, a gift she deserves more than anything.

An idea blooms in my head, a way to give her a taste of what's beyond her fence line. But it'll take some research and work, something I'm completely willing to give. I keep my mouth shut for now, though, hoping to surprise her. Something tells me Shayanne likes surprises.

"Prettiest girl at all the ranches you've been to?" she asks playfully.

This answer I can give her gladly. But first, I pull her on top of me, her knees going astride my hips as our bodies align.

"You fishing for compliments, honey?" I tease, kissing and

licking along the column of her neck. She purrs deep in her throat, urging me on as she tilts her head to give me room to work. "And with a trick question too?" I scold, biting the rope of muscle connecting her neck and shoulder as she stills on top of me with a needy gasp. "The prettiest *woman* I've ever seen was right next door the whole damn time. I was just too stupid to see it."

Her hands splay on my chest, and I arch into her touch. "Not. Stupid." Her words are stilted, punctuated by the kisses she's pressing to my skin now. Along my scruffy jaw, down my neck, on my chest. "I was just hiding away while you were running away."

The truth of that, both of us escaping into what we know best, becomes secondary as all I want to do is escape into her, into us. Into *this*. Ignore the future where she'll want me to stay, ignore that I'll always have to go, and pretend that she can come with me.

I roll us, flipping our positions and settling between her spread thighs. I prop myself on one elbow, my other hand delving into her honey waves as our eyes lock together, telling her seriously, "No more hiding. No more running, okay? I know we can't tell your brothers yet and I'll have to travel for work. That's our lives right now, but I don't want any escape routes between us. You and me, Shayanne. Promise."

She bites her lip, her eyes wide and filled with innocent hope. I kiss her, pulling her lip free with my teeth and soothing the bite. She moans into our shared air, her voice soft and intense. "Promise."

My heart flies up in my chest like the roller coaster ride she takes me on just dropped out beneath me in favor of a damn airplane takeoff. I'm flying, something I've done so many times before, but never like this. Never with her.

The kiss catches fire, the heat turning to molten lava in my gut as my cock thickens against her. She squirms beneath me, rubbing herself along the ridge inside my jeans. I meet her thrust for thrust, but after only a few moments of grinding, I can't take it. I need more.

I sit up on my knees, running my hands up her long legs to her waistband where I don't bother teasing. This might not be silk sheets and fine wine, but it's us. Pure. Simple. Honest.

I need her too much. Want *more* with her.

I pull the sweatpants down her legs, revealing cotton panties, white with pink hearts on them. On anyone else, they might be juvenile, but on Shayanne, they're so sexy they send a jolt straight through my body with the way they ride high over the curve of her hip and dip low over her mound. But I don't take long to appreciate them either, pulling them down and off her as well.

Thankful to the moon for shining so brightly tonight, I stare at her soft, sweetly formed pussy. She scrambles for the blanket as a shiver shakes her body, but I push the cover off her legs, promising, "I'll keep your lower half warm."

She makes a squeaky noise, realizing exactly what I mean, but there's no fear in her eyes, only heated want for me to show her everything she's been missing, everything I want her to experience, but only with me. She will only ever need to be with me.

I drop down in the V of her legs, her thighs draped over my shoulders. I lay my cheek along her thigh, nuzzling her and listening to the scraping sound of my rough beard along her soft skin that's even more delicious than I dreamed it'd be. Her hips lift, bucking toward my mouth, hungry for me to get on with it.

I chuckle darkly. "You want me to lick you, honey? Run my tongue all over your clit and dip inside your pussy to lap at your sweetness?" I spread her lips with my thumbs, letting my breath blow over her, the heat of my exhales mixing with the cool air of the night.

"Yes," she moans. "Do it." A thread of bossiness enters her tone, and I love that she's with me, not just taking what I want to give her but demanding what she needs.

So I oblige. I lick along the wet folds of her lips with feather-light strokes, finally getting the full-strength taste of her. She's delicious, a sweet and earthy natural sugar that makes me high. I slip deeper, wanting more, but she grips my hair, guiding me higher.

I take her cue, happy to worship her every nook and cranny just as she wants. There'll be time for 'exploration' later. My tongue swirls over her clit and her back arches like she's been shot through with lightning. "Holy fuck! That's . . . that's . . . oh, my God, I didn't know —"

"Fuck, Shay," I think I say, but it comes out just a moan because I can't stop licking at her. My tongue circles her clit as her cries get higher and louder. They're music to my ears, but I know they'll carry out here and I can't chance someone finding us, not when she's about to come in my mouth for the first time.

I move to sit on my knees, looking her in the eyes. "Gotta be quiet, honey. I'm still your dirty little secret, but you're about to tell everyone in three counties that I've got your pussy about to come all over me."

A full-body shudder racks through her, shoulders to toes as her eyes roll. Fuck, this woman likes it when I talk dirty to her, but I need my mouth for other things right now.

Gently, I lay a hand over her mouth, and she nods that she's fine. I'm not one for restraints and gags, but sometimes, necessity is the devil. I tease along her opening with my other hand and she whimpers into my palm.

Her wetness coats my fingers, letting me slip one into her easily. A few strokes, and she can take a second. But three is tight, so I go slower, letting her get used to the stretch. "That's it, Shay. Take me." I lean forward, our eyes locked on one another, and her brows pull together, silently begging.

I don't lick her this time. Instead, I suck her clit into my mouth, fluttering my tongue across it as fast as I can. I match the pace with my fingers, thrusting them into her harder and rougher now, brushing over the front wall of her pussy with every stroke. She cries into my hand, her hips spasming, and then she freezes.

That perfect moment on the edge of possibilities, when everything somehow seems both limitlessly large and impossibly small, stretches out for an eternity for both of us. And then, with the softest stroke of my tongue on the tip of her clit, she explodes, calling out my name against my hand. Waves of pleasure visibly rush through her as she contorts and thrashes, more of her sweetness leaking onto my hand.

As she falls back to the blanket, lax in pleasure, I take my hand from her mouth to fumble with my jeans. Button undone and zipper mostly shoved down, I pull myself from my underwear.

"Let me suck you too," she says, trying to get up again, but she's weak with how hard she just came.

I shake my head, placing my hand over her racing heart. "No, I want that pussy, Shayanne. I need you." She opens her legs wider in invitation, not a single doubt on her face. When I look down, her pussy lips are shiny with slickness, gleaming in the moonlight. Stroking my cock up and down through her lips, I spread her honey all over me, bumping at her clit with my crown.

She moans, oversensitive at my rough handling of her most tender parts. That sound lets me know it's not going to be tonight, not here in the moonlight in the dirt. She deserves better and I know it, but I'm so far gone, I need something. I can't just go home to spank into the haymow.

Instead, I thrust against her, not entering her but letting

her lips kiss along my shaft and the ridge of my cockhead slip over her clit. Again and again, I fuck her without fucking her and she bucks back against me.

Both of us look at the point where we're connecting, not completely, but as close as we can tonight. "Not like this, Shay. But soon. Soon, I'm not going to hump you like a damn teenager. I'm going to fill you with my cock, my cum. Claim you in the damn town square, if that's what it takes. Because you're mine, and I'm yours."

My balls pull up tight at the idea of walking hand-in-hand with Shayanne, not giving a single solitary shit about who sees us and knowing that she's proud to be with me too. That idea is the sexiest damn fantasy I can imagine. We wrap our fingers together, tightly holding hands against her thighs as we almost-fuck.

"Come, Luke. Come in me, on me, I don't care. Just do it, please." Her voice is breathy, but the thread of something stronger is woven into her tone. She's on edge again too.

I unlock my right hand from hers and guide her fingers to her clit. "Rub yourself for me, honey. Make yourself come again because I'm gonna come all over you."

Her fingers obey even before her lust-clouded eyes clear, and I follow suit, jacking myself roughly. My cockhead bumps into her hand every few strokes, adding another element of pleasure.

We both watch, mesmerized by each other in more ways than just this moment in the moonlight.

"Fuck, Shay. I'm coming," I manage to grit out. My eyes clench shut as my cum jets from my crown, but when she cries out too, I force my eyes to open, needing to see her.

My hot cum is covering her hand, her clit, her pussy where she's holding herself open for me like the sexiest damn target I've ever seen. She pauses for a split second, artfully painted in the evidence of my desire, before she begins stroking herself again.

She spreads my cum into her skin, mixing it with her own juices, and then she bucks again, her hips rising as she moans long and deep, her thighs quivering with the effort. I let her lips sweetly kiss along the length of my cock, feeling the pulses as she comes. When her fingers still, I take their place, lazily swiping across her clit a few more times to draw it out longer.

She pulls away, a smile lifting the corners of her mouth. "Mmm, too much. I can't."

I can't help the cocky grin, and I lean down, kissing the tip of her nose. "Wore you out already?"

"Not even close," she argues back, though she's laid out on the blanket like she could fall asleep at any moment.

I want that. To fuck her to utter exhaustion and then cuddle her all night as she sleeps in my arms, to wake up in the morning and have her be the first thing I see as I greet the day. And I remember my idea of a surprise. I'm going to knock Shayanne's socks off, but I'm going to need some help.

CHAPTER 14

SHAYANNE

*T*he truck roars its way down the driveway, a tan cloud of dust swirling behind it like the hounds of hells are nipping on its heels.

I'm already opening the door, running for the front drive to meet it. Well, drive is a bit of misnomer since it's really just the patch of grass we all park on, but it's where I head.

Unable to contain my excitement by jumping up and down, I don't even flinch when the horn blares a little tune as the tires stop with the smallest slide on the flattened grass. I run for the driver's side, opening the door.

"Sophie! Get out here and hug me!" I tell her, fighting back the urge to pull her from the truck while she's still got a seatbelt wrapped around her belly. Finally, she gets free and steps out.

"Shayanne, I've missed you!"

It's been all of three weeks, plus a few days, since we've seen each other at Hank's, but it feels like forever because so much has changed. Not that she knows that. Luke's top secret and all, definitely not something to share in a text or a phone call where I might be overheard.

We hug like it's been ages, squealing and carrying on, as Daddy calls it. She asks to see the goats, and we wander into the pen so she can pet them. Usually, she'll plop right down in the dirt and let them crawl all over her, calling it her favorite form of goat yoga, though there's very little down dog happening. Usually, it's more of us telling the ornery goats to 'get down'. She's more careful today, though, feet spread wide and stable and bending forward to scratch at their wiry hair. Her round belly lays on her thighs, and I swear she's glowing as she grins at me, a woman totally happy and fulfilled with life.

"Damn, you have popped. You sure you ain't got twins in there?" I tease her, knowing that even as big as she is, she's not that big for being six months along with a Bennett. Early on, she told me through hormonal tears that Mama Louise warned her that all her boys were around nine pounds.

She stands back upright, one hand going to rub her belly and the other to her back. "Don't I know it, but definitely not twins. Sonogram and the doctor both say so."

I give her an analyzing look, holding up my hands like I'm a cameraman finding the best frame. "Maybe pick a couple of names, just in case," I say seriously. She smacks at my hands, cursing a blue streak, and then we both dissolve into giggles. "Just kidding, Soph. You look great."

"I will, after this weekend. You ready?" she asks, looking toward the house.

"Yeah, let me grab my bag and fend off the boys so we can get outta here." I stomp up the front steps, and the screen slams behind us both as we enter the house. Ever the animal lover, Sophie pets Murphy too, promising him extra biscuits next time he comes to see Doc Jones for his shots.

"Guys!" I shout out. "I'm leaving!" Two words sure to get them to drop whatever they're doing and make an appearance.

Like magic, doors open upstairs and a herd of elephants

tromps down the stairs. Or the boys. Could go either way until their dark heads pop into the kitchen, throwing the odds.

"Hey, Sophie," Brody greets her. It's not much, but it's a hell of a lot better than his snarled acknowledgements used to be. Once, I'd even heard him call her a Bennett Bitch, but one very intense, pissed off conversation between us put a stop to that real quick. She's my only and best friend, and I'm not going to have him mucking it up, thank you very much.

She smiles back, recognizing the progress. "Hey, Brody! Brutal, Bobby," she says, just as kindly as she always is. "Thanks for letting me steal Shayanne this weekend. I need a good girls' getaway before this alien forces its way out of me." She mindlessly rests her hands on her belly, her smile belying the silly insult against her unborn baby.

"Sure. Of course," Brody says, but then he turns to me. "Everything taken care of?"

I resist the urge to tell him, 'yes, Dad,' because around here, that'd be an insult, and besides, Daddy hasn't cared enough to keep track of us in a while. That's been Brody's gig for a long time now, I realize. He's done so much for us, being more of a father figure than I ever gave him credit for. I step up on my tiptoes, kissing his cheek in appreciation, and he starts. "What's that for? You buttering me up for something?"

His slight flush tells me that he appreciates the affection despite his incredulous words, and I chuckle, patting him on an unshaven cheek.

"Nah, just gonna miss your ugly mug," I reply. I do the same cheek kiss to Bruce and Bobby, not wanting them to feel left out. "And yours, and yours too . . . maybe, just a little."

I hold up my finger and thumb an inch apart.

"Food's all in the fridge, labeled by meal with instructions to heat stuff up," I reply, but I really hope they take a night to go into town and unwind a little. "I bought an extra twelve-pack of beer and hid it in the barn fridge so y'all could have a little fun too. But don't get into any trouble. I'll be too busy to bail you out until Monday."

I say that last bit fake-harshly, holding out an accusing finger and daring them to get up to too much.

"Yes, Mom," Bobby teases. That doesn't hold any of the bad juju my dad thought did and instead feels like a nice compliment. "For real, since Dad's gone, we'll probably just hang out, or if we get ambitious, maybe go to Hank's for open mic night. We can handle ourselves, dear sis. No need to worry about us."

The words are all right, but the looks they're giving each other tell me they've got bigger plans than Bobby is letting on. At this point, I don't want to know. As long as Sheriff Downs doesn't call me, I'm gonna say it's a winner, winner, chicken dinner weekend for the Tannens.

"And what, exactly, do you ladies have planned?" Bruce queries, giving me a raised eyebrow that says he thinks something's up with my impromptu trip to Great Falls.

Sophie answers for me, giving my brothers all the sass they deserve. "Triple-S. Shopping, sausage pizza, and the spa. A girl's best friends. By the time I bring Shayanne back, you won't recognize her. Mani-pedi, massage, haircut, facial, and an actual dress."

Bobby's nose screws up, like Sophie just passed gas. "Whatcha need a dress for? Not like you're gonna feed the goats in that."

His laugh is a deep baritone, and Brody and Bruce roll their eyes at his ridiculousness.

"The hell I won't. I'll be strutting out there in heels, owning that catwalk." I do my best impression, making Sophie snort while Bobby just looks horrified at the idea. "For real, though, I'll let you in on a little secret, Bobby, because I know you forget sometimes." I lean in close, stage whispering, "I'm a

woman, girly parts and all, and I like doing girly shit sometimes, just for the hell of it."

"Ahh," he hollers. "Don't say shit like that, Shayanne.
Next, you're gonna say the V-word."

I laugh, pushing my luck and his boundaries. Batting my
eyes as innocently as I can, I say, "What? You mean, vagina?
Should I say pussy instead? Or cunt?"

Brody stops me, his voice pretty hard for him. "Goddamn
it, Shayanne. Have some fucking manners in front of a guest."

He looks to Sophie, shaking his head like he's the long-
suffering one who has to put up with all our antics. Truth be
told, we learned half our craziness from him.

"Sorry," I tell him, obviously not sorry in the least. "Guess
I'd better go before my mouth gets me in any more trouble."

I grab my bag, blowing air kisses their way. "Bye, guys.
For real, don't call me unless something's on fire."

Outside, we hop in Sophie's truck and she heads down the
driveway. The gate closes behind us as we hit the asphalt, and
my breath escapes with a huge smile. "Freeeedom!" I yell out
the open window.

Sophie's laugh is big and boisterous, and I feel like we're
Thelma and Louise on the cusp of a great adventure.

THE BAGS OF CLOTHES SOPHIE TALKED ME INTO ARE STORED
by the customer service-conscious receptionist at the spa while
inside, I'm wearing nothing but a fluffy cotton robe and a big
ol' smile. I definitely went overboard, but it'd been hard not to
when Sophie was oohing and ahhing over every stitch and
begging me to let her live vicariously through me since she's
stuck in maternity stretchy crap for a few more months.

Now, we've been rubbed, scrubbed, and pampered beyond
measure. The only thing left is the mani-pedi, which is why

we're sitting with our feet soaking and hands being worked over while my hair's wrapped in another huge cotton towel, my skin feeling flushed and soft.

For two women who work hard with our hands, this might be more necessity than treat, but I still picked a pretty bright pink color. It'll chip in days, but for the moment, I'm ignoring that fact.

"Which dress are you going to wear tonight?" Sophie asks me, though her eyes are closed and her head is thrown back on the pillow-cushioned chair.

"I think the green one," I reply, remembering the way I'd felt curvy and feminine in it, two things I rarely feel. "Where are we going to dinner again?"

Sophie's eyes crack open and sly smirk steals across her face. "I didn't say. It's a surprise."

I can't move my right hand because the lady is filing my nails, but I shove at her with my left, trying not to move. "Surprise? You didn't tell me you were hiding things from me. So no sausage pizza?"

"Pshaw, sausage pizza? Honey, tonight's about anything but sausage . . . pizza. And I'm not the one hiding things. Such as, Shayanne Tannen, I saw you and Luke making all kinds of eyes at each other at the clinic. What's up with that?"

Luke said Sophie threw him under the bus about that little non-incident, but I wasn't prepared for her to hit me up on it too. Thinking fast on my feet, even though they're currently soaking in mango-scented bubbly water, I grin innocently, shrugging.

"What? That was weeks ago. No big deal at all." *That sounded normal*, I think, though my voice might be a smidgen tight.

"And he's virtually running away from the family dinner table at night," Sophie continues. "I mean, he's a bit of a loner sometimes, but it's not like we've suddenly started smelling bad and he needs the fresh air." She drops her chin, looking at me through narrowed eyes. "Though I do smell some manure. Of the . . . bullish variety."

Damn, I forgot about Sophie going out there for family dinners so frequently. I'm so busted.

It's been hard keeping this from her, anyway. She's my best friend, and I know she'll be happy for me. Just as importantly, she can keep her mouth shut so that my dad and brothers, save Bruce, don't find out.

I make the decision to spill my guts, partially because I need to celebrate this momentous thing with someone and partly because I really do value her input. She's a smart cookie and way more experienced with guys than I am, though that's not a hard barometer to pass.

"Soph, you have to promise me . . . not a single word to anyone," I whisper, serious as can be, and she crosses her heart with a maroon-tipped finger, much to the not-delight of the manicurist.

"Okay, so we danced, and we might've run into each other a few times since then and hung out." Even though the words seem casual, my tone tells an entirely different story and she raises a skeptical brow.

"Hung out?"

"Or more than hung out. We're . . . dating, I guess? Though we don't really go out, just to the tree, or the barn, or on walks or rides. But that's dating, right?" My tongue is running away like a leaky faucet, spilling all the dirt in one big gush that I'm powerless to stop.

Sophie's grin is one of smug satisfaction. "I knew it. You little minx, sneaking all around, getting your freak on with my damn brother-in-law. I should be mad," she says, giving me a long, pregnant pause before chuckling, "but I'm too happy for you both to work up much of a fuss." She looks to the manicurist again, a brow raised in defeat as she sits still. "Honestly,

LAUREN LANDISH

though, if I could give you a high-five and a smack upside the head, I so would."

The manicurist, probably just being careful, grips Sophie's fingers tightly, not letting her move, and Sophie rolls her eyes good-naturedly.

Sophie sits up straight, all prim and proper. "Okay, hit me with it. I want the full story, every dirty detail. And don't leave a single thing out. You owe me that, at least."

My smile feels giddy, like there are bubbles shooting through my body and fireworks sparkling on my skin. I'm not sure where to start, but somehow, I find the brain power to tell her everything. It's a gigantic jumbled mess, starting with the chemistry we both felt at Hank's and ending somewhere around our dinner date at the tree.

I still try to be careful, though, because while I'm spilling my guts to Sophie, I don't want every damn person in the salon to hear what Luke and I get up to. So in a voice so low I can barely hear it myself, I even tell her about my first trip to the barn and how sweet and slow Luke's been taking it with me.

"Is that what you want? Slow and sweet? Not that there's anything wrong with waiting, but are you a ring-first sort?" Sophie asks. We've talked about my virgin status, but not at length. It's just not the kind of thing I go around announcing.

"Fuck, no. Have you seen Luke?" I ask incredulously, and Sophie shakes her head as she laughs. "I've been so close to jumping his bones and riding him like a damn pony that I can barely stand it." Oops, that was kinda loud, judging by the laughter the two nail ladies are fighting. Shit . . . and the ladies in the chairs across the way. I'd assumed they were watching the television over our heads, but it seems their eyes are drifting down to Sophie and me, and they're probably eaves-dropping more than watching the latest *Fixer Upper* episode.

Lowering my voice, I try again. "I just never met anyone, had time to care about someone until now. My brothers were

170

this huge threat when I was in school, and even after that, I think they scared off any guy who even considered approaching me."

"But not Luke," Sophie reminds me in sing-song tones. "He's not scared of anything, I don't think. Even though your brothers would probably slice and dice him if they caught him near you. Luke's brave, though, traipsing all over the continental US, doing his thing with zero fucks given to the old-boys school that says a young guy like him doesn't have a place in a world of big-money horses, but he's been making winners and money left and right. And now, stealing away the heart of my best friend in the whole world right under the nose of her big, mean brothers."

Her insult's said in a playful tone, so I don't feel the need to defend the family name with Sophie. At least not this time, because she's right. My brothers have been known to be big and mean. They're doing better, growing up and maturing, but reputations are hard to change, especially when folks' minds can be more stagnant than they should be.

Also, I suspect that Sophie actually likes my brothers a little. She's worked out at our farm, and she knows them well enough to see underneath their rough exteriors. And Sophie just likes most people, in general.

Especially her new in-laws. "Luke's just a quiet sort of courageous, dependable and steady and solid like an oak tree."

I never really thought about Luke that way. To me, he feels adventurous, and that's not just because he's some dirty little secret or there's a taboo 'don't get caught' risk. It's because he makes my heart race, my body heat, and my brain short-circuit.

But I can see Sophie's point. Even when Luke's driving me wild or getting me to do things I'd never even considered, like rubbing one off in front of him, he does it with surety and confidence, a swagger that says he knows what he's doing. I'm always comfortable with him, feeling like nothing could ever go wrong when I'm safe in his arms.

My face must show some firestorm of emotions because Sophie is looking at me carefully. "Shayanne?"

I meet her eyes, my wide hazel ones to her blue. "Shit, Soph. I've really fallen for him."

Instead of being worried, Sophie's face breaks out into a huge, delighted grin. "Well, congratu-fucking-lations. It's about damn time."

I laugh and think she might be right. It's definitely time.

I COME OUT OF THE HOTEL ROOM BATHROOM TO CATCALLS and whistles. "Whoo, Shayanne! You look hotter than a jalapeño fart!"

I do a solid 360 twirl, capping it off with a curtsy. Though I've never been a ballerina, I think it's passably graceful. If not, it's as graceful as I get, so it'll have to do. "You think? This okay for dinner?"

Sophie hums approval, but she's looking at her phone. "You said you had the all-clear for the weekend, right? Nobody expecting you home until late Sunday night?"

"Yeah, why? Everything okay?" I ask, worried that James is texting her or she's not feeling well. I know pregnancy can be a roller coaster, feeling fine one second and wanting to crash onto the nearest couch the next. It wouldn't be the first time Sophie-the-Go-Getter has overdone it, and we did have a busy day. "We can do room service if you'd rather?"

Before she answers, there's a knock at the door and Sophie looks up. Her bottom lip is behind her teeth and she looks as guilty as sin.

"Could you get that?" she blurts out.

I give her a weird look but move toward the door.

"Hey, if it's room—" I start before my voice dies in my throat.

Luke. He's dressed up in a pressed white dress shirt and black jeans that are darker than velvet, and overall, he just looks . . .

My heart jumps into overdrive.

His face switches from nerves to a blossoming smile as he sees my eyes widen in recognition and then happiness. I watch the way it spreads across his face, the flash of white teeth only brightened by the spark in his eyes as he sees me in all my fancy-schmancy glory. The heat burning in him calls to the butterflies in my belly, like polar magnets pulling together.

"Hey, honey," he drawls out, casual as can be.

No fair. He's using that voice, the gravelly baritone that tells me to 'fucking come on me, woman' when he's fingers deep inside me and about to lose control. Like Pavlov's dogs, I'm trained, and I'm instantly wet.

"Luke." I'm breathless with surprise. With happiness. With need.

At that moment, Sophie scoots between us, her weekender bag already tossed on her shoulder. "Be good, kids." She points at Luke, her voice still light. "You owe me big time, buster. Drop her off on Sunday and I'll take her home."

She winks at me and then she's gone.

I'm alone with Luke Bennett, apparently for the weekend, at a hotel with a bed . . . right . . . here.

Hell fucking yeah!

CHAPTER 15

LUKE

*T*o say that Shayanne looks stunning is an understatement. I'm just not poetic enough to properly describe her. She's wearing a green lacy thing that's riding her curves almost as tightly as I want to, and her hair is styled and curled, sculpted in a way that makes the ends caress her breasts, and her eyes are almost as wide as the O of her surprised mouth.

When she says my name in that panting husky way, quiet enough that only I can hear her, every bit of blood in my body rushes south and my best jeans are suddenly way the fuck too tight.

Thankfully, Sophie interrupts the eye fuck with her blasé attitude as she scoots between us. I don't hear a word she says. My attention's too locked on Shay to pay Sophie any mind, but I get that she's pointing at me and issuing some directive. Whatever. I'll deal with her later. Much later.

After I get to spend the whole damn weekend with my woman. Just me and Shay.

"What did you do?" Shayanne asks, but the shock is starting to give way as the situation dawns on her.

I push in closer, pinning her up against the door frame as I loom over her. I feel like I could engulf her, consume her, devour her and that she'd be right on board with that too. But that's not the plan, and I'm sticking to the plan. She deserves it. She deserves everything and more.

"I might've enlisted a little help in the form of a city girl turned vet and conspired to steal you away for the weekend," I tell her, letting the cocky arrogance that I pulled one over on her, her dad, and her brothers sink in.

Her eyes spark with merry devilment. "Why, Luke Bennett, are you saying I'm stuck with you for the next thirty-six hours, give or take? Whatever will you do with me?" Honey coats her tongue as she coyly flirts, knowing damn well what I'm going to do with her.

I know exactly what she wants. The same thing I want.

But it's going to have to wait because though I'm desperate for her, I'm not an asshole. Going out in public with her, to dinner and dancing, feels just as important as what we're going to do in this hotel. It's the point of this plan, to show her off, to stand by her side and declare to everyone we can that she's mine and I'm hers.

We need this, maybe as much as we need to push back inside this hotel room and not come up for oxygen until Sunday night. I could survive just breathing her in, I'm sure of it.

"Anything we damn well please, honey. Now grab your shoes while I wait right here."

Her bare toe, in a pretty shade of pink I've never seen on her before, digs into the carpet. "You don't want to come in?" she asks, a sexy siren leading me to the rocky shores of her body. Her lips pout, making me want to kiss them into a smile.

So I do.

I lay a rough hand on her waist, squeezing the swerve where her hip dips in as I pull her tighter, pressing her body against me. Lowering my lips to her, I catch the slightest whisper of candy. It must be her lip gloss, or maybe it's just her addictive sweetness. I savor it, slow and easy, as I drive us both to the edge. The thrill that we're right here in a hotel hallway, barely contained in the doorway, just adds to the feeling.

Against her lips, I murmur darkly, "If I come in there, honey, you know as well as I do that we're not coming out until we have to. I aim to take you out on a proper date, dinner and dancing. You deserve at least a little bit of courting, Shayanne."

The intensity of my tone sends a ripple through her, and her breath hitches sexily. I want to chase that sound down her throat, press my lips there and feel the vibration as she does it again and again.

But I stay strong. One step at a time.

"Now, Shay. Git!" I order, popping her ass sharply with a smirk.

She jumps and laughs, swatting at my chest. "Just you wait, Luke. You'd better eat well tonight because when we get back here, I'm going to make you pay for your conspiring and sneaking around."

I'll gladly take any punishment she wants to dole out. "Promise?" I tease, hitching my thumbs in my belt loops. "I hate having debts."

She huffs like she's accepting that challenge, and I know I'm in for quite the night with this firecracker.

Two minutes later, I realize just how woefully unprepared I am.

Shay doesn't walk back out so much as she struts out in heels I've only heard called 'fuck me pumps', and damned if that's not exactly what I want to do to her. They lift her already delectable ass, and as she walks, my mind floods with images.

I want to push her legs up high over my shoulders as I pound into her. I want to wrap her legs around my waist and let those spikes dig into my ass as she prods me on. I want to turn her over and ride those upturned globes as I pull her hair, making her mine forever.

I am so fucked, and we haven't even left for dinner yet.

THIS IS THE FANCIEST PLACE I'VE EVER EATEN. BY FAR, BY like nine levels of white tablecloths, French accents that might actually be real, and more forks than any man needs to eat a single meal.

Shayanne looks like a kid in a candy store, or maybe a peasant invited to dinner at Buckingham Palace.

That's basically how I feel too.

We're dressed for this, her in that sexy as hell green dress that makes her eyes seem more mossy and deeper than usual, and me in a black suit coat I've only worn a few times before. I was just glad to have a reason to wear it besides to discuss money or for a funeral.

Still, all the fancy trappings don't mean this place is us.

"I knew this place was supposed to be swanky, but I'm not sure I was expecting this. I feel like a bull in a china shop," I tell Shay softly, a private confession between the two of us.

Her wide eyes look around at the tables gleaming with crystal, the black tuxedo-wearing waitstaff, and even up to the high ceiling that's been painted in some sort of Renaissance scene. Finally, her eyes return to me, a spark there that warns me to steel myself for what she's about to say because it's gonna be a zinger.

"One, you said *schwanky*, and that's funny as hell coming outta your mouth. Two, you look stiff, so shake it off, man." She wiggles a bit in her cushy upholstered seat and my eyes catch on the fullness of her breasts as they jiggle too. Her smirk is pure 'gotcha', but I wasn't trying to hide my appreciation of her assets. I take her suggestion and move a bit, letting my tense muscles relax. "Good, and three, then why the hell did you bring me here?"

I shrug, slightly embarrassed. "Okay, don't laugh, but I spilled my guts to Sophie so she'd help arrange all this," I say, gesturing from her to me. "And when I told her I wanted to take you out on the town and blow your socks off, she said we had to come here. Something about Michelin stars and food to die for, and it sounded like a good idea. Hell, she had to help me get the reservation by dropping her brother's name, I think."

I've only met Sophie's brother a handful of times, but he's definitely in another realm. For all the dirt and grit Sophie can handle, her brother is suits and business dinners. And richer than God himself.

Though I told her not to, Shay laughs lightly. "That sneaky bitch!" Her voice is quiet, but judging by the sharp look the severe-looking lady at the table next to us shoots our way, not quiet enough. Shay doesn't even notice, which I find endearing somehow. "Sophie was asking all kinds of questions today, poking and prodding like I was a cow needing a checkup. And she knew all along, that co-conspirator." Her eyes drift off a bit, like she's remembering their conversation from today. "Yeah, she's sneaky."

She doesn't sound it, but I check anyway. "You mad that we went behind your back? Even if was good intentioned to surprise you?"

She refocuses on me, shaking her head. "Nah, this is honestly the sweetest thing anyone's ever done for me. You guys went through all this trouble to surprise me, and you did it in a way that we could go out in public without fists being thrown over it. I feel like you thought of everything."

She reaches across the table, and I meet her, clasping her

LAUREN LANDISH

fingers in a strong but gentle grip. I slide my thumb along the soft skin between her thumb and finger.

Heat builds just from that slight touch, like we're both imagining me doing it other places on her body, all over her body. We've waited, we've let the anticipation build . . . and it just makes this moment all the more important. It makes every breath we share more important.

"Can I let you in on a secret?" she whispers.

"Anything," I say truthfully.

The slightest flush pinkens her cheeks, and I wait on pins and needles for her to divulge her deepest, darkest desires. "You don't have to wine and dine me, Luke Bennett. You blow my socks off every day, just sitting on the hard ground under a tree, eating roast beef sandwiches."

Her eyes don't waver from me, her attention and her truth floating in the buzzing air between us. And that truth is that with this relationship, before we've ever really 'done the full deed,' we've jumped so much deeper into an emotional bond than I ever expected.

I am so gone for this woman. Not because she can clean up well and do this fancy shit, or because she's as down to earth as they come, but somehow, it's both. She's . . . complete.

The strength of her spirit and the softness of her soul, the sweetness of her heart and the salty words that come out of her mouth, the innocence she possesses and the dirty things she inspires in me. It's all of it. It's her. It's my Shayanne.

I'm on the verge of spilling all of that in a verbal torrent, but the waiter chooses that moment to appear at the edge of our table. I hadn't even noticed his approach, too lost in her eyes and my own heart's whisperings.

"Mr. Stone requested the chef's special for your dining pleasure tonight. I trust that's acceptable?"

It's on the tip of my tongue to say fuck it and get the hell out of here, scoop Shay up in my arms and run for the truck

180

and drive pell-mell for the hotel. I can tell Shay is thinking the same thing.

But I can also see the chandeliers reflecting in her eyes. Tonight's going to be a big night for us both, and I want her to have the absolute best of everything. So I nod for the waiter, never looking away from Shayanne. "Yes, thank you."

He disappears, and the heat between us scorches the air as the promise of an entire dinner evening at this table looms. I'm just thankful for the long, white tablecloth hanging above my lap. I doubt the snooty lady at the next table over would approve of the throbbing tent in my jeans or the fact that I'm nearly lifting up the table with my crotch.

I lean forward and Shay follows suit, closing the distance across the narrow table. I cup her face, stretching to whisper in her other ear. My voice is smoke and gravel, all the things I'm not saying in the rough rumble as I tell her, "You amaze me every day too. I'm completely in awe of you."

I feel her breath hitch and know she understands what I'm not saying . . . yet. But I need more, so much more. "I'll tell you everything later, when I'm balls deep in your pussy for the first time, claiming you, making you come all over me, owning your pleasure like you own my heart."

She shudders, the slightest quiver rushing through her body as she leans into me. I trace my thumb along her cheekbone and then lay the softest, slightest feather of a kiss along her lips. "Soon."

Dinner is delicious, I'm sure of it. I'm sure the chef put all of his or her years of skill into the preparation of something exquisite. But it could be taco truck burritos, for all I care. I don't taste a single thing. I'm too lost in Shayanne's eyes, in the promise of the night.

After we eat, I'm trembling with want, so close to cutting off the rest of the plan and rushing back to the hotel, but I hold myself steady. For her. She deserves this, a night on the town, something she rarely gets at all and never like this, in the big city.

Compared to the fancy pants restaurant, our next stop is much more our speed. It's a 'country bar', more of a citified version of Hank's, where this all started, which seems fitting. Like we truly have come full-circle in a way.

The fanciness slides off us like an uncomfortable skin, and I undo a few buttons and roll up my sleeves, having already shucked my jacket and tie back in my truck. I don't quite feel back home, but the jeans, boots, and shirt at least look normal here.

"Two beers, please." The bartender doesn't bat an eye or ask for Shay's ID, which only reminds me that she's young and I need to control myself.

Slow and steady, Luke. Like James used to tease you, use the Force.

She lifts the bottle to her mouth, puckering to take a long drag, and all I can imagine is her mouth opening to take my cock. The images superimpose themselves in my mind, and she damn well knows it.

Setting the bottle down, she dabs at the corner of her mouth with a pink-tipped finger. "Whatcha thinkin' 'bout, cowboy?"

I don't give her the answer she's looking for because it'll lead us right out the door. Instead, I guzzle half my beer in one go, then take her hand. "Thinking about spinning you around the dance floor until you're so dizzy that all you can focus on is me. That even though the very ground beneath your feet feels uncertain, you know I've got you steady in my arms and won't let you down."

A flash of something shoots through her eyes, gone before I can recognize it. The smile she flashes my way is easy to read, though. "Show me what you've got, then," she dares. "We'll see who makes who dizzy."

The first few songs are fast, and I do my best to show her

off, keeping in mind that though our shoes are slick, she's not used to dancing in heels. It's a big floor with a lot of talented dancers, so though we're doing some fancy tricks, no one pays us much mind. Seems the city folks have some moves too.

Over and over, I spin her away and then pull her back, catching her against my body in a teasing torment. I dip her, swooping her off her feet into the air where she points her toes and bends one knee, her head falling back to expose the long line of her neck. When I set her upright, I can't help but press a kiss there, inhaling her and counting the rapid beat of her pulse.

I don't have words right now, but she hears my soft growl. "I know, me too," she says softly, but with her mouth by my ear, I hear her loud and clear.

She follows my every lead like we choreographed this, but truthfully, we're just making it up as we go. We can just read each other that well. I can see her focusing when I do complicated hand grabs, can feel the slight delay as she trails her fingers around my waist when I send her behind my back, and I can see both the laughter and heat building in her quickening breaths.

Like I'd slipped the DJ a twenty, he switches songs to something slow and grinding. Chase Rice's *Ride* coats the dance floor in a sultry groove, and I keep Shayanne pressed against me, slowly spinning us both in place. I bring her hands to my neck and rest mine on her hips, joining us in an embrace that's anything but gentlemanly. This isn't about dancing and moving around the floor anymore.

This is foreplay.

Heated, roiling need burns through us as we edge ourselves closer and closer to the point of no return.

Shay's voice has an edge to it as she speaks against my chest, "Luke, we need to go. I need . . . I'm . . . I can't wait anymore."

I flip her around, pulling her back to my front, and with her heels on, her ass cradles my hard cock. It takes every bit of restraint I have to not grind against her, to take her right here on the dance floor, but I still hold her tightly, so close only the thin layers of fabric separate us.

I slip my hand up to her jaw, tilting her head so I can murmur into her ear. "You feel what you're doing to me, honey? You're damn near driving me insane. I want inside you so badly."

"Let's go." It's more order than request, and I love that she's not shy in the least about what she wants.

But I remind her that she's not the boss, not tonight. This is important, and I won't let her rush it, won't let me rush it either. I'm going to go slowly and torture us both until she needs me more than she even realizes she can.

I press against her, splaying my free hand on her belly. "You want me to take you like this? Drop you to your knees on the bed, push you forward until you catch yourself on your hands, and then fuck you from behind, rough and dirty?"

I feel the goosebumps flash on her skin, though she's molten in my arms.

My chuckle is deep and dark. "I will, but not the first time, honey. I want you underneath me, want to slide inside you slow and easy so I get to know every inch of your sweet pussy for the first time. I want to watch your eyes as you take me deep, feel you stretch around my cock, knowing that you'll never be the same, that in this, you'll always be mine and I'll always be your first."

I hold back from saying 'and your last', but just barely. Yeah, I want her forever right now . . . but that's her choice. I need to earn that gift, not demand it.

She sighs, her head falling back against my shoulder for a moment, and I wonder if she's going to detonate right here on the dance floor from just my words. I feel like I fucking could with just the smallest grind of her against my cock.

Without preamble, she steps away from me, grabbing my hand and dragging me with her toward the door. "You can do what you're promising or watch me get myself off. Either way, we're going to the hotel right fucking now."

She's talking over her shoulder as she stomps toward the door, me in tow. I glare menacingly at the guy who happens to catch her say 'get myself off' as we walk by, and he flashes me a bro-grin. Normally, I'd tell him to fuck off and mind his own business, but Shay's not giving me a chance as she drags me along.

She's ready. And I'm so fucking ready.

So I do the one thing my manners require. "Yes, ma'am!" And then I'm the one shoving her toward the door and into my truck.

CHAPTER 16

SHAYANNE

We stumble into the hotel, trying not to run, but I'm about as close as I can get without breaking one of my brand-new heels. The elevator is a moment of privacy that at least allows us to kiss. Hot, wet liquid desire rushes through me. He tastes vaguely like beer and mint, but beneath, it's him. Pure Luke, strong and potent, addicting me to him more with every touch of our tongues. The rising elevator makes my belly swoop almost as much as he does.

Fumbling down the hall, our hands run over each other, scrambling to get to what we both want. I feel the need to touch him everywhere at once, and he seems similarly minded, judging by the grasping handfuls of my flesh he's groping. He pushes me backward, almost like it's a long line of dance steps, until he backs me against the wall next to the room. The door opens with a click and a green light, and then we're inside.

Alone. In a hotel. Me, Shayanne Tannen, with Luke Bennett. About to get our freak on.

Oh, God, don't say it like that, Shay.

I chastise myself but then lose all coherent thought as Luke forgoes undoing the rest of his buttons and simply pulls his shirt over his head. My brain just goes into spasms . . . *hubba, hubba, hubba*.

Pull it together.

This is not a damn rom-com movie where I'm gonna be the silly girl. I'm a woman, and I know what to do with a man like Luke Bennett. Well, I know what I want to do, which is touch him, taste him, and take him. Everything he's promised and more, everything I've read about and seen in movies, everything Sophie has shared. Just everything, all at once.

That's totally possible, right?

But I'm not the cool chick. I'm just Shayanne, who has her mind overloading with possibilities. Instead of being the smooth seductress I thought I could be, my mouth is gaping like I'm seeing him for the first time. I can't help it, he's just so beautiful. It's not the right word to describe a rough cowboy like him, but it's what he is to me. He's muscles carved by hard work, skin tanned and lined from the sun, a smattering of blond hair that thickens low on his belly. And that cocky smirk that silently asks me if I like what I'm seeing.

"Honey?" he rumbles, hands pressed to his sides like he's holding himself back from me. Like he's waiting for me to say the word before he unleashes himself on me.

I don't give permission. I take control instead, flinging myself at him. He catches me, like I knew he would, meeting my lips in a flurry of kisses. I can feel the need burning bright and hot, almost blue fire inside me.

But he tempers it, wrestling me back to my feet and holding my head still in his large hands. Between kisses, he says, "Easy, Shay. I don't want to rush this. We have all night, and I want to make this good for you."

"It will be," I promise him. "Because it's you."

He groans, like my words bring him pain. Confused for a moment, I search his eyes and realize that it's not pain at all. It's pleasure. A fine line between the two comes into sharp focus, and I feel myself take another step on my path to womanhood. I know what his words do to me, and I want to have the same effect on him.

Bravely, I swallow and tell him, "I've wanted this for weeks with you, Luke. I've gone home after our nights at the tree and gotten myself off, even when I just came on your fingers or your tongue. I needed more then, and I'm so ready for you to finally give me more tonight. Now. Please."

I can hear the plea in my voice, the hopeful sound echoing through the room that's silent save for our panting breaths.

His growl is feral, a primal uttering of desire. "Turn around."

I think for a moment that I pushed him into taking me roughly from behind, and my inner wanton slut does a clapping happy dance.

Hell to the yes for that!

Slowly, so slowly he's still torturing me with how he's drawing this out, he lowers the zipper on my dress, and I realize he just needed access. But as he kisses his way down the bumps of my spine, I'm not disappointed in the least. How could I be when his scruff is roughing along my back, contrasting with the softness of his lips?

My dress puddles at my feet, and I step out of it as he directs me to turn back to him. His eyes are dark and stormy as they sweep over me, taking in the black lace bra and panty set Sophie had insisted I get to wear beneath the dress. Sneaky girl knew exactly what it was going to be for, and judging by the look on Luke's face, I owe my bestie a huge thank you.

"Fuck, you're gorgeous, Shayanne. So damn pretty." His thick finger traces the strap from my shoulder down to my cleavage. Before he even gets there, my nipples are already hard, standing up to beg for his attention. He gives it, reverently running his thumbs over the sheer material cupping my breasts. I reach behind my back, undoing the bra myself, and it floats down to the floor, already forgotten when his eyes lick along my bared chest.

He spreads his hands over my ribcage, lifting and guiding me to arch as he urges my breasts toward him. He lowers himself to me, taking my offering like a sexual god, sucking and licking and nibbling my tender pink flesh. My hands twist into his hair, holding him to me, holding on to Earth because I feel like my feet are leaving the ground.

Actually, I'm standing on tiptoe, trying to get as close to him as I can. But he's got me, like he always does, holding me in place and not letting me fall.

With a wet smack, he lets go of my breast and I sink back to the floor, sliding down his body. "Let's take these off," he says, pulling at the scrap of material ghosting over my hipbones. He slides the black lace down my legs, dropping to his knees in front of me.

I step out of the panties, standing over him in just my heels as he looks me over from head to toe and back up again. It may have felt like he's a god, but now he makes me feel like a goddess as he kneels before me, worship in his every touch, every glance, every breath.

He moves to pick up my foot, slipping my heel off. "I've got about a dozen different fantasies involving these shoes, but not this time. I want it to be just you and me, 'kay?"

I grin, nodding. "Okay, but only if you promise to tell me each one of those fantasies."

He nods, his face serious as he stands back up. "Lie back for me," he says, lifting his chin toward the bed. "I want to see you, honey."

I do, feeling the cool softness of expensive cotton beneath my heated skin. But the real treat is that Luke is undoing his belt, then his jeans, which fall to the floor and out of my sight. He kicks out of his dress boots, something I thought I'd never see him wearing. Slowly, he teases me with his boxer briefs, his thumbs looping into the waistband.

I prop up to my elbows, encouraging him. "Get on with it. Let me see you again." I mean for it to be a bit sassy, hell, maybe even bossy. But it comes out too airy to have any bite. Still, I try to be flirty. "Are you afraid I'll bite?"

"Hardly," he says as he follows the order anyway and his cock fills my vision again. Beautiful. I know I already had this conversation with myself, but it's the God's honest truth. Luke is a stunningly beautiful man, rough-hewn around the edges, but that just increases his perfection in my eyes. He's like a natural gemstone, not needing any polishing to put stars in my eyes.

His cock is thick and long, and I wonder how in the hell he's going to fit inside me. But I have faith that we'll make it work. That he'll make it work.

I see the shine of pre-cum on his crown, and my mouth waters to taste him the way he has me so many times already, so I sit up. Grabbing at his hips, I pull him toward me, my intention clear.

"Shay." My name is a groan on his lips. "You don't have to. I've got a hairpin trigger where you're concerned right now."

I take the compliment, but I don't relent. "Gimme, and then you can do me until you're ready to go again."

He looks at me like I just promised him the Holy Grail, and he must decide that sounds like a fine plan because he steps closer. I run my palm up and down his shaft, feeling the silk over steel of his cock and spreading the slickness from his head. Then I stroke him, not too tight but not too loose, just like he's shown me he likes, and bring my tongue to him.

The first taste is a revelation. Man, musk, and earth, but sweet too.

I run my tongue in a circle, lapping at him before wrapping

my lips around him and sucking. His grunt is deep and soulful, a sound I cherish and want to pull from him again.

I work him deeper into my mouth, tasting him an inch at a time until my lips meet my fist. I find a rhythm, slurping and sucking as I jack him off, keeping my lips and fist connected in the up and down strokes. He arches, giving me more, his hands on my shoulders to keep from falling backward. "Fuck, Shay . . ." he cries out, and I feel him grow impossibly harder in my mouth.

He's close, so close, and I want him to come in my mouth.

He pushes into my mouth a little farther, and I gag slightly. Reflexively, I pull back, my eyes watering. "Sorry," I say, a little embarrassed.

"No, I'm sorry. Got carried away. You okay?" he says seriously, his eyes locked on mine. He runs a thumb along my lower lip, slipping through the accumulated spit stringing toward his cock. I nod, and he quietly asks, "Can I tell you something?"

He doesn't wait for me to nod, but he can tell me anything, anytime, and I'd want to hear it.

His voice is deep, a secret murmur in the soft light of the room. "I liked that, slipping into your throat so that you have more me than oxygen. But not yet. For now, touch me, suck me how you want. I'll be still."

I swallow thickly, my mind awhirl and my body on fire. "I liked it too, just surprised me," I admit honestly. I look up at him through my lashes and lick my lips. "Together?"

His jaw tightens, and I know he gets my meaning. I'm not ready for a full-on face fuck, but I don't want him to be still. I want him to lose control a bit. For me, because of me.

His crown passes my lips, and I taste his skin again, cupping my tongue around him. His hand delves into my hair, not forcing me but guiding me like he does when we dance. I feel like everything with Luke is a dance, an invitation to follow but not a demand, a willingness to lead with my desires at the forefront of his mind every step of the way.

Together, we work him deeper into my mouth, slipping into my throat every few strokes as he hisses. "Yessss, that's it. Relax and let me in."

It feels like a bigger statement than just about me sucking him. I need to relax and let him into my whole life, not just this secret section I've cordoned off for him. Because he's taking up more and more of my mind, my heart, and my soul.

"Shay." His voice is strangled tight in warning, and I suck him harder, letting him bump the back of my throat and moaning my permission—no, my *demand*—for him to come. He roars above me as hot pulses of his cum jet into my mouth, and I feel this sense of power and accomplishment flood me.

I did this.

Me.

Not wanting to forget the lesson, I swallow as much as I can, but some escapes, dribbling down my chin.

He strokes into me three more times and then pulls free of my mouth, his chest heaving so hard his abs are outlined in stark relief. He looks like he's just had a spiritual experience. I know I have.

"Holy fuck," he says, a slight crack in his ragged breath. And then his lips are on mine, giving no thought to his cum still on my lips, his taste still on my tongue. "God damn, honey."

He pushes at me, and I lie back on the bed, bending and opening my knees brazenly in invitation.

His eyes wander over me, heat licking along the trail of his gaze. "You look so pretty right now. Pink and wet. Think you're ready for me?" His hands trail up my thighs, squeezing and massaging as he gets higher.

He spreads me open with his thumbs, and I've never felt sexier or more vulnerable. My hips buck beneath his hands, begging, and he obliges, swiping through my juices to spread them up to my clit.

His attention is focused, a man on a mission as he takes me higher and higher, faster and faster. He knows my body now, having coaxed orgasms out of me in mere minutes or drawn them out for an eternity. In the barn, under the tree, by the light of the moon and the heat of the sun.

But never in a bed. Never like this. Like this is something special. Like *I'm* something special.

I try to hold on to my sanity, to reality, but it's snatched away in a tidal wave of release as he demands an orgasm from my body and it gives in so willingly. Black spots dot my vision as I shatter to pieces, flying apart and then slamming back together, back to reality.

I blink hard, finally seeing Luke again on the other side of whatever he just did to me. His jaw is clenched, that bump of muscle appearing and disappearing beneath the scruff. He needs me, probably as much as I need him. Maybe more.

"For the love of God, fuck me, Luke. Please, make me yours."

He climbs on the bed, scooting me up until my head rests on the pillow. Like I could be going to sleep. I'm definitely not going to sleep, not with him looming over me.

I'm going to lose my virginity to Luke Bennett, right here, right now. I've never wanted anything more.

He takes my hands, interweaving our fingers, and lays them over my head. His eyes meet mine, and there's a serious-ness there I don't expect. Not that I think this is some fling for either of us, but Luke seems intensely solemn.

"Shayanne," he starts, and my heart is hammering in my chest, trying to break free and fly around the room like a lost hummingbird. His gulp is audible as his Adam's apple bobs before letting out the words he hinted at while we were at dinner. "I love you. I need you to know that. I love you."

Whatever I thought he was going to say, it wasn't that. Hot tears prick at my eyes, euphoria and disbelief battling it out inside me.

The Big L. I knew it could happen someday. I'd seen it up close with Sophie and James.

But for me? And with Luke?

It stops my breath, and I have to force myself to breathe again. There's only one answer to that, and I lick my lips, a smile tilting the trembling corners upward. "I love you too."

With no other words needed, he's kissing me, tasting the words as we murmur them again and again. My eyes fly open as his cock spears through my lips, dipping in incrementally as he works his hips against me.

He lets go of my hands, and they instantly wrap around his shoulders, holding him to me like I think he's going to get away. He grips my hips, holding me down and not letting me help as he carefully pushes deeper into me.

It's not pain, just an incredible sense of fullness that washes through me as he works his way in slowly. "Relax . . ." he whispers, and I don't know if it's to me or to himself, but I will my muscles to soften and let him inside.

There's a moment of pain, but it subsides quickly. He slides all the way inside me, both of us freezing as the importance of the moment sinks in. I really am his now.

I'm his woman.

"You feel so good, Shay. Velvet squeezing me so fucking tight. Shit, honey."

His words are stilted but sexy as fuck, and they turn me on. I want to tell him too. "I feel . . ." I start, but my brain shuts down, lost to pleasure.

His strokes become longer, filling me and then retreating to leave me wanting. Each thrust cracks something open inside me, making me more vulnerable, more lost to the pleasure of this moment, more in love with him. It's more than physical, though that part's amazing. It's all-encompassing.

"What do you feel, honey?"

"Mmpfh. I feel . . . complete," I try, but I shake my head. That's not it. "I didn't know I was empty without you."

That's it. In so many ways, I didn't know I was merely existing, not living before Luke came into my life. I didn't know that my body could feel like this, that my heart could swell this big, that my soul was searching for his.

The man next door who I never knew was my missing piece.

But finally . . . finally, I'm no longer empty.

I'm filled—with love *for* him, with love *from* him. And as he begins to stroke deep inside me, touching places I never dreamed, I'm also filled with so much cock and cum, just like he promised all those weeks ago.

My first time. It's beautiful in its roughness, lovely in its powerful fragility, and sexy in all its raw crudeness. It's perfect.

I had no idea it could be like this, but with Luke, I believe.

I believe in miracles and adventures and possibilities, right here at home.

CHAPTER 17

LUKE

"I planned for us to go down to the Fall Festival and walk around a bit," I tell Shayanne, though my actions don't match my words as I open her hotel robe to expose her shoulder, laying a line of kisses along the soft skin there. "I honestly figured we might need a break. Well, I thought *you* might need one," I admit, because I feel like a damn teenager, already raring to go again.

The first time was sweet and slow and romantic, everything she deserved. But since then, we've been ravenous, unable to get enough of each other. I've had her twice more on my cock, and I've lost count of how many times she's come on my fingers and tongue. It's been a two-person orgy, a buffet of every carnal desire that crosses our minds.

Our last round, she'd begged me to fuck her hard and I'd had to oblige. Fuck, I'd wanted to desperately. With every bit of strength I had left, I'd flipped her over and taken her from behind with punishing strokes as we watched ourselves in the big mirror over the dresser. I don't think I've ever seen a prettier sight than Shayanne Tannen impaled on my cock, coming with my name crossing her lips like a prayer.

It's been the best twenty-four hours of my life. We've slept in bits and fits of exhaustion, nibbled room service from each other's fingers, and now we're standing in the windows overlooking town. The Fall Festival I'd planned to take Shayanne to is in full swing. From here, I can see twinkling orange lights outlining the trees against the dark night sky, a big campfire with kids roasting marshmallows, and couples walking hand in hand. The chill of the glass tells the story of the passing season.

When Shayanne and I first danced at Hank's, it was barely September, just after Mark and Katelyn's August wedding. Now, we've passed Halloween and we're rushing headlong into Thanksgiving and the holiday season.

If I were ticking off days on a calendar, it wouldn't seem like much, but it feels like an eternity because I don't remember a time before Shayanne. Or at least, I don't want to.

And though the days might be short, the nights with her wrapped in my arms with only the stars and moon as witnesses have been absolutely everything. I meant it when I told her that I love her, and I can feel that she means it too.

She leans back into me, humming happily. "I don't want to put on clothes and go out there. Can we just watch from here?" She sounds dreamy, content. Like a kitten who's gotten her fill of cream. My chest rumbles at the thought of how true that is.

"We can do whatever you want, honey." I spin her in place, pinning her against the window, my hands on her hips. "Just tell me what that is."

It's a dare, and the acceptance of the challenge flares in her eyes. I wait, my breath held in my chest, knowing I'm at the top of the hill on her roller coaster and so fucking ready for her dips and swerves, the unknown twists and turns she'll take me on.

She bites her lip and bats her lashes, letting the tension build expertly, playing me like a damn fiddle. "I want . . ." Her lips quirk and then she lifts up to her toes, her hand wrapping around my neck to pull me down. In my ear, her breath is hot and full of promise. "I want . . . pancakes. And strawberries. Ooh, and a mimosa. I've never had one of those. I want the whole fancy breakfast deal."

She drops back to her flat feet, the happiest of grins brightening her face and telling me just how pleased she is with herself.

I can't help but match the smile. She's a playful little minx, and I love her for it. "You do know it's eight o'clock . . . in the evening, right? Sure you don't want dinner?"

The freshly-fucked mess of her honey waves bobs as she shakes her head. "Nope, breakfast for dinner. It's a thing. Look it up." She taps her pink-tipped finger to my nose. "Sophie told me. She knows these things."

"Breakfast for dinner it is, then," I agree.

A quick phone call later, and her food order is on its way. Plus bacon, because I need some protein to refuel after our aerobic endeavors.

Struck with an idea, I grab the comforter from the floor where we kicked it off and a couple of pillows too. Shay turns, giving me a questioning look.

"Felt a little fancy after all this time sitting in chairs and lying on a bed with you. Figured it was time to return to our roots. Well, as close as we can get up here." I move to the sliding door and kick it open, stepping out to the small balcony.

It's probably generous to call it a balcony, but it'll fit the two of us just fine, especially as close as I plan to be with Shayanne. "We might not be on the ground under our tree, but a romantic picnic overlooking the festival sounds good."

She seems to agree because she's already following me outside. I get the bedding piled up on the concrete, angling to get the best view through the iron railings, and with perfect timing, room service knocks on the door.

I set the food on the edge of the blanket and sit down, my legs splayed wide as I lean back against the pillow-cushioned brick of the building. "Come here," I tell her, and she moves to sit in front of me. We recline, her back to my chest, and I feed her a bright red strawberry. While she chews, I roll up a butter-soaked pancake taquito-style and hand it to her. She bites off the end, mumbling something that vaguely sounds like 'delicious'.

Right on cue, the band at the festival starts up. A moody violin cries into the night, poetic and beautiful all at once, and then an airy voice joins in. I've never heard it before, but a beautiful song about lost love and forgotten dreams washes through the night.

I feel like I have my love and my dream right here in my arms. I must make some noise, a purr of happiness, maybe, because she tilts her head, looking back at me.

"Whatcha thinking 'bout?"

I stumble over my lack of words, a jumble in my brain flashing images of Shay. The past, the present, the possibilities of a future, all of it rushing through my head, but I don't know how to explain. For her, I try, anyway.

"The song," I say, gesturing to the street below with my chin even though she can't see me behind her. "I was thinking that it's sad she's alone because I have exactly what I've always wanted right here in my arms. It doesn't seem fair, but I'm not giving you up, either. And I don't give two shits if that makes me a selfish prick." I pull her to me tighter, like a kid who won't share their favorite toy.

Her giggle is sweet, bubbly like the mimosa she's barely sipped. "Selfish is not a word I'd ever use to describe you, considering our current tally."

I run my hand down her bare thigh, thankful for the covers of night and cotton fluffiness which conceal my somewhat public display. I growl threateningly, "You keeping score?

Hell, if I'd have known that, I would've gone for a few more." I tease up, inching closer to her center, and damn near roar like a possessive monster when she spreads for me.

Her breath hitches, and I'm belatedly thankful she wasn't chewing. I take the pancake with my free hand and stuff the remainder into my mouth.

"Hey, that was mine!" she balks.

Through the crumbs, I mumble, "Sharing is caring, honey."

I almost expect her to mouth back, but I slip my thumb over her clit and anything she was going to say is lost in the moan that rolls in her throat. "You too sore, or you think you can take me again?" I whisper in her ear.

Her answer is broken off before she can say anything by the ringing of her phone. She whines, squirming against my hand. "Leave it."

I pet her soft slickness, wanting to make sure I don't wear her out, and the phone silences. The peace lasts only a moment before it rings again. "Ugh, sorry," she huffs. "Hang on."

She picks up her phone, glancing at the caller ID, and rolls her eyes. "Brody, don't tell me you can't fend for yourself for a weekend."

At Brody's answer, the smile melts off her face, replaced by horror. "What?"

I can hear the fear in her tone, instantly sitting upright and letting the blanket fall to my lap.

She's talking, and I'm only catching her side of the conversation, but I can tell something's seriously wrong. She's shuffling around the room, searching for something, and when her eyes meet mine, I know.

She needs to go. Our bubble just popped.

I get up, instantly in mode to help her handle whatever's going on. I grab a T-shirt from my bag and slip it over her head. She barely takes the phone away from her ear to let it settle over her shoulders. I find her sweatpants and hold them out for her to step into.

I yank my own jeans up and toss another shirt over my head, shoving into my boots. She's got flipflops from somewhere and is heading toward the door.

"What did the paramedic say?" she says, her voice shaky but amazingly strong.

Shit.

SHAYANNE HASN'T SPOKEN. NOT SINCE SHE HUNG UP AND said that they're rushing her dad to Great Falls Memorial.

I put the pedal to metal and pull her to my side, curling my arm around her shaking shoulders. She's crying softly, and I hold her, praying that her dad is okay. I don't particularly care for the man, but Shay does and that's all that matters.

At a red light, she leans toward the glove box and grabs a napkin to wipe the tears from her eyes. I hand her a ponytailer from the gear shifter. "It's Sophie's. She leaves her stuff everywhere," I say by way of explanation, but Shayanne doesn't seem to even hear me. She takes it silently and mindlessly does some magic twisting trick that leaves her hair in a careless knot on her head.

She feels distant, like she's a shell of her usual self as she's disappeared into her own head. I still don't know what's happening, but whatever it is, we'll handle it together.

As soon as I shut the engine off, she's pushing me out of the truck and making a run for the emergency room doors. I follow close behind, jogging to keep pace. She damn near falls against the desk, immediately blurting to the receptionist. "Paul Tannen? My brother said they were bringing him here."

The lady behind the counter looks cool as a cucumber

compared to Shay's wide-eyed panic. "By ambulance or on his own?"

"Ambulance," Shay says. The lady does a bit of clicking, but the doors open behind us and a tornado of Tannens rolls in.

"Hang tight, Dad. We're here," a deep voice says.

Shayanne and I turn to see Paul on a gurney, surrounded by her brothers. Paul's shirt is pulled open, his soft, pale belly exposed except where there are wires running to a beeping machine. An oxygen mask covers the lower half of his face, but he looks pale and clammy.

She runs for him. "Daddy!" Her voice is too loud, too high-pitched. As she takes his hand, it's softer but pained. "Daddy?"

He pulls at the mask. "I'm fine, Shayannie. Brody's just overreacting is all." His bluster is right, pure cowboy bullshit, but he's obviously weak. He looks at her sweetly, and I can see the father he once was. For all the wrongs he might've done, he has done some things right. Shayanne is proof of that.

Shayanne goes to reply, but Paul's eyes find me in the deserted room. "Bennett? What the hell are you doing here?"

It takes less than half a second for his eyes to tick to Shayanne and then back to me.

"Stay the hell away from my little girl, Bennett! I'll fucking kill you . . . no, Shay—" His fury is cut short as he gasps for air, gripping at his chest.

The paramedics interrupt, rushing Paul onward. "Everyone back."

The doors swing shut as the gurney passes through, and time stretches silently, an instant feeling infinitely full of dire possibilities.

Shayanne breaks down, tears tracking down her face in rivers. Brody lays a hand on her shoulder, but he glares at me.

"What the fuck are you doing here, Bennett?" He's in denial. His dad saw it instantly, but he doesn't want to. Especially not now.

Shay sobs loudly, her hands coming up to cover her face. "Come here, honey," I say gently, though it might as well be a sledgehammer for the effect the words have. She turns and buries her face in my chest as I wrap my arms around her, comforting her.

"Get your hands off her before I beat the shit out of you," Brody snarls. His chest is puffed up, his eyes a bit wild and flashing, and both of his fists are clenched at his side. It feels like we've been here before, but things are different now.

I don't move except to rub soothing circles on Shay's back, forcing myself to stay calm and not react to his imminent threat. My voice is quiet but hard, broaching no discussion of the current state of our affairs. "Not now, Brody. You can beat me up later. Right now, *she needs me.*"

The promise of a future beatdown seems to surprise him, or maybe the reality of the situation is just sinking in, because his bravado falters. Brutal takes control, stepping between us to move Brody back. He angles Brody toward a chair, which he sags into.

"Bobby, will you get us all a coffee? Think it's gonna be a long night," Brutal says.

Bobby is looking between us all like we've sprouted second heads or he's entered the Twilight Zone. Hell, I know the feeling. This was coming, sooner or later. But I wouldn't have sprung it on them like this. I would have preferred to walk up to them, man to man, in a neutral place . . . or really, anywhere other than here and under these circumstances.

Nothing to do about it now, though. The cat's out of the bag, and we'll have to make do without shitting kittens.

The waiting room of a hospital is heavy place to be. I've never spent much time in them, but the uncertainty of life clings to every corner, shadows of death no matter how bright the lights might be.

Shay sits in my lap, our coffees forgotten on the chair next to us as time drags on. Brutal's sitting two chairs down, and Brody and Bobby sit across from me. If looks could kill, I'd be dead about a thousand times over and then burned to a crisp just for good measure.

Shay looks up. Quietly but with more strength than she should possess, she asks, "What happened, Brod?"

His brows furrow, and he looks pained. His dark eyes are bright as they flick to me. I know he's trying to decide how much he wants to say in front of me, but he gives in for Shayanne.

I know the feeling, man.

"Dad came home early, said he wasn't feeling good. Knew it had to be bad for him to be home on a Saturday night, but I thought he'd just lost big." The bitterness is apparent. "He sat down on the couch and was watching TV. I was in the kitchen and heard a thud. I went running in there, and he was on the living room floor." His eyes are glassy, looking through us like he's back home in that moment again.

"I thought he fucking died right there." He shakes his head and runs his hand through his hair. "I thought . . . Jesus, the other day, I thought he was just overheated. But maybe not? Don't worry, baby girl. He's a tough old bastard. Too tough to die."

Brutal takes over. "Brody called out and we came downstairs. Called 9-1-1 and you. And here *we all are.*"

It's about as much acknowledgement of the elephant in the room as I expect. The elephant? Oh, that's totally me. I might as well be wearing a huge hat and carrying a banner that says, *Yeah, Shayanne was fucking me at a hotel all weekend and we lied about it too.*

A woman in scrubs appears, her voice calm and professional. "Brody Tannen?"

He stands up, his reply pitching an octave high in worry. "Yes?"

We all reflexively stand too, trying to be ready for any news, good or bad, she might deliver.

She looks at us and smiles compassionately. "Just Mr. Tannen for now. He's asking for you, if you'll follow me."

Brody disappears behind the double swinging doors. And then there were four.

"What the hell, Shayanne?" Bobby snarls, and she flinches but glares at him. I settle her back in my lap, holding her tightly, protecting her. Not from her brother, because I know he wouldn't actually hurt her. But from his words, which are just as sharply painful, especially right now. They're all going through something, but I won't let him take the fear and adrenaline of the night out on Shay.

Brutal sighs. "Not the best way to spill this particular news, Sis."

He leans back in his chair, crossing his arms over his chest and stretching his legs out in front of him before letting his eyes slip shut. He looks like he could be taking a well-earned break after a long day, not a care in the world. For all his casual appearances and previous acceptance of me and Shay, I'm wary of him. Of the three brothers, he's the one most likely to 'accidentally' kill me with a single punch.

Shayanne nods, even though Brutal can't see her through his closed lids. "I know. Brody called and we just . . . came as fast as we could." His meaning dawns, and she gives him a long look. "You knew about this weekend?"

Brutal cracks one eye and peers at her. "It's Fall Festival in Great Falls and you spent damn near twenty minutes telling me how sick apples make Sophie less than a month ago. Didn't figure she'd want to spend the weekend surrounded by the smell of apple cider, even if there was a mani-pedi involved." He glances at her nails. "Pretty."

"Thanks."

They seem okay, and Brutal doesn't seem like he's about

to sneak attack me, especially given the news that he figured out my secret plans for the weekend. It strikes me as surprising that he knows Sophie can't stand apples. I didn't even know that, and I eat dinner with her more nights than not.

Bobby is still looking between us like it's not computing, but he's taking his lead from Brody. "You knew about *this*?" he asks Brutal, tipping his head our way. When he nods dismissively, Bobby turns back to Shayanne and me, his ire lighting him up inside. "You saw what this did to Dad, right? He was talking, doing better. Until *he* showed up."

It's more accusation than she can take right now. She's made of steel, but her heart is fragile and her brother is shitting all over that. Thankfully, Brutal says something before I do.

"Bobby, for now . . . shut up," he growls. I see it then, the mask of calm he's thrown over his stress, the disguise he's using to hide how hard tonight has already been. He's holding it together, but it's taking everything he's got.

His words are just as much for me, and I nod in response.

Once upon a time, me and my brothers were where they are right now. A life of hard work, big meals of butter-laden foods, and time caught up to Pops. He'd died peacefully in the front yard underneath the tree he planted for Mama. And we'd been left to pick up the pieces. We'd had good training, love, and Mama on our sides, though.

The Tannens don't have any of that.

Once upon a time, maybe they did. But they've been making their own way for so long. They're held together by sheer stubborn will, spit, and duct tape.

Even so, losing a parent is hard. Losing your only remaining parent is unfathomable. Even if it's Paul Tannen.

The door opens again and Brody's back. His face is red, his jaw clenched, his breath jagged as hot anger rolls off him.

"You." He's locked on me like a cat chasing a laser beam,

knowing it'll inevitably catch it and looking forward to the domination and destruction it'll wreak.

Apparently, this is happening now despite Brutal's edict.

I'm prepared for it, though. Brody needs this. He needs to rage, to fight, to scream at the unfairness of it all. And he's only got a few options on how to do that. I'm his best target. Hell, I'm his only target.

As soon as I saw Shay, I knew I had to have her and that this was going to happen. They talk about water under the bridge, but the bridge between the Tannens and the Bennetts has had too much sewage flow underneath it for anything else. When they found out about Shay and me, hell was gonna come looking to be paid, but the angst of the night only makes it that much more necessary.

I hold up a hand, silently telling him to wait a second. I shift, picking Shayanne up and setting her in the chair next to Brutal. I give him a look, begging him to look after her.

His answering glare tells me everything I need to know.

With that, I stand and face Brody Tannen.

He's a man in pain, a man filled with fear—of losing his dad, of losing his sister, of taking on a mantle that already weighs heavily on him. A man I respect for the work he does and the love he has for Shayanne. A man I hope will someday respect me. Because I love his sister, and I'm not letting her go, no matter what.

"Fucking Bennetts." My name is as much a curse as the F-bomb is.

I lift my fists, knowing this has to happen. I give him my right side, hoping he'll take the open target and praying his left arm is weaker as I give him the free shot.

He pounds into me with two quick uppercuts to my gut, sending my breath wheezing out harshly. Okay . . . he's got a good left, too.

Shayanne cries out, but I can't risk a look her way. I have

to trust that Brutal is a man of his word, even the unspoken ones, and that he'll hold her back.

Brody wraps his arms around my torso, squeezing me tightly, and I know he's prepping to pick me and throw me to the waxy linoleum. I drop my hips, just like I learned long ago when Mark would do the same thing to me, and we jockey for position. Finally, I drop an elbow to his shoulder, not to hurt him but to get him to let me go. He grunts and his grip slips.

I push him off me, and we take each other's measure. Distantly, I can hear the lady at the front desk calling for security, her voice bored like this is a regular Saturday night occurrence.

"Just get the fuck out of here," he barks.

Suddenly, Shay is between us once again. This time, she's not holding us back from each other. Her attention is on me as she gives Brody her back. Her hands go to my chest, snatching my shirt. "What the hell?"

Her tears are dry, angry sparks taking their place. If they could, I'd bet her curls would be standing on end from all the fireworks rushing through her. She's a cat with her claws out and her back arched, fire aimed at me and Brody because we're right here, but even more so at the fear of what's happening with her dad behind those doors.

Brody chuffs behind her, a hint of vindication in his smug face.

"I'm fine, honey." I slip a tendril of hair that's come loose from her messy bun behind her ear, answering the question she didn't ask. "It was coming. We both knew that."

She sags, her shoulders dropping from her ears, resolved to that truth. "I think you should go," she says in a flat, exhausted voice. "I'll call you later."

It hurts. I don't want to leave her. Not now, when she needs support. Not ever. Even though she's being so fucking brave, so strong, there are things that nobody should go through alone.

But I understand. She does have family, and though they're already in a bad spot, they've got each other's backs. And my being here isn't helping.

Well, it probably helped Brody a bit to have a punching bag for some of his shit, but unless I want a repeat of that, and I don't, I should go.

"I love you," I say, knowing they'll all hear me but not giving a fuck.

"I love you too," she answers softly, honestly.

I'm just enough of a shit to admit to myself that I take some sick, twisted pleasure in her saying it in front of her brothers. Finally.

CHAPTER 18

SHAYANNE

*T*he hours stretch out, made even longer by the fact that I'm just utterly exhausted. It's the longest night of my life. At least, I think it's still night outside. We moved to a waiting area upstairs when Daddy was admitted to the ICU, and there are no windows here.

Only the ticking of the clock on the wall, a sound so annoyingly painful I want to rip it down and chuck it across the room, tells me that time is passing. I dozed for a bit, but I haven't seen Brody shut his eyes once.

He's alternating between pacing and sitting in various chairs, knees spread wide and head hanging low. He hasn't said a word to me since Luke left. Minutes ago, hours ago, days ago? Who knows.

The door opens, and we all look up, hope and fear warring that it's news, some sort of update. Sophie comes in, struggling to carry a brown grocery bag and a smaller white paper bag in one hand and a drink carrier in the other. Her belly isn't doing her any favors, only adding to her load.

"Hey, guys, figured you need a pick-me-up. Coffees all around, and I got everyone some breakfast." She's chattering brightly, as if her appearing like a fairy godmother is no big deal, handing out liquid fuel and bacon, egg, and cheese sandwiches on thick toast.

My brothers take her offerings without hesitation, a sure sign that hell has frozen over.

Okay, that's not fair.

They know I'm friends with Sophie, and they listen to my stories about her since we're best friends, but I tend to hang out with her at her house. It's just safer, considering her relationship with James.

When she does come to the farm, it's usually in her role as Doc's vet assistant, and Brody treats her professionally, and on the rare friendly visit, they usually make themselves scarce. Insinuating herself into our family this way is not our norm, but they're not even batting an eye. Not even Brody.

Maybe they're just hungry. I know I've got a vague ache turning in my stomach, half hunger, half guilt. That's my job, to keep everyone fed. I should've done that, but I feel like I'm hanging on by a thread and don't have any spare bits of me to parcel out right now.

"Have you heard anything?" she says carefully, sitting down next to me.

I shake my head. "Not since he got to ICU. They said it's a wait and see situation."

I feel drained, exhaustion licking at me from deep inside, and my tone remains flat even after sipping on whatever high-octane coffee she got. It's better than the hospital swill, that's for sure.

"Okay, well, don't worry. You all stay here in case anything changes. We've got the farm covered, and I'll bring your clothes back with dinner."

Brody looks up at that, confusion written on his face. "Got the farm covered?"

He glances up at the clock and we all follow his sightline. It takes me a second to decipher the time with my bleary eyes. It's almost seven in the morning. "Shit, I've got to check on the cows. They've been in that pasture all night."

He stands up, reaching to adjust the hat that's usually on his head, but it's not there. He must've left in too much of a hurry to grab it. His hand falls uselessly to his side.

Sophie smiles softly and waves Brody back down. "We've got it, Brody. James, Luke, and I went over this morning, did checks on all the animals, and got everyone fed and watered. It's all taken care of for now. Tell me where you want your cows, and we'll get them over there tonight, keep it all running smoothly."

His jaw drops the smallest bit and then he licks his lips. I can see the tense set of his shoulders and know he's not happy about Luke being anywhere near his animals. Or me. It's a tangled web of possessiveness and dislike. Even so, it's a sweet gesture, neighborly and friendly.

Brody collapses to the chair, sullen and spent. "Uh, thanks, I guess." He's doing his best to be polite despite his current state. "But I'll head out there tonight. We'll need to grab a shower and a change of clothes."

Sophie looks at me, less sure in her words. "About that, I extended the hotel reservation for another couple of days." Something about the way she says it makes me think she had less to do with it than Luke did. "That way, you can stay in town and take showers or get some sleep. I went ahead and left some toiletries and clean T-shirts in the room too. I could bring them here if you want, though?"

Brody's jaw ticks. "No, that's very kind. Thank you," he grits out like it's painful to thank her for doing something nice.

"Okay, well, I'm going to get to work," Sophie says with a crisp nod. "Please call me if you need anything. And I'll go by tonight for evening rounds unless Shayanne texts me otherwise. We'll take care of everything. You just do what you need to here."

She points at the brown bag. "There are big water bottles and some snacks in there. A few magazines, a deck of cards, and a phone charger too."

Looking at each of us, her eyes are sad but determined. She stands in front of me, and I rise to hug her. Or more accurately, to be hugged by her. She wraps her arms around me, pulling my head to her shoulder and petting my greasy hair without judgement. I sigh into her, not realizing how much I needed this until she offered.

She kisses my cheek and whispers quietly, "Hang in there, Shayanne. You can do this. You're the fiercest bitch I know."

I can't laugh, but my breath is the slightest bit easier at the crude pep talk.

Unflinchingly, Sophie moves to Bruce and opens her arms. He hesitates but stands and hugs her. It's awkward, but I know he feels better too. She does the same to Bobby, who still looks like the rug has been swept out from beneath his feet. When she stands in front of Brody, he shakes his head grumpily.

Undeterred, she kicks at his booted foot with her own. "Stand up and give me a hug or I'm taking that coffee back. And it's the best thing you're gonna drink today unless you hit the mini-bar at the hotel." She's slick, reminding him of what she's done in a light, joking way and not giving him the option to skip the hug. He's on full alert and needs to be forced to let his guard down even the barest bit right now.

Grudgingly, he stands up and wraps his big arms around her. She hugs him tight, not letting him go for a second longer than he prefers. I know Sophie. She's not trying to establish dominance but is trying to give him a little more comfort, knowing he could use it but would never say as much.

And like the whirlwind she is, she's gone.

By early afternoon, we're all going stir-crazy. We are not indoor people. We are not 'sit in a chair on our asses' sorts. Lack of action, lack of information, and lack of surety are leading us to madness.

Brody stands for the first time in hours. I think he did finally sleep a bit, though, after the doctor peeked out to let us know that things looked as stable as we could hope.

"I'm gonna hit the shower and that mini-bar. Grab some lunch." He picks up the white keycard from the stack of stuff Sophie left and heads down the hall.

Bruce lifts his chin at me. "Good luck, Shay. Best follow him and face the music."

I sigh, forcing my stiff body to follow after Brody. These chairs are torture devices, numbing you so you don't realize how painful they truly are.

I trail behind his broad back, working to keep up with his fast strides only to hop in his truck and find country music blaring from the radio, letting me know he doesn't want to talk. He maintains his silence until we get into the hotel room, where he stops on a dime so fast, I run into his back. I look to see what made him freeze up, but the room is neat and tidy, freshly put back together the way it was when Sophie and I arrived yesterday.

"Oh, shit. Is this . . . did you . . . ?" He turns and looks at me, his eyes wide with some undercurrent running through their dark depths. "Did you fuck Luke Bennett in this room?"

If he'd said it mean-spiritedly, more sneer than shock, I'd be sure-fired to snap back at him. I'm on edge too, damn it. But his tone isn't cruel or disgusted, more stunned that the thought had just occurred to him.

He runs his fingers through his thick hair, waves fluffing up from the repeated movement, and I know he's missing his hat again.

We don't do this. We don't talk about sex, we don't accuse each other of perfectly normal things like they're somehow wrong, and most importantly, we don't turn on each other. Especially not when the shit's hitting the fan.

Brody is my brother, but of the four kids, it's always been him and me leading this bus. Truth be told, Bruce and Bobby spend hours together in the fields, and Brody and I work together with the smaller animals and keeping the house running. We're a family of four, in teams of two. But we all pull together, having each other's back no matter what.

I think that's part of the reason I wanted to keep quiet about Luke, I realize. I knew it was going to get ugly, and I didn't want this to affect the way I see Brody or the way he sees me. I don't know that I ever truly cared what Daddy thought about Luke, but I care what Brody thinks.

My voice is quiet but steady and strong. "Yes, Brody. I fucked him here, and it was my first time, so don't ruin it for me. And I made love with him here, first time for that too. Because I do . . . I love him. And he loves me. So you need to get onboard with that because it's happening."

"How long?" he snaps. He's mad, but I know him, and underneath his brutish behavior, he's hurt. Hurt that I hid this from him.

"It seemed necessary. It was my idea. I was hiding him, not him hiding me," I reply, skipping to the heart of the matter. I know that's an important distinction, and though I was never ashamed of being with Luke, keeping him a secret felt exciting and risky, like an adventure for the country girl who's never had one. The risks haven't paid off because I've hurt the people I care about with my sneaking around.

"How. Long. Shay?" Brody's eyes are hard as they stare holes in my soul.

"A little over two months. I see him almost every day when you're in the fields or at night when everyone's asleep. We talk and text and leave each other notes at the tree." I hold my head high, no longer hiding anything and ready to face his judgement. "I love him, Brody," I repeat, hoping he'll see reason.

He growls, deep and low, but I hear the muttered "Mother-fucker." He turns away from me, beelining for the bathroom, and the door closes with a click that cuts through the air with harsh finality. An incongruously small sound for such a bullet to the gut.

The shower starts, and I take my phone from my back pocket.

Thank you.

I'm not even sure what I'm thanking him for. All of it, I guess.

Anything, anytime, honey. What do you need?

He doesn't ask how Daddy is like everyone else has, but I feel like that's intentional. His focus is on me. For the first time in longer than I can contemplate, I'm someone's first priority.

I didn't even know, but you did.

There's so much to it that I can't even begin to explain. He knew I'd need him and went into the lion's den of that hospital willingly, though he'd be exposed. He knew Brody needed to let off steam, and he took that hit so my brother wouldn't self-destruct in the middle of a maelstrom. He knew we'd need the farm taken care of, that I'd need Sophie, that we'd need a place to crash, even if just for a minute.

This is what he does. Luke is a caregiver, a lot like me. But different. He's taken care of his family and his ranch silently and in the background for years, and he's gone out and helped take care of other people's animals, their ranches' futures too. And now he's taking care of me and my family.

Luke's list of people he truly lets in might be small, but the

217

list of people he cares for is long. Still, it feels like a gift to be at the top of that list, knowing that he'll do anything for me.

It's what family is supposed to be. It's what neighbors and small towns are supposed to be. And it lives inside him, everywhere he goes.

My phone dings in my hand and a picture pops up.

It's Luke, a goofy smile on his face because Troll, my favorite goat, is licking his scruffy cheek.

Don't be jealous, but this one is a helluva kisser.

The bark of laughter feels good and wrong at the same time, but it's perfect. The slightest balm against another painful moment.

Thank you. I needed that.

I've got you, honey. I love you.

I love you too.

CHAPTER 19

LUKE

"Thanks for sitting down with me. I called this family meeting for something important," I say, mindful of the five pairs of eyes staring back at me unblinkingly.

"Well, then, quit your hemming and hawing and get on with it then. I've got shit to do," Mark barks. He doesn't mean to. It's just his normal tone of voice, so I ignore him. Especially when Katelyn swats at his chest scoldingly. He looks at her, the 'what?' apparent in his eyes, though his frowning expression doesn't change.

Mama's eyes are laser beams locked on me, but she says out of the side of her mouth to Mark, "Language."

There's a whirling swirl of noise as everyone starts talking over each other. I try to let it be, but eventually, I'm unable to take it a second longer, and I whistle loudly. Mark winces, which gives me a small amount of joy. He literally won the county fair with his whistle and can do it so loudly, we can hear him pastures away. But in this little room, my attempt at getting their attention is a pretty good challenge to his little trophy.

"Good one," he deadpans, then waves his hands for me to

get on with it.

"Look, I've got something to tell you that might come as a shock, but it's serious." I take a deep breath, fortifying myself and expecting an explosion.

Maybe it'll be a small one, just a single stick of dynamite's worth, I think hopefully. Or maybe like one of those demo deals where the whole building collapses in on itself.

Fuck, I hope it's not that one.

Though if it is, if our families won't stand beside us, worst-case scenario is that Shay and I will just leave. I haven't talked to her about it, but I'll take her anywhere she wants to go, across the whole US of A. My work could let us do that if I play my cards right. I've got connections, and I've gotten offers sometimes from some of the stables I've been to, looking to lock down a talented breeder for their own lines. But that's not what I want, not really. I need this place to come back to, and so does she.

Home. Mine is with her, but together, our home is here on this land.

"I'm seeing Shayanne Tannen."

I clench my jaw, waiting for yells and anger. I wait for my brothers to flip their lids, or worst of all, for Mama to be disappointed in me.

But instead, nothing happens. Zero response from the peanut gallery.

I look at them, but they're looking at each other. Brows are pulled down, shoulders shrugged up in confusion. Finally, Mama prompts me, "And . . . ?"

I give her a careful once-over, and I can see fireworks dancing there. But she doesn't look mad at all. It almost looks like she's . . . happy? But that doesn't make any sense, so I try again.

"I love her, Mama. And she loves me," I say proudly, hoping against hope that it's enough.

She claps her hands and kicks her booted feet, grinning like a fool. "Hot damn, it's about time, boy!"

No one calls Mama on the fact that she just cussed, though she'll damn near yank your ear off for doing it, especially if you say the F-word at her kitchen table. Don't ask me how I know. Unthinkingly, my hand drifts to my left ear.

Now, I'm the one looking confused, though. All five pairs of eyes are looking at me like they're barely holding back laughter. "What?" I stutter. "What?"

Mama gets up from her chair, coming over and hugging me. She's tiny, barely chest-high on me these days, but I still fold into her arms because she's my mama and that's what you're supposed to do.

Realization dawns.

"You all knew?" I ask incredulously.

James breaks first. "Hell, man, you've been home for almost two months straight, and how many times have I stopped by the barn? I can tell you it hasn't been near as many as usual. Figured you needed your, ah, *privacy*."

Mama smirks, but she still swats at him. "James Bennett, you watch your mouth."

He grins like butter wouldn't melt in his mouth, shrugging. "Mama, I didn't say a single cuss word at all. Not my fault if I was being brotherly and not interrupting Luke's afternoon distractions."

Even Mama blushes at that. And so do I.

They knew. They know.

I'd even thought about why Mark and James weren't coming by the barn very often. Hell, on one hand, I'd thought it was a damn good thing, giving me some privacy just like James said. But on the other hand, it'd felt like a dismissal. Like even though I've been here for a longer stretch than usual, they just didn't care as long as my work got done, which it always does.

It hadn't occurred to me that they were doing it on purpose, knowing that whatever was going on, it was mine to share when I was ready. I mean, I figured that Sophie'd talked to James . . . but probably not until the last day or two.

What an idiot I've been. For all the shit we give each other and all the times I feel a bit invisible around here, maybe they're better brothers than I sometimes give them credit for.

Katelyn laughs, looking at Mark. "Afternoon delights? I didn't know about that. We just knew about your midnight treks out to the pasture. For what it's worth, that dim little flashlight you use to avoid cow paddies might as well be a blazing shooting star when you're walking through a pitch-black field."

"Thought you were coming over for an uninvited, ill-timed visit the first time we saw you stalking around. Damn near broke my leg shoving Katelyn off the back porch and into the house." He growls out the story, and I realize just how close to death I came. If I'd seen what was surely a naked Katelyn, my body probably would've never been found.

I glance to Mama, who just spreads her hands. "A mother knows things." She's never been one to divulge her near-magical methods of knowing what her boys are up to. I've always sworn she has spies all over town and probably implanted us with microchips when we were babies. "Did she like the Fall Festival?"

I glare at Sophie, wondering how much she's told. "Thought you said you could keep a secret, Sis?"

She smirks, shaking her head and holding out both palms in a 'don't blame me' motion. "I didn't tell that part."

James wraps his arms around her, teasing, "You told me that part."

Her voice is quiet and she blushes. "That was different. I had to."

I pinch the bridge of my nose, looking up and praying for

some fucking patience. "Why did you have to tell him? You promised me when we whipped that plan together that it'd be top-secret, remember?"

"I had to do the reservation so I could check us in, which means that I got an email confirmation," Sophie explains, "and James saw it and got all excited thinking I booked us for a babymoon getaway. I tried telling him it was for Shayanne and me, but it's not like he wouldn't question it when I came home Friday night."

"That . . . makes sense."

She glares at James, punching her husband lightly in the shoulder. "So I swore him to secrecy, which apparently means jack squat." Back to me, she says, "Sorry, but not sorry. This should've happened ages ago." She gestures to the room, getting nods all around.

"She didn't tell me," Mama says, corroborating Sophie's story. "I just figured it out. The Festival is so lovely. Did Shayanne like it?" she asks again.

I sag, utterly defeated, not by harshness but just by love. Dammit. "We had a great weekend and were just getting ready to enjoy the rest when Brody called. I'm afraid I've got some bad news. Seems Paul Tannen had a heart attack last night."

I tell them everything I know and everything that happened. They're quiet, the news hitting pretty close to home, literally, since the Tannens are neighbors and it echoes so similarly to what happened with Pops.

"What do they need?" Mama says as I wrap up my story. That's Mama. The source of my can-do attitude. Give either of us a checklist of things that need tending to, and we'll make sure they're all done before the sun sinks below the horizon line. No muss, no fuss, just get it done.

And she's not going to hold a grudge. Paul Tannen offended her, yes. He said some things that weren't gentlemanly. But for Louise Bennett, that's the past. Today is about helping a family and helping neighbors.

"Sophie and I tended the animals and set them up to use the hotel so they could stay in town. I'm heading over there in a minute to do the evening checks. Figured I'd order dinner to be delivered to them so they'll have something to eat. Rinse and repeat tomorrow. Shay asked me to go for now. I think my being there made it harder on the boys, and that's the last thing I want to do, especially right now."

Mama nods. "I'll handle dinner. Don't worry about that. It's been a while since I've seen those kids and wish it was under better circumstances, but it is what it is. They need a Mama, and good thing I am one."

She's not bragging, just proud that it's the truth. Mama is a motherly woman for anyone and everyone she meets. I just hope they greet her with more kindness and openness than they did me. Though I don't think any of the Tannens would send away a piece of Mama's famous pie.

"Might take pie to ease your way in," I advise, and she smiles softly like she'd already thought of that.

"NICE SETUP THEY'VE GOT," MARK SAYS ADMIRINGLY, looking around.

He'd offered to come over to the Tannens' instead of Sophie so that she could get off her feet after the long day. James had shot him a grateful smile and herded her off to the truck while I was grateful for the physical help. Not that she needed herding, but she's huge for seven months along and I'm still wondering about the doctor's assessment that she's only carrying one baby.

"Yeah, Sophie told me Brody does a top-notch job, especially considering the animals aren't their primary income like they are ours. The Tannens make most of their money from their harvests, Shayanne says. Either at the markets or this season, with her pumpkin puree. The goat milk soaps are doing really well too. She's taking trips to the resort twice a month to restock because they're selling like hotcakes up there."

I rattle off the details of their family businesses based on countless conversations with Shayanne about them. She's the money person in their operation, and I've heard everything from celebrations at her soap sales at the resort to worries over the smaller than usual pear crop they had.

Mark eyes me thoughtfully, mouth in a straight line. Finally, he sighs and crosses his arms over his chest. "You sure about this?"

It's only four words, but I know he's asking so much more. Am I sure about Shayanne, about helping her family, about getting tangled up in the mess that's sure to come of this?

I nod, glad Mark's open to listening. "She's it. And I'm not some grumpy asshole who's fighting it the whole way." His left brow raises at the dig at how Katelyn had to damn near bop him over the head to make him see how perfect they are together. "I'm all in with Shay. Have been for a while now."

That's apparently all he needs to jump fully onboard with my relationship because he nods and lets out one of his infamous grunts that could mean anything from 'fuck off' to 'I love you'. I think this one is more the latter.

Knowing that I have my family at my back eases the knot inside me I didn't know was pulled tight. There are going to be some tough days ahead, for Paul as he recovers and for Shay and me, because I'm pretty sure that Paul, at least, is going to try and tear us apart. And I doubt her brothers are being too supportive, either. The feud has gone on too long, been too ingrained in the Tannen boys for them to let it go easily.

Though at least Brutal seems okay with it, so maybe there's hope. I pray there's hope for us all.

CHAPTER 20

SHAYANNE

"One for you, and here's another," Mama Louise says, her voice threaded with kindness.

She's handing out Tupperware containers of ranch chicken casserole, one for each of us to go with the other containers she's handed out. Magically, they're still warm, like she packed them in the insulated cooler straight out of the oven.

She probably did. She's good like that. Or she used to be. I don't know her that well these days, I guess. But her inherent goodness shines out of her, making her a beacon of comfort we all need right now, even if the boys aren't willing to admit it.

But they take the offered food and mumble their appreciation in an approximation of manners that I think would make Mom proud.

"Have you heard anything else?" Mama Louise asks Brody, deferring to his role as the eldest and leader. I suspect she's gotten a quick download from Luke or Sophie, but either way, she's dead on.

He shrugs, his voice flat and robotic, even if he does peel open his Tupperware almost immediately. "Doc says it's still touch and go. Won't be out of the woods until he has forty-eight hours with a clean EKG, and so far, he's not going more than a few hours without an episode. They're not even willing to do surgery on him right now, said that's a sure-fire death sentence with him being so unstable."

He's given the same report several times to various friends of Daddy's who've shown up to lend their support. It's sweet that they're willing to come visit but hard to keep hearing the words that sound so uncomfortably foreign about my dad. He's this big, strong, can't-keep-him-down beast of a man in my eyes, and the sudden change to weak and sickly is head-spinning and heartbreaking. I can't imagine how hard it is for Brody to keep repeating the doctor's words, and I imagine they're turning over and over in his head on a loop.

Mama Louise nods, not offering useless sympathies or reassurances that she doesn't know will actually hold true.

He'll be fine.

Too tough to let this keep him down.

I'm sorry.

All of them are said with good intentions, but none of them fix the problem at hand. Only time and the doctors can do that.

"Eat," Mama Louise orders. "You need to keep your strength up. Sitting in a waiting room is hard work."

That sounds strange, but truer words have never been spoken. I'm more exhausted, mentally and physically, than I am after a long day working at the farm, but I've barely moved from this chair.

We do, mindlessly making the casserole disappear into our empty bellies. She produces cobbler from another bag, making apologies that she didn't think pie would travel well, and we eat that too.

And as delicious as I'm sure it is, it's all bland mush in my gut. Not because of Mama Louise's cooking, which is excellent as always, I'm sure, but just because I can't taste anything, feel anything.

I'm numb.

Mama Louise gathers up the Tupperware and quietly says she'll take them over to Sophie's to wash up, but she'll stay close. After she leaves, the minutes and hours pass.

At midnight, Bobby and Bruce make a trip to the hotel and come back with droplets of water still hanging onto the curling ends of their hair, their breaths emanating the smell of hotel lobby coffee.

And still, we sit.

The door opens and we all look up reflexively.

Dr. Taylor walks into the waiting room, looking grim. "Mr. Tannen?"

Brody stands up abruptly and we all follow suit. Brody throws an arm around me, pulling me to his side like he did when we were younger. And I'm so glad because I need his strength right now.

Because we all know, it's in the way he said 'Mr. Tannen' and not 'Brody'. Before Dr. Taylor can even say another word, we know from the set of his shoulders and the resigned look on his face.

"I'm sorry. We did everything we could, but the damage to his heart was too extensive."

He says other things, but I don't hear them because I bury my face in Brody's thick chest as the sobs shake through me.

He's gone. Daddy's dead.

Shayannie.

Suddenly, the nickname that always drove me a little crazy seems painfully missed. I'd give anything to hear Daddy call me that again, to make me pissed off again at his bullshit . . . anything.

Thank God for the big hands and strong backs that surround me right now, though. I'm not alone, not really. Brody, Bruce, Bobby, and me gather each other close. I don't know if they're crying, my vision too blurred by own tears, but I can feel the pain inside them as sharply as my own.

We're alone, but we're together. And Tannens are tough. We'll get through this. There's no other option.

———

"Do you know what he wanted for his service?" Mama Louise asks Brody gently. She came immediately when I called. Despite the hours, despite the time. She's been there for us, and I love her for it.

We've each had our turns to go into his room and say our goodbyes. The room felt empty, like Daddy's big personality was missing and instead there was just a cold, clinical hospital generic-ness surrounding me.

But I said my piece and had found some small sliver of peace at his bedside, holding his hand and oddly thankful that it was still warm so I could pretend he was sleeping.

Brody meets her gaze, but his eyes are glassy and hard as marbles. "I'll figure it out."

Mama Louise nods, her voice clear, calm, and supportive. "I know you will, but you don't have to do it alone. I'm sad to say that I've done this a couple of times in my life. Once was for your mother, and Paul and I had some conversations. I'm not saying I knew your dad well these last few years, but I'd like to help you with this."

Brody bristles, his voice cold. "Don't need any help, least of all, from a Bennett."

I flinch, knowing the dig is at me and that he's lashing out, but it still stings on my already battered heart.

Mama Louise eyes Brody, the moment stretching out, and I can see her mind working as she analyzes Brody. Finally, she says firmly, "Not helping you. I'm helping Paul, who was a friend of mine and of John's for a lot of years before everything got so messed up. He was a husband to the best friend I've ever had, Martha Tannen. I'm helping a man who may not have always done the best thing or even the right thing, but he deserves to be laid to peace properly. So get off your keister and follow me. There's work to be done, and you're in charge now, Brody Tannen. Lead your family the way I know you can."

Chee-sus and crackers. Mama Louise is a fierce, heavy-handed beast of a woman. I want to be her one day.

I think for a moment that Brody is going to snap at her. His huge, chest-filling breath says he's getting ready to unleash his fury in a verbal spew that will melt her in a puddle where she sits.

And then the air escapes him in a sigh of futility and he stands. "Let's get this shit over with."

Mama Louise dips her chin once in agreement then reminds Brody softly, "Language."

He looks at her incredulously. "My dad just died and you're bitching about my language? I'll say whatever the fuck I want, you hear?"

Her lips tilt down the slightest bit, understanding but disappointed in what Brody just said. "Of course, you can. But how you carry yourself reflects not only on you but on that man you're getting ready to pay final respects to. And it sets the tone for your whole family. Choose wisely."

He walks through the door, and Mama Louise follows, tossing back a sad smile to us. They're meeting with the morgue director and funeral director to set up the transfer to the funeral home. Brody will then have to have another meeting to make decisions on the funeral itself. I feel like I should be helping with this, but he told me and the boys to let him handle it.

I'm weak enough that I'm glad he's doing it because I don't know if I could. But one look at Mama Louise tells me that I'm stronger than I think I am, and if I had to, I could do this. I'm still glad I don't have to, though, even if I feel a little guilty at leaving Brody to do the dirty work.

PAUL TANNEN WAS A SON OF A BITCH. THE BEST I KNEW. HE'D HELP you out in a pinch and call you on your bullshit with a big old grin on his face. I remember a time I got stuck out in my back field and Paul came charging up in that fancy new truck of his, and I knew he didn't want to get so much as a speck of dirt on that thing. But you know what he did? He hooked a winch up on that big, fancy truck and got to pulling. Got my beater truck out in a jiffy and then bought me a beer that night, said I needed it after the crap day I'd had.

A tear leaks out before I can catch it with the white handkerchief in my hand. The handwriting's scraggly, pure country boy who doesn't do much writing past scribbling a shopping list, but it's beautiful to me. I look down at the next one, but before I can start reading, someone stands at his wake to start speaking.

"Paul loved to play cards and he had a hell of a poker face," says the man, who I think I've seen down at the farmer's market from time to time. Jerry, I think. "You could never tell what was in his hand until that last second where he laid 'em down. He played big, he played hard, but there was one thing he had zero bluff about. How much he loved his kids. He'd talk about the farm sometimes, but it was always tied up in how proud he was of them. I might've heard him say once or twice that they were so good, they didn't even need him to keep it running. I hope that's true because if there's one thing Paul would've wanted, it's for his good name to go on with you four and that farm."

Gee, thanks. No pressure, I think to myself sarcastically.

Someone else gets up, looking uncomfortable in his suit,

but when he speaks, his voice is clear and filled with emotion. "Paul Tannen was a study in before and after. Before Martha died, he was a family man through and through. They were the best team I'd ever seen. She balanced his rough edges and he drove her a little crazy. Man, he loved her and she loved him. And born out of that love were four kids they doted on. After Martha passed, he wasn't ever the same, and I think we all knew that. He was broken inside and doing his best to hold his pieces together. He tried hard to do right by you kids, but I know the weight of being left behind weighed on him. I hope he's happier now, holding Martha again the way he always wanted to. They're watching over you now, kids, your mom and dad, holding hands and proud of you."

The man isn't even someone I know, which seems sad because he obviously knew Daddy well. I like the picture he paints of my mom and dad, back together and happy. I don't know whether I believe that's real or not, but it does ease the pain a bit.

The service is lovely. People wax poetic about a man who only vaguely sounds like Daddy.

There are some stories that I've never heard and some I've heard a million times, all little pieces of tape that hold my heart together. I lose track of the number of people who tell me that I'm the spitting image of my mom, and I wonder if Daddy thought so and if that was why it was hard for him to be around me as I got older. Maybe I reminded him a little too much of what he'd lost?

I'd thought I was numb before, when questions were looming overhead and my ass was sore from the uncomfortable chairs. But now, this is true numbness. I'm on autopilot, going through the motions—shake hands, nod politely, and thank you for coming.

Can I get out of here yet?

Back home, there's a houseful of people I wish would just

go away. I feel like I'm on display, a bug in a jar for everyone to peer at.

Is she about to break down?

What are these kids going to do? Poor things.

Did you hear who she showed up at the hospital with? Paul would've never allowed that.

The last one is the one that irritates me the most. Since Luke left the hospital that night, he's been my rock.

He's been handling things behind the scenes, like the farm and sending Mama Louise and Sophie. He found the time to take me on a walk to a treed courtyard at the hospital, knowing I needed a moment to fall apart in private.

He even met me at our tree last night to just hold me silently as I raged, letting me take out my anger and sadness at the unfairness of it all.

Today, Brody and he have reached a temporary truce, and I'm so thankful for it. Because I need Luke by my side. He's here, with me, dressed in a black suit that fits him perfectly. I thought his being dressed up was dashing just a few short days ago. Now, I never want to see him in a tie ever again.

I want things back like they were, T-shirts and ripped jeans. Silly goats and silly dreams. But they never will be again.

For my family, though, I'm holding strong. Even if Luke's holding me up, literally and figuratively.

CHAPTER 21

LUKE

*L*ooking over during the wake, I can only think one thing. Shayanne is so damn strong. Her nose is red and her eyes are puffy, but her face is dry and her back is ramrod straight.

I know she's crumbling inside, but you'd never know it. She's playing hostess, offering sweet tea and beers to people like this is a damn party. But I can see the flinch every time someone offers their condolences.

I remember feeling like that back when Pops died. Like I had to be the strong one, the tough one, keeping up a façade of normalcy when my world had been shattered by the loss of a man I loved so much.

I take a sip of the beer I'm holding, not surprised to find it's gone lukewarm in the overheated house.

Pops, I could use a bit of guidance here. Tell me how to help her, how to help them.

Across the room, I meet Mark's eyes and then, next to him, James's. I remember, and I know they do too. Funerals are always awful, but I'm sure this brings up some tough memories

235

for them just like it does for me. It's too close to home, too similar to Pops, too soon.

Part of me wonders if it'll always be too soon or if at some point, the years will make it more bearable.

A memory works its way to the front of my mind. The night of Pops's funeral, afterward, my brothers and I, still in our suits, headed down to the pond. We built a big campfire and sat around for hours, telling stories and reminiscing. Mama checked on us once from the porch but left us to our own little ceremony. She understood that it'd been our private way of connecting with Pops, not a public display like this.

The Tannens need that. Maybe more than my brothers and I did. We were steady, solid as a family, and we have Mama.

But they've got this wedge shoved in between them all.

Paul is some of that wedge, the mindfuck of losing a man you loved, a man you respected but a man who frustrated and disappointed you, too, throwing everything into a giant Gordian knot. It's hard to find that balance in the grief. Thinking ill of him in his passing feels like a betrayal, but he wasn't perfect. No one is.

I'm sad to say that I'm a section of that wedge too, causing strife for the brothers, but I won't change it. I love Shayanne too much, and I'm a selfish prick who wants her at any cost. Plus, she needs me.

I lift my chin at Mark, not willing to leave Shay's side as I trail along with her as she works the room.

He reads me and comes closer, and I say quietly, "Remember the night after Pops's service?" He blinks, which I take as a yes. "Can you set that up out back somewhere?"

His lips press into a thin line, but he nods. I think I see a flash of something in his eyes, pride, maybe, but it's gone too fast for me to be sure.

My brothers disappear quietly, not wanting to make a

scene and knowing that the whole damn town knows about the bad blood between the Tannens and Bennetts, even if they don't quite know why the feud exists. But we're all being watched, gossip hanging on the vine and ready to bloom, warranted or not.

Wakes are an odd thing. Some people feel a need to share their grief, sobbing and wailing in what seems to be almost more show than emotion. Others wish they could have some privacy or want to just pretend like nothing's wrong. There are as many ways to grieve as there are people on Earth, none more right or wrong, just different and as individual as each person. But somehow, the support of a circle of people is supposed to lessen the pain of the process. I'm not sure if it actually works, but it's what's always been done, so it's what we do.

Finally, slowly, the house begins to clear out as people take their leave.

Until eventually, it's just the Tannens, me, and Mama. She's in the kitchen, cleaning up empty glasses and putting the stacks of labeled casseroles in the freezer.

As Mama closes the freezer for the last time, I can feel that the truce Brody and I silently adopted today is over. It's time for me to go.

I clear my throat, looking around at the four Tannens. "I won't tell you that I know how you feel. Paul was your father. But in some ways, I've been where you are. When Pops died, it was hard." I swallow thickly, not used to talking about emotional shit, and definitely not with people I barely know and who are eyeing me like they'd just as soon beat the shit out me as listen to me share my feelings.

I look around the empty house, wondering momentarily what's going to become of it. "After everyone left, we felt like we needed something more . . . personal, private to say our goodbyes." Shayanne's breath hitches, and I pull her to my side. "My brothers and I had a campfire, told stories about Pops, and it was hard. So fucking hard, but it was good."

A tear burns at my eye, not at the loss of Paul Tannen but at the pain I know they're feeling because I felt it too. "We set up a campfire outside for y'all tonight, if you want. There's some beer and a couple of wine coolers and some crappy snacks. I don't know shit about your grief, but I know you need to heal, to huddle together and figure some shit out. Tell stories about your dad, get it all out, or just sit there silently and watch the flames. Whatever you need to do, just hold on to each other."

Brutal covers the distance between us in three strides, his jaw set and his hands clenched at his side. I'm this close to shoving Shay away in preparation for his attack when he sticks his hand out. Surprised, I shake it. "Thanks, Luke. You've been a big help these last few days."

I nod my head in appreciation, not needing accolades.

I don't expect Brody or Bobby to be nearly as kind in their goodbyes, so I focus on Shayanne. I hug her tightly, not giving a single fuck that her brothers can see, and then press a soft kiss to her forehead. "Anything you need, honey."

She nods in recognition, and I'm so damn proud of her for how fierce she is. I don't know how I ever thought she was young. Maybe in years, but she's the most responsible and mature person I think I know. Her exuberance is dampened in sadness right now, but she's resilient, and I know she'll bounce back from this.

She'll be sunshine again, someday. And I'll wait for her to shine again, help her find her light if she needs me to.

I spin her, pushing her toward Brody. Our eyes meet, my blue ones beseeching, his brown ones hard and unreadable. He licks his lips, his voice calm as the lazy creek that runs along the back stretch of our properties. "Family meeting outside."

Without another word, he turns and takes Shayanne with him. Brutal and Bobby follow with hollow eyes and uncertain frowns.

I escort Mama out, helping her into my truck so we can head home ourselves.

KNOCK-KNOCK-KNOCK.

I wake from a fitful sleep, tossing my thrashed blankets off as I try to decipher what woke me. There was a sound. A knock?

I get up and quietly step to the front of the house, toward the front door. I open it a crack, not sure who in the hell is knocking on my door.

For one, no one knocks on this door. I live in the ranch hand house, and though we don't currently have a ranch hand hired, this house is a bit free-reign, all of us coming and going at will since we've all lived here at one point or another. And two, it's the middle of the fucking night.

The porch light is blinding, and I blink until I see Shayanne standing there, surrounded in the yellow glow like a damn angel dropped down from heaven to my porch.

"Shay? Honey?" I stutter, not expecting to see her tonight. I figured she'd have had family time and then collapsed asleep, as exhausted as she must be.

She's got on pajamas, little cotton shorts with a ruffle along the hem and a sweatshirt. Her feet are hidden by fluffy Ugg boots that are stained and worn from farm life. She looks cold, from the chill in the November night air and probably from the ice inside her.

"Get in here, woman! You're going to freeze," I say, pulling her inside.

I flip on the lights to grab a blanket off the couch and wrap it around her. As the warmth of the house hits her, her teeth begin to chatter. I set her on the couch and quickly move to make her a cup of hot chocolate. I don't usually have the childhood treat in the kitchen, but Carson, our last ranch hand, loved the stuff and left almost a full box of the instant mix in the cupboard. I send him a silent thanks on the night wind.

She sips at the steaming sweetness gratefully, and I sit down beside her, pulling her into my lap. She lays her head on my shoulder and I can feel the stress and strain melting off her.

"You okay, honey?" I ask finally, not wanting to pry but worried about what sent her to my doorstep tonight. I'd hoped the campfire would be a good first step toward some healing, but maybe I was wrong. Regardless, she shouldn't be out in this cold, walking acres from her door to mine. She had to have walked because I know I didn't hear an ATV or Gator, and there are no horses outside. I would've heard any of those long before her quiet knock.

Her shrug is small, her voice smaller. "Couldn't sleep." She's quiet for a moment, then speaks again. "Funny thing is, I've never had problems sleeping when Daddy's gone. Never thought about it one way or another, but tonight, the house felt emptier somehow. Like he's not just gone for the weekend, but gone . . . forever."

Her pain kills me, sharp thorns against my skin as I curse that I can't take the heartbreak from her. I'd gladly take every bit of it if she didn't have to suffer.

I trace circles along her back, soothing and comforting her as best I can, even though it feels like it's not nearly enough. I let her decide where the conversation goes and share what she needs to.

"The campfire was good. Thank you for that," she says after another sip of hot chocolate.

"I'm glad. It was good for us. I just hoped it would help

y'all too." She's quiet, so I continue, filling the air between us with confessions that I've never shared with anyone.

"We got so drunk that night, even Mark, who can drink a horse under the table. We cried until we laughed at how pitiful we were, and we laughed at stories about Pops until happy tears came pouring out again. Eventually, we were cried out and our bellies hurt from the jostling beer and laughter. We had a service for Pops with the whole town and all that pomp and circumstance rigmarole, but that night by the campfire, that was when I said my goodbyes to him. Just his boys around a fire. I think he would've liked that."

The memory feels fresh, like it just happened. I think it's because I still feel him every day. He's in the land I live on, in the horses I work with, in my families' hearts, and in ways, big and small, in all the things we do. We learned this life by his side and live it in his honor with everything we do.

"And Mama Louise?"

I stroke her hair, shaking my head softly. "I heard crying from time to time, but Mama grieved in her own way. I do know that when she got back in the kitchen, we spent a whole week eating nothing but Pops's favorites. It was her way, I guess."

I can feel Shayanne's cheek puff up against my chest, and I realize she's smiling. Even the smallest lift in her spirits makes me feel like a fucking hero. She needs that right now, any little sparking moment of happiness I can give her.

Though I know her night with her brothers was just as personal and private as ours for Pops, she shares with me. "We didn't get drunk, though I think the boys put down that whole case of Modelo, saying they'd never had fancy beer before. I'll have to remember to thank James for that because I know it's from his private stash."

I kiss her head, humming. James did pick up a few bad

habits during his time on the rodeo circuit, fancy beer being one of them. "He was glad to help. We all are, honey."

"We talked about Daddy, though. It felt good, even though it hurt. I told them what he'd said in the hospital." She drops her voice low like Paul's. "'So damn proud of each of you, love you all with my whole heart, even if this ticker's not working right.' I think he told us all that."

"We mostly told stories about when we were kids, back when things were still . . ." Her voice cracks, and she swallows, not wanting to go there. "Back when Mom was still alive too."

She disappears into the past in her mind, though she stays in my arms, and I give her time to live in those happy memories.

"Did you know that I was supposed to be a boy?" she asks, and I shake my head. "Brody said he remembered Mom being pregnant with me, them talking about how we were going to have a house full of boys and how proud Daddy was. And then I was born . . . not a boy."

I twirl a curl of her honey waves around my finger, knowing that she's all woman even if she's a hell of a tomboy in a lot of ways.

"Apparently, he was stunned, but before he'd taken me and Mom home from the hospital, he'd gone full-princess-mode. I've seen pictures of me when I was little, always in pink and ruffles, but I figured that was Mom's doing. Apparently not, though. I remember getting the dresses so dirty when I'd play outside, wanting to keep up with all the boys. Hell, my first rifle was even pink. I thought it was because he thought I was less than the boys, somehow not as good as them with my cutesy stuff. Seems maybe I was wrong and he was glad I was a girl. *His girl.*"

Her admission that she didn't like being called 'girl' seems tragically ironic now, and I know she's seeing so many memories through a different lens with the new information she's learned about a man she thought she knew.

But can a child ever really know their parent? There's always a generational difference, and any good parent protects their child as best they can, making sure they grow up healthy and happy, knowing as little pain as possible. I wonder now whether Paul stepped away from his family in an attempt to save them from his own pain as he found a way to dull the sharp edges for himself.

Maybe my perception of Paul Tannen is askew too, colored by my own loss and his appearance when the hurt was so fresh. I know that Shayanne has so many good memories, but I was all too ready to bastardize him for the one thing he did that I disagreed with. Of course, he made the same mistake, so maybe we're all a bit culpable in this weird and needless feud between our families.

She starts to sob, and I take the mug from her hands, setting in on the coffee table. Gathering her close, I rock with her, cooing and whispering in her ear as she gets it out.

"I keep feeling like at some point, I'll be out of tears. Surely, that's true, right?" she asks, not wanting an answer. Her eyes meet mine, her voice soft and raw. "Can I sleep here tonight? I don't know if I can handle going home."

"Of course, honey," I tell her gladly because I don't know if I'd be strong enough to drive her home and drop her off to sleep alone, not when she sought me out and I'm all too willing to hold her. I pick her up in my arms, carrying her to my bed.

I've wanted this, her in my space, in my bed. But it's never happened, the nights outside too beautiful and the days too rushed. The barn and tree are our places. I wanted this under different circumstances, though. I'd imagined finally being able to have her in my bed without secrets, but not like this. Not with her in pain.

I set her on the edge of my bed, adjusting the pillows for her. "Get comfortable. Let me turn off the living room lights."

I'm gone just an instant, but when I return, I'm struck by a powerful sight. Shayanne has pulled off her sweatshirt, leaving on the matching tank top and her shorts. She's curled up in the center of my bed on her side, her hands folded beneath her cheek like an angel. Her waist dips down and her hip sways high, and the cheeks of her ass are peeking out of her shorts.

It's wrong in so many ways, but I have to adjust myself before I lie down behind her. She's just so magnificent that even broken down like this, her strength and beauty shine through.

"Can you keep the lamp on?" she asks softly, like she's embarrassed by the understandable need.

I leave it and curl up behind her, matching us along the lines of our bodies. Knees to knees, hips to hips, chest to back, and I press a kiss to the bare skin of her shoulder. She lifts her head, and I slip my arm beneath her, wrapping her in the cocoon of my embrace as she snuggles against me.

"Thank you," she whispers, like she doesn't want to break the quiet of the room.

I squeeze her in answer and she stills. I listen to her breathing, feeling each slow and steady rise and fall, waiting for her body to finally relax into sleep before I allow myself to succumb.

"Luke?" she says on an exhale.

"Yeah?" I rumble against her back.

"Can you . . ." she starts and then stops. "I mean . . . never mind."

I open my arms, rolling her to her back so I can see her pretty face in the shadows of the room. "What, Shay?" I ask gently, running my thumb along her cheekbone as I cup her face. "What do you need?"

Her eyes are glittery, tears and pain and love all mingling

with the hazel swirls of green, brown, and grey. "Can you make me forget for a minute? Just take all the pain away?"

It takes two breaths for her meaning to sink in. "Honey, are you sure? We don't . . . I don't think that's—"

She cuts me off, putting a finger to my lips. "Please."

Her plea is my undoing. I press the softest feather of a kiss to her mouth and she moves her lips beneath mine. She tastes salty like the tears she's been crying. I move to lay a line of kisses along her jaw toward her ear. "Tell me if you need to stop, honey. But I'll make you feel good. I'll make you forget as long as I can."

Her sigh is one of relief and gratitude. I consider pressing her hands to the mattress and just worshipping her body, but she needs the freedom to do anything she desires. This is for her, and if she needs to touch me, I'll happily take her fingers dancing along my skin.

I move the tiny strap of her tank top, kissing my way down her chest, tasting and loving every inch of her as I expose more and more. Her nipple is hard, the pink areola already pulled tight to the air of the cool room. Shay moans, her hands delving into my hair and holding me to her.

I let a hand trace down the curve of her side, squeezing the flesh at her hip in question. She bucks beneath me, seeking more. I slip into her sleep shorts and then beneath her panties, sliding my thumb along her seam. She's not even wet yet, not like how she usually is for me, and I groan at the velvety feel of her soft skin.

"Shay," I growl in warning, needing to make sure she's okay with this. Or at least as okay as she can be right now. One of her hands drops to my forearm, holding me to her, and she works her hips against me, using me to chase her own pleasure.

"Fuck, honey." I can feel her wetness growing, finally

coating my fingers like she always does, and I spread it to her clit.

I let her nipple go with a soft pop and lift up to see her face. Slowly, I circle her clit, watching as she begins to keen for me. Her brows pull together, and she's muttering, "Yes, yes, yes," over and over. I move faster, knowing what she needs to get there but drawing it out, giving her as much distraction and peace as I can.

It may not be right, probably some degree of gross misconduct to fuck her on the night of her father's funeral, but I get it. It's cleansing, a rain of pleasure to wash the hurt away, even if it's only for a moment.

"Luke, please," she begs.

I move over her, covering her with my body as she spreads her legs for me. One hand on either side of her head, I press into her slowly as I stare into her eyes, not wanting to add to her pain. I begin to move, inch by inch, retreating and then filling her as she grips me so tightly. Her lashes flutter as her eyes roll back in her head.

"Nu-uh, keep your eyes open. Look at me, Shay. Stay here with me, honey, in this moment right here," I tell her, and her eyes pop open. They're bloodshot, but I can see my woman in their depths, the strength she always shows falling away for me. Only for me. With me, she's vulnerable, she's soft, and I'll protect that sweet innocence inside her at all costs.

Even if it's by giving her a rough fucking that will take her mind off everything outside these four walls and our writhing bodies.

I stroke into her harder, my hips slamming into hers as I keep the slow pace that will drive her wild with need. Each thrust damn near shoves her up the bed, and she lets go of the grip she has on my back to press her hands to the headboard above her for leverage. The air hits my skin, and I hiss, feeling the raw spots where I know she's left half-moon-shaped marks along my spine.

She cries out, and I lick my thumb before slipping it between us. I massage her clit in strokes that match the pounding of my cock inside her.

"Come for me, honey. Feel everything about this moment — your sweet pussy squeezing me tight, my cock rock hard inside you, your hard clit pearling up for me, your tits bouncing with every stroke. Feel me loving you, right now and forever." My words are growled vibrations through gritted teeth as I try to hang on for her.

Thankfully, she detonates beneath me, her cry coming from her soul, loud and cathartic. "There you go, honey. Keep going, keep coming for me," I tell her, keeping my punishing pace as she rides the first orgasm into another. I fly then, meeting her in the dark abyss of pleasure.

I am deeply, completely, utterly lost in the sea of her. Before, I'd felt like she was taking me on a roller coaster, but now it feels more like riding the waves of the ocean. Sometimes fierce and wildly untamed in its up and down swells, sometimes softly lapping at the sandy foundation of shore but always constant in the way it surrounds and fills me.

That's my Shayanne.

With a shudder, she comes back to life. There are tears tracking down into her hair, and I wipe them away gently. "Shayanne?" I ask, my voice hoarse from my own cries of pleasure.

She nods. "I'm good. Thank you. I . . ." Her voice trails off as she gives me the barest hint of a smile, reassuring me that she's okay. As okay as she can be after everything that's happened the last few days, but definitely all right after what we just did.

This was different. Not quite fucking, not quite making

love. Therapy, solace, a life-affirming connection, a way to feel something other than loss.

Soft now, my cock leaves the warm heaven of her. I turn her back to her side, wrapping my arms back around her in a cocoon once more. "Get some sleep, honey. I love you," I tell her, burying my nose in her hair to press a kiss to her crown.

"I love you, too," she sighs.

Within minutes, she's asleep. Her breathing is a steady hum in the dark room, but it's a long time before I fall asleep too.

CHAPTER 22

SHAYANNE

*W*aking up in Luke's bed is everything I'd dreamed it'd be when I set out in the November chill last night. It's warm and safe, a haven against the storm roiling in my heart and through my family.

But the bright light of morning invades the sweetness of my escape into his arms, into his bed.

Time to rise and grind. Pull up your big girl panties and get shit done.

Except I don't have on panties. Or shorts, or anything else, for that matter. Luke's naked body is pressed to my back, and I remember last night, how sweet and caring he was, how far he was willing to go to make me feel better.

I'd seen the uncertainty in his eyes when I begged him to make me forget for a moment, and I'd seen the moment he gave in. Not for himself, but for me. His gaze had been heavy on me the whole time, his blue eyes never leaving my face as he searched for my every reaction, ready to give me whatever I needed.

God, I love this man. And just as importantly, he loves me. It feels unreal, but also the most real thing I've ever experienced. He's my anchor as the world churns around me, and I snuggle back into him, wanting the harbor that only he can offer me, wanting to pretend that tragedy isn't lurking outside the door for just a little bit longer.

His morning wood presses against my back, and I grind my ass against him, tempting him, teasing myself. Seems the dam's broken, and I can't get enough. He groans in his sleep, hips surging forward, and I shudder, ready for the escape he can give me again.

His hand tightens on my hip, squeezing me hard enough to stop my movement. "Shayanne."

His voice is rough and deep with sleep, a note of warning threading through the drawled syllables of my name. He pulls us together, not a breath of space between us, his cock sandwiched against the fullness of my ass.

"Honey, use me anyway you need to," he growls in my ear, "anytime, always. But I think you need to get home before your family comes stomping over here, shotguns ready, to find you naked in my bed, impaled on my cock."

My eyes flutter open and I realize how bright it is in the room. I'd studiously avoided thoughts of what time it might be, what I might be missing at home, and what responsibilities I'm shirking by skipping out into the night. His words drive me mad with want, but he's right.

I sigh, sagging in his arms, and he rolls me to my back, watching me lovingly. His fingers dance along my hairline, smoothing the riotous mess of tangles I rock every morning. I should probably be embarrassed by the wild hair, puffy eyes, and morning breath, but Luke's quiet eyes tell me he still thinks I'm beautiful. Even broken and weak as I am now.

"What do you want, honey?" he asks, letting me make the decision for myself. It's another thing to love about this man. He sees my strength even when I don't. He knows my most vulnerable parts, is probably the only person who truly does, and he gently cares for them while never making me feel like that's all I am.

I blink slowly, digging deep and finding the core of steel that's trying damn hard to crack. But I refuse to fail my brothers, not when they need me. "I need to go home."

Luke's kiss is unexpected. He has zero cares about my breath or his own, both of which could probably wilt an oak tree and together are evilly potent. But it's raw and real, the soft support I need. When he pulls back, there's a light in his eyes like he's proud of me. "There's my woman. Let's get you home so you can handle your shit."

He stands up, and I mourn the loss of his warmth in the bed. His cock juts out from his body, drawing my eye even though I just agreed with him that I need to go. His big, rough hands cover the goods and he tsks lightly. "Ma'am, are you ogling me?" His teasing tone is just what I need to break the somber spell I'm under. A small smile tentatively breaks across my face, feeling foreign when he jokes, "Just a piece of meat to some people."

He grabs for my hand, pulling me to stand before picking me up in his arms and carrying me to the bathroom, setting me back on my feet but letting me slide down his body. He cups my face in his palms, his face serious. "Honey, just know that you're always beautiful to me," he says cryptically before kissing my forehead, and my brows knit together in confusion.

"Huh?"

He spins me in place and I see my reflection in the mirror over the sink.

Oh, shit.

I'd figured I was a mess, but I didn't realize that I never took off the makeup I wore for the funeral. It's now trailing in dried black rivers down my face and smudged to the side in a wash of dirty specks. Waterproof, my ass.

"Luke Bennett, why didn't you tell me I look like the before in a waterproof mascara commercial?" I'm already scrubbing beneath my eyes after licking my fingers, figuring spit's better than nothing. "Shit, I might as well be a damn raccoon."

Luke's unsuccessfully trying to hold back a smile. "Like I said, always beautiful." He opens a drawer, and it's a veritable cornucopia of feminine hygiene products, everything from face masks to tampons and enough ponytailers to tie up an entire cheer squad. "Is any of this what you need?"

I grab for a makeup remover wipe and glare at him. "Do I want to know whose shit this is?" Jealousy is hot and sour in my blood and apparent in my biting question.

Luke's smile grows, no longer restrained. "It's Sophie's, honey. Can I tell you a secret?"

The slight reassurance that it's Sophie's and not some one-night-stand concierge drawer soothes me . . . slightly. I nod, not sure I want to hear it if it's got anything to do with who else Luke's been friendly with.

"You're the first woman to ever sleep in that bed with me." He says it straight-faced though I'm sure he's lying through his perfect white teeth. I narrow my eyes, looking for the tell. But what I see is a slight pink hue tinting his cheeks. He's embarrassed but apparently, he's telling the truth.

I must look shocked, because he lifts my chin with one thick finger. "To be clear, I'm not a saint, but I never wanted anyone in my space before. The barn and my home, they're my sanctuary, you know?"

"And now?" I press, not caring in the least that I sound like a needy, greedy bitch.

He steps closer, capturing me between the vanity and his body. "Now, I want you everywhere. My barn, my bed, hell, around Mama's dining room table." For a cowboy like Luke, that's serious. If he wants to take you home to his mama, you're this close to walking down the aisle.

Goosebumps pop out on my bare flesh and he brushes his

calloused fingers along them. "Know what else?" I swallow, shaking my head. "Jealousy looks good on you, honey. But you've got no reason to be, ever." He hunches over, breath hot in my ear, and whispers, "I love you, Shayanne Tannen."

No way am I letting that go to waste.

I hop up on the vanity to get at cock-level, ready to go. Not for an escape this time but because I want this. Us. Luke squeezes my hips, helping me get situated on the edge of the thankfully sturdy sink cabinet.

This man is going to be the death of me.

The errant thought is a common turn of phrase, but *'death'* stops me in my tracks as the rest of the world hits me like a freight train. I freeze, and Luke's eyes narrow. "Shay?"

I shake my head, trying to smile. "Sorry. My mind ran away for a second, but I'm here. I'm good."

He pulls me to him, my cheek hitting his chest and his hands tangling in my hair. The mood between us shifts, cooling but deep like ocean waters. "I think it'll always happen. Something will be an unexpected trigger, and it'll remind you. It happens a lot at first, less as time goes on. And you get better at not letting it define the moment. Now, I can see something that makes me think of Pops and it's not a fresh stabbing pain. It's more like a soothing hand on my shoulder. Does that make sense?"

I nod against him, as comforted as if he'd wiped away fresh tears though none come. I guess I'm all cried out after the last few days. Instead, he takes the makeup wipe from my hand and gently dabs it along my face and under my eyes, cleaning up the mess.

He tosses the wipe in the trash and hands me a scrunchie. "Sophie's." Then he opens another drawer and hands me a packaged toothbrush, like you'd get at a hotel. "For the ranch hands who sometimes come through."

He smirks knowingly, and I should feel embarrassed by my

jealous outburst, but instead, he makes it seem cute and adorable.

He leaves me to it, disappearing only to come back dressed in jeans, a flannel work shirt, and boots. He looks damn good, I'll admit, but nothing tops a naked Luke.

Except maybe me, I think, forcing my brain back to more pleasant thoughts. Being on top becomes a new adventure on the list of things I want to do, see, try, and experience.

He's got my pajamas plus a pair of his sweatpants in his hands. "It's too chilly out for you to go back in shorts," he says, a gentle reminder that I'd been close to freezing last night by the time I got to his door. But it'd been a distant discomfort, nothing compared to the pain in my heart.

I nod, not arguing and he seems relieved, like he'd expected me to put up a fight about it.

Once I'm ready, he leads me over to the barn. "Figured we could ride to your house?" I nod and he gets Duster saddled up quickly, his movements efficient from years of practice.

I stand back, enjoying the grace of his body as he works and letting the calm of the animals soak into my soul as I scratch Demon's cheeks and nuzzle his nose for kisses.

Luke looks over and shakes his head, a twitch to his lips. "Damn horse whisperer."

It's a compliment of the utmost degree from him.

He climbs up and holds out a hand to help me up. Sitting behind him, I lean in, pressing my breasts to his back and wrapping my arms around his waist. He pats my hand comfortingly, though it seems more to reassure himself that I'm secure than anything. I like that he cares for me without smothering me. It feels . . . good . . . different . . . empowering.

Outside, the chill hits me even with Luke as a windbreak. I can see Duster's hot breath misting in the fall morning air. But it's beautifully sunny, miles of green and gold as far as the eye can see.

The clop-clop of Duster's hooves is the only sound as my heart slows to match the slow, undulating walk. And for a precious moment, I feel . . . peace.

As soon as our homestead appears, that serenity evaporates on the wind. Brody is in the goat pen, tossing out their morning feed, his eyes burning through Luke and me as we approach on Duster.

Luke lowers a hand to my thigh, rubbing soothingly without a word. There's a question in the caress, too.

What do you want me to do?

"I've got this. I ain't scared of Brody. Only problem is, he ain't scared of me neither. But he should be," I reply softly, ready for war.

He's going to have to get used to this. He has to because I need him and I need Luke. I don't ask for much in this life, but right now, I'm asking any damn power that's listening to make Brody see reason in this.

I see Luke's nod of agreement out of the corner of my eye because I'm laser-locked on Brody, a challenge and a dare in my hard glare. He pulls his hat off, curling the already rounded brim a bit more before jamming it back on his head angrily.

I climb down off Duster, patting his haunch in appreciation of the ride, and Luke follows suit, doing the same.

"G'morning, Brody," I say, nice as apple pie. Well, maybe cinnamon-apple pie, because while I let my usual sweetness shine, there's a hint of spice beneath the warmth.

He grunts in response, his eyes dark as onyx as they sweep down my nightwear outfit. I swear I can see the thoughts stumbling through his mind right now.

Luke tries too, holding out his hand. "Brody."

Brody drops his eyes to Luke's outstretched hand but then

255

holds his up, showing that his hands are covered in feed dust. "Bennett."

He's sticking with last names, apparently. I'd bet that even if his hands were clean, he wouldn't shake Luke's right now.

Feeling like that's as good as it's going to get, I take Luke's hand. "I'll call you later, 'kay?"

He wraps his arms around my shoulders and I enjoy the softly worn flannel at his ridged belly. I feel the gentle press of his lips to my forehead. "Anytime, honey. Love you."

I glance up to see that though he's speaking to me, he hasn't taken his eyes off Brody. He's expecting a sucker punch, I'm guessing. Eye on the threat and all that.

"Love you too."

With that, Luke steps back and climbs onto Duster. With a two-fingered wave, he starts to ride away. After a few dozen yards, he lets Duster loose and they begin a quick gallop. At Duster's age, he can't hold that pace for long, but it probably feels good to be a little wild, for both horse and rider.

I turn back to Brody to see his mouth is pressed in a flat line.

"Brody," I start.

He shakes his head. "Don't want to hear it, Shayanne. We've got enough shit to do. Gotta catch up from your playing hooky this morning." He says it distastefully, like the thought is bitter.

I sigh, resigned. "Fine. I'm going inside to eat breakfast and get to work on some paperwork."

"He didn't even feed you breakfast?" Brody snaps. "Asshole."

"He didn't feed me breakfast because he knew I needed to get home," I retort. "It was because he cares, not because he was being an asshole. Though it seems like you're an expert on the topic of assholery."

The comment is acidic, but it pours from my mouth automatically. It's not our usual teasing but real and painful.

I stomp toward the house, hating this. I don't want tension and anger between us, but I don't know how to fix it. Not and get everything I want, everything I need.

CHAPTER 23

SHAYANNE

a quick shower washes the grit out of my eyes and the fire out of my attitude, both of which should be a good thing. Instead, as I dry off, I feel raw and sullen.

Looking at myself in the mirror, I attempt a pep talk.

Time to cowboy up, Shayanne. Find your power, step back into your role, and get done what needs gettin' done. Take care of yourself and take care of the family.

My chest lifts with the air I force into my lungs. I hold it until it's uncomfortable, fighting to feel, wanting to live. With a whoosh, it lets loose, and I feel somehow reinvigorated at the reminder that I have a life to live, a job to do, and I'd best get to it. Ain't no one else gonna do it, that's for damn sure.

We've all got our role to play.

I pull on jeans and a flannel shirt, rolling the sleeves up as a sign of my intention to work. Murphy whines as I make my way down the hall, and I can't help but pause long enough to scratch behind his ears. "Sorry, boy. I've got to do this . . . now or never."

I stop at the doorway to Daddy's room, though, frozen in the empty space.

His bed is made, the navy comforter pulled up and the two pillows, one dented from his head and the other puffy from lack of use, laid neatly against the headboard. The closet door is open, showing the carefully sorted sections of dress shirts, work shirts, and pressed jeans. His cowboy hat hangs on a hook on the wall. We'd wanted to bury him in it, a true picture of how he looked every day, but it hadn't fit right in the casket.

The thought is painful, bringing up the memory of him laid out in the satin-lined box. He'd looked peaceful, and I'd pretended he was just sleeping. I still want to pretend he's just on an overnight trip to the casino.

But he's not.

With shaking hands, I take the hat off the hook and settle it on my head. It's too big, but it fits better now than the last time I wore it. I couldn't have been more than twelve or thirteen then.

I'm in the passenger seat of Daddy's old truck, the too-loud single cab with a bench seat, worn vinyl covered by a quilted moving blanket. The windows are down and the wind blows loudly, whipping my loose hair into my face, tying it in knots. Daddy takes his hat off, dropping it on my head. I give him a thankful smile, flashing teeth too big for my still-young face. I feel safe, loved, and special to get to go into town with him today while the boys work at home.

Back in the present, I run a finger along the worn rim of the felt hat. That memory had been shortly before Mom got sick and Daddy disappeared on us, not literally but figuratively.

With a bit of time and some different points of view from the funeral, I can see Daddy a little differently now. I've been mad for so long, frustrated and disillusioned when he fell off the pedestal I'd put him on.

But the truth is, he was just a man, with both strengths and flaws, multi-faceted and in pain over the unexpected path his life took.

Grimly, I tell the room, "I love you, Daddy."

There's no answering rustle of the curtains or cool breeze to let me know he heard me, and that disappoints me. He might not be here now, not in the room, not in this world, but he left me with something meaningful. Work and a work ethic, family and love.

I move to the desk where I sit and pay bills every month. This time, there's more to be done. So much more. Mama Louise wrote me a list of how to handle someone's estate and make sure we address everything that needs to be checked off before we see the lawyer. At least Daddy had a will. After Mom died, he made sure to take care of that for us.

I check my notebook, reading the bulleted list I wrote as Mama Louise handed out advice from her voice of experience. She'd been such a help planning Daddy's service. I don't know how to thank someone for that. Anything I can think of seems piddly in light of the load she helped us carry.

The next hours pass in a blur.

I log into the bank accounts on the old computer, checking and double-checking that everything's been paid on time and the scheduled transactions are all correct. I go through old files and discover a small insurance policy I didn't know about, so I shoot off an email to see if it's still valid. I find an old metal box in the bottom drawer, but when I open it half-expecting to find tools, I discover a stack of old photographs.

I thumb through them, seeing pictures of Mom and Daddy, of each of us kids as babies, of animals long since gone. I wonder if Daddy flipped through these and how he selected these pictures for this box because they're from a mish-mash of years and not in any order I can discern. Finally, I put the pictures back in the box, telling myself that I should go through those with the boys, together. With a hand laid on the closed lid, I take a steadying breath, thankful for a moment that there are no more tears left in me.

LAUREN LANDISH

I return to my digging, checking each file folder and letting my fingers trace over the ones with Mom's looping cursive and Daddy's block print. Their handwriting was as different as they were, soft and sweet and hard and gruff, but they were in perfect balance.

I'm struck again by how hard it must've been for him to lose Mom. All of the people telling me how much I look like her come back to mind, and I wonder if I was a good reminder of her or a painful one.

Dinner is quiet and tense, the four of us taking our usual spots around the table. We've had dinner without Daddy sitting in his place at the head of the table countless times, but it still feels different now.

There's a void instead of a vacancy, the distinction subtle but definite.

"I went through Daddy's desk today, made sure everything's on track," I tell the boys, breaking the awkward silence of us passing serving platters of food around the table. I made another pot roast today, knowing that I'd likely be tied up all day, but I did make Brody's favorite sourdough rolls as an olive branch. He's got two on his plate already, so hopefully, that's a good sign.

"I found a box of pictures I thought we could go through together," I continue, not getting any response. "Doesn't have to be tonight, but sometime, you know?"

Bruce lifts his eyes from his plate, looking supportive. "That'd be nice, but maybe not yet."

It's not a question, and his eyes flick from me to Brody and back like he's trying to read the airwaves between us to see what's not being said.

"Yeah, sure, of course," I say agreeably. I turn to Brody,

262

not letting him ride beneath the radar any longer. "I found paperwork on a safety deposit box at the bank, too. You know anything about that?"

Forced into a corner by the direct question, he grinds his jaw. "Nope." He pops the P, dismissively ending that line of conversation, but he adds a shrug of one shoulder.

"Figured I'd go to town tomorrow and see what's in it, but I'm betting you'll have to go too, seeing as you're the oldest. Think you can get away from the critters for a bit to go?"

"Guess it depends on whether I have to do your chores or not." His voice is flat and emotionless, which hurts more than if he were yelling and stomping.

Brody isn't the hothead people sometimes think he is. He's just a rough old country boy. But one thing he never is is apathetic. You'd never know that right now, though, because it's as if he's looking straight through me and couldn't be bothered to care.

"I said I was sorry for missing breakfast this morning. I'll be here to make your damn biscuits and fry your bacon tomorrow." My voice is loud, making up for Brody's quiet.

He flinches the tiniest bit at my words but holds his eyes steady on mine as we enter some battle of wills like we're kids again.

It's Bobby's choked voice that makes me lose focus. "You were gone, Shayanne. We didn't know where you were, not really, though we guessed. But you were *gone*."

And like a lightning bolt shot down through the sky to my heart, I realize something hard. We all just lost our father. I mean, I knew that, of course. But was I too tied up in my own loss to really consider theirs?

They lost their father too. And the first morning without parents, they woke up to find me gone, our family routine broken, our circle untied.

Guilt runs through me.

Brody has held us together so well and for so long, putting his own hopes and dreams on hold for us, and I'm sure he's afraid I'm gonna leave him like Mom and Dad did. Bruce has this farm and his oversensitive heart that's hidden by an exterior that scares the shit out people before he's even said a word. And Bobby is the brother who escapes into a world of his own making, just him and a guitar, bringing the music he hears in his head to life.

They needed me. Not to make breakfast but to be there for them. To be the glue, just like Mom was. And I wasn't.

"I'm sorry, guys," I say softly, meeting each of their eyes. "I was selfish, didn't think of what it would be like for you this morning. I couldn't sleep and so I just went . . ." I glance out the window to the setting sun, the pinks and oranges painting the sky as darkness chases them down the horizon. "I should've told you."

"You could've come to me," Brody says. It's a huge admission on his part, not an olive branch but a whole damn tree, tied up in a question of where my loyalties lie.

I look back to him, feeling Bruce's and Bobby's eyes on me, waiting to see if we'll get this sorted out.

"Brody, you are an amazing brother and a great leader for this family," I start.

He interrupts, his voice tight and his jaw hard. "I sense there's a *but* coming."

I smile wanly, shaking my head. "*And*, I have never wanted to do anything but be by your side and care for this family. Not really. I think I honestly never considered that there might be more for me, you know?"

His slow blink tells me he understands that, at least.

I know he always dreamed of taking over this farm, of being the next generation to love this land, but surely, he had other dreams too? A wife, a family, a trip around the world? But he got stuck here sure as I did, never seeing a way out or a different path. It doesn't mean we don't love our lives, but maybe that we can still think fondly of the other paths we might've taken.

"I still want this—this life, this land, this family." I can feel the relief in the air around us, so it's hard to continue.

"But I want something else too. Luke Bennett. And he wants me. He lets me be vulnerable, soft, a woman, I guess. But he holds me up and tells me that I can do anything. And so I pick myself right back up, dust the dirt off, and handle our shit. I need both. I can be both. But you have to let me. Please, Brody . . . let me be your sister, a part of this family, and a woman in love with the boy next door."

It's my line in the sand.

It has to be.

I don't know what I'll do if he says no. I can't foresee losing either of them, my family or Luke. I don't want to imagine it.

He growls, getting up from the table to pace, twisting his hat in his hands. Bruce and Bobby meet my eyes, sadness already swirling in their dark depths.

"You know what Dad said when I went back there to see him that first time?" He doesn't wait for us to answer but continues in a ramble more similar to my chatterbox style than his own usually measured speech. "He was lucid, and he was mad as a hornet's nest. Damn near spitting as he ranted about the Bennetts and how they were stealing you away." He drops his voice, mimicking Dad's. "Sneaky sons of bitches, turning my girl to their side."

He looks me squarely in the eye and in his own baritone says, "It was damn near his deathbed wish that you never be with Luke Bennett, Shayanne."

I gasp, the pain of that truth unexpectedly sharp. "Brody!"

His decision could be a declaration of war between us, but I can feel his hesitation, the barest hint of hope. His heart is hard and unyielding, though, at least for now as indecision pushes us to the limit. The proverbial rock and hard place have nothing on us.

His breath heaves, chest rising and falling too fast, and his shoulders are hunched up to his ears. I can see the toll this is taking on him, the weight of the world bearing down on him, and though I feel a bit guilty about it, I'm not trying to make his life harder.

I'm just trying to live mine too.

He licks his lips, the verdict on the tip of his tongue, but then he swallows and turns. The back door opens and then slams shut. Even through the solid wood, I can hear his choked, "Fuck!"

It hurts so fucking bad.

But he didn't say no.

It's not that I need his permission or blessing, but I can feel the fierce pulling along the seams of my heart, poison leeching into our family connection by my announcement that I want more.

But it doesn't have to be this way.

I desperately want it to not be like this. And though it's wrong to speak ill of the dead, I don't feel the least bit guilty for thinking that this is all Daddy's fault. He stirred up this hornet's nest, created this bad blood for no good goddamn reason, and we're the ones to pay for his stubborn as a mule, stupid pride.

I'm the one to pay.

With my heart broken either way . . . by my family or by losing Luke.

CHAPTER 24

LUKE

"Saw your girl a few minutes ago. She said to tell you hello."

Mama's voice is calm and no-nonsense, coming from the doorway to my stall-turned-office. I look up to find her watching me with a steady gaze, but when I meet her eyes, she glances around.

"Haven't been out here in awhile. Like what you've done with the place."

I follow her line of sight, seeing the awards Mark nailed up on the far wall. I nod, one corner of my mouth tilting up a little. "Mark hung up 'em up. I ain't bragging or nothing. Probably did it more to give me hell than anything."

Her eyes snap back, shaking her head. "He's proud of you. You might be humble, but he brags on his famous horse breeding and training brother about as much as he does his famous bull riding brother."

I know as well as she does that Mark likes to give James as much shit as he can, but to anyone else, he only has pride for our youngest brother. That he says the same things about me is . . . something. Surprising? Reassuring? I'm not sure of the label, but it feels good. I know that, at least.

Like a true cowboy, I change the subject to avoid any emotional shit. "You say you saw Shay?"

Mama nods, knowing exactly what I'm doing but allowing it anyway. "I did. She said to tell you hello," she repeats, but there's a question in the tone this time.

I swallow, revealing what Mama likely already knows. "She was coming over every night after dinner and going back to make breakfast and get to work for the day. But she hasn't come over the last couple of nights. Said she was beat after making her pies and just needed to crash."

I'd offered to help make or deliver pies. Hell, I'd told her to cancel the orders if that's what she needed to do. People would understand, considering the turmoil their family's going through. But she'd said the distraction was a good thing.

And there's been a lot of distraction needed.

Distraction from her and Brody still being at odds, dancing around each other in an awkward politeness that's killing her.

Distraction from Brutal and Bobby stepping back and letting Brody and Shay figure out their shit. Though having Brutal on her side is a salve, at least, and Bobby is hanging out in town more than at home, Shay says.

Distraction from a stack of papers they'd found in a safe deposit box that seemed to be Paul's ledger of wins and losses, monies collected and owed. She'd even found documents of another bank account she hadn't known about, but with the lawyer's help, she and Brody transferred those funds into the household account.

Distraction from the loss of her dad, the man he was and the mythical creature she still sometimes thought he was or could be.

So she's spent the last few days in her kitchen, whipping up her smashed pumpkin pies for holiday deliveries, running herself ragged, and not wanting or allowing any help.

Mama's lips purse thoughtfully. "She dropped off my holiday order, so that makes sense. Just so you know, I invited the Tannens to Thanksgiving." She says it casually, like it's not a damn bomb.

Meanwhile, my eyes damn near bug out of their sockets. "Not sure that's a good idea, Mama." Understatement of the fucking century, and I should get an award for the steadiness of my voice.

I can picture the food fight now, and I know it'd turn to blows. Three on three ain't bad odds, except one of their three is Bruce 'Brutal' Tannen, who I once saw take on an entire offensive line single-handedly, so it's more like five on three. And I'm not feeling good about that.

Mama's eyes sparkle and an evilly sweet smile lifts her lips. It's like a wolf's challenge in sheep's clothing. "Which is exactly why I didn't ask for your opinion, nor did I need your permission. I'm simply informing you of what I've already done so you can plan accordingly. Understood?"

Properly put in my place, I nod. "Yes, ma'am." After a pause to let the unspoken apology of my dropped chin and shrug sink in, I ask, "Did she say yes?"

Mama's smile is truly kind now, and she nods. "Of course, she did! Think she's gonna tell an old woman no? Pshaw."

She makes a dismissive sound as if no one would consider telling her no. Funny thing is, she's absolutely right. No one would dare to tell Louise Bennett no about a damn thing, at least not and live to tell about it.

The fight imagery is still on my mind, but I'll admit that I like the idea of Shayanne sitting next to me at Mama's table. We haven't done that, and with it being a holiday, it feels even more weighted with importance.

I must smile or make some unconscious movement of excitement because Mama shoots a hard tap at my chest with the back of her hand. "This isn't for you, Son, much as I do like to make you boys happy. This is for those kids, so you'll be on your best behavior. For me, for Shayanne, and for her brothers. Or I'll kick you out before you get any smashed pumpkin pie."

I can't help but tease back. "I can probably get pie from Shayanne if you kick me out."

"Don't be talking about a girl's pie with me, young man. I'm your mama and don't need to know a bit about that." Her hands are on her hips, but there's an undercurrent of laughter to the words.

Holy shit, Mama just made a joke . . . about my sex life. At least, I think that's what she's teasing about. My brows shoot up my forehead in surprise and question.

"Don't go looking so surprised, Luke Bennett. I loved your Pops and he loved me too. Wanna hear a secret?" she asks. I shake my head so hard my brain damn near rattles around, not wanting to hear this in the least. But she winks and tells me anyway. "It's not like we only did it three times in the dark to get you boys."

I shove my fingers in my ears, scrunching up my face. "La-la-la-la. Nope, don't want to hear that."

Her laughter is bright and loud as she bends over, hands on her knees like she can't catch her breath.

"Good lord, sometimes you boys are so easy." She laughs while I stare, slack-jawed and horrified. Eventually, she rights herself, though her breath is still a bit wheezy. "Seriously, though, this is their first holiday without either parent and it's bound to be a tough one. I don't know what they did after Martha passed, but I'm going to make this one a bit easier if I can. You'd best be on good behavior."

Her narrowed eyes brook no argument. "Yes, ma'am."

She pats my chest nicely this time before heading out the open main door and back to the house. She's got on tennis shoes, so I'm guessing she's spending some time in her garden today.

She's the epitome of work-till-you-die stock, and they don't much make them like her anymore. She's worked every day of her life since she was a teen, waitressing, ranching, and mothering our motley crew. I know she's looking forward to grandmothering James and Sophie's little one as soon as it makes an appearance.

As soon as the barn's quiet, I hear the side door open.

"Coast clear?" I hear a disembodied whisper.

I chuckle. "Yeah, Mama's gone. What the hell are you up to? Watching to make sure the coast is clear?"

James comes into view around the corner, Mark behind him.

James plops down in the chair on the other side of my desk, instantly lifting his feet to set his dirty boots on the wooden surface. Mark sets a big hand on either side of the doorframe, blocking us in.

Though I asked James, Mark answers my question. "We saw Mama heading over here and thought we'd make sure everything was okay without getting in the way."

"You mean you didn't want her to make a target outta you too."

He grunts, which I take as agreement.

James claps, leaning back more so that only the back two chair legs are on the floor. "So spill. What's Mama up to now? We also saw Shayanne stop by, so I know there's something going on. Mama works in mysterious ways, but sometimes, she's about as transparent as a glass window." He points a thick finger my way and then Mark's. "And if you tell her I said that, you're a dead man."

I almost look behind him with wide eyes to make him think

Mama is back and overheard his mouthiness, which is one of James's favorite pranks to pull, but I don't have it in me right now.

I shake my head, swallowing my concern. "She invited the Tannens to Thanksgiving."

I might as well have set off a bomb in the room, which is the proper reaction to that news.

"Shiiiiiit," James drawls out in a hiss.

"Fuck." That bark of reaction to damn near everything bad is totally Mark.

I nod. "I know. She warned me that she's doing this for them and that we'd better be on our best behavior."

I'm quiet for a moment, looking at my hands as I pick at a ragged cuticle. "Can I tell you something, though?" I look up to find two pairs of blue eyes, bright as the summer sky and so similar to my own, staring back at me. "I'm kinda excited about it. For Shayanne, at least. I like the idea of her having holiday dinner with us."

James smiles, but Mark frowns, their reactions as different as the men they've become, even if they do bear a striking family resemblance. We all do.

"I get why you'd feel that way. If anyone understands wanting to be with your girl twenty-four seven, it's me," Mark says humorlessly because he's literally not kidding in the slightest about how he feels about Katelyn. "But Shayanne's a package deal, Luke. The Tannen brother drama isn't quite finished, so don't go making problems for her. You want her, but they need her."

"I need her too," I argue, "and she needs me."

Mark sighs and looks up at the exposed rafters, running his hands through his hair like he's searching for something in his mind. "Imagine if James had brought home a girl we hated on sight, some prissy gold-digging bitch who didn't understand our family ways and wanted to take him away from us. How would we have felt about a woman like that?"

"Hey!" James balks, "Sophie ain't like that!"

Mark barely blinks. "Ain't talking about Sophie. You know we love her more than we love you, asshole."

James grins and nods, knowing it's partially true. What can I say? Sophie's a hell of a woman.

Back to me, he says, "What would we have thought—done —to make him see sense?"

"Anything," I answer, not seeing his point.

"To them, that's you." I start to mouth off, but he holds up a staying hand. "They've been tainted against you by Paul, plus, you travel the whole world. You're this fancy-schmancy horse-man, not a ranch or farm-working hand like the rest of us. It ain't your fault, but I reckon that's how they see you. Like a snake oil salesman who's selling their baby sister on a life of ease far away from them."

"That's not what I'm trying to do. I mean, I'll admit that I've thought about taking her with me on trips because this long stretch home isn't my norm, but we haven't even talked about that. I know this is her home. Hell, it's my home too." I shake my head and get up to pace, replaying conversations in my head and seeing them in a new light. "And I mean, I've tried to make things easier on her, on all of them, really, by helping out any way I can. But that's just what I do. I wanna help."

My voice trails off, and Mark grunts as he puts a heavy hand on my shoulder. "You do help. We all know that," he says pointedly, and I think again how wrong I was about my role here on the ranch. I've never been invisible, not to them, and it was only my own misguided perception that made me think I was. "Just make sure they see that too. Hell, Brody is about as upfront as you can get. Just tell him outright that you love

Shayanne and want to marry her and have a whole litter of honey-haired kids running around their property, right where they belong. It'd probably ease his nerves considerably."

He grins so big his rarely-spotted dimple pops out on his cheek.

Holy fuck.

That sends a shock through my system. But not a bad one. No, not bad at all. I imagine a whole herd of little girls with Shayanne's waves and my blue eyes, each with a goat in their arms.

James's laughter brings me back to Earth. "Ooh, boy, did you see his face? He went all dreamy and shit. Fuckin' *Hallmark* movie special in there," he says, tapping his temple.

I narrow my eyes and shove his shitkickers off my desk, but he's still chuckling. To Mark, I say, "Sounds like you're trying to get me killed by Brody Tannen and kicked out from Mama's table all at once. You wouldn't be making a play to get all the pumpkin pie to yourself, now would you?"

"If I need more of Shayanne's smashed pumpkin pie, I'll just buy it. No need to swipe yours," he says gruffly, swatting at my head in a brotherly smackdown.

I give him a bit of side-eye, not letting this go. "Just tell Brody I love his sister and wanna knock her up so I can see little Shay-Lukes running around? That's your big plan, huh?"

He presses his lips together. "I get where Brody's coming from. He's got a lot on his plate, and trying to herd a family of assholes is usually more force than finesse." His eyebrow arches as he looks between James and me. "Maybe don't say 'knock up', either."

James raises his hand like he's in school. "I vote for Luke-Annes. It rolls off the tongue better." With a smirk, he drawls out, "Luuuke-Aaaaanne."

"Sophie picked a baby name yet?" I ask him, redirecting his wild tangent.

He starts to say something and then flashes his middle finger at me. "Don't be trying to trick me. We ain't telling names until that little one is in our arms."

Suddenly, he's the one who looks all cartoon dreamy.

CHAPTER 25

SHAYANNE

"*J*'m not going." Brody might as well sound like a drill sergeant, laying down the law.

"If he's not, I'm not," Bobby follows suit, albeit in a slightly less aggressively volatile fashion.

I have had it. Day in, day out, we're tippy-toeing around each other.

Simultaneously, I've been busting my ass making dozens of pies to fill the orders that were placed as far back as September. Some people indulge all season, but primarily, these pies are a hallmark of so many families' holiday tradition, which I love being a part of, but the increased sales this year are a double-edged sword when I'm the only baker. I've made upward of one hundred pies in the last week, most of those in the last three days. My new record.

To their credit, the boys have done deliveries while keeping up with their own chores, including yesterday's trip to take twenty of those pies to the resort restaurant for their holiday feast. But driving all over town isn't nearly the work that making pie crust is. My hair is a near-perpetual frizzy mess from the humid kitchen that's been so hot I turned off the heat yesterday and let the oven warm the whole damn house.

Plus, I've done all the prep work for another batch of goat milk soap because the December farmer's market is mere days after Thanksgiving. I've got my list of scents in my notebook, along with quantities of each, and have already printed the labels and cut ribbons to wrap each slab of yummy, soapy goodness. This market's gonna be huge and our last chance to close out the year with a big profit. Well, big for a one-woman, thirty-goat operation.

Add all that together with the fact that I haven't seen Luke in days because I've literally fallen into bed after completing my daily checklist, and I'm at the end of my rope.

Throwing one hand on my hip and pointing a finger at Brody, I tell him in my fiercest voice, "The hell you're not, mister! Mama Louise has been a major help to us while Daddy was in the hospital and with all the arrangements, and you damn well know it. And she has *kindly* invited us to Thanksgiving, knowing that I'm plum worn out and can't make a whole meal without losing my ever-fluffing mind right now. So, you are going to get off your tantrum-throwing, pouty ass, slap an appreciative smile on that ugly mug, and play nice for two hours like the adult I know you can be. Capiche?"

Bobby doesn't say a word, but he gets up and high-steps it to the kitchen where I see him grabbing foil-covered dishes off the stove like a good soldier. He stands next to Bruce, who's trying unsuccessfully to hide a smile at my outburst.

Brody rolls his eyes and sighs like an annoyed teenager. "Fine," he surrenders. "Two hours, and I don't want to see any lovey-dovey shit between you and Bennett."

"I will sit in his lap and suck gravy from his fingers if I damn well want to, and you will do nothing but smile and tell Mama Louise, 'Thank you for dinner.'"

I'll do nothing of the sort, but I'm not letting Brody ruin this for me.

I need to see Luke. I need to not have the whole meal and our holiday's success or failure resting on my shoulders. Which makes me realize again how much Brody has on his.

I go over and hug him by force, trying really hard not to let the fact that he doesn't hug me back stab into my heart. "Thank you. I love you, even if you are a stubborn jackass."

He grunts and picks up the last foil-covered dish. "Let's get this over with."

MAMA LOUISE IS ALREADY HOLDING THE DOOR OPEN FOR US as we climb out of Brody's truck. It's older and seen better days, and eventually, he'll probably switch over to Daddy's newer truck, but for now, that seems weird, so it's sitting in the garage like a token of his presence even in his absence.

"Get on in this house before you catch cold," she warns, but the smile on her face is welcoming and warm.

"Thank you for inviting us," I say in polite greeting as I head straight for the kitchen. I'd sat in it only days ago when I delivered her smashed pumpkin pie order. Behind me, I can hear each of the boys mumbling some sort of hello too, though quite a bit less appreciative than me.

When I turn around, I see why. Mama Louise is taking advantage of the boys' full hands and hugging each one of them. They look stiff and uncomfortable, but they're at least well-mannered enough to not balk too much. Mama Louise winks at me, letting me know she's well aware that she's pushing them. They need it, though, that bit of motherly love, and she seems comfortable doling that out like ice cream on a hot day in summer.

"Oh, just put the food on the counter," a voice says, smacks between every word. "We'll get everything all arranged."

I glance over to see Katelyn sitting on the kitchen table and Mark feeding her a slice of turkey.

Okay, so maybe my little joke wasn't so far off, I think with a small grin of shock. Brody looks at me, daggers shooting out like little warnings of 'fuck, no' with a big dose of 'don't you dare.'

I don't know Katelyn that well, only having hung out with her at Hank's a couple of times with Sophie being our six degrees of Kevin Bacon connector. But she's seemed sweet on those outings.

Admittedly, I've wondered what magical, mystical witchy power she must possess to have captured Mark's heart, the near-declared bachelor Bennett brother having never given anyone so much as a second glance and barely a word before she swooped in and claimed him. Or he claimed her? I'm not sure, but there's a story there, according to Sophie, even if she won't gossip enough to tell me what it is.

"Hi, Katelyn, Mark. Happy Thanksgiving! Here okay?" I ask, setting my casserole dish and bag of goodies on the counter.

"Absolutely," Katelyn says with a smile. But when Mama Louise marches in the kitchen, directing my brothers on where to put things, she hops off the table like she's afraid she's about to get busted.

For their part, my brothers look a bit shell-shocked but are following orders. I suspect that everyone pretty much does what Mama Louise says all the time. She's a spitfire, and I'd hate to be on her bad side.

She claps, getting all of our attention.

"Okay," she says, looking around her kitchen and not seeing us at all. "Ladies, help me get the food set up, please. Boys, if you'll move that table out to the back porch, that'd be great. We don't have a table big enough for everyone . . . such a good problem to have," she interjects wistfully. "So, we'll push the two together and call it good."

She claps again and we all get to hustling, doing her bidding.

"Mark," Mama Louise says. He looks at her just in time to catch the rag she throws his way. "Clean off the table, please. We sit on chairs, not tables."

He has the decency to look scolded for a half-second before a light sparkles in his eyes. It's a good look on him, and unexpected, given his reputation around town. "Well, I kept putting Katelyn in my lap, but you vetoed that too. Figured the table was the safest place since you said we needed to be here to greet our guests."

She huffs and rolls her eyes, looking ever beleaguered by her sons, and I can feel her familiar torment on a cellular level myself.

Sensing her proximity to killing him, Mark starts wiping. I see Bruce lean over and whisper something in his ear, and Mark's small smile seems like a promising response.

Together, the guys complete their assignment, moving the table to the screened-in porch and setting up space heaters to keep us all toasty while we eat. Mama Louise, Katelyn, and I get the food all ready.

Mama Louise tells me, "Luke should be back any minute. He went into town to get James and Sophie loaded up. Don't tell her I said so, but I think he's there mostly to help get Sophie into James's big truck."

She winks at me like that's big gossip, and I have to grin.

I haven't seen Sophie since the funeral, but we talk on the phone almost every day. She's been checking in on me like a good friend and keeping me entertained with pregnancy woes. Her recent reports have been focused on her inability to see her feet and her worries that James thinks she's bigger than the broad side of a barn. In the next instant, she'll hush me, though she was the one talking, and say the baby's moving through happy tears.

She's going to be a great mother, I just know it.

As if her words conjured him out of thin air, I hear a door slam outside. Seconds later, the front door opens and Luke swirls in like a tornado, all energy and power.

"Shay?" he calls, his voice a rumble I feel to my toes.

I peek around the corner, a dishtowel in one hand and a serving spoon covered in stuffing in the other. Luke's face lights up as he sees me, and then he immediately scoops me into his arms, spinning me around as I try to keep the stuffing from flying all over Mama Louise's kitchen.

"Whoa," I cry out.

"Fuck, I missed you, woman."

Distantly, I hear Mama Louise mutter, "Language."

But Luke keeps talking, not paying her any mind. "You get everything delivered? Did you get some sleep? How'd everything go at the lawyer's?" His questions pop out like gunfire, but he doesn't let me respond. Instead, he takes my lips in a sweet kiss, tasting my answers and soothing every frayed nerve, tired muscle, and overfired synapse in my body.

I melt into him, and the spoon clatters to the floor, reminding me of where we are.

"Oh, uhm . . . sorry, Mama Louise."

My apology seems unneeded given the smile on her face, though. She looks at Luke and raises one eyebrow. "Two minutes to say hello properly . . . not in my busy kitchen. And not a second more, or I'll send Brody out to hunt you down."

Luke doesn't waste a bit of our one hundred and twenty seconds, making a grab for my hand. Behind me, I hear Mama Louise laugh and say, "Katelyn, can you wash that spoon for me, please?"

On the back porch, Luke presses me up against the wall,

just out of view of the prying eyes inside. I expect him to basically maul me for the short time we have, but his touch is
gentle as he cups my face. His eyes search mine as he slips a
lock of hair behind my ear. "You are a sight for sore eyes,
honey. I've missed you so much, been so worried. Are you
okay?"

He truly wants an answer, and that means more to me than
he could possibly imagine. He's not telling me what he thinks,
not demanding anything from me. He simply wants to know
what I'm feeling. Good, bad, or ugly, he'll hear me out.

"I'm good. Even better now."

His breath is jagged, like my words have relieved some
wound inside him. "You okay?"

"I am now," he says. The words are breathed against my
lips as he finally kisses me.

Somewhere in the back of my brain, I can hear a ticking
clock. *Sixty seconds, Shayanne. Make them count.*

I hook my fingers into his belt loops, pulling him to me and
matching him move for move as we reacquaint ourselves with
each other. He tastes like mint, smells like leather, and feels like
home.

He must have an internal alarm, too, because all too soon,
he pulls back and presses his forehead to mine. "Love you,
honey."

I smile, knowing he can see the lift of my cheeks even if
he's too close to see my mouth. "Love you too."

"You ready for this? Eating dinner at my mama's table is
kind of a big deal. The holiday makes it even more so."

He says it carefully, like he's testing me out.

"You think I don't know that? I changed clothes three
times before I even went downstairs. But you know what?" I
pause, and he waits for me to continue. "Inviting someone to
dinner might be a major thing for you and me, but my whole

family's being here is a big deal too. It's a step in the right direction, even if I had to kick 'em to get them out the door."

He grins, pulling away so I can see the way it makes his eyes glitter. "I can't wait to hear that story, but we'd better get inside before Mama sends Brody to find us and I've got his little sister pinned up against the wall, doing filthy things to her."

I groan, his words making me want him to take me against this wall.

Okay, maybe not this one, and definitely not right now with our families ten feet away. But ooh, he knows how to light me up.

"That's a dirty trick, Luke Bennett. I'll remember that later," I tease.

He laughs and then sobers. "You look beautiful, Shayanne. Happy Thanksgiving."

DINNER'S ACTUALLY NOT THAT BAD, ONCE WE GET ROLLING. I'd been afraid it'd be long stretches of silence and awkward get-to-know-you questions, but the food is the great denominator and brings everyone together.

We sit around the makeshift extra-long table, even having a few empty spaces with the two pushed together, and pass the platters around. There's plenty of food, both Mama Louise and me outdoing ourselves if I do say so myself, and each dish is more delicious than the last.

"Mama Louise, you'll have to give me the recipe for your green bean casserole. I've only ever made the one off the can of fried onions, and I can tell there's something extra in your version," I venture.

Sophie moans her appreciation over her second helping. "It's the best, even better than turkey. Not that the turkey's not

delicious, but green beans are suddenly my new favorite food."
Her eyes roll back in her head and her lashes flutter as she
takes another bite.

We all look at her, internally laughing at her exaggerated
adoration over vegetables, of all things, but she's got no shame
as she digs in for another forkful. James looks at her tenderly
as he spoons the ones from his plate onto Sophie's. Her chip-
munk-full cheeks lift and she points her fork at him. "You're
the best, you know that?"

"It's not a big secret, I'm afraid," Mama Louise admits. "I
just add freshly fried bacon, onions, and mushrooms to the
green bean mixture. I dice them all up and sauté them down so
they're invisible before adding them. Had a few picky eaters
who wouldn't eat it if there were 'chunks' in it." She says it
with a smile, like a selectively choosy kid is just one of those
things.

"I'll definitely try that," I tell her, wishing I had my notebook to jot down her tips. I left it at home today, a symbolic
gesture that this is my day off. No lists, no diary entries, no
reminders. Just living in the moment, thankful for the gifts of
today.

Family.

Friends.

Love.

Another day on this Earth.

Because none of those things are a given.

At some point, conversation turns to cows, which is
another surefire conversational safe zone with this crowd.
Brody even joins in when Mark and Sophie talk about a trip to
the winter auction to buy and sell a few more head of cattle.

I swear that pigs are flying when they joke about some big
wannabe cowboy who showed up last year, not knowing a
damn thing. Apparently, he bought all beef cattle thinking he
was gonna raise them for milk.

The vibe around the table is relaxed, even friendly as Mama Louise serves up one of my smashed pumpkin pies for dessert. But I know it's like getting comfortable on a tightrope. Just when you think everything is all good, that's when you misstep and go tumbling down.

Baby steps, careful steps, slow and steady.

"Luke, when are you going out next? You're not gonna miss the birth of your niece or nephew, are you?" James says, but there's an undercurrent to the words I can't figure out. He yelps, his eyes cutting to Mark. "Damn, just asking."

I've seen that reaction at my own house. Mark just kicked James underneath the table, I'm sure of it. But why?

Luke takes a soft breath, his palm going to my thigh where he rubs a soothing pattern. Or it would be soothing if it wasn't him and wasn't my thigh. Or maybe if it hadn't been days since I'd been under him or on top of him.

"I won't miss it. I have to head out for a three-day weekend next week, but they're well aware that if Sophie goes into labor early, I'm on the next plane out to get home. I *always* come back home."

His last words are spoken to Brody, though James asked the question, and a ripple runs through the quiet air around the table. I can feel everyone's eyes on me, Luke, and Brody, ping-ponging between us.

"Actually, I wanted to ask . . ." Luke looks at me with those blue eyes that make me want to dive into them and backstroke for the rest of my life. "Shayanne, would you like to go with me? It'll be a quick trip, and I'll have to work, but you can see another working ranch and meet their horses."

Erk, record scratch. What?

My jaw drops open in surprise as excitement bubbles up in my belly.

Brody pops the bubbles like they're nothing, though, his

voice deep and threatening. "That's Shayanne's birthday. No."
He says it like his word is law.

Luke licks his lips, trying to please Brody, I can see. "Her
birthday is on Monday, and we'd be back Sunday night. Plenty of
time to celebrate. I wouldn't interfere with that, especially not a big
birthday like twenty-one. The farmer's market is that weekend, so
you'll probably be staying in town, anyway. And it's karaoke open
mic at Hank's," Luke says, turning to Bobby. "Could be fun?"

He's thought of everything.

Except they're talking about me like I'm not sitting right
the fuck here.

"I would love to go," I blurt out. Steadier, I declare, "Yes,
I'll go."

Brody looks at me, flames rising in his eyes. He pushes
back from the table, the chair legs making a screeching noise
on the wooden patio floor, and walks to Mama Louise's side,
who looks up at him with some emotion running through her
eyes. Disappointment, maybe?

He sticks out his hand. "Thank you for Thanksgiving
dinner, ma'am." She shakes his hand, looking like she's biting
her tongue to hold back whatever she wants to say. I imagine
that's not something she does particularly often.

Bobby stands next and does the same, a handshake and
thank you before following Brody back into the house and
toward the front door.

Bruce does it last, following suit, though I can tell he's
doing it reluctantly. Before he leaves, he looks back at me. "I'll
try to talk some sense into him. We'll see you in the morning
for breakfast?"

I nod glumly, all Thanksgiving progress having gone out
the window into the cold fall night.

When it's just the Bennetts and me, Mark glares at James.
"Seriously?"

He throws his hands out to the side. "What? I was trying to give him an opening to tell Brody about the Luke-Annes. He's the one who botched it!" he accuses.

My brows furrow. "Luke-Annes? Is that like when you 'ship' something? Like Jennifer Anniston and Ben Affleck were Bennifer? So we're Luke-Annes?"

Luke groans, putting his head in his hands. "Sort of, but no? I'll explain later, 'kay? After I kick James's ass."

"Language. And no one is kicking anyone's ass on Thanksgiving," Mama Louise announces, still calmly eating her pie like World War III didn't just start around her. I notice that no one mentions her slip of the tongue.

I SWEAR I MEANT TO HAVE CRAZY I-MISSED-YOU SEX WITH Luke the instant we walk into his house after the chilly ending to what had been a lovely dinner and significant progress. But the last thing I remember is lying down while he got ready for bed. Lying down in his soft, warm, fluffy bed. Vaguely, I remember snuggling into his arms, feeling his body conform to mine from behind. And then . . . darkness.

It's the best sleep I've had in weeks.

CHAPTER 26

LUKE

"You sure about this?" I ask, hoping down to my guts that she says yes but occasionally being a decent enough guy to give her an out if she needs it. But I want this. If she's changed her mind, I might just throw her over my shoulder and make a run for it. I'm sure I could eventually make her see reason with my tongue between her legs.

Her eyes light up instead, her gray sweater somehow making them seem brighter. Relief washes through me, and her smile eliminates any further worries.

"Of course. I've been busting my ass all week to get the soaps ready for the market and stock the fridge with food and beer, and I told Brody to get over himself no fewer than ten times before I left. I both hugged and flipped him off. Balance, you know."

She kicks at her small pink suitcase by my front door with her boot. "I'm ready, *so ready*. I'm doing this, so let's get to it," she says, snapping her fingers at me, or maybe it's at the situation.

There's my woman, sass and fire and a healthy dose of country crazy. Fuck, I love her.

I've been worried about how buried she's been, burning the candle at both ends for weeks. I know this is usually a busy time of year for her, and she's had record-setting sales for her pies, but I think she's going a little harder than usual to stay distracted. It's a valid coping mechanism for grief but probably not the best one.

"All right, then. Your chariot awaits, honey."

Outside sits Mark's truck. He offered to drive us so that I wouldn't have to leave my truck at the airport, and to no one's surprise, he's already sitting in the driver's seat. We climb in and Shayanne relaxes into the warm air of the cab.

The drive goes by quickly as Shayanne chatters on about the new scents she made for this month's farmer's market. She seems most proud of her holiday lines, having created a 'Gingerbread Cookies and Ma-a-a-lk' scent and one she laughingly calls 'Jolly Old Man', which she explains is a blend of peppermint and pipe smoke to make her version of what Santa smells like.

Though she's being funny, I can tell she's nervous, filling the moments with her rambles to keep from focusing on the short flight we have in front of us. If Sophie weren't pregnant, I would've driven for this visit, but with time being of the essence, the flight seemed the best bet. Plus, I know Shayanne hasn't flown before and this is a small taste of the adventures I want to take her on. She deserves this type of thing.

Before I know it, we're telling Mark goodbye with him promising to call me if anything happens with Sophie. He pulls away and I grab our bags. "Ready?"

Her smile is soft, in contrast to her furrowed brows. She takes a steadying breath and the tilt of her lips lifts a bit more. "Ready."

THE FLIGHT IS UNEVENTFUL, SAVE FOR SHAYANNE'S SQUEAL
of jumpy delight when we take off and her excited applause
when we land, but I love the feel of her hand in mine for the
duration of our time thirty thousand feet above the Earth and
the look on her face as she points out the window.

A stable hand from the facility I'm here to visit meets us at
their airport. "Hey, J.R. How's it going, man?" I say, shaking
his hand. He's got on the requisite boots, jeans, and dirt-
smeared T-shirt, likely having left the stables just in time to
make it to the airport.

He smiles in return, crinkles popping at the corners of his
brown eyes. He's not that old, mid-forties, maybe, but the long
days in the sun take their toll. "Can't complain. Don't think I'm
doing as well as you are, though." His eyes turn to Shayanne
and he offers her a nod. "Ma'am."

I make introductions and we head for his truck. He raises
his eyebrow in approval as we climb in, likely wondering how
an asshole like me landed a woman as stunning as Shay. I just
grin back like the cat that got the cream.

"How's Bonnie doing?" I ask.

"She's all right," he hums, "but I think she needs you to
work your magic."

Shayanne stiffens next to me, almost imperceptibly, and I
can't help but smirk. "Bonnie's their quarter horse, a successful
breeding from a couple of seasons ago. Good and agile, but
she's not a track horse."

J.R. laughs, sounding every bit the pack a day smoker he's
been for as long as I've known him. "Hell, you sound sad about
that. The boss loves that little mistake, considering the others
from that visit. We both know you ain't here to train her,
though. You're here to train me on that rodeo stuff, and I'm a
good enough horseman to admit it. Boss's daughter wants to
barrel race her when she's old enough."

I already knew that and made the plan accordingly, but

Shay seems interested. She asks a few questions, and I sit back, letting her and J.R. talk. I watch her instead, mesmerized as she slips right into my world with ease.

She must feel my gaze because she pushes her hair behind her ear, glancing at me from the corner of her eye. Her small smile lets me know that she likes my eyes on her. As if they'd be anywhere else.

When we arrive at the ranch, J.R. grabs our bags from the back of the truck. "Boss said to put you in the apartment over the barn instead of the ranch house, seeing as you brought a friend."

Shayanne balks, looking shocked. "Oh, please don't go through any trouble for us. I'm sure we'd be just fine in the ranch house, if that's easier." Her eyes order me to tell J.R. that too.

"Thank you, man. Appreciate it," I tell J.R. instead.

Some ranches have rules against females in their ranch house, and honestly, I haven't seen their living arrangements here. For all I know, it's bunk beds, a feed-trough urinal, and an outhouse bathroom. Wouldn't be the first time I've seen that. So I'll happily take a barn apartment and cross my fingers and toes for heating and plumbing like the pansy ass I am. Plus, a bit of privacy with Shay can only be a good thing.

For one, I'm ready to hold her in my arms and really make sure she's doing okay. And two, if she is all right, I want to spend the night buried inside her.

"You wanna go relax for a bit, or would you rather meet Bonnie?" I ask Shayanne, changing the subject.

"Bonnie," she says definitively. The wry twist of her lip tells me she noticed I didn't do as she said, but the smile she's fighting says she knows why too.

We spend the whole afternoon in the chill of the late fall air, sunshine sparkling against the field of winter rye in the distance as I watch Bonnie and J.R. work their way around the dirt. I can do all the research, ask all the right questions, watch videos of my equine client, and make all the plans, but nothing is as useful as watching the horse in person. Their personality, their strengths, and their limits all play a major part. Bonnie is a fine animal and will do well with barrels if her rider is good too.

That's where the training comes in. I have to get Bonnie ready to learn with her rider because eventually, they'll be a close-knit team if everything goes as it should.

I lose track of time as J.R. and I work with Bonnie, gauging her responsiveness to things as mundane as a stranger's touch to her willingness to follow a lead. A loud round of laughter breaks my concentration and draws my attention. When I look over, I see Shayanne sitting on the fence with a gaggle of cowboys surrounding her. She's damn near holding court like a fucking queen as she listens raptly to some story an old guy is telling is her. Everyone laughs again at whatever he's saying, his hands waving animatedly through the air.

She's absolutely fucking stunning. And she's mine.

She looks back to me and waves. I can see the older guys around her looking on knowingly, likely recognizing our love and feeling sentimental, though they're too rough to ever admit it.

I notice a couple of the young bucks silently taking my measure, too. They can fuck off. I know Shayanne doesn't want anyone but me, and the feeling's mutual.

Still, a little territory staking ain't a bad thing. I hold up a finger to J.R. and strut across the arena to Shay. She watches my approach, eyes taking in every roll of my hips and the burning look I'm shooting her. Her lips quirk like she knows exactly what I'm doing and approves.

"Hey, Luke. Looks like Bonnie's doing well," she says,

sweet as candy when I stand in front of her, one of my dirty hands on each of her denim-clad knees.

I nod, looking up at her on her fence perch. "She is. But I'm more interested in how you're doing, honey." I let my voice drop low, my bedroom voice as she calls it, knowing it drives her fucking crazy.

She doesn't take her eyes off me, and I can see the fires dancing in their depths. "I'm just fine."

She's feigning being unaffected, but I feel the clench of her thighs under my palms. I don't fight the kiss we know is coming, lifting to my toes to reach her as she bends forward to meet me halfway. It's over too fast but communicates my need to her and my claim to every fucker leaning on the fence wishing he were me.

"Be done soon. Got dinner plans for you tonight," I tell her mysteriously. I boop her nose and toss her a playful wink before heading back to J.R., who's watching the show with a shit-eating grin.

Behind me, I hear someone sullenly mouthing, "Damn near pissing on his territory like a dog."

Another voice responds, "Wouldn't you too?"

DINNER PLANS MIGHT'VE BEEN OVERSTATING MATTERS. More like J.R. offered to bring us plates so we could stay in. He's a good guy, and when I'd told him I was bringing my girlfriend because she was going through some tough times at home, he'd promised to do anything he could to make it a good weekend away for her.

And as promised, the chopped sirloin, steak fries, and cinnamon apples are delicious and a testament to the ranch's kitchen.

"Thank you for coming with me," I say, shoveling food in

my mouth. I'm not usually such a monster, but today was a lot of work, both physically and mentally, to get Bonnie where she needs to be.

Shayanne is much more mannered and nibbles at a large fry. "Of course. It was fun to watch you in action today. The guys all seemed to respect you, other than telling me a tale of you once getting knocked on your ass into a pile of manure. But even that was said with affection, I'm *sure* of it."

Her eyes dance, knowing damn well those fellows were just trying to make me look bad in front of her. Little do they know, I'd lay down in shit if it'd make her laugh. Hell, I'd do anything to bring a smile to her gorgeous face.

"Fuckers. There's supposed to be a code, you know? Rule number one, don't go spreading stories that'll knock a guy down, especially to his woman." I fake an angry scowl, not giving a damn about their sharing the story. It's a funny one, seeing as how both me and the horse were okay, just in need of a good scrubbing bath.

Shay pats my hand like she's soothing me, but it's all sarcasm. "There, there. It's fine. I still think you're a big, strong cowboy. Those mean boys didn't make me think any less of you."

Her voice is pitched like she's talking to a whiny five-year-old, and I laugh. I lay a gentlemanly kiss to the back of her hand, then trail down to her fingers, pressing my lips to the pads of each one. I lick at her index finger, tasting the salt from the fries before sucking it into my mouth for a nibble.

At her gasp, I kiss her palm, her fingers cupping my scruffy cheek. Her breath is faster, her chest rising and falling and her eyes glazing over.

I'm *this close* to shoving the dinner dishes out of the way and taking her. But not yet. I need to know if she's okay.

I lean into her touch, hungry for it, for her. I force the

strangled words out. "How are you doing, honey? I mean for real, not the charade you've damn near perfected."

Her sigh sounds resigned to having this conversation, even though she'd rather not. Her whole body sags as she sheds the shield of strength she wears with ease. Only with me does she melt into a puddle of honesty.

Quietly, she asks a question I don't expect. "Does it make me an awful person if I say I'm doing okay?"

"No, but are you?" I follow up.

Her hands drop to her lap, where she fidgets and twists them. She looks down like they're fascinating. "I feel like there's been so much . . ." Her voice trails off, and I give her time to collect her thoughts. "Mostly, I'm upset about Brody, not Daddy. God, that's awful."

Her eyes go wide, horrified at her own feelings as she covers her mouth. I take her hands again, holding my gaze steady. "That's perfectly reasonable, Shayanne. Tell me," I order, but it's soft, more a request than a demand.

She shakes her whole body, like a dog getting water off its back. I can feel she's trying to do the same with the emotions coursing through her.

"Just let it out. I'm not here to judge, just to listen."

She licks her lips. "Okay, I'll try to make sense of the jumble in my head."

Like a dam breaking free, it all comes loose in a torrent.

"In a way, I lost Daddy a long time ago, you know? He stepped back after Mom died, and I tried like a demon to hold onto him, keep him with us. I tried to do everything I could to be *her*. I can see now that he was heartbroken, but at the time, it felt like he abandoned us. Like I wasn't good enough. But still, I kept him on that pedestal. Even when he fell and I saw how wrong he could be, it was like I still had hope he'd come around. Does that make sense?"

I nod, not interrupting her.

"Even that withered away, though, and I was just . . . resigned. He was alive, sitting at the dinner table most nights, but he was already gone. I feel like I mourned Daddy a long time ago, in a lot of ways. What could've been, who we might've been to each other. His death hit me hard, but it was more because that last little seed of hope died than anything else. And I really do think he's finally at peace, in a way. I hope that's true, at least, because it gives me a little peace."

Her eyes are dry as a bone, and I'm amazed again at how strong she is. Even laying her heart bare, she's unflinchingly tough.

"Brody's a whole different thing, though. I didn't expect him to fight me on this, on you. I figured he'd grump around and tell me I couldn't do this, can't do that. But I didn't dream he'd be this much of a stubborn ass. And I'm furious he can't just let me be *me*." There's the smallest, cutest growl in her throat as she rants about her brother.

I shrug, not worried. "He'll come around. He just needs time."

She looks at me, the fire in her veins licking at me now. "Seriously? That's your big plan? Give him time?"

I nod. "Yep, that's all I've got. He's not gonna change his mind because I make some grand gesture. He wouldn't respect me if I groveled and begged him for permission, and to be honest, he's just fighting to hold on, his fingertips on the edge to keep everything together. He's a family man and his flock is going through some major shit. He's making progress, though. He came to dinner and didn't tie you up in the barn to keep you from leaving with me. He just needs time."

Her mouth opens and closes, gaping like a fish out of water. "That's not . . . he should . . ." Her shoulders drop as she realizes what I'm getting at. "Oh, my chee-sus and crackers, you're right. He is doing better, but I'm focusing on the stomping around, huffing and puffing, and judgy glares."

297

I grin. "He's an asshole, no doubt about that. But he's an asshole who loves you and thinks you deserve better than me. For the record, he's not wrong. I'm the worst."

She smiles back. "You're something, I'll give you that. Not sure it's the worst or the best, though. You might have to remind me, let me see for myself again."

She's got her sultry voice on, seduction in her every cell. Reassured that she's truly doing well and just busy because it's needed, not because she's shoving down painful emotions, I stand and walk around the table.

She turns to face me, her chair scooting on the floor. I drop to my knees between her spread thighs. I let my eyes follow my words, down her body.

"Fuck, I want to taste you, honey, the fiery sass of your mouth," I say as my eyes land on the plump fullness of her lips, "the chill of the day on your skin . . ." My gaze glances over the collarbone peeking out of her flannel shirt. "And the sweetness you hide between your thighs and only share with me."

I bend down, placing my cheek on her thigh, and run my palm up the other, getting closer and closer to her heaven.

She nods breathlessly, without words, for a change. But I see a spark in her eyes as they darken. "Best get to it, then, cowboy."

"Yes, ma'am," I say cheekily as I move up to take her mouth.

It's instant ignition, no slow burn or teasing left in either of us. It's been too long since I've had her, and my need hits me hard. Our mouths fight for control, devouring each other as our teeth clash and tongues taste our shared breath.

She whimpers, and I growl, loving the way she shamelessly gives in to our need. I stand, gripping her ass, and pick her up, her legs going astride my hips. I toss her to the bed in the corner of the all-in-one room and gruffly tell her, "Strip."

I wonder if she's going to argue with me about it, but when

I rip my own flannel shirt off and then reach behind my neck for my T-shirt, she gets to it. Matching me move for move, we strip ourselves faster than we could've each other.

Bared before me, I'm reminded again how beautiful she is. I didn't forget. I just tend to think I'm embellishing in my head, my memory hazy and rose-colored by how good she feels. But the real thing laid out before me is even better than I remember.

Her honey skin is dotted with goosebumps from the slight chill in the air, and I can see her slit glistening with anticipation. She runs her hands up her belly, tracing the curve of the underside of her tits and pleading, "Just fuck me, Luke. I need you."

A jolt of electricity runs through me, ending in my cock, and I have to grip myself hard to keep from coming from just her words. Still standing at the bedside, I bend forward, licking a long, slow line along her pussy and swirling over her clit. "Just need one taste, honey."

She writhes against me, searching for more. I give in, always still surprised and thankful to be invited into her body, into her heart, into her life.

I lift her legs to my shoulders and slam into her in one fierce motion, filling her balls-deep and holding her there as she instantly spasms around me. She gasps, coming just from one thrust.

"Fuck, Shay. Already?" I rasp in shock. I give her small thrusts, riding her through her orgasm as she cries out my name and her head thrashes on the bed. She's gonna have knots in her hair, something that oddly makes me proud. I'm the only one who can drive her wild that way.

I'm the only one who ever will.

Her eyes open, dark and heated as she returns to me from whatever orgasmic bliss she traveled through. She's with me, against all odds, against her family's wishes. A primal instinct roars through me, and I pull out, telling her, "Flip over. Hands and knees."

She does as I command, presenting the perfectly full apple of her ass to me. One day, I'll take that virginity too, if she wants me to. But right now, I need back inside her. I gently grab a handful of her tangles, ordering, "Arch for me."

My free hand traces down the bumps of her spine, and I slip two fingers into her wet pussy. "One more taste," I say, licking her juices from my fingers.

She moans, pressing toward me needily. Gripping her hips with both hands, I push through the kissing caress of her lips until my thighs press to hers. She bucks against me, moaning, "Fuck me, Luke. Make me come again."

Such a bossy thing, but that sounds like a damn fine plan to me.

I fuck her hard, no mercy given as I slam into her relentlessly. The only thing keeping her from faceplanting on the bed is me pulling her back onto my cock with every stroke. It's rough, raw, another level to our connection.

"Rub your clit, Shay. Come all over my cock and I'll fill you up with my cum. Fuck, honey, it's been so long, I don't know if you'll even be able to hold it all. I'm gonna make us messy with our cum."

It's only been a couple of weeks since our softer session after the funeral, but the nights we have had together haven't been ones of physical lovemaking. Instead, I've held her in my arms, keeping the sadness and pain away, giving her a place to just be, no show needed.

But now, that's not what she needs at all. It's not what I need, either. We need this powerful fucking, a cleansing start to a new phase. One where she's mine and I'm hers. One without her dad, one where Brody is going to have to get the fuck used to this. Because I love her and she's mine.

One day, I'm going to make it official, but for now, impaled on my cock, her velvet walls squeezing me in a grip so tight it edges me on the line of pain and pleasure, I know it.

I love her so goddamn much. She's it for me. Forever.

Her pussy spasms and she cries out, her arms collapsing as she falls to the bed. I fall over her, covering her with my body, my chest pressed to her back. I ride her like this, using the bounce of the bed to work her onto my cock as I stroke into her.

My balls pull up tight, and I grunt out her name as cum jets from my cock in pulses, painting her pussy, marking her as mine. Her sugar cum coats me too, claiming me as hers. Our sweat makes us slippery, but it's just one more way we're together.

Two bodies, one heart.

CHAPTER 27

SHAYANNE

"*S*hh! Be quiet, motherfucker. Don't wake her up before we're ready!" The whisper-yell is more than enough to wake me from my sleep. As is the responding *thwack* that signals someone just got smacked.

I stretch in my bed, sore but in a good way. The trip with Luke was fun, a great adventure, just like I knew it would be. I met new people, saw some gorgeous horses, and had lots of deliciously rough sex that made me appreciate all the ways Luke can love my body. Soft and sweet, hard and wild, and every shade in between. I'm a lucky woman.

Which is also evidenced by what my brothers are doing right now. It's a Tannen family tradition, one my mom started when Brody was a toddler. Birthday pancakes, a monstrosity of fluffy goodness layered with piles of fluffy whipped cream and doused in sprinkles.

She made them every year for each of us, from the time we were able to eat a pancake, and I continued the tradition after she was gone. It never occurred to me how sweet it is that the boys do it for me every year too. I'm glad that this year is no different, considering the tension we've been working through.

Brody hadn't even come home last night before I'd gone to bed, and a small part of me had been scared he'd skip the tradition this year. Though I didn't admit that, not even to myself, until right this minute.

A knock pounds on my door, ending the charade. "Rise and shine, Shayannie. Got a little surprise for ya. And if you don't hurry, I'm gonna eat it all myself." Bobby's already laughing, the threat not even worth the oxygen he put into saying it because we both know he's not going to eat my birthday breakfast.

Still, I throw the blankets off and hop out of bed, feeling like a kid again. I fling open the door, ready to run down the stairs to the kitchen table, but I pull up short at my three brothers all standing in the hallway.

This is not part of the tradition, I think with trepidation.

"Happy birthday, Sis," Brody says, his face straight even though he's smiling. He hugs me tightly and I melt into his arms.

"Thanks, Brody," I say softly to his thick chest.

Next up is Bruce and then Bobby, each of whom do the same hug and greeting.

"Sooo . . . breakfast waiting?" I say, not sure why we're still standing in the hallway.

Bruce's grin is the epitome of *I know something you don't*, which makes me nervous as hell.

Brody scratches at his lower lip with his thumb. "Yeah, breakfast in a minute, but I wanted to give you fair warning so you could plan ahead." His pregnant pause gives me time to let all sorts of awful scenarios run through my head. "See, I was at the market this weekend when Sophie came by. Do you know how many kids she's got in there? Gotta be at least a litter's worth."

My breath hitches at the news that he saw Sophie. This could be really good, like maybe she talked some sense into him, or really bad, because Sophie's not a shy wallflower. She'll tell you straight up if you're a fuckup. That's why we get along like birds of a feather, no soft edges on either of us. And pregnancy has made Sophie even a little sharper, if anything.

Danger! a voice shouts in my head.

"Just the one, so the doctor says. But she still has one more month till her due date, so I agree there might be at least one more hiding from the sonogram," I answer warily, focusing on the least volatile bit of information.

Brody looks understandably doubtful that Sophie's got one baby in her belly—and that she'll make it another month.

"Anyway, she had an idea. I wasn't sure, but she basically beat me over the head and said she was doing it, so I'd best get with the program if I wanted any say-so." He quirks his brow at me. "So I'm with Sophie. We all are," he says, suddenly remembering that Bruce and Bobby are standing next to him.

"With her on what?" I say leerily, looking at each of them in search of some sort of answer as to what the hell's going on.

Bobby has met his limit of staying still and keeping quiet. He bounces on the toes of his boots, grinning. "Your twenty-first birthday party at Hank's tonight. Sophie and Brody arranged everything while he was in town all weekend."

Bobby's grin is one of relief. He's not much on secrets, and the surest way to spread a story is to tell him. If you want it to make the go-round even faster, tell him not to tell a soul. Boom . . . whole town'll know in record time.

It's not a flaw, though. He's just a 'what you see is what you get' kinda guy, so he's transparent about everything.

I look to Brody in shock. "You planned a birthday party for me?" I ask, my lower lip trembling.

"Well, yeah," he says, looking totally uncomfortable. "It's a big birthday for you. Seems appropriate that your big" —he pauses to look at Bruce and Bobby— "well, that your biggest brother should buy your first official beer."

I can't help but grin. He's well aware I drink on occasion, and he even stocks the fruity wine coolers I prefer when we have bonfires in the summer. But this will be a first. A beer with my brothers, bought from Hank himself.

The even bigger deal is that he planned something for me. With *Sophie*. Sophie *Bennett*.

"Thank you," I say, pressing a kiss to his stubbled cheek.

He rocks on his feet, heels . . . toes . . . heels . . . toes. "There's, uh, there's more."

I lift my brows and clasp my hands together. "Brody Tannen, did you get me a new goat?" For some girls, that'd probably be the worst present ever, but for me? I'd be happier than a pig in slop to get a new goat.

Country girl, party of one . . . right here!

He smiles, knowing that I'd love that. "Well, I did say we'd add to the herd, but that's not your gift. Sophie helped me invite a few people, get a cake and balloons, and some other stuff. We're not just eating and drinking at Hank's. This is a legit party. For you."

I hear the record screech as he speaks. "Invite a few folks?" I look to Bruce and Bobby, who have remarkably straight faces. I narrow my eyes at Bobby, knowing he's the weak link of information spilling.

But Brody gives in first. "She said that she needed to invite your girls night out group. Her, Katelyn, her sister, and then she said something about the girl at the resort you work with in the gift shop?" I nod like a bobblehead, excitement pouring into my veins and waking me up better than a cup of coffee or sugar-doused pancake ever could.

"And Doc, of course." I nod again, waiting and hoping. I cross my fingers behind my back.

Brody sighs, unable to hold it back. "And the Bennetts. Felt like we should invite Mama Louise after how nice she's been, which means the boys are coming. They said they'd tell

Luke. Unless you cut him loose after a shitty weekend away?"

His hope is real, but even he knows the chances of that are slim to none.

I squeal, literally out loud, like a pig demanding some dinner. I jump into Brody's arms and he catches me easily. I pepper his cheeks with kisses. "Thank you, Brody! I swear, you're gonna grow to like him."

He grumbles, setting me down. "Let's eat some pancakes. We've got work to do if we're cutting out early to head to town."

Brody's gruff response isn't the turnaround I'd hoped the party was a sign of, but it's progress, like Luke said.

Baby steps, one by one.

He'll come around.

HANK'S IS IN FULL SWING. EVERYONE I KNOW AND CARE FOR is here, plus most of the folks in our rural area because no one is passing up a birthday party with free cake, and word gets around fast, even in our remote region.

We've eaten dinner, my favorite chicken fried steak and 'taters sitting in my full belly, and I stood on the bar, a huge no-no, to raise my first official beer to cheers from the crowd. Hank had shaken his head when I'd chugged the whole thing in one go. Might be my first official, but it ain't my first by a long shot. And I've been spun around the floor more times than I can count by just about every guy here, even Hank himself, who I've never seen cut a rug.

Almost as importantly as the celebration, Brody and Luke haven't come to blows. Yet. Though the glares they're tossing at each other are damn near deadly.

"Holy shit, is that Roxy?" I hear someone exclaim. I turn to see Sophie's sister-in-law walking in, followed closely by Jake, her brother. Though Sophie doesn't tell many folks, her sister-in-law is famous. Like of the one-name variety, hence the shock in the loud question.

She comes up and gives me a hug, telling me happy birthday, and Jake does the same. I'm happily surprised to see her. Her tour schedule doesn't always allow her to hang out with us, but I always enjoy her company when she comes to our girls' night out get-togethers. She doesn't understand our love of farm animals, but she's as real as they come.

"Think I could do a song for you?"

A bark of laughter escapes from my chest. "Uhm, you're *the* Roxy. I think you can do whatever the hell you wanna do," I joke, "and I know I'd sure appreciate it even if there's someone in here who wouldn't."

I glance around, my brow fake-furrowed as I look for a nonexistent Roxy-hater. We both know that every single person in this place would love to hear her sing.

She grins and points a stiletto-tipped navy-blue nail my way, grinning hugely. "Sassy bitch. That's why I like you."

She pats Jake on the chest, letting him know she's fine to mingle with the masses, but he nods at a guy in a black T-shirt who strategically moves to follow Roxy. Security. I can't imagine needing that just to get a beer at a friend's birthday party.

Luke appears at my side, offering a handshake to Jake. "I know Sophie passed along my appreciation, but thanks for helping me surprise my woman. She's a tough cookie, but I think the delicious dinner you arranged really put me over the edge with her."

He winks at me, knowing full well we'd spent the better part of that fancy-schmancy dinner wishing we were back at the hotel eating fast food so we could get into bed sooner.

"No problem, glad I could help." Jake's pretty lowkey too.

If Sophie hadn't told me, I would've never known that he's some big-wig with more money than God and part-owner of one of the fanciest nightclubs in existence. I like that about him.

"Does anyone mind if I sing a little song for my friend's birthday?" Roxy's voice comes through the speakers. I look over, and it's probably the smallest stage she's ever graced with her presence. More of a raised step than a true stage, to tell the truth. But she looks right at home, especially when everyone starts cheering.

"This one's for you, Shayanne. Thanks for introducing me to bull fries. Never would've thought I'd like those." Her face screws up in disgust. "But you were right. Drop anything in batter to fry it up, and it's edible. Might not be delicious, but it's *edible-ish.*" She grins, raising an invisible glass, and everyone follows her lead, beer bottles filling the air. "May you have many more years of being right, trying new things, and having every wish come true."

Her sultry voice fills the small bar. It's one of her pop songs. Hank would never put it on his jukebox, but it's perfect and beautiful. Luke asks Jake to excuse us, and he sways with me on the dance floor. No fancy tricks this time. We just let the music and atmosphere wash over us.

"All for you, honey. Hope you feel the love because Sophie and Brody really went all out to make you feel special. Happy birthday." His voice is breathy, just for me, and then he quiets so we can hear Roxy sing.

All around us, couples rock back and forth in each other's arms, filling the floor to get a better view of the famous pop star. She holds the last note longer than should be humanly possible, and applause erupts.

She smiles and dips her chin, her mass of curls bouncing forward to cover her face. When she looks back up, her cheeks are pink with happiness. "Thank you. Now, I'd thought about

singing *Happy Birthday*, but I was informed by a little birdie . . .
ahem, Sophie . . . that someone was already doing that.
Bobby?"

I gasp, turning to watch Bobby approach the stage.

He sings and plays guitar, we all know that. But somewhere along the way, it became *his* thing. He'll play in the barn
or out in the fields, and I know Bruce hears him sometimes
when they're working. But he never wants us to come to
Hank's when he does open mic nights and rarely sings around
the house anymore. His humming seems pitch perfect, so I
don't know what his deal is, but I know that him singing for
me tonight is a big fucking deal.

A gift from him to me.

Tears burn my eyes as I smile at him and mouth, "Thank
you."

He smiles back and sits down on a stool someone has stuck
up on the stage. He gets his guitar situated and strums a couple
of chords. "Happy birthday, Shayanne. I love you and hope
you get what you're wishing for."

I choke, knowing he's talking about me and Luke, and me
and Brody. He's still following Brody's edict and isn't sure if
Luke is as good as he seems to be, but tonight, at least, he's
willing to wish for my happiness, whatever form that takes.

He sings the basic *Happy Birthday* song that's been sung for
years, but with his voice, it takes on new life. *Holy shit, Bobby
can saaaaang!*

His voice the last time I heard him was good but occasionally broken by puberty cracks that I know embarrassed him.
Now, his voice is smoky whiskey over gravel as he plays
slowly, cutting the song's peppy tempo by more than half. Even
Roxy seems surprised, if her raised brows are any sign. She
moves to Bobby's side, and with silent agreement, she harmo-
nizes with him.

Normally, people will start to sing along with the birthday

song. But no one makes a sound, not even so much as breathing to break the spell Bobby and Roxy are weaving with the simplest of tunes. They sing it through twice, the second time more runs and 'oohs' than words, but it's absolutely beautiful.

When they close the final note, the place explodes in applause. I make my way to the stage just as Bobby finishes helping Roxy step down. I tackle him in a hug, crushing his guitar between us, and he laughs. "Don't hurt Betty!" When I pull back, he's holding his guitar like I might've injured it with my attack.

"Thank you, Bobby. That was amazing."

He looks wide-eyed. "No shit, Sis. I mean, happy birthday and all, but did you see me fucking *sing with Roxy?*" I love that he was willing to sing for me, and I love even more that in making a wish come true for me, one I didn't even know I had, he had one come true too. "Hell, I could die a happy man, right now!"

Jake appears at Roxy's elbow and overhears. "I feel the same way every time I look at her, man." He could be exaggerating, but the look of adoration on his face says it's the God's honest truth.

Next, Sophie and Brody appear with a cake big enough to feed the whole city. It's lit up with candles that are throwing sparks like the 4th of July and seem likely to set off Hank's smoke detectors. This time, everyone sings, and I close my eyes, making a wish for peace in my family . . . my whole family, Luke and my brothers and me.

I blow out the candles, making sure each one is smoking before I breathe again.

CHAPTER 28

SHAYANNE

J'm vacuuming the living room when I hear a loud knock on the front door. That's weird. I mean, the front gate opens automatically unless we set it to lockdown mode, but most folks will call before showing up all the way out here. We're not really 'in the neighborhood' for anyone except the Bennetts.

Maybe it's Mama Louise?

She's come over a few times since Daddy's passing with casseroles or pies, along with a kind smile to check on us. I feel like she's kind of adopted us, even though we're all grown.

I turn off the vacuum, leaving it in the middle of the floor to open the door, a smile already on my face as I wonder what delicious thing she 'made too much of' today.

Except it's not Mama Louise. And there is definitely not a casserole or smile to be seen.

Instead, there are five guys standing on my porch. One to the front and four others standing a step back. They're all big and tough-looking, but in a citified way. The man in front is wearing a black turtleneck and has his hair slicked back into a

313

ponytail that's laying over his shoulder. He slips his sunglasses up onto his head, revealing eyes as dark as his shirt.

"Can I help you?" I say, my manners automatic even as I'm thinking *what the fuck?* Irrationally, I'm glad for the screen door between us, though it'd be as useful as an umbrella in a tornado if they make any sort of move. I'm also aware that the shotgun we keep for coyotes around our herd is way over on the other side of the living room above the fireplace and that Murphy is upstairs in Bruce's bedroom, asleep on the rug. Not that the old dog would be much help against this crew.

Turtleneck guy bares his teeth. I'd guess he thinks it's a smile, but it makes the hairs at the base of my neck stand up. "Yes, Miss Tannen. My name is Edward Franks. I'm a friend of your father's. I wanted to pay my respects. So sorry for your loss."

The words are right, and ones expressed endlessly in the days after Daddy died. But something about this Edward guy is all wrong.

"Thank you. How did you know him?" I reply warily. A dangerous thought is taking shape in my gut about who these guys are, about what they want.

"Oh, old friends. Nothing he would've shared, I'm afraid," he says, not answering. "Is Brody around?" He looks left and right, and I realize that his every word is designed to make sure I realize that he knows more about me than I do him.

I hold up a finger, playing dumb. "Just one second. I'll give him a call." I shut the door gently, even though I want to slam it and make a run for the back door. I grab my phone and dial Brody's number.

He finally picks up on the third ring. "What's up, Shayanne?" His voice is chirpy, happier than I've heard him in weeks. There's still a thread of uncertain tension between us over Luke, but it's been better-ish.

"Brody, get to the house NOW," I hiss. "Some of Daddy's

314

friends stopped by. An Edward Franks?"

"Shit," he says, not sounding surprised, and I wonder how much of Daddy's activities Brody was aware of. "I'll get Brutal and Bobby. We'll be right there. Shay—" he says warningly.

"Just get up here," I snarl, fight or flight warring inside me along with fear and anger. Thinking fast, I text Luke too, figuring some backup might not be a bad thing.

Need help at my house. 9-1-1. NOW.

I've barely hit *Send* when the door opens behind me. Embarrassingly, I squeak like a mouse and Edward's grin is one of pure delight, predatory and evil.

He steps inside, his goons following him.

I step back, mentally measuring the distance from my feet to the back door and finding my odds slim. Instead, I find some backbone. My voice is firm as I tell him, "Brody will be up in just a second. Now, I don't want a mess on my clean floor, so I'll just set y'all up with some tea on the porch. Scooch!"

I gesture to the vacuum and then make a shooing motion, pointedly telling him to step back outside, but he just flashes that piranha smile again.

"We'll wait inside, if it's all the same. It's quite chilly out there."

It's a standoff, our eyes staring into one another. On one side, you've got five feet of fury, on the other six feet of slickness . . . with backup.

Not fair.

What must be minutes later but feels much longer, I hear the growl of Brody's ATV. He was in the back pasture with the cows today, so he must've opened the throttle wide to be here already. The engine quiets and I hear the farm truck too.

The back door opens and my three brothers rush in.

Edward drops our staredown, but I don't feel like the winner when he looks to Brody and says, "Now that we're all here, there are things we should discuss."

315

CHAPTER 29

LUKE

*T*he ringing chime of Shay's text automatically brings a smile to my face, but that evaporates when I see her message.

What the fuck?

In an instant, my mind runs away with possibilities, each worse than the last. Whatever the hell is going on, Shayanne needs me. 9-1-1 makes me think it's bad, and I take a quick minute to grab the walkie-talkie off my desk. We all have cell phones, but with spotty reception out here, the walkies are more dependable when time is of the essence. Like now.

"Guys? You there? It's important," I say, pressing the button.

"Yep," Mark replies. I don't wait for James's response, hoping they're together in the pasture.

"Shay just texted me, 'Help, 9-1-1.'"

I don't even get the chance to ask as Mark's reply cuts through. "On my way, meet you at their house. James too."

I run out of the barn toward my truck only to find Mama sitting in the driver's seat, revving the engine. Out the open window, she yells, "Get in!"

I don't think, just jump in, and she's off like a demon, my engine screaming at the mistreatment.

Mama's not the best driver, but she's not the worst either. But right now, she's got the pedal pressed down hard as she skips the long-way-around paved road between our home and the Tannens', instead taking the crow's-flight route. She's bouncing over the dips and bumps of the grassy pasture, getting us there as fast as possible.

I grip the oh-shit handle over my head with one hand and the dash with the other. "Mama! Be careful!" I yell.

"Be ready," is all she replies. I follow her line of sight to see a big, shiny, black Suburban sitting in the grass in front of Shay's house. It looks like a foreshadowing of doom and my gut drops.

Mama slams on the brakes, skidding to a stop. I'm out before she's even got it in park. Somehow managing to time it just right, Mark and James are dismounting from their horses a few yards away. They must have jumped the fence between the back pastures . . . crazy bastards.

Mark's eyes question me, but I have no answers. Instead, we go barreling in like a herd of country boys do.

Inside is absolute pandemonium.

Brody, Brutal, and Bobby are all fighting with some bigass motherfuckers. Fists are flying and punches are landing with *oomphs*, but it's not a fair fight, not with the size of these guys.

"Luke!" Shay cries out.

I turn to follow her voice and I see absolute red. Another guy has her held by the arms, but she's fighting his restraint like a fucking champ, yanking and pulling her arms and stomping on his feet. Unfortunately, she's barefoot, because she could do some real damage if she had on boots. If anything, though, he's not hurting her, just holding her back from her brothers.

That's my Shayanne!

I have no idea what's brought this all on, but I know whose side I'm on. Shayanne's.

Mark and James must have the same thought because we all join in, tackling the newcomers.

Welcome to town, fuckers! Try a good old country boy ass-kicking as a thanks for stopping by!

With improved odds, we make some real headway, but the guys we're fighting aren't just big for show. They're skilled, and the bruises blooming on the Tannens' faces show that. Hell, Brody's nose is bleeding when I join the fight he's waging.

Punches pound flesh, a sick sound filling the room as we all take hits. It's a mess of arms and legs, bodies fighting for dominance. I just keep aiming for the guys in black shirts mixed in with the chaotic heap of our battle.

An uppercut hits my gut, and I feel my rib complain. I can see that Brody threw it. On accident or on purpose, I don't know, and we don't have time right now to address our own shit.

Almost too quiet to hear, a voice says, "Enough."

Just like that, the black shirt-wearing guys stop fighting. They push off us, totally nonchalant, done with the fight because they were instructed to be. Brody throws one more solid punch at the guy closest to him and a crack of a nose answers.

Judging by the blood-tinted smile Brody gives the guy, it's payback for his own smashed schnoz.

I turn to see a guy in a turtleneck sitting on the couch, examining his nails like we weren't all just fighting for our lives. He actually looks bored.

He stands, scanning the room, his dark eyes landing on Brody. "One way or the other, I'll have my money." He looks around again. "Though, rest assured, I wouldn't dream of living in a place like this. I'll sell it."

Shayanne gasps and my brow furrows. What the hell is this asshole talking about?

He doesn't answer my unspoken question. He simply walks out the front door, his men following him. We all hold our breaths until we hear their SUV start and drive away. It'll still be a solid minute until they hit the other side of the fence, but the immediate threat is gone.

"What the fuck?" I say, my breath pained from exertion and my now aching ribs.

"What the fuck is right! What are you doing here?" Brody yells at me, anger reddening his face and making his nose bleed faster.

Incredulously, I sputter. "What? I'm saving your ass! You're welcome, by the way."

"Didn't ask for your fucking help, Bennett!" he roars. Suddenly, he runs at me, tackling me to the floor.

A flurry of punches batters my body as I keep my guard up to protect my face. I buck my hips, setting him off balance and tossing him off me. I quickly hop to my feet, but he comes at me again and I'm forced to fight back. I throw a solid cross to his jaw, avoiding the cheap shot at his nose, and follow up with a hit to his gut too.

Doesn't feel so good, does it, asshole?

He growls, and I realize that was out loud, not in my head. He lands a good hit to my cheekbone and pain blooms bright and hot as I feel blood trickle down where the skin split.

Bad part is, I still don't know why he's attacking me.

Shayanne cries out, "Stop! Brody . . . stop!" I chance a glance her way to see Mark holding her back. I'm glad because I know her and she'd run pell-mell into the middle of whatever this is and get hurt. I don't want that.

But if Brody needs to bleed me, so be it. I don't know what we walked into over here, but I'm damn sure gonna see it through.

We trade a few more punches, each throwing more than we land and our breath jagged with exhaustion. Mark whistles loudly, his county fair-winning piercing edition, and everyone cringes. Mama covers her ears with her hands but nods her approval.

"As that nasty fellow who left said, *enough*," Mama declares. "Now let's get you all cleaned up and we can figure out what the fuck's going on."

Everyone freezes. Mama just dropped an F-bomb. I can count on one hand the number of times that's happened in my lifetime and not even need all five fingers. It's a sure sign that she's done with whatever fighting we're doing and we'd best get ourselves straight right quick or she'll be the one to do it. It's a threat I've heard before, and I don't even know what it means. I've never pushed hard enough to find out, and I'm certainly not gonna start today.

"Yes, ma'am," I say, daring Brody with my eyes to say anything contrary.

Instead, he growls and points a crooked finger at me. "I can handle my own family shit. Back the fuck off." He spins on his heel and stalks to the front door. The screen door slams behind him loudly, and through the windows, I see him punch a porch post as he yells out, "Fuck!"

He buries his hands in his hair, pulling at the strands.

Mama dips her chin, her lips pressed together in a thin line that makes the wrinkles above her lip flash. "We'll let Brody cool off while I deal with the rest of you. Shayanne, can you lead us to the kitchen and hand me some towels that we can use for cleanup?"

No one says a word as Mama and Shayanne tend to our wounds. For the most part, it's bruising, so we don't ruin many of Shay's kitchen towels, but we do use almost every bag of frozen vegetables she has in the freezer.

Mark's got one on his right hand and one on his left shoulder. James has one to his jaw, holding it with the back of his bruised hand in a multi-tasking necessity because Brutal and Bobby have a couple of bags each. Brutal's got one on each hand—and I make a note that he's seriously ambidextrous when he punches—and one resting on his thrown-back forehead to soothe his busted brow. Bobby's flexing his hand slowly, and I hope he's not too hurt to play guitar again because that'd be a shame. He drops the bag of peas back onto it with a grimace, but he doesn't seem too upset, so that's a good sign. His other hand moves to hold a bag to his jaw.

We look like the losers, but somehow, just getting out of that fight alive feels like a victory.

"What happened, kids?" Mama asks.

Brutal and Bobby look to Shayanne, the apparent family leader in Brody's absence.

She tells us about Edward Franks and his goons coming over, wanting to see Brody, and how she'd called in the cavalry because she'd felt like this was going to be bad.

She'd been right, unfortunately. And we're all paying the price.

"So, what does this Franks guy want?" Mama asks Shayanne. "He said he wanted his money and that he'd sell this place."

Shayanne looks at Brutal and Bobby, shaking her head and throwing her palms up like she doesn't even know how to begin to answer that.

Brutal clears his throat. "He said he was a *friend* of Dad's."

Even that little bit answers so much. Paul Tannen was a good man for a lot of years, a less good man for some, but recently, his escape into gambling had been scandalous. Win big, lose big, play hard either way. And Edward Franks's appearance becomes seriously concerning.

"He said Dad signed a line of credit to keep the cashflow rolling after we cut him off . . . and put up the farm as the collateral. It's payable on death after all heirs reach the age of twenty-one, so we can either pay off the huge loan Dad ran up or Edward'll take the farm to pay the debt," Brutal finishes.

Shay growls, literal fury rolling in her chest. "The one damn thing Daddy could've done right, but he even managed to fuck that up by dying weeks before my birthday."

Brutal shrugs. "At least we're dealing with it now, with slightly clearer heads. I don't know what would've happened if that guy had shown up to the funeral talking about taking the farm."

"We would've run him out of town, that's what," Mama scoffs. "He came now because that's what the contract said, but make no mistake, he came knowing you kids would be blind-sided by this. He wanted the upper hand." She *tsks* like that's a shameful thing. "Do you even know if this is true? I mean, does he have paperwork with Paul's signature?"

Shayanne shakes her head, and Brutal's and Bobby's brows rise. A glimmer of hope that maybe this is all some misunderstanding tries to lighten my anger.

Then Brody comes back in the back door. He's obviously been listening from the porch, judging by the hard line of his jaw. His nose is straighter than it was before, so I guess he set it himself, which must've hurt like a son of a bitch. Tough fucker, that one.

Mama tosses a bag of okra to him, which he catches with ease in one hand, but I see the slight grimace. The other holds a manila envelope.

"Asshole left this on the front porch. Seems he might have a leg to stand on," he says, his voice deep and angry. But I can see how tired he is, the weariness etched in every line of his face and the set of his shoulders.

Shayanne gasps, her hands covering her mouth, but in the next heartbeat, she's pissed as a raging bull. "No! We will fight this with everything we have." Her nail digs into the wood of the table as she makes her point. "I'm not leaving my home because Daddy messed up and fucked us over."

I know how hard it hurts her to say that, to know it down to her soul. Brody licks his lips and winces when he tastes the blood from the fresh split there.

He goes to Shayanne, an invisible thread pulling them together. He hauls her into his arms and she curls against his chest. She doesn't cry, not now. She's holding strong, gearing up and getting ready for battle. There's a part of me that wishes she was seeking comfort from me, but I know she needs this from her brother.

The connection between them has been fraying, unraveling bit by bit as they battle it out over Shay and me. But in this moment, I think we all realize that there are bigger problems looming, and whom Shayanne loves doesn't matter in the least as long as we all love each other.

Okay, so I don't love Brody Tannen, and he certainly doesn't love me. But as long as we both love Shayanne and tolerate each other, that's got to be enough, right?

I meet his eyes and see more than I expect.

He attacked me today, bled me over interfering in his family, with Shayanne and with the shitstorm that landed on his front porch. But I can see his silent apology, his pain as he struggles to be everything to everyone and his hope that his family can just be happy. I remember that Mark seemed to feel a kinship with the eldest Tannen son, and if I can manage to understand Mark's grunts, maybe I can learn to translate Brody's fists into the words he truly means to say.

Family — Protect. Love. Survive.

Farm — Work. Support. Provide.

That's all there is to him, all that matters.

I nod my chin once, and in some type of cowboy conversation, a truce is made.

"Bennetts, thank you for coming today. But can we get a

little privacy now? We have some things to discuss as a family," Brody says flatly.

We stand up from the kitchen table and begin a circle jerk of careful handshakes, brothers to brothers. Mama goes in for a hug with each of them, fussing over their cuts and telling Brutal that he needs to put Steri-strips on his brow. He agrees, though we all know he'll do nothing of the sort.

I kiss Shay on the forehead, and she closes her eyes and whispers, "Thank you."

"Anytime, honey," I promise her.

Last but not least, I shake Brody's hand. It's a tight grip for both of us, one last pissing match that hurts both of our abused hands. But he growls, "Thank you."

I know it cost him a lot to say that, especially to me.

So I let him off the hook he's uncomfortably twisting on and let him know that we're good. "Next time you throw hands at me, I'll go for your nose instead of being nice and getting your jaw."

He smirks like the cocky bastard he is. "You can try, motherfucker."

It's not a pretty ceasefire, but it's ours and I'll take it.

CHAPTER 30

SHAYANNE

*J*don't bother with a real dinner, not after the battle royale of the afternoon. I toss microwaved ham steaks, box macaroni, and cold biscuits on the table and call it done. It all tastes like sawdust, anyway.

"So, what are we gonna do, Brody?" I ask, jumping into the deep end with both feet.

He swallows a bite of ham and lays his hand on the stack of papers he read out loud to us. Seems Daddy really did sign a contract with Edward Franks.

The gist of it is that Daddy had a line of credit and was making payments up until a week before he died. He managed to get a clause in the contract that we all had to be twenty-one for the collateral to be actionable, which would've been a small kindness if we'd been younger and wanting to stay on the farm until we grew up. But since we're all of age, we have no time, no money, and no options.

Brody looks like a man drowning in his insufficiency, but I don't think any of us were ready for something like this. I always thought Daddy was funding his gambling with his own wins and the little 'allowance' we gave him. At least, that's what he assured us was happening.

Guess not, huh, Daddy?

"First things first, we need to see the lawyer in the morning. He handled Dad's will and estate stuff, and he probably knows more about contracts than any of us, so maybe he can give us some advice on where to start."

"Uhm, not that Mr. Jacobsen isn't good," I ask, biting my lip, "but do you think this might be a bit outside his norm?"

Brody sighs but looks choiceless. Thankfully, I have an idea.

"I think I'll call Sophie tonight too. Her brother's that big shot, and I'm sure he's got some bulldog lawyer he can recommend. 'Kay?"

"He probably does, but we can't afford some high-dollar suit, Shayanne," Bobby says miserably.

"We have to," I argue. "The safe deposit box had a few thousand dollars in it, not enough to make a dent in Daddy's debt, but maybe enough to get us some real advice, at least. We can't lose the farm because we don't know what we're doing. None of us are stupid, but this isn't something we can begin to handle on our own. I mean, look at y'all."

My eyes tick around the table to my brothers, each one with bruises still blooming in ugly swatches of black and blue.

"I can handle our shit, Shayanne," Brody protests. "Always have, always will."

I don't respond, just glare back. This is so far beyond the scope of anything he or I have ever done, and we can't just start now. Now when the stakes are so high. Hell, we could end up losing a lot more than just the farm.

Brody blinks silently and then begrudgingly agrees. "Fine, call Sophie. See if someone can meet us anytime tomorrow, in town or out here. We need to act fast because I don't trust that

Franks won't come back out here. I'm scared he won't give you a chance to call me next time."

A hush falls over the table. I've never felt vulnerable at home before. We've always been safe, and the folks out here in our remote area are kind and friendly, the sort that'd give you the shirt off their backs. But today, I'd been alone with danger. It went badly for our family, but it could've been worse, much worse.

"I'll lock the front gate and set it to manual before I go to bed tonight," Bruce says. "No one will get in without a remote."

"Unless they're on foot and just climb over," I correct.

Bruce sighs, knowing I'm right.

Silence reigns for several minutes, the only sound the scraping of forks on plates and Brody's slightly wheezy breathing from where his nose still ain't quite right.

Bobby finally speaks. "We gonna talk about the other thing? About the Bennetts?"

It's a bold move on his part. We're in the eye of a tornado and he just threw fire into the mix.

Is a fire-nado a thing?

I don't know, but it feels like it's swirling all around us right now, real or not.

Brody gets up from the table, refilling his tea and dropping it to the table so hard it sloshes over the rim. His mood's gone dark, his eyes black as soot. We can all feel the shift, and I'm honestly scared of what Brody's going to say.

"You know what I think?" He scoffs at some thought only he can hear in his mind, his paces across the kitchen floor picking up speed as my heart races. "I think Dad didn't know shit. Maybe once upon a time, he did, but here lately, he was mean, Shay. Mean to those people next door, mean to us." He looks at Bruce and Bobby, whose heads have dropped. "He was wrong."

I wonder if Daddy was a different man to them than he was to me. I've had some eye-opening thoughts about who Daddy was and what might've made him devolve into the man he'd become, but maybe even that's not the whole picture. Today's definitely proof of that.

We each had a relationship with him, but that doesn't mean it was the same for each of us. There's a saying I heard once. Hell, it was probably one that I repeated with a 'Daddy says' at one time or another.

Some people say I'm sweet as an angel. Some people say I'm cruel as the devil. They're both right. Just depends on who you are to me.

I wonder if I got the nicer version of Daddy as 'his girl' and what that means the boys got from him.

I don't have time to contemplate, though, because Brody is laying down his verdict.

"It was good of them to come over today," he starts.

I can't help but interrupt. "You beat Luke up for that."

Captain Obvious, shut up and let the man speak!

Brody shrugs, smiling a little. "Well, he got in the way of me whipping those guys' asses."

No one acknowledges that that wasn't what was happening at all and that if the Bennetts hadn't shown up, we'd be a lot worse off than we are. Pride is a dangerous thing, but I'll let Brody protect his if that's what he needs.

"You're not leaving." Brody says it as an order, but I hear the hint of a question and nod. "You love him." A statement, but I nod again. "And he loves you, treats you right?" That's a question, and even though I'm nervous at where he's going with this, a slight smile lifts my lips as I continue my bobblehead action.

"Yes, yes, and yes," I say, reassuring him.

"Fine," he says, rolling his eyes. "You can date the asshole next door."

I hop up from the table and tackle him. He catches me

around the waist, trying to get away from the kisses I'm peppering his cheek with. I see him wince and remember too late that his face is probably pretty pained right now. "Sorry. Thank you, Brody."

"Good thing you came to your senses," I only half-tease him, "because I wasn't going to let this go."

He lifts one eyebrow, deadpanning, "No shit? I couldn't tell, Sis."

Bruce huffs a tiny laugh, his fork clenched in his purple paw of a hand. "Can we eat now, before all this gets cold?"

Bobby looks around, a smile blooming on his face, which looks odd because one side is so swollen it looks like he's got the mumps. "So, does this mean we ain't feuding with the Bennetts no more?"

I pick up my fork, holding it high and declaring, "This means we ain't feuding no more."

The atmosphere feels lighter, even with the uncertainty of this contract and what it'll mean weighing on each of us. At least one drama is handled. And we'll face the other as Tannens. Too tough to give in.

Brody and I sit back down, and we all dig in as a family.

Brody still leans over, talking as he eats. "Okay, rule number one . . . he ain't sleeping over here. I'm not listening to anyone, Bennett or not, rail my sister, and these walls are too damn thin for any real privacy."

I blush fiercely. We don't do this, but now that he mentions it . . .

"Where do y'all get laid?" I ask around my mouthful of food. "You just go to the girl's place and then creep out before dawn for a walk of shame?"

I look to each of them to find their brows all creeping up toward their hairlines, looking guilty as sin. Finally, Bobby smiles. "More like a walk of fame when they're begging, 'Come back, Bobby!'" He aims for a falsetto, but it's barely an octave higher than his usual deep voice.

Bruce's mouth quirks up and I can't wait for the zing he's about to throw out. "They're probably saying that because you didn't get the job done, fucker. Ladies first ain't just for opening doors, you know."

Bobby grabs what's left of Bruce's biscuit, holding it hostage as he taunts. "'Least I'm getting some, not mooning and holding out, lover boy." With that, he shoves the whole thing in his mouth, which has to hurt. I wonder what Bobby knows that I don't, but for now, I'll let it go.

We're here, together. And that's enough.

"Fine, I'll sneak out as per usual each night, and you pretend you know nothing," I reply with a big, fake wink. "I'll get my freak on with Luke and sashay back over in the morning to make breakfast. Do I need to sneak back in too?"

Brody's smile is small but important. A true sign of acceptance of Luke and me. "No, you don't have to sneak around. But I don't want to see your PDAs. You're still my little sister, even when you're a pain in my ass."

I nod, acting like I'm taking notes in the air because my notebook is in my nightstand. "Oh, question, though, now that we're being all out-in-the-open with relationship stuff. What can you tell me about reverse cowgirl?" I flutter my lashes, the very picture of innocence.

Bruce and Bobby both groan, but Brody goes one step further. "I'm out," Brody says, getting up and walking out of the kitchen. But I notice he takes his biscuit with him. He pokes his head back in, pointing a finger at me and talking around his mouthful of bread. "Lawyer tomorrow after breakfast. Bright and early."

"Think I'll eat upstairs tonight so I can chew a little more carefully," Bobby adds, getting up too. I knew that mouthful of biscuit was too much for his sore jaw.

Before he passes the door, I call out, "Come back, Bobby!" My falsetto sucks just as bad as his does, and I can't help but giggle at his groan of frustration.

Bruce reaches for Brody's plate, spearing his abandoned chunk of ham with his fork and moving it over to his plate. He takes a big bite, chewing thoughtfully. "Whatcha need to know about reverse cowgirl? And do we need to have the birth control talk?"

Now I'm the one crying out. "Ugh! I was kidding! No, I don't want to talk sex positions with my brothers, and I'm good on the birth control."

He winks, pointing at me with his fork. "Gotcha!"

I smile, enjoying this moment of banter. We're all masking some feelings, playing on the surface where it's light and easy, but the water's scarily churning below and full of sharks. That's okay, though. It's Get Through Shit 101, focus on the moments of good and fake the rest till you make it out the other side.

CHAPTER 31

LUKE

"So, what'd the lawyer say?" I ask, my fingertips swirling a mindless pattern on Shay's belly.

We're at the tree, my back pressed to the bark through a wool blanket. Shay's between my spread legs, leaned back against my chest. Together, we make up one big, fluffy burrito of blankets to ward off the chill of the night.

We could've gone to my perfectly warm house, but it'd seemed right to meet here tonight. She needs the open vastness of the night to spill the hard details of her day, now more than ever. The darkness, broken by the moonlight, is like its own blanket, insulating us from the issues we're facing, a protective shield in its own way.

But that shield only goes so far.

"Basically that we're fucked. Ten times over and twice on Sunday," Shay responds sadly.

I squeeze her in the circle of my arms, a silent request for her to spill it.

She sighs and looks up at the stars. "From what the lawyers can tell, the contract's legit. Which means it's binding and we have to pay up. There's not enough in Daddy's estate or any of the accounts to make even a dent in the balance he has. So the only way to make it right is to give them the farm or sell it and pay them off. Either way, we lose."

She sniffles and then wipes her eyes on the blanket. "I can't lose my home, Luke. I don't know what to do because it seems like it's all falling apart no matter what. Brody damn near lost his mind today and then took off like a demon in his truck after the meeting. I don't even know where he went, but Bruce said to let him go, that he'd be okay, just needed to figure some shit out. But there's nothing to figure out! We're just up shit creek without a paddle."

"Shay, honey . . ." I start, not knowing how to take this pain away but wishing hard that I could.

She's not done, though.

"The worst part of it is that I am so *furious* at Daddy. *He* did this to us. Franks isn't a good guy, and I sure haven't forgotten the sight of his goons beating up everyone I care about, but he's just holding up a contract he signed in good faith. It's not his fault, not really. It's Daddy's. He took that money knowing he couldn't pay it back and that we'd be the ones to pay the price when he died. I've gone back and forth emotionally at losing him, but right now, I'm so mad I could spit nails. If I could, I would strangle him with my bare hands."

Shock courses through her at her own words, her body going rigid. She mumbles something that sounds like regret, but I soothe her, pulling a hand out of the blanket to rub along her wavy hair, twirling a lock around my finger.

"It's okay to be mad at him. Just because he's gone doesn't mean that he's now some reverent saint you can't ever speak ill of. He was a man, with all the inherent flaws that go along with that. Maybe he had more than his fair share of hurts and weaknesses, but it's okay to be upset that what he did is fucking you over."

It's as much of a kindness as I can say about the man right now. Shay's right. If I could bring him to life to kill him again for hurting her like this, I would. In a heartbeat.

But I can't. We're where we are, with what we've got. And we'll have to cope.

"So, what's the plan, then?" I venture.

Anything she says will suck. I know it, she knows it, and her brothers know it. There's no way they're getting out of this with their farm intact. At this point, they'll be lucky to have their family intact.

"The lawyer Sophie's brother recommended . . . his name's Mr. Branford. He said if we give in to Franks and complete the contract, there's no real cushion. It'd be a true hand-over of the property and we'd walk away with the money in the accounts and the clothes on our backs. We could take the herd, but we'd have nowhere to raise them, so our best bet would be to sell them so we'd have a little money to set ourselves back up for a fresh start."

She chuckles humorlessly, both of us knowing that none of her family wants a new life somewhere else. They *are* that farm, just like we are our ranch. I get how impossible starting over sounds to them. We'd be devastated too if something like that happened.

"Second option is to find a buyer who wants it as an investment property. Basically, just a silent owner who'd let us keep running it like we always have. But we'd have to answer to someone. It wouldn't be *ours*."

I nod, my chin digging into the top of her head. "But you could stay. Your brothers could stay. Would someone do that?"

She twists, looking at me in the dark. "I asked Sophie if her brother or Roxy would. Do you know how hard that was for me to do? I mean, she's my best friend and I would never want to use her like that, but I didn't see any other way. Desperate times, you know? So I swallowed my pride and asked."

My breath is frozen in my chest. "What'd she say?"

"She cried and said that if she could, she would. She tried, she even checked her own bank balances. She has a trust from when her parents died, and they have James's bull riding money, but it's not enough. And with the baby coming . . . she can't. Jake and Roxy couldn't either, something about having just made a big long-term business investment, which I get, but I just . . . I don't know what to do."

She shivers, but it's more from the cold in her veins than the night. Still, I need to get her inside where it's warm.

"C'mon, honey. Let's go home," I tell her, my voice raspy with emotion.

She gets up, standing like a zombie as I slip a blanket over her shoulders. I toss another around my own and then my arm around her to lead her toward my house. All the fight's gone out of her and she lets me guide her through the darkness.

I don't bother turning on the lights at home. We just shuffle inside to the bedroom, where I strip Shay down to her panties. She doesn't move other than to step out of her sweats and lift her lifeless arms as I pull her shirt over her head. She's a shell of herself, all vibrancy and fire snuffed out. Lying in my bed, she looks forlorn, a lost kitten whose final hope at kindness in the world has been ripped away.

I strip to my underwear and curl up behind her, a buffer to the storm raging around her family. But I can't do anything about the storm inside her heart.

Or can I?

"I know it's not much, but your goats . . . they can stay here. We've never had any, but we can help take care of them, and that way, you can still make your soaps. If it comes down to it, Mark'd probably buy your herd for the going rate. He was gonna buy some at the winter sale, anyway." I'm talking out of my ass, not having a clue whether Mark was going to add to our herd or not but knowing that he'll do it for the Tannens. For Shayanne. For me.

It's the smallest gesture, but it's all I can think of right now. Shay's voice is small, broken. "Thank you."

And then she drifts off into a fitful sleep. Meanwhile, I stay awake for hours, thinking and planning, wishing and hoping.

For a future with Shay. For an answer to her family's problem. Hell, around two in the morning, I think I make a wish for world fucking peace. All I know is, I can't let this woman in my arms go and I'll do anything to make her happy.

THREE DAYS LATER, MARK AND I ARE SITTING AT A DESK IN town. There's a stack of papers in front of me with neon yellow flags sticking out the edge.

The portly man across from us smiles, his cheeks lifting so high his eyes look squinty. "If you'll just read through this, initial and sign as noted."

Mark puts his big hand flat on the papers, stopping me. His eyes bore into mine, his breath slow and his voice a growl. "You sure about this? It's not on you, Luke. And they're going to be pissed as hornets. They're gonna fight against it and might not even take us up on it."

I press my lips together, knowing he's right. But after hours of thinking, several long and hard conversations, and a long ride on Duster's back to talk with Pops in my head, it's the best I've come up with.

"I'm sure," I say, my voice sure and steady even if my hand is shaking a bit.

Courage is not the absence of fear. It's doing what you need to do even when you wanna piss yourself. Hell, sometimes, it's doing it while the piss is running down your leg.

Pops's gross bastardization of the famous quote runs through my head.

Mark nods. "Thought so. Just had to be sure. Damn proud of you, Luke."

CHAPTER 32

SHAYANNE

I know Mama Louise is being nice, but I really don't feel like a big family dinner tonight. But she'd insisted, telling me not to cook a thing and just to show up with my brothers. And by *insisted*, I mean virtually dared me to disobey.

So dinner at the Bennetts' it is.

We sit around the mish-mash of tables on the back porch again, space heaters whirring in each corner. Through the window screens, you can see the last leaves leaving the trees and the bare yellow-grey of the grass for miles around us.

"Ooh, it is colder than Christmas out here. Gonna have to figure out a better solution for dinners before the real winter weather hits."

Mama's offhand words cut deeply because we won't be here to see the winter snow covering the acres of land. I mean, I'll still come over to see Luke, of course.

But it's not the same. It won't ever be the same again.

Mark says a quick prayer over the food and then Mama takes over. "Dig in before the chill takes the warmth outta dinner," she says chirpily.

341

We each grab the nearest platter or bowl and serve ourselves as the passing of dishes circles the table. I look down to see chicken fried steak with white pepper gravy, mashed potatoes drowning in brown gravy, fat green beans with bacon, and a roll on my plate. I don't remember putting any of it there and don't want to eat in the least.

The table's quiet, sounds of food disappearing into people's bellies the only breach of the silence. Mama Louise clears her throat once, and then again.

I look up from my glum stare at the steak, like it's the thing that's offended me. Mama is looking pointedly at Mark, who swallows his food with a gulp.

He looks to Brody, hesitation in his eyes. "So, I know you don't want to talk about this, Brody. And I wish I could respect your wishes, but I can't."

Brody's eyes are coals, hard and barely covering the fire burning through him. He hated swallowing his pride to ask Sophie for help with the lawyer, and I didn't even tell him that I'd begged her to buy the farm because I knew he'd have never allowed it, not that it mattered in the end. But the truce with the Bennetts is too fresh for a challenge. Especially not by Mark, who's the equivalent to Brody in our family.

The leader.

Not when Mark is doing well, keeping his family stable and safe, and Brody feels like he's failing. He's not. The failure is all Daddy's doing, but Brody feels responsible all the same, and nothing we've said has persuaded him from that line of thinking.

"No," Brody snaps back immediately, his jaw clenching.

"Hear me out," Mark says, not a question in his hard words. But at least not an order. "Please."

I can only imagine what it cost Mark to tell Brody 'please' since neither of them is known for their softness or kindness.

I swallow, a gnawing in my gut telling me that something's

going on. I glance around the table. Bruce and Bobby are doing the same as me, looking around in confusion. Mama Louise, Luke, and James are all looking at Mark like he's holding court. Sophie and Katelyn are looking at me, though, a message in their eyes I can't decipher.

Luke drops his hand to my thigh, squeezing tight. He's trying to tell me something too, but I don't know what it is.

Brody doesn't agree to listen, but he doesn't get up from the table either, so Mark goes on. "We know that the lawyer said your best option was a silent investor."

A tiny ridiculous hope blooms in my heart as my eyes widen. Is Mark gonna offer to be a silent investor for us so we can keep our farm?

"I've been accused of being quiet, that's for sure. But I ain't silent, I can guarantee you that." And poof, that hope disappears like cotton candy into water.

Brody looks at him, his eyes narrowed. "What are you saying?"

Mark's eyes tick to Mama Louise, who nods. Her face is straight, something I've never seen before. She's not usually a bluffer—when she's happy, she smiles, when she's sad, she frowns, and when she's mad, she'll bite your fool head off while you apologize for causing a ruckus. This is different . . . scary.

"I want you to hear me out before you say no. You owe that to yourself and to your family," Mark decrees. Brody doesn't agree, but he doesn't argue.

I feel like I'm watching continents move, slow but powerful, quiet but fierce.

"I propose that you sell your farm to us." Brody flinches at Mark's words, but Mark plows ahead. "We'll give you market value for it so you'll have the money to pay off Franks, plus some in the bank. Just as importantly, your family will be safe from their threat."

Brody growls and Mark growls right back.

343

Not continents. Beasts, ready to battle.

"There's more. The entire property will become Bennett Ranch, and herds will be combined and worked across all the pastures. You ready for the good part yet?" Mark's lips twitch, and I get the sense that he's enjoying this somehow, which pisses me off.

I'm about to say something, yell at the injustice, or more likely, tell him to fuck off for taking advantage of our loss the way Daddy tried to do to them when their dad died. Daddy was wrong when he did it, and so is Mark. Fucking hypocrite, that's what he is.

Luke gives up on squeezing my thigh and pinches me instead to get my attention. I swat at his hand, glaring at him in anger. "Wait," he mouths silently, for nobody but me.

"We can't work all that land, all those animals. Not with just three of us. Not with Luke being gone a lot of the time and James about to have a baby. We're gonna need some help. That's where you Tannens come in. I ain't ever worked fields, don't know shit about farming or orchards. But you two do." He lifts his chin toward Bruce and Bobby. "And I can't care for the herd alone."

Brody scoffs, his words more a sneer than anything. "So you wanna buy our land out from underneath us and then hire us back on as workers?"

Mark's shoulder lifts and then drops. "You can see it that way if you want, and I guess in a way, that's true. There ain't no shame in what we do. We're all ranch and farm hands." He points around the table at everyone except for Sophie and Katelyn, who have their own careers that don't depend on the land surrounding us. Well, Sophie does, kinda . . . but the point's made. "Some of us just have to worry about the budget sheet, and some of us just do the work and fall into bed at night."

He pauses, and I can see the reality sinking in for Brody, heavy and painful.

"And what ranch hand do you know who has their own family home? You all can stay over there or build your own house somewhere on the property, if you'd rather. And one last thing, and this is a big deal no other buyer is gonna give you, so listen up . . . we'll include in the contract that if we ever choose to sell your original acreage, you'll have right of first refusal. We won't ever be able to sell your family land without you passing on it first."

Mark sighs, like saying that many words in one go was hard as hell for him. I see Katelyn lay her hand over his, her red-tipped thumb swirling across his tanned skin.

It sounds . . . good? I think. I mean, it's definitely better than anything we've come up with in the last few days. Luke resumes the swirling pattern on my thigh, letting me think, but I can feel his eyes on me. Heavy, hopeful. Like my heart.

Brody's head falls, though. "I can't. I don't know if I can—" He looks up, his glassy eyes meeting mine, Bruce's, and Bobby's before he looks up at the ceiling, shaking his head in denial at the inevitability of our losing the farm.

Mama Louise's voice is soft, serenity rolling through the air in waves from her end of the table. "Here's what I think, Brody Tannen." He doesn't look at her, but she keeps speaking to him. "You are a good man, one who has done far too much for far too long, probably more than any of us even realize. And it's time for you to get to live your life too."

"This is my life," he strangles out. "I don't know anything else."

Mama Louise smiles. "And you know it better than just about anyone, save maybe one or two people at this table." She looks at Mark, and I see a slight flush wash over his scruffy cheeks. "Mark's all business, and I think you are too in a lot of ways. Shoot, I think you two'd make a good team. The business makes sense, you know it does. But let me tell you what I see."

Her eyes move around the table, meeting each of ours, and I can see the love pouring out of her, changing the very atmosphere surrounding us to one of . . . home.

"I've been blessed to spend a few years on this Earth, more than your mother, your father, and my John. What I've learned is that *family* is what matters. My family, your family . . . and what could, if you'll let it, be *our* family. It's not always made by blood. Sometimes, if you're lucky enough, it's made by choice. Look around this table, Brody."

Though she's telling my brother, I do as she says too and see the shock on my brothers' faces and the surety in the Bennetts'.

"Shay and I could tear this kitchen up, whipping up some dinners like you've never dreamed of, or she could focus on her soaps if she wants, because I'd love nothing more than to feed a full household every night. That's my life, my love to my boys, and now, my girls too." She looks at Sophie, then Katelyn, and then me. And I feel something I haven't in a long time. A mother's love, honest and pure . . . and mine. It feels warm and good, like sealant over a crack in my heart that's been fighting to heal.

"You and Mark could work an even bigger herd together, though the good Lord knows, you'll have to figure out how to speak in more than grunts and fists. But you are two peas in a pod, and I think you'd be friends if you both managed to get your heads out of your asses."

I can't help the tiny giggle at Mama's cussing because I think she's right about their being alike in a lot of ways.

"Your brothers' lives don't have to change unless they wanted something different. And even then, they'd have the *choice*, something none of you have now. The only thing that's changed by this plan is the worry on your shoulders, the weight you carry every day, the boundaries still caging you in. You don't have to do it alone. Let us all help carry that load so you can be free to do what you love, where you love the land, without worries."

Brody looks at Mark, so much swirling in his eyes that I can't tell what he's thinking, which scares me. This sounds too good to be true. It sounds like the solution we've all been praying for, and I just hope he can see that. We're losing the farm no matter what, but at least this way, we keep our lives the way we've always lived them. Dare I say, it might even be a better quality of life than the worry-filled one we've had these last few years.

"You got funds for a purchase this big? I mean, not to put too fine a point on it, but our farm ain't small potatoes. And given the current situation, I'd advise against putting up your ranch as collateral." He laughs, but it's a bitter, painful sound.

Mark looks at Luke, who I see nod beside me in some brotherly version of a conversation.

"Well, I did take that lesson to heart. And to be quite honest, I wouldn't put Pops's land up for anything in the world. But we needed collateral to secure the loan. Good thing we've got some damn fine thoroughbreds in the barn. For some reason, Luke seems to fancy you more than them."

Brody looks at Luke incredulously. "You did that for us?"

Luke grins, cocky bravado that I know is for Brody's benefit, to let him save a little face in a situation he likely feels humbled by. "Well, I figured I owed you after sneaking around with your little sister. How about we call it even now?" He throws his arm over the back of my chair possessively, dangerously comfortable with his PDAs considering Brody's precariously on edge and close enough to throw a solid punch. "Plus, I've got no intention of defaulting on that loan and losing my babies. Between you working the herd, the boys working the

347

land, and me working the horses, we'll make each of the payments early, just to be sure."

It's a promise as sure as I've ever heard one. My heart leaps at the picture they're painting, wanting it so badly. Brody and I have been through so much together, the ragtag glue holding our family together, but the Bennetts are promising something much better than a quick fix or the make-do we've had to settle for.

They're promising a family, a forever.

Brody blinks and then swallows thickly, not taking the lightness Luke offered. His voice is choked, rough as he tells the table, "This is . . . a lot. Thank you so much. I guess we need to talk about this as a family."

Mark nods and gets up. "Katelyn planned hot chocolate and s'mores for us around the campfire pit out back as dessert. We'll go get everything set up and light the fire. Take your time, though. It doesn't have to be tonight if you're not ready. Or ever, if you don't want to. Gotta say, though, I don't think we'd ever get better neighbors than you."

He sets a manila envelope on the table next to Brody. "I took the liberty of having Sophie's hotshot lawyer draw up the contract. He said he made a few notes for you, so read over it carefully. It's all in there."

"WHAT DO YOU THINK?" BRODY ASKS US WHEN SILENCE descends again.

We've read over the contract page by page, and it's exactly what Mark said. Mr. Branford's notes had basically said, *Sign this now!* so we know what his advice is.

"I hate it," Bobby says, surprising us all.

"What?" I screech, my voice pitched high enough to shatter glass.

"I hate that we're here, stuck in this position," he says, wincing but holding up a hand. "But that's Dad's fault, ain't it? He left his mess for us to clean up, same as always. His problem has been ours for too long. And of all the options we've gone through, this is the best. Far better than I think we even dreamed."

Bruce looks thoughtful and zeroes in on Brody. "For us, this is all emotional shit to some degree. If we do this, it's mostly the loss of a piece of paper and a name on the front gate, but we're gonna keep doing exactly what we've been doing our whole lives. For you, though . . . you think you can work with Mark? More importantly, you think you could work *for* him? I mean, if we sell to someone else, you're probably going to be a ranch hand somewhere, so you're gonna have a boss no matter what. But it wouldn't have to be Mark Bennett."

Brody's jaw clenches as he looks to the ceiling. He seems to be watching the lights shine, or maybe seeing beyond them?

"I think that what we've been told about them for a lot of years was fundamentally wrong, and this is proof of that. As far as working for Mark Bennett, I could do worse. He's a straight shooter, responsible, and someone I can respect. He's a hard worker, and that goes a long way, in my book. And this way, at least we're all still together. That means a lot."

He's right. Our staying together means *everything*.

I bump Brody with my shoulder and give him the slightest smile. "Fundamentally? Five whole syllables? Wish I had my notebook to write down the date."

His answering smile is sad. "I think we'll remember this day for a long time, Shayannie."

Decision made, Brody picks up a pen. He sighs, a shudder rolling through his body. He looks up one more time, pen pressed to the page. "Fuck you, Dad. Hope you're rolling in your grave and flaming in hell."

Shiiiit.

That's somehow harsher than I thought Brody would be. I mean, I'm still furious at Daddy, but I wonder again if Brody got something different from Daddy than I did. But that's a conversation for another day. Right now, we're signing away one dream, one life, and starting a fresh one with a bigger family right next door.

Brody signs.

Bruce signs.

Bobby signs.

I sign.

We go outside, the cold night a deadly shock through me. We approach the rising fire as a unit, one family joining another, the sum greater than its individual parts.

I sit on the ground between Luke's spread knees. He wraps his arms around me and kisses the crown of my head, the warmth of the fire and his body bleeding into me, bringing me back to life and filling me with love, with family.

CHAPTER 33

LUKE

"How'd it go?" I ask Shay from my perch on the front porch. Her boots have barely hit the dirt, but I've been watching the drive for her to get here for too long to be patient now. Plus, I can already see by the look on her face that it went about as well as we'd expected. Which was pretty damn shitty.

"Ugh, such a slimeball!" she hollers. "Do you know that after all was said and done and Brody signed over the check to Franks, he wanted to chit-chat about Daddy? Like we were best friends or kissing cousins or some shit. No, thank you, hope to never see ya again!"

She's pointing a finger and stomping her feet on the front steps to Mama's house, her waves bouncing around in a riotous halo. I hate to see her mad, but she looks pretty with the pink coloring her cheeks. I'm a smart enough man to never, ever tell her that, though.

I know today was hard on her, hard on Brody too. But they've been doing amazingly well with this whole transition. Better than I would've, that's for sure, and I'm so damn proud of Shayanne. Of all the Tannens, really, though I won't be telling the boys that anytime soon because they don't want that touchy-feely shit from me.

We finished the contract and loan with the bank two days ago, and we are officially the owners of the entire two thousand acres, a new and expanded Bennett Ranch. Once that was handled, Brody had to meet with Edward Franks to pay off the debt Paul racked up.

To be on the safe side, we'd coordinated. The meeting took place in Mr. Branford's office with a personal guard. I didn't ask what kind of work he usually does to have a security detail on speed-dial, but I'm betting it's not ugly divorces. Brody, Mark, and Shay had gone to town for that. Mama, Bobby, and I had sat on our front porch, with Brutal and James on the Tannens', just in case Franks sent his goons back for a go-round while the meeting was taking place.

But thankfully, everything was fine on our end. Just a quiet few hours of some get-to-know-you chatter. I think Bobby's the last real hold-out of the Tannens, which surprises me. I thought he was pretty mellow, but there's something about him. He reminds me of the saying, *'Still waters run deep,'* but I'm not sure what's in his head or his heart. I can just feel the distance, but maybe that'll get better with time, something we'll have plenty of now.

And hell, for all I know, he's still grieving over his dad. I know all the Tannens are to some degree, even with the anger they feel at him. You never 'get over' loss, not really. It changes you and then you move forward. They're mourning the man he was and who they wish he would've been, all the while having these sparks of happy memories that don't seem to coincide with who he'd become. Add to that being forced to lose the deed to their land, and it's a lot. So I'm willing to cut Bobby some slack for burying that pain down a bit.

"I'm guessing you told Franks where he could shove his

nostalgia? With some style, I'm sure." I wiggle my eyebrows at her, hoping to douse her fire with my silliness.

I already know from Mark's text that it went all right, and we'll hash it out with a play-by-play over dinner. So for now, I just want to soothe her ruffled feathers.

She groans, eyes rolling heavenward. "You are the worst. I've got a good hissy fit worked up here, and you're ruining it for no good-goddamn reason. Just let me whine for a minute!"

"Don't be a salty heifer, woman," I tease. "You finished your business, he's an ass, and now it's time to move on. We've got bigger and better fish to fry."

It's a risky attempt at distraction, and I have to work to keep my face straight, really fucking hoping she hears the humor. Otherwise, I'm a dead man. Rest in pieces, because there won't be any peace from a pissed off Shayanne.

"Did you just call me . . . a salty heifer?" she retorts, her mouth dropping into a gape. "Are you for real, Luke Bennett? I should tan your hide for mouthing at me like that."

She might sound outraged, but she's got a thread of laughter working through the words, too, and I let my smile loose, throwing in a good chuckle too.

"Woman, if anyone's getting spanked around here, it's you. Not me." I point at her and then myself to emphasize the point.

"Hmm, maybe. We'll have to see about that," she sasses back. She walks past me into the house, dragging a blunt nail over my sweatshirt-covered chest. I turn to watch her go, appreciating every look of her apple ass I can get. Before I can follow, she turns back and winks. "Not."

She laughs and runs into the safety of the house before I can even get up to chase her.

I like this. Her smiles, her teasing laughter, her comfort in my family home, her place in my heart.

And somehow, it's working.

It will be even better when I have to travel again after the

LAUREN LANDISH

holidays. With our families combining into this mish-mash of support, Shay will be able to go with me and her brothers will still be cared for by Mama. It's a freedom Shayanne's never known.

And it's a mother's love the Tannens haven't had in too long. Mama won't ever replace their mom, but I think being 'adopted' by Mama is pretty much the best thing that could happen to anyone. Plus, she can tell them stories they've never heard about Martha Tannen. Maybe one day, about Paul too, but that's still a pretty touchy subject for now.

I get up and follow Shay's voice to the kitchen. From the doorway, I watch silently as my woman and my mama chatter away like old friends with a platter of chicken, a bowl of egg wash, and a plate of seasoned flour in front of them.

It makes warm fuzzies crawl all through my skin and my heart race a bit. I saw this moment when Mark and James found their women. Mama sharing her county fair prize-winning, super-secret fried chicken recipe is a sign of acceptance. A big one. It's her stamp of approval on her entry to our family.

I scratch at my lip with my thumb, my smile bright. "You teaching her to make your fried chicken, Mama? I know what that means." Shay's eyes ping-pong between us in cute, wrinkled-brow confusion.

Mama looks at me and then back at Shayanne, a softness to her face that I can't decipher. She looks out the window where Sophie and Katelyn are pulling up into the grassy drive after their day of work in town. Any minute now, all the guys are gonna come rolling in too, and we'll have family dinner around the brand-new, big-enough-to-fit-an-army table we bought.

Finally, Mama speaks, her voice wistful. "When James met Sophie and Mark met Katelyn, I knew they were the ones for my boys. I worried about you, though, always gone, always searching for something." She looks back at me and I realize how much she saw, how much she always saw. "I worried you'd find your match out there somewhere and leave us. I would've been okay with that, if it'd made you happy." She blinks, though, and I'm not sure that's entirely true.

"But you found what you were looking for right here at home." Her smile is one of pure pride. "No, I'm not teaching Shayanne to make my fried chicken. I'm sure she's got her own recipe, been making it for years just like her mama made it, I reckon." To Shayanne, she says, "There are lots of things I can teach you, but I won't mess with a good thing you've already got going."

This isn't a stamp of approval or a welcoming into the fold. This is respect on a whole other level. As equals, as friends, as family.

Shay's eyes water, and she lifts her shoulder to catch the single errant tear that falls because her hands are messy with globs of flour. "Do not make me cry, Mama Louise. I already salted the chicken!" That's my sassy spitfire, my emotional roller coaster ride . . . my woman. And I wouldn't have her any other way.

CHAPTER 34

SHAYANNE

"*L*et's go, let's go!" I know I look like a kid hyped up on sugar-crack cereal—eyes wide in my flushed face, jumping up and down like a jack in the box, with my hands clapping out a rhythmless pattern. But Luke is slower than Christmas this morning!

Well, maybe not exactly, because Christmas ain't slow today. It's here!

My first Christmas with Luke.

Our first Christmas without Daddy.

Our first Christmas with the Bennetts.

It's a big day, and I'm ready to get it rolling. If only he would get his lazy ass outta our bed. "You sure pajamas are okay? Do I need to get dressed, fix my hair, or anything?" I say, standing beside the bed. Okay, not standing. More like kicking the bed with my shins so Luke's prone form bounces a bit.

He rolls over, his bare chest mighty distracting from my rush to get to the main house. "C'mere, woman." He holds wiggling grabby fingers out to me, and even though I know I should scoot back so he'll get up, I lean over so he can reach me.

He pulls me to him, and I let out a holler of surprise at the sudden movement. My tummy swoops, not from the movement but just from him. I still can't believe this is my life.

That he is my life.

Every day, we work on the ranch, with horses and goats and soaps, oh my! And every night, we fall into bed, into each other, and a little more in love.

He presses a kiss to my forehead, then one to each cheek, and then finally, with a sigh of relief, he covers my mouth with his. His morning kisses are the best, sweet reminders that I'm his dream come true. He told me that, word for word one morning, and I damn near lit up like a firework. Luke Bennett is better with words than he thinks he is and more romantic than I'll ever let him know.

Gotta keep him twisting on the hook just a little every once in a while.

"You look beautiful, just as you are. Pajamas around the tree in the morning are kind of a tradition. We'll do Santa gifts this morning, usually one small thing that's just for fun, and then a big breakfast. Tonight, we'll do the main tree with gifts to one another and dinner. So you're good in your nightgown."

He looks down my body with wolfish eyes, but I'm not sure what he's looking at so hungrily. My hair is a literal rat's nest of tangled curls, my face is completely bare, as per usual, and my 'nightgown', as he called it, is really just a huge, long T-shirt that falls to my knees.

When his eyes peruse back up, he meets mine, blue to hazel, and I wonder what color our kids will have. Our little Luke-Annes. He'd finally explained that reference, and my ovaries had nearly exploded on the spot.

"You look perfect, but maybe we ought to brush our teeth before we go?"

I cry out, covering my mouth with one hand and his with the other. "Oh, my God, is it bad this morning? It's you, not me," I declare, daring him to disagree. "My breath smells like roses and sunshine. No, like mint and lavender." I don't think he understands a word I'm saying because I'm mumbling into my palm, but I feel his lips smile against my other one, and then, he licks me.

I move my hand from my mouth, letting him see my evil smirk for one second before I smear my wet hand over his face. "Ahh! Gross. Move your ass, woman! We've got places to be."

He bumps his hips, setting me right on the floor with both of us grinning like loons. We aim for the bathroom in the hallway to brush our teeth. Maybe some mouthwash too, I decide.

Halfway there, we meet sleepy-eyed Sophie and James. They'd stayed out here in the ranch house last night so we'd all be close to Mama Louise's for morning festivities. Thankfully, they're both dressed in pajamas too, Sophie in maternity yoga pants and a tank and James in flannel pants and no shirt, which makes me feel a little more comfortable about my attire.

Sophie has a laughing smile on her face, and her hands are resting on her humongous belly. I meet her smile, both of us so, so happy.

James smirks at Luke. "Let me give you a tip, brother. Never, ever say 'gross' about anything that happens in the bedroom."

Oh, my chee-sus and crackers . . . they could hear us.

And if they could hear our silly antics this morning, they could probably hear us last night too. We weren't exactly quiet when Luke was teasingly calling me Mrs. Claus and telling me he was gonna 'eat all my cookies'.

My cheeks burn pink and hot, embarrassment rushing through my body.

But Luke is calm as ever, giving his brother a shrug as he

throws an arm over my shoulders. "Hey, man, you do it your way, and I'll do it mine. Ain't getting no complaints."

"Teeth!" I blurt out and then realize that sounds like I'm adding to their conversation. Which I'm definitely not. "I mean, I need to brush my teeth." I skedaddle the rest of the way down the hall and shut the door behind me.

I can hear the deep timbre of Luke's laugh. "Guess I'd better go apologize for embarrassing my woman. You go ahead and head over to Mama's. We'll be along shortly."

Oh, God. How can I be embarrassed, turned on, and really excited to go open presents all at the same time?

But when the bathroom door opens and Luke steps inside, only one of those emotions takes center stage. "Get on the counter for me, honey. I want my morning taste of your sugar." At least he keeps his voice down, though right now, I don't know if I'd care if he shouted it.

He's got my panties pulled to the side and is three slow licks in when I hear the front door open. James's voice calls out, "Make it fast, lovebirds, or Mama will be hunting you down."

I should be flushed with embarrassment again, but the only thing bringing pink to the surface of my skin is my need for Luke.

"Better make it quick, I guess," he rumbles into my core.

With that decree, he sucks my clit into his mouth hard and batters it with his tongue. He knows my body, knows that'll send me flying fast, and after only a couple of seconds, I plunge over into bliss. My hips buck off the counter, and I hold on to keep from falling, even though I know he'd catch me. He locks his arms around my hips, hands fastened tight over my mound to hold me to him for another lick, and then one more, making me so sensitive.

While my pussy is still pulsing, he stands up and guides me to turn around. I bend over the counter, and he shoves my panties down my legs before lining himself up with my opening. I watch him in the mirror, see the need lining his face as he watches his cock disappear inside me. "How's the view?"

His eyes tick up to mine in the mirror and stay. "So fucking sexy, beautiful. So fucking *mine*."

His fingers dig into my hips, letting me know that he's about to unleash on me. Once upon a time, I'd been nervous about sex with him, not because of anything he'd done but because it was my first time and I wanted him so badly. But he's shown me that there's nothing to be nervous about. We fit together perfectly, every time.

I nod, biting my lip. He thrusts deep and hard, slamming into me over and over. I lift to my tippy toes, letting him have all of me and taking all of him. "Fuck me, Luke. Give me a creamy white Christmas."

I've gotten a little looser with the dirty talk too, though he's still loads better at it than me. Get it? *Loads*. I crack myself up.

"Fuck, Shay." His voice is strangled, his eyes still locked on mine. "Yes," he hisses, and I feel his heat fill me. His head tosses back, the cords in his neck popping out as he groans his release.

He sags, his head lolling to the side as he recovers. "Guess we'd better get going, huh?" he says. I can see in his eyes that he'd just as soon take me to bed and hide away for the day.

I whimper when he leaves my body, and he hands me a tissue from the box on the counter. "Thank you," I say. "You'd better wash your junk, too, or everyone's gonna know what we've been doing from the smell of sex surrounding us."

He grins the cocky boy smile that I love. "Honey, they already know what we've been doing. We're late, for sure."

Shit!

Not my first Christmas! I want to make a good impression. Not that any of them have given me an indication that I need to. We've been welcomed into the family like long-lost cousins. But this is Christmas!

I shove Luke off me and turn into a whirling dervish of get-ready. My hair goes into a knot on my head, teeth are already brushed, fresh panties on under my gown, socks and boots on.

"Let's go!" I yell, but Luke's already standing at the front door.

He looks good, his flannel pants tucked haphazardly into boots and a coat over his T-shirt. I look down at myself, worried. "Are you sure?"

His eyes lick down me, from my messy bed head, to my pink cheeks, to my Carhartt coat over my T-shirt nightgown, to the white athletic knee socks, to my dirty Uggs. "You've never looked more gorgeous, Shayanne. You're the best Christmas present I've ever woken up to."

My heart melts into a puddle of goo again. "I love you," I say breathlessly.

"I know. It's hard not to," he says fake-sadly, shaking his head.

HE'S RIGHT. EVERYONE KNOWS WHY WE'RE LATE. BUT other than Brody giving Luke a bit of a stink eye, which Luke answers with a grin, it seems okay. Though that's probably because everyone's fussing over Sophie.

She's due any day now and has basically taken to sitting in the closest chair and having people wait on her hand and foot. She says she feels bad about it, but I think she secretly loves it. Who wouldn't?

Plus, I think she's really uncomfortable, given the way she's pressing on one side of her belly. I raise an eyebrow in question and she says, "Foot in my rib. I think this one is gonna be a soccer player. Or a drummer, maybe."

I watch, fascinated as her belly morphs and shifts before my very eyes. It's cool and weird and gross, and I wanna feel that one day too. But not yet. Luke and I have still have a lot to learn about each other, even more to do, and an actual list in my notebook of places he wants to take me before we settle down with a baby.

Though it's only been a couple of weeks since the big family merge, things are going well and looking even better for the future.

The herds combined well under Mark and Brody's watchful eyes, and they're developing some grunting short-hand of conversation that only they understand. Peas in a pod for sure, according to James, who has been working with them when he's not taking care of Sophie.

Bruce and Bobby pretty much do the same thing they've always done, except they report to a different table for dinner each night. Bobby even asked us if we'd all come down to Hank's to watch him perform on New Year's Eve when they have an open mic.

Luke's working with his horses, making calls to check on his charges and scheduling next spring's breedings. Our next trip is almost a month away. We're going to Kentucky, which will be a checkmark on my new map of the fifty states. The goal is to check them all off together, and Luke says he can probably get a client in most of them. If not, we'll go just for us. And there's no timeline, so if it takes us forever, that's just fine.

With Brody being busy with the cattle, I've taken over caring for my newly expanded goat herd. My goat soap business is all mine now, from milk to bathtub. And it's going great. I had to do two more batches of the holiday scents for the resort, and Sophie's spent some of her downtime helping me research an Etsy shop. I never thought I could do that, and honestly, Daddy would've never let me. But now, I do whatever the hell I want and grow my business my way.

My hope is to get the online shop up and running before spring and summer fruit seasons hit because I know I'll be super busy then. I'm expecting my carrot cake, strawberry jam, and blackberry cobbler sales to be just as high as my pumpkin pie figures since I've already signed a contract with the restaurant at the resort for those.

And I'm really excited for a new recipe I found—watermelon mint *agua fresca*. It's supposed to be delicious on its own, or even better with a kick of tequila. I think the folks out here are gonna go nuts over a lemonade alternative, and I've already sourced gallon jugs for delivery. Bruce teased me that instead of being the milkman, I'm gonna be the watermelon woman for the summer. Delivery on demand. He was kidding, but I kinda hope he's right.

It's like I've found the best of both worlds in a way I'd never dreamed, a thriving business right here at home, where I can take care of my family, but also, a way to see beyond my little corner of the world.

And all with the man I love beside me.

Mama Louise comes in with one more present and carefully slips it under the tree. "Sorry! Santa must've gotten lost when he delivered that one."

The smile on her face says she's up to something, but I'm not sure what. We've gotten really close over the last few weeks, and she's shared lots of stories about 'back in the day,' as she calls it, when Pops was alive and they were friendly with Mom and Daddy. I know she's trying to help me remember the good times, and I'm thankful for it. I'm not as furious at Daddy as I was, but there's still a good chunk of bitterness at how everything played out, even if this does feel like home now.

"James, will you do the honors?" He nods and gets up from Sophie's side to pass the presents out.

One by one, we go around the big circle of our blended family, tearing into paper, ripping open boxes, and digging into bags. I don't know if Mama plays Santa by herself or the boys helped her, but everyone has something they happily exclaim over.

Last but not least, it's my turn. I pick up the box from the floor in front of me and Luke says, "Careful, it's fragile."

I look back and ask sassily, "How do you know? I thought Santa brought it?"

James makes some comment about Luke being Santa enough for my cookies, and Sophie smacks him. But they both grin and laugh as I blush.

Carefully, I lift the lid to find . . . a teeny, tiny, pink pig.

"Oh, my God, you got me a PIG?" I scream, eyes jumping from Luke to the pig, Luke to the pig. I don't know whether to hug him or the pig first.

The pig wins.

I scoop the tiny critter out of the box where it makes a snorting sound that's not quite an oink.

Luke laughs as it curls up under my chin and my eyes water. There must be something in the air because I am not crying over a pig. An adorable, snuggly, snuffling pig *of my very own*.

"Why do I get the feeling I'm about to get kicked out of my own bed?" he rumbles, but it's good-natured. I think.

"No, we'll put her between us," I say, not caring at all that I've got a sappy smile on my face and my eyes are still watering. "Wait, is it a her?"

Sophie nods. "You remember that client of Doc's with a miniature pig she kept feeding people food? Well, she got better, learned about her animal, and bred a litter not too long ago. That's one of Bacon's offspring."

Like a lightning bolt through my mind, I know her name.

"Bacon Seed, that's what I'll call her. Cute, right? Because of her momma."

Everyone freezes, eyes wide in shock, and then a raucous laughter busts through the room. "Bacon Seed?" Brody says, wheezing because he's busting a gut so hard. "Only you, Shayanne. Only you."

I nod, curling Bacon Seed in closer and petting her little leg down to her hoof, which I'm going to paint pink like toenails. I might not be girly in the least, but my pig is definitely going to be.

"Who's my good girl?" I coo to her. And then I pitch my voice high, answering for Bacon Seed in the princess-y snooty voice I've already assigned to her, "Well, that would totes be me, obviously."

She's such a diva already.

Everyone wants to pet her, but I make them come to me because I'm not letting her go. Except for Sophie. I get up and go over to her so she doesn't have to move because I'm a good friend like that. Especially since she helped get me a pig for Christmas.

CHAPTER 35

SHAYANNE

*T*wo days later, we've finally finished all the Christmas leftovers. No more turkey sandwiches for lunch, no more sweet potato casserole, and no more cinnamon apple pie.

Bacon Seed is doing great. Turns out, she sleeps better in her kennel than in bed with us, and Luke has added pig training to his research. He says they're super smart and can almost be dog-like as pets. I told him I knew my little girl was brilliant, and she's way better than any old dog. Unless he got me one of those too. Then they could be little pet-pal siblings as they grew up.

I thought it sounded like a fine idea, but he'd said no. Apparently, he's already asked Mama Louise to pig-sit while we go to Kentucky, but he thinks pig- and puppy-sitting might be a bit much. Begrudgingly, I'd agreed and snuggled Bacon Seed closer while I pouted just a little bit.

From the back pasture, I hear a truck blazing up like fire, loud and fast. I look up and see Mark's work truck sliding to a stop, and James jumps out.

He's yelling something I can't hear, and then I read his lips. "Sophie!"

LAUREN LANDISH

"Oh, shit! She's in labor!" I answer, just as loud, even though he can't hear me through the window either.

Mass chaos reigns, or least it feels like it. But mostly, it's just James freaking out. Mama Louise picks up the walkie-talkie and presses the button. "It's time. Everyone to their stations."

She thought that'd be a funny alert, but it's pretty close to the truth. I know that acres away, Bruce and Bobby are hopping in their truck, Mark and James are already here, and I can hear Brody's ATV whining as he gets closer. Luke's in the barn, but I bet he's already got every horse put away safely. I grab Bacon Seed and run for the house. I set her down in her kennel with a little pig feed and promises of all the snuggles tonight when I get home.

She snorts, so I take that as agreement.

We all load up, though it takes two trucks to carry us all. "What'd Sophie say?" Mama Louise asks James.

His eyes are wide, wild. "She said, 'Don't freak out, I'm fine. My water broke and Doc's taking me to the hospital so he doesn't have to see my hoo-ha and deliver this baby.'"

Mama Louise pats his hand. "Then don't freak out. She's in good hands either way."

"Doc Jones, the veterinarian, is not delivering my baby!" he says, as if his words can make it true.

Minutes later, we park at the hospital and rush in like a wild pack of animals. Or cowboys. Same thing.

"Sophie Bennett?" James says to the receptionist. She looks him up and down and then leans over to look at the rest of us. I swear her eyes linger on Brody for a second longer, though. "She's having a baby!"

The receptionist smiles professionally, not at all ruffled by James's outburst. "Labor and delivery is on the second floor, sir." She points and James is off like a shot, all of us following behind at a slightly less frantic pace.

He smacks a metal pad by a set of double doors and then forces his way through sideways before they even open halfway. A woman in scrubs stops him with a raised hand. "You must be the Bennetts? We've been expecting you, though when Mrs. Bennett said a herd of buffalo was coming, we thought she was exaggerating."

She laughs like the joke is funny, but James is too far gone. "Where is she?"

Her smile is sweet and warm, like she's used to dads-to-be freaking out.

"Mr. Bennett, if you'll follow me? The rest of you can step into the family area around the corner. There's free coffee and vending machines, if you'd like something. It's probably going to be a long night."

James is gone, following the doctor, and we all shuffle around the corner as directed. Katelyn is already there, sitting primly in the feminine skirt and heels combo she usually wears to work. I guess she made it faster than we did since the resort is so much closer. We sit down with her to wait.

It doesn't take long for the memories to come back. The ass-numbing chairs, the uncertainty, the antiseptic smells teasing at my nose.

None of us have been in a hospital since Daddy passed. It hasn't been long by the calendar, but so much has happened, it feels like a lifetime ago.

It feels like a family ago.

I look around and meet Brody's dark eyes. He lifts a brow, asking me if I'm okay, and I nod. I do the same back to him, and his shoulder lifts a centimeter before dropping again. I watch as Bruce and Bobby nod back to Brody's silent question too.

At some point, Jake and Roxy show up and sit vigil with us. Jake looks sick with worry and Roxy pats his hand, whispering in his ear.

Hours later, a frazzled James pops his head in. His blond hair is standing straight up and his eyes are bloodshot. He looks exhausted so I can only imagine what Sophie looks like. "She's about to start pushing. It'll be soon. I'm gonna be a Daddy, guys."

His eyes shine with unshed tears, but he looks happy. He sees Jake and Roxy and asks if they want to see her for a minute. They nod and the three of them disappear.

"Will you join me?" Mama Louise says. She stands, and we all stand with her, making a circle. She takes Mark's hand on her right and Brody's on her left, and we each take the hand of the person next to us, completing the connection.

Mama Louise closes her eyes. "Please protect Sophie, guide her along the journey she faces, and help her baby join this family. We have a lot of love to share, with each other and with the next generation. May her delivery be as pain-free as it can be, as beautiful as Sophie is, and may her baby bring her as much joy as I have received from all my children."

A mix of deep timbres gruffly says, "Amen." Katelyn and I sniffle and whisper it too.

And then we sit back down to wait. As a family. To greet our newest member.

I HAVE NEVER TRULY SEEN *BLISS* BEFORE. IT'S A WORD I'VE said, a word I've read, but I've never truly seen it for myself until James comes back into the waiting room. His face is pure, unadulterated bliss.

"It's a girl. A beautiful, gorgeous, squalling pink girl. Both her and her pretty momma are doing well."

We erupt in cheers, the boys all patting his back too hard and us girls blubbering like faucets. "Congratulations!" we all say over and over.

"What's her name?" Mama Louise asks.

"Cindy Louise. We named her for Sophie's mom and you," James says. Mama Louise cries some more and pulls on James's shoulders so he'll bend down to hug her.

"Thank you, that's so sweet. I never . . . thank you."

When Mama Louise lets him go, he laughs. "The other good thing is, I won the bet. Thank God!"

He looks up, his palms spread wide, and we look at him in confusion. When he looks back at us, he explains. "Oh, Sophie didn't tell you? She made me promise that I did not put a ten-pound baby in her. I guess that was her big fear after Mama's comments about Bennett babies and her belly being so big. She said if it was ten pounds, we were done, no more babies. Good news, though. Nine pounds, ten ounces! So there's a chance there will be a next time."

He looks relieved, and I know that Sophie is too, both because ten pounds of baby sounds painful as hell and I know she wants a bunch of kids. She and her brother grew up alone, him raising her after their parents passed when she was just a kid, so she's always wanted a big family.

Though maybe *big* is relative . . . like maybe two, if they're nine-pounders. Ouch!

"Doctor said she can have visitors, but only one at a time. Wanna come meet your granddaughter, Mama?"

She nods, a tissue pressed to her eyes.

We sit down, happiness weaving through us like sparklers, invisible to the naked eye. But I can feel it. We were already making our way, growing into something greater, but this baby is going to tie us together in a whole new way. We're all gonna love that little girl like mad. We'll teach her to be country crazy, love animals and the land, and take care of each other just like we all do.

Because we're a family, by blood and by choice. And that's what family does.

EPILOGUE

LUKE - SIX MONTHS LATER

"**Y**ou think she's gonna like it?" I ask Brody, who's squinting like the diamond is ridiculously small.

To be clear, it's not. It's a modest, respectable size, I think. Well, I hope. It's also made to hold the diamond super-secure because the lady at the jewelry store said if my bride-to-be is hard on her hands, it's important. And since Shay typically has an animal in her arms, dirt under her nails, and smells of hay and sunshine, I figured safety first was a good move. Because this is definitely for the long run . . . or forever, whichever comes last.

"Fuck if I know what she likes," Brody finally says with a shrug. "I would've said she'd shoot you on sight, and look how that turned out."

I laugh at his grumpiness. It's not nearly as bad as it was six months ago. He's lighter, friendlier, and dare I say . . . funnier. As long you can take a solid verbal smackdown. The guy's a pro at dry, eviscerating one-liners.

I smack his shoulder, another thing that wouldn't have happened months ago. "Seriously, fucker. It's good, right?"

He smiles, finally giving in. "Yeah, it's pretty and sparkly and all that girly shit. You sure you shouldn't get her one of those silicone rings instead? She's kinda . . . well, you've met her. She's rough and country, more one of the guys than princess-like."

I nod, knowing my eyes look starry and not giving a single fuck. "I know. She's *perfect*. And she is girly with me, sometimes. But I love her just how she is."

"Good fucking thing, otherwise, I'da had to kill you a long time ago," he says, succeeding in looking menacing. I haven't forgotten the couple of shots he's taken on me, and he hasn't forgotten the ones I got on him either. But they seem more like brotherly fights now, not territorial disputes over my bride-to-be and where her loyalties lie.

Essentially, we're all one big happy family now. Like the fucking Brady Bunch Goes Country or some shit.

"You tried," I respond with a shrug.

He grins, the camaraderie easier and getting better every day. "Okay, fuck stick. Tell me how you're gonna do it so I can tell you it sucks." He stands with his arms crossed and his jaw clenched tight. Judging me.

But when I'm done telling him my plan, he smiles and shakes my hand. "She'll love it. Don't fuck it up."

It's a blessing I didn't think I'd ever get when Shay and I first started sneaking around. But through loss, recovery, teamwork, and family, we've done more than dismantle a useless feud. We've made something greater.

"WHAT'S UP, HOT STUFF?" SHAY ASKS FROM THE BARN doorway. She's got on denim shorts, boots, and plain white tank top, her hair braided in plaits, and she's got my favorite dirty straw hat perched on her head.

She looks stunningly sexy. I want to throw her over my

shoulder, run home with her, and fuck her so senseless, she doesn't even notice when I slip this ring on her finger. Maybe that makes me a fucking caveman, but I don't give a damn right now.

But she shoots me that shy smile, though we both know good and well that she's not shy in the slightest, and I know I can't steal away with her. I want to give her tonight, complete with all the grand gestures and romance she can stand. This will be the story we tell our kids, not that I fucked her into marrying me.

I walk to her, letting her soak in my intentions, and then wrap my arms around her waist, dipping her back the slightest bit before kissing the line of her neck. I drop my voice down to the rumble I know drives her wild and makes her heart race beneath the press of my lips.

"You look good enough to eat, honey."

"You taking Duster out?" she asks breathlessly, looking over my shoulder, though I'm doing my damnedest to distract her with more kisses.

"Hmm? No, not me, we. *We're* taking Duster out. I've got plans for you, Shayanne Tannen," I tell the full lushness of her tits where they're pressed up against the neckline of her tank.

Her arms wrap around my head, holding me to her. I could suffocate in her tits and die a happy man, but I settle for teasing her nipples through her shirt and kissing every inch of skin I can get at.

"You sure about that? I was thinking we could visit your office over there and reenact one of our first dates again. I could hop up on your desk and you could sit in your chair in front of me, maybe get an up close and personal view of my pussy while you put on a show for me too?" She looks hopeful, fluttering her lashes at me like I'd be doing her a damn favor.

Holy fuck.

She's gotten good, too good, and I'm this close to doing

what she suggests and then heading out for my plans. But if we do that, we'll miss the sunset.

I sigh heavily, my need for her and the dirty things she promises riding me hard. But I persevere because I'm not a pansy ass. I can be strong for her. I can wait a little bit to get inside her because I know damn well that I'm getting inside her tonight.

"No." She blinks at me, not understanding the word, so I try again, trying to get the blood to flow north to my brain instead of south to my cock. "No, I've got other plans for you tonight, and I won't be deterred."

Shit, I might as well have waved a red cape at a bull. She's all 'challenge accepted' anytime someone lays down the law.

But she surprises me again by smiling sweetly. "All right, then. Take me places and show me things. Whatcha got in mind?"

"It's a surprise," I say, kissing her smile so I can taste her happiness, the happiness I bring her just by being here at the end of the day, wherever *here* might be. The ranch, our house, another city, another state, and one day soon, another country, if I can swing a few things for a trip to see a special horse. But as long as I'm by her side, she's happy.

And making her happy makes me happy, so it's perfect.

I lead her over to Duster and climb up, helping her get situated behind me. I let Duster take his time. He's getting older and sometimes is a little fussy about having to go for his daily walks. But he's always more spry if he keeps moving. A couple of days lazing around the barn and he's about good for nothing but nose kisses and neck scratches.

Our tree comes into view, and Shayanne presses her cheek to my back. I hum happily, knowing she'll get a tickle from the vibration. I feel her smile and pat her hands around my waist.

We get down, and I let Duster roam to eat the fresh grass

in the area, knowing he'll come back when I call for him. Shay walks toward the tree. "Hey! There's something there."

She reaches for the piece of white paper, sitting beneath a rock on the lowest branch. We haven't left notes for each other like this in ages, though I'll sometimes scribble something in her notebook for her to find unexpectedly.

She reads the words I wrote for her. Ones of promise, ones of future, ones of love.

She's already crying when she turns around. I'm down on one knee, ready for this moment.

"Shayanne Tannen, when I first saw you, I thought you were an annoying brat of a munchkin." She laughs through the tears just like I'd hoped she would when I worked on this speech, wanting to get it right.

"But when I saw you again, I realized you'd grown up into something truly spectacular. You were the worst kind of off-limits, but I've never been much on rule-following, anyway, and neither have you, my little tomboy badass firecracker." She swats at my shoulder, and I grab her hand to kiss it and hold in mine.

"Somewhere along the way, I fell head over heels in love with you. You make everything better—my heart, my home, my life. And if you'll let me, I'd like to spend the rest of my life doing everything I can to love you. Will you marry me?"

She nods, her bottom lip tucked behind her teeth. "Gonna need the word, honey. Just so we're clear those aren't tears of pity."

She tackles me, my legs flailing out from beneath me, and I'm suddenly really glad I spread a blanket on the ground when I was here with Brody earlier because she's kissing me all over, each smack punctuated with a resounding "Yes!"

Before I know it, we're naked except for the ring on Shay's finger, with only the setting sun to see our celebration. Shayanne sits on top of me, riding me like a damn cowgirl, with her tits bouncing and her hips lifting and lowering in a wave, and I fall in love all over again with my sassy spitfire.

Her resilience, her kindness, her caring heart, and her untamed zero-fucks-given approach to everything. She is who she is, and you can take it or leave it.

And I'm definitely going to take it. And love her for the rest of my life.

At some point, we collapse into each other, spent and exhausted. She snuggles into my side, her head on my chest and my arm wrapped around her as the full June moon rises in the purple sky. "Everyone's waiting at Hank's for drinks and dancing to celebrate with us. I told them we'd be there when we got there."

Shay squeals and kicks her feet in the air. She holds her hand up, looking at the diamond.

"I can't believe they almost double-handedly ruined this for me," she says, shaking her head.

"Huh? Double-handedly?" I answer, not following her in the slightest but loving that she still surprises and confuses me sometimes. It keeps me on my toes.

"Yeah, double-handedly." She looks up at me like I'm stupid when she's over here making up words. "It's like single-handedly, but there's two of them. Hence, double-handedly."

"Uh, okay. So they almost double-handedly ruined this?"

You ever say a nonsense word so many times that it starts to make sense? Or a real word so many times it begins to sound like gibberish? That's what I'm feeling right now. It might have something to do with the blood flow not recirculating through my body yet, though. It's still rather centrally focused at the moment since Shay's naked and pressed against me.

Her nod is definitive, like she's glad we got that out of the way and I understand her now. I don't, but I'm not gonna highlight my failures if she's not.

"Daddy and Brody, they almost ruined this with their feud and fighting, and I'm glad they didn't get their way. I'm really glad Brody came around, because having us all together is better than I ever could have dreamed."

Ah, that makes more sense, I think, catching her meaning now.

She lifts up to her elbow, staring into my eyes. "You are better than I ever dreamed. I love you, Luke Bennett."

She lowers her mouth to meet mine in a kiss, and my breath ghosts over her lips. "I love you too, Shayanne Tannen-Bennett."

And our future is sealed with a kiss.

Later, we'll walk Duster back to the barn and go see our family at Hank's. I'll spin Shayanne around the floor until she's dizzy and heavy in my arms. I'll take her home and make love to her again, slowly worshipping her because we have all the time in the world.

And then we'll make our life together, one day at a time and one state at a time.

I hope you've enjoyed the Bennett Boys as much as me, and while this is the end of this series, there will be more in this world! The Tannen Boys went from being the bullies next door to men who've done the best they can with what they had. There's something to be said for their resilience, grit, and strength . . . and I think they deserve their own story! Their story will be of how, in losing everything, they became part of something even bigger. And, of course they add to the crazy mix with sassy, sexy women of their own. Be on the lookout for it later this year!

ABOUT THE AUTHOR

Bennett Boys Ranch:
Buck Wild ‖ Riding Hard ‖ Racing Hearts

Dirty Fairy Tales:
Beauty and the Billionaire ‖ Not So Prince Charming ‖
Happily Never After

Get Dirty:
Dirty Talk ‖ Dirty Laundry ‖ Dirty Deeds ‖ Dirty Secrets

Irresistible Bachelors:
Anaconda ‖ Mr. Fiance ‖ Heartstopper
Stud Muffin ‖ Mr. Fixit ‖ Matchmaker
Motorhead ‖ Baby Daddy ‖ Untamed

Connect with Lauren Landish
www.laurenlandish.com
admin@laurenlandish.com
www.facebook.com/lauren.landish

If you enjoyed this book, stay in contact! You can join my
mailing list here. You'll never miss a new release and you'll
even get 2 FREE ebooks!

Printed in Great Britain
by Amazon